**Four delightful Regencies—
available for the first time in one volume!**

**Praise for the novels
of Barbara Metzger**

"Metzger's prose absolutely tickles the funny bone."
—*L.A. Life Daily News*

"Barbara Metzger's voice is always fresh! With wit
and inimitable style, she dares to go beyond the cliché
to create uniquely Metzger stories."
—*The Literary Times*

"One of the freshest voices in the Regency genre."
—*Rave Reviews*

**Praise for the novels
of Margaret Evans Porter**

"As rich and savory as a box of chocolates."
—Teresa Medeiros

"Interesting . . . cleverly told . . . quite believable."
—*Library Journal*

"Margaret Evans Porter is a delight!"
—*The Literary Times*

"Fabulous."
—*Midwest Book Review*

Valentines

Barbara Metzger

— and —

Road to Ruin

Margaret Evans Porter

A SIGNET BOOK

SIGNET
Published by New American Library, a division of
Penguin Group (USA) Inc., 375 Hudson Street,
New York, New York 10014, U.S.A.
Penguin Books Ltd, 80 Strand,
London WC2R ORL, England
Penguin Books Australia Ltd, 250 Camberwell Road,
Camberwell, Victoria 3124, Australia
Penguin Books Canada Ltd, 10 Alcorn Avenue,
Toronto, Ontario, Canada M4V 3B2
Penguin Books (N.Z.) Ltd, Cnr Rosedale and Airborne Roads,
Albany, Auckland 1310, New Zealand

Penguin Books Ltd, Registered Offices:
80 Strand, London WC2R ORL, England

Published by Signet, an imprint of New American Library, a division of Penguin Group (USA) Inc. *Valentines* was previously published by Fawcett Crest, an imprint of Ballantine Books, in February 1996. *Road to Ruin* was previously published by Signet in December 1992 by arrangement with Walker & Company. For information address Walker & Company, 435 Hudson Street, New York, NY 10014.

First Signet Printing (Double Edition), February 2004
10 9 8 7 6 5 4 3 2 1

Valentines

To Mr. and Mrs. Neal Pruzan in honor of their wedding.
I should have been there.
Congratulations and Happy Anniversary

Contents

Bald Lies

Chapter One

*T*here was fog. There was the dark of night. There was smoke from candles and smudge from cigars. Mostly, however, there was a cloud of gloom hanging over the corner table at White's Club that cold January evening.

Three friends sat slumped around the table, each too deep in despair to notice the card games going on around them, the wagering or the tongue-wagging. No acquaintances stopped by with offers of a hand of whist, or for opinions on a fine piece of horseflesh, or comments on the finer flesh of the new horseback rider at Astley's. Only the silent waiters dared approach, with bottle after bottle of liquor. There was enough brandy splashed that night to flambé an entire cherry orchard. There was enough melancholy to produce *Hamlet* thrice over.

Other than the maudlin pall, the three gentlemen shared little in common at first glance. One was a veteran of the Peninsula campaign, a tanned and hardened Corinthian. One was a leading light in his party's political future, solid and comfortable. One was a Tulip, with pomaded locks and yellow cossack trousers. His shirt points were so high, he would have been blinded

had he chosen to examine anything but the wet ring his
glass was leaving on the table.

The gentlemen did share a dawning familiarity with
three decades of life, and all were peers of the realm: an
earl, a viscount, and a baron. And they were best of
friends since schoolboy days, pulling each other
through scrapes and Suetonius, sharing vacations, al-
lowances, and confidences. Now they were well past
adolescent pranks, but they still shared each other's
woes.

Gordon, Viscount Halbersham, was the first to speak.
The young Whig reformer cleared his throat, almost as
if he were about to address the House of Lords. Instead
of his usual ringing Parliamentary tones, though, he uttered a pitiful whine: "I think Vi is having an affair."

Neither of his friends disputed him. Neither pair of
eyes could meet his. How could they deny his wife was
cuckolding him, when it was the talk of London? There
were wagers entered in White's own betting book to
that effect.

"And with Fitzroy-Hughes, of all men!" the viscount
went on, more to himself than to his unresponsive table-
mates. "A blasted Tory."

"He dresses well," put in Lord Frances Podell, the
fashionable but drooping baron.

"Now, that's a fine lot of sympathy, Franny." Viscount Halbersham rounded on his foppish friend. "Very
helpful." He swallowed another glass of brandy.

"Damn, what's a man to expect from such a fribble?
Orange and purple butterflies on your waistcoat, by
George. It's a miracle you weren't set upon by some
wild-eyed lepidopterist."

Franny ignored the slur, knowing Gordon only spoke
from his own despondency—and poor taste. "Then run
the dastard through and be done with it."

"What, and have to flee the country? We're at war
with every place worth visiting. Of course, there are the

Antipodes. A duel would put paid to my career anyway."

Another silence ensued until Maxim, the Earl of Blanford, lifted his dark eyes from the contemplation of his own personal hell in the bottom of his brandy glass. "Come now, Gordie, things can't be as bad as all that. You don't know for sure Lady Viola is playing you false. Just because she made sure Fitzroy-Hughes was invited to that New Year's house party is no reason to suspect the worst."

"She did dance with him a lot," Franny put in, earning glares from both men.

"But you don't like to dance, Gordie," Lord Blanford offered. "And Lady Vi does."

"They both disappeared for an hour during the ball."

The earl brushed that aside. "Coincidence only."

"She kissed him at twelve o'clock."

"You were across the room."

"I caught him wandering down the wrong hall that night."

"Have you considered Jamaica? I hear the scenery is nice, but the climate . . ."

They all had another drink.

"Deuce take it," Blanford eventually said. "There has to be another way. Why the devil don't you get the chit pregnant already? Motherhood will settle her down well enough. It works for broody mares. Get her mind off anything but filling her nursery. You've been married, what? Two years now since we stood up with you. What in blazes have you been doing?"

"I guess we all know what he hasn't been doing," Franny put in, "if Lady Vi's making sheep's eyes at Fitzroy-Hughes."

"Confound it, it ain't my fault!" Lord Halbersham exploded. "She's off at some ball or rout or theater party till dawn, then she's asleep till midday, when I've got to be at the House. By the time I get home, she's dressing for another blasted outing, and it's 'Oh no,

5

"Gordie, you'll muss my gown,' or 'Sorry, Gordie, my maid has already done my hair.' Women, bah!"

Max was studying his fingertips. "I don't think it's women as much as London. It sounds like the social rounds are your real competition. Lady Vi is a beautiful little baggage; that's why you married her in the first place. But if not Fitzroy-Hughes—and I'm not saying he is poaching on your preserves—then you'll be worrying over someone else soon enough. Best to get the minx out of Town altogether. Spend some time together at your country place, work on propagating the species and extending the line, all that rot. You've been talking about setting up a stud farm for years. Tell Viola you're going to do it now, as an excuse for rural-izing."

"Things are slow in Town anyway. The real parties won't start up again until the spring," Franny added.

"And you said yourself things are quiet at Whitehall with so many members in the shires over the winter."

The viscount's brow cleared for a minute, then the frown lines returned. "Vi hates the country. She won't go."

"Confound it, man, she's your wife. She doesn't have a choice."

"Spoken like a real bachelor," Halbersham replied. "You believe all that legal argle-bargle of a wife being man's chattel, and that oath stuff about her swearing to honor and obey. It's a hum, all of it. Wives have ways of getting what they want, let me tell you. Cold meals, overstarched linen, exorbitant dressmakers' bills. That's just the start! Then there are the tears. No, Max, a wise man doesn't start ordering his wife around like some kind of servant, making her do what she doesn't want. Viola would make my life hell."

"Seems to me," pronounced Lord Blanford, watching his friend sink back into his dolorous stupor, "that she's already got you halfway there."

Viscount Halbersham took a deep swallow of oblivion, and another when the first wasn't working.

It was Lord Podell who spoke next, after a few moments of reflection on his companion's sorry state, and his own. "Seems to me it would be cheaper, too," he said.

"What, a duel? Are you still of a mind to second me at dawn then? Deuce take a fellow if his own friends are so anxious for his blood."

"No, I meant the country. Got to be a sight less costly than Town. Why, no one would care if a chap wore the same waistcoat to dinner twice in a week."

"They would if it was one like yours," Gordie muttered, but Max shook himself out of his own doldrums to take a careful look at his dandified friend. Between Podell's intricate neckcloth and curling-tonged tresses were worry lines, sleepless shadows. "What, dipped again, Franny?" He started to reach for his purse. It was no secret the baron was punting on River Tick.

Franny held up a manicured hand. "Thanks, but it's bellows to mend with me. A loan won't cover it this time, and a fellow can't keep borrowing from his friends, especially when he knows he's got no way to pay them back. Mightn't have a brass farthing, but I've got m'honor."

"Don't be a gudgeon, Fran. Surely a monkey will see you through. You'll come about, old son, and Max will never notice the loss," Gordie volunteered. "Rich as Golden Ball, our boy Blanford." The viscount peered through a drunken haze at his somber friend. "I say, Max, you ain't lost your fortune, too, have you? Mean to say, here you are, blue-deviled as the two of us, and you ain't even got a wife."

Max just shook his head, his hand still poised at his waistcoat pocket and one eyebrow raised in inquiry toward Podell.

Franny had to repeat, "It won't fadge, Max. You might buy the duns away from my door today, but what

7

about tomorrow? We all know the dibs are never going to be in tune.''

Gordon lifted his quizzing glass in an unsteady grip, but still managed to get a better look at Lord Podell's ensemble. ''Dash it, Franny, if you didn't spend all your blunt on some Bedlamite tailor, you might have enough put by for the rent.''

Franny sniffed. ''A fellow has to keep up appearances, don't you know.''

''Maybe you should consider going to the country for a while after all,'' Max suggested. ''As you said, the pigs and sheep won't care if your outfit is bang up to the mark.''

''Outrun the bailiffs, you mean.'' Franny gave a dry laugh. ''I would if I could. But the Hall is leased out, don't you know. The rent money is the only thing paying the mortgage, else the cents-per-centers would have the ancestral heap, too. The rent's not enough to cover major investment, new equipment, better conditions for the tenants, I can't turn a profit.''

Gordon nodded. His wealth came from the land, too. ''Surprised you managed to hold on to the place this long, in the condition you inherited it.''

Franny sat up a little straighter. ''It's been in the family for centuries.''

''It was your father's family home, too. Forgive me for speaking ill of the dead, but he didn't seem to give a groat about the place.''

Franny sank back into his chair, and into his misery. ''Gambling fever. Fatal flaw, don't you know.''

Gordon snorted. ''Fatal is one thing, foolish is another. Spending your last shillings on silver buttons.''

Franny started to say that the buttons weren't paid for when Max spoke up: ''What you need, Franny, is a wife.''

''What, after Gordie's tale of woe as recommenda-tion? No, thank you. I'd rather go to debtors' prison.''

"Stubble it, I don't mean a wife like Gordie's."

Gordie was on his feet. "Now, wait a minute—"

Max waved him down. "No insult intended. Lady Halbersham is a diamond of the first water, a Toast since her come-out. But there's no getting around that she's an expensive piece of goods. That's not what Franny needs. He needs an heiress."

Franny managed a shaky laugh. "Then I'm safe. Heiresses are watched as carefully as eggs on a griddle. No rich papa's going to let any down-at-heels baron within a mile of his precious daughter. 'Sides, I ain't in the petticoat line."

Max ignored the last, and continued his deliberations out loud while Gordon nodded sagely. "Not an heiress of the *beau monde* then—"

"Hold on, I ain't about to buckle myself to some Cit's platter-faced gal just so she can call herself baroness and try to drag her family into the ton on my coattails."

"No, that's not what you need. Gordie had to have a wife with elegance, social standing, a regular darling of the nobility to be his perfect political hostess." He raised his glass in a toast to Halbersham's absent, if erring, wife. "You need a wealthy chit from the gentry who's used to the country and won't mind staying there. You install her and her papa's money at the Hall, give the old man a grandson to call heir to a barony, and you are free to take up your London life right where you left off."

"Here, here," Gordie seconded.

"But I ain't in the petticoat line, I tell you," Franny said in a near whimper.

Once again he was ignored. Max was staring at the ceiling through a smoke ring he'd blown. "In fact, you ought to go on home to Bedford with Gordie and Lady Vi. Get you away from your creditors for a time, and a chance to look at the crop of local beauties before they

9

make their bows in Town and get spoiled by city ways."

Gordie wasn't sure if his wife had been insulted again. He was so far in his cups, he wasn't sure of anything except that he might have a chance of convincing Viola to accompany him to the country if they made a house party out of it. "There's nothing Vi likes better than matchmaking," he said, toasting the earl's brilliance with another glass. "We'll do it!"

After a few more glasses, even Franny began to see the merits of the plan. What other choice did he have? He swallowed, and nodded.

Gordie slapped him on the back. "That's the ticket. You'll see, we'll all come about." He stood to leave, anxious to confront his wife while his enthusiasm—and courage—were high. Before he left, offering Franny a ride in his coach, he turned to the earl. "I say, Max, why don't you come along? We can get in some shooting and you can help keep Vi from missing the pleasures of Town. Besides, I really do mean to set up the stud, and there's no better judge of horseflesh than you."

"And you know I'll be bound to make mice feet of any courtship. Need your advice," Franny declared firmly, more firm than his wavering stance, held up by his sturdier friend. "Not in the petticoat line."

Max waved them on. "I'll think about it."

"You do that," Gordon turned to go again, half dragging Franny. He stopped at the edge of the table, temporarily propping his lordship against a passing footman, to whom Franny was confiding his anxieties about the female species, to the fellow's disgust and horror. "Oh, by the by," Gordon said, "never did get to ask what had you so moped. I mean, what are friends for, if not to listen to a chap's troubles?"

Lord Blanford merely raised his glass again in acknowledgment. "Go on, get Franny home before he is arrested. It's nothing worth mentioning anyway."

Max poured himself another glassful, alone there in the corner. Nothing worth mentioning, right? His life was over, that was all, but no, it wasn't worth mentioning.

Chapter Two

Max could not have opened his budget to Gordon or Franny anyway. His problem was not something to discuss even with one's best friends; they couldn't understand, not having the same experience. Besides, it was so terrible, so personal, so blasted depressing, Max didn't want to talk about it. Gordie's marriage was in peril and poor Franny's finances were at *point non plus*, earning them both his sympathy and compassion . . . but he, Maxim Blanding, Earl of Blanford, late of His Majesty's Cavalry, was going bald.

Oh Lord, bald! His hair wasn't just receding, it was retreating with the lightning speed of one of Wellesley's tactical withdrawals. At this rate, he'd be — No, it didn't bear contemplating.

Max told himself, not for the first time, that it wasn't just vanity that made him wince with every hair left in the teeth of his comb. He never thought his looks were much of an asset in the first place, with a crooked nose from a long-forgotten cricket match and new scars from the more recent army days. Always dark-complexioned, he now had a weathered appearance, like an unpainted shutter.

The incipient resemblance to a hen's offering didn't

even bother Max as a *memento mori*. He'd faced death on the battlefield often enough to accept his own mortality. No, he saw each fall of dark thread, each ebony remnant on his pillow slip, as a sign of betrayal. His body was playing him false by growing old. Old. Max Blanding, first cricketer, Lieutenant Lord Blanford—growing old? How had that happened? He was only two and thirty. He couldn't be old yet.

Max had studied his friends this evening, searching for signs of decay. Gordie was gaining some girth, but he was still the rosy-cheeked lad from school days. And Franny, despite his affectations in dress, was still a blond, blue-eyed cherub. They were all of an age, so how was Max the only one getting old?

He pondered the question while he waited for the footman to bring another bottle to the table. At this rate, he estimated, in less than a decade his teeth would be coming loose and his stomach would be straining toward his knees, no matter how hard he worked at Gentleman Jackson's. He sucked in those muscles with a gasp.

"Are you all right, my lord?" the worried servant asked.

Max scowled the waiter away. He didn't feel old, that was the rub. Gordie could settle into middle age with his career and his flighty wife; Max wasn't ready. Perhaps because he'd given three years to Wellesley's campaign, he felt cheated. There was too much he hadn't done, like secure his own succession, for one. Here he was chiding Gordie, and he had naught but a chinless cousin to inherit. He'd thought to have plenty of time, at least until he was forty, before starting his nursery. Now who knew how soon before he lost that, too? Zeus, by the time he found a suitable bride, he'd likely be wearing whalebone corsets and ivory teeth. Held together by dead creatures, by George, he'd creak when he stooped to one knee to make his offer, and have to be helped up by some smirking chit who'd have to shout her acceptance into his ear trumpet.

Not that Max doubted she'd accept, whichever woman he chose to bear his sons. He was still an earl with deep pockets, no matter that he was nearing his dotage. Unfortunately, he was enough of the dreamer to regret being accepted for his title and wealth alone. Name, fortune, and an acceptable appearance made a much better bargain. A shiny pate was no more acceptable to Maxim than stains on his linen.

He sighed. Perhaps he should take the advice he'd so blithely offered to Franny and find himself a comfortable wife now, while there were still strands long enough to pull across his forehead. Hair today, groom tomorrow.

The glittering London belles held no appeal for him. He'd dread seeing his scalp reflected back in his fashionable wife's cold, disapproving eyes. No, he'd think about going into the country with his friends to look over the provincial possibilities—tomorrow. For tonight he had to concentrate on getting home without looking like he couldn't hold his liquor anymore, either.

He made it across the floor without mishap, and waited with studied nonchalance for the doorman to hand over his hat and gloves.

"Best to bundle up, my lord," the man offered with a smile. "It's cold enough out there to freeze the whiskers off a rat."

Hair jokes? Was he now to be the butt of hair jokes? Lord Blanford changed the doorman's tip to a smaller coin, crammed his curly-brimmed beaver down over his ears, and stalked off into the night.

Gordon, Lord Halbersham, managed to convince his pretty young wife to leave the gaiety of the capital without too much effort. Viola was already contemplating a visit to Bedfordshire anyway, with London so thin of company. With all those starchy dowagers giving her gimlet looks, Viola thought she'd do well to let memories of that New Year's party fade a bit lest she find certain doors closed to her at the start of the real Season.

So Gordie merely had to promise her a new set of diamonds, the refurbishment of Briarwoods, his country seat, in time for a lavish Valentine's Day ball, and the management of Lord Frances Podell's love life.

"Let me see. There's Lord Craymorc's daughter. Ten thousand a year. She's been on the shelf so long, even Franny's empty pockets should look good." She chewed on the stub of her pencil, adding names to the list. "That awful Mr. Martin's girl should be out by now. He's in trade, rich as Croesus, but the mother was acceptable. And Pamela Feswick is always on the lookout for a husband."

"Dash it, Vi, the Feswick woman is thirty if she's a day, and a shrew. Think of poor Franny."

"Exactly. Poor. And awkward around strange women."

"That Feswick woman is as strange as they come. Remember we'll have to entertain them now and again. Don't mean to give up Franny's friendship."

Pamela Feswick was crossed off the list. "Too bad it's not Blanford looking for a wife. There'd be no trouble there finding any number of acceptable girls." And her house party would be the most notable success of the year, instead of being a humiliating repairing lease.

Gordie laughed. "There have been acceptable and not-so-acceptable females throwing themselves at Max's head since he was out of short pants. He wouldn't need us to find him a bride, were he looking to get legshackled. Which he ain't, so don't get that look in your eye. Max ain't one to put up with anyone meddling in his personal life."

"Still, if he came, we could attract more women for Franny to look over. Max is definitely a prize worth pursuing, even if he doesn't permit himself to be caught."

"Dash it, I hate having my friends put up as bait."

"And I hate your making marriage out to be a fate worse than death," she replied with a scowl.

Gordie cleared his throat and made a strategic retreat.

"Not at all, my dear. Not at all. It's just that Max will do what he wants to do. Always has. Went and joined the army, didn't he, even though he was the old earl's heir? No, you worry about Franny." His lordship mean-dered about the sitting room between their bedcham-bers. "Ah, Vi, it's late. You can fret about the party tomorrow. Why don't you, ah, come along to bed now?"

Viola shooed him off with an absentminded wave of her beringed fingers. "You go on, Gordie. I'm going to write an invitation to Max begging him to come. For Franny's sake."

Viola's note reached Max about noontime the next day, along with his morning coffee.

"Are we ready to arise, my lord?" his valet inquired.

"We are ready for the last rites, Thistlewaite," Max groaned from the depths of a pounding headache. He was definitely too old for this.

Thistlewaite left to return with a potent, noxious-smelling brew calculated to cure hangovers, or kill the sufferer. "Drink up, my lord. We'll feel more the thing after a shave."

Only if he could hold the razor to Thistlewaite's throat, Max thought, but he drank while the valet bus-tled about with hot water and lather. Thistlewaite had been in the family forever, like the suits of armor in the hall. The man was about as companionable as those clanking hulks, but Max could no more get rid of the servant than he could sell off the family plate. He'd tried. Thistlewaite wouldn't go, looking after the Earls of Blanford being his God-given mission in life, accord-ing to Thistlewaite. At least he gave a good shave. While dabbing warm lather on the earl's face,

Thistlewaite asked, "Shall we be exercising at Gentleman Jackson's Boxing Saloon this afternoon, my lord?"

"*I* shall be going a few rounds with the Gentleman himself. *You* shall start packing." He indicated the invitation he'd set aside as the valet approached with the razor. "I am thinking of joining Lord and Lady Halbersham at their Bedfordshire property."

Making firm, even strokes, Thistlewaite commented, "Very good, my lord. Lord Podell will be relieved. He called earlier this morning to discuss the invitation."

"And what did you tell him?"

"That we hadn't decided yet, but it was an excellent idea."

"What, getting him out of Town?" .

Thistlewaite was applying the damp towel now. "No, finding him a wealthy bride. When a gentleman reaches a certain age, he owes it to his lineage to—"

"Please, Thistlewaite, no lectures this morning."

"Very good, my lord." The valet replaced the towel and other equipment on the shaving stand. "Perhaps a bit of boot polish would do."

Max sat up, too suddenly for his aching head. "What the devil . . . ?"

"Here, this bare spot in the back. If we cover it with blacking, perhaps no one will notice."

Max jumped up and craned his neck around toward the mirror. "The back? You mean there's a bare spot on the back, too, not just the receding hairline?"

Thistlewaite silently held up a hand mirror so the earl could see his back's reflection. "Oh Lud." He sank back into his chair.

"The boot polish, my lord?"

"What, and have it drip down my back as soon as I break a sweat at Jackson's? No, just comb it across as best you can," Max said with resignation.

"Very good, my lord. I suppose we cannot consider some rice powder for the, ah, forehead then, to take away the shine?"

17

Max grabbed for the mirror again. "Shine? There's no blasted shine. It's the light, that's all."

Thistlewaite stared at the wall behind his employer. "When a gentleman reaches a certain age . . ."

"I know, I know! Dash it, I've already decided to look around at the available chits Lady Halbersham trots out for Franny. Better get the job done while I still have some grass in the meadow."

"Excellent plan, my lord. There are some fine country families in Bedford."

Max stood up to have his coat fitted across his broad shoulders. "I'm glad you approve. For a moment I was worried you'd hold out for a bride from the social columns, some starched-up aristocrat."

Thistlewaite brushed at the sleeves. "Since a dowry is not the first consideration, although not to be disdained if one is available, character is more important in our countess. A kind heart, a loving nature."

Those were more or less the requirements Max had arrived at, since he'd not yet stumbled across a woman who inspired eternal devotion. Of course, he couldn't admit to his valet that he was willing to settle for comfort instead of passion. "Why, Thistlewaite, you old dog you, I didn't know you had such a soft streak. I thought you'd have me make one of those dynastic arranged marriages of titles, lands, and money. Lud knows you've been nattering on about this debutante ball or that duke's daughter for ages."

"Exactly, my lord. And nothing came of it."

"Oh, so now you are willing to accept a lesser mortal, to see me in parson's mousetrap. Female, fertile and friendly, that's all, eh? Well, I suppose a fellow could do worse." Max gave one last swipe of the comb across his head, then looked longingly at the hairs left in the comb's teeth. "A lot worse."

Thistlewaite followed his eyes. "Perhaps it is time to consider a hairpiece, my lord."

"What, a wig?" Max practically shouted. "Never!"

"Not an old-fashioned full wig, just a subtle addition to your own hair. The ladies do it all the time, with false curls or added braids for height."

"Good grief, I'm not that vain, man."

"But we do have an appearance to maintain. It's not like buckram wadding to broaden our shoulders, or, heaven forfend, sawdust to pad our calves. We have no need to resort to such subterfuges. But a discreet bit of hair . . ."

"Dash it, I'm not going to wear a dead rat on my head! I'd be the laughingstock of London."

"In London, perhaps, but in Bedfordshire, where no one knows us? 'Twould make a better impression on the young ladies."

Max thought of some sweet young female cringing at his looks, forced by her family to accept his suit. "So I make a better impression. What happens after the wedding night when my new little wife goes to run her fingers through my hair? Surprise, sweetheart, your husband is as bald as a baby's behind?"

Thistlewaite clucked his tongue. "We wear a nightcap for a month or two until she grows used to it."

"Blast it, *we*'re not getting into bed with some silly chit who's going to set up a screech when she finds she's married a plucked goose. I am!" Max snatched up his gloves and headed toward the door. His last glimpse was of Thistlewaite pulling hairs out of his brush, shaking his head. "Deuce take it, I'll think about it. But don't go cutting off the tails of my horses."

Chapter Three

Bachelors in the neighborhood! Bachelors in the neighborhood! It didn't have quite the ring of "For God, King, and Country," but as far as battle calls, it was an effective rally cry. Every proud mama in Bedford, every despairing papa, took note as soon as Lady Halbersham's instructions were delivered to her housekeeper at Briarwoods, the Halbersham estate.

The housekeeper had a cousin, the butler had a crony at the Spotted Dog. A footman was walking out with a maid at Squire's place, and the potboy went home to his mum in the village at night. Every servant in the county soon knew Lady Viola's plans, and every cottager, local merchant, and so on, until word reached those most interested, the wellborn or well-to-do—and their daughters. In the country where every eligible *parti* was known since leading strings, strange gentlemen were noteworthy indeed, especially if they happened to be London swells.

From Lady Halbersham's designations of the rooms to be aired, it was understood that Lord Halbersham's boon companions were to attend. The usual sources—afternoon teas, whispered conferences at the lending library, hasty searches through the back issues of social columns—immediately ascertained that the higher-ranking Lord Blanford was a top-of-the-trees Corinthian, and a confirmed bachelor. No matter. No one is more hopeful than the mother of a pretty girl. That he was reputed to be something of a rake merely added spice. Lord Podell was said to be most unfortunately pockets-to-let, likely on the lookout for an heiress. The poorer girls sighed, for the baron was reportedly as handsome as he could stare. Still, there were bound to be parties and dinners, and even a ball to look forward to in the middle of winter.

Parents started praying, dressmakers started stitching. The local merchants and draymen all found cause to toast Lord Halbersham and his friends. The house party was a success before anyone arrived.

And to Miss Audrina Rowe, it was a godsend. She'd heard at the little vicarage where she called every day to wish her father good morning and make sure Mrs. Dodd had his breakfast eggs cooked just the way he wished. Mrs. Dodd knew all about the house party, from her nevvy who was groom at Briarwoods Manor. Jem Cochlin, delivering the bread, added his bits of information, and even young Master Timothy from Squire's come for his Latin lesson was bursting with the news.

While Audrina was helping Vicar Rowe with his sermon, they even discussed if he should write in a welcome to the strangers to the congregation, for he was liable to forget without his notes.

"I'm not sure such fine London gentlemen will attend our tiny village chapel, Papa. From what I hear, they are not precisely the devout types." Her mind was already full of scraps about gambling, drinking, womanizing, horse-racing. "No, I do not expect to see them in St. Margaret's."

The vicar patted his beloved daughter on the hand. "Now, Audrina, we mustn't listen to gossip, you know, or prejudge guests to our community. I'm sure our Lord Halbersham only knows fine, upstanding gentlemen."

Since anyone, even his eighteen-year-old daughter who'd never been farther afield than an assembly in Upper Throckton, was more worldly than Vicar Rowe, his opinion was suspect. Dree wanted to disagree, but she knew better than to argue with her father, who'd find some good in Lucifer himself. She merely kissed the vicar good-bye.

"Yes, hurry along, Audrina. I'm sure your cousin Carinne will be needing you."

No, Carinne didn't need Dree, except to hand over fresh handkerchiefs to mop up her tears. What Carrie needed was a miracle, and Dree might just have found it—or him. Audrina didn't care if those London toffs were pagan fire-worshipers or peep-o'-day boys. They were young and titled. Either one had to make Carinne a better husband than Lord Prendergast. Now all she had to do was convince Carinne's father, Uncle Augustus Martin, of the fact.

On her way back to White Oaks, her uncle's estate, Dree pondered ways to convince him, since Uncle Augustus was even more set in his opinions than dear Papa. Papa could never hold with thinking ill of anyone; Mr. Martin could never hold with anyone else's thinking, particularly not a female, and a harum-scarum young female to boot. Audrina reminded herself to try to put her flyaway hair in some kind of order before scratching on the door of his library. She shuddered, and not from the cold winter wind.

That library was where Uncle Augustus was wont to shout at servants, scold his daughter, and upbraid his niece for Carinne's shortcomings, as if Dree could make her dear cousin into anything but the loveliest, sweetest girl in all of Bedfordshire. No, Audrina Rowe did not want to face her foul-tempered uncle, but she would, for Carrie's sake.

How could she not, when she owed her cousin so much? Why, the warm cloak she wore right now was a gift, as was the made-over dress she had under it. Dree could never forget the broths and healthful foods Carrie sent down to the vicarage when Papa was so sick last year, and how sometimes she'd sent Dree a coin or two, from her pin money, she said, because the vicar would give his income away in charity. And she did it all despite the wishes of a father she was petrified of, a man who didn't have an ounce of charity in him.

Uncle Augustus gave Audrina room and board now, not out of the goodness of his heart, but so he wouldn't have to hire a companion for his daughter. Not that Dree could show her older cousin how to go on; the fancy boarding school Carrie had attended was supposed to have accomplished that. Dree's purpose was to satisfy conventions, that Mr. Martin's daughter was not traipsing unchaperoned about the countryside like a hoyden. The fact that his niece had to complete the two-mile walk any time she wished to check on Papa mattered naught to Mr. Martin, certainly not enough to permit one of his footmen to accompany her, or a groom to hitch up a pony cart for her. Dree kicked a rock out of her way. She supposed she should be grateful he didn't put her to work mucking out the stalls on the stableboys' half days off. As it was, she already helped the housekeeper with the mending and the butler with the polishing, menial jobs Carrie was never permitted to do as they were considered less than ladylike.

Audrina didn't mind, really, since this was the least hard she'd ever worked in her life. And she did feel lucky to be close to her cousin while helping Papa with the pittance Uncle Augustus gave her, instead of tending someone's spoiled children or testy grandmother. Besides, she'd promised her aunt when that lady passed on that she'd stand Carinne's friend, for Aunt Estelle knew that her sweet-natured daughter would never be able to stand up to Augustus Martin. No one did.

Aunt Estelle and Audrina's own mama were sisters, but what different paths their lives had taken. They were pampered daughters of a marquis, but one with six

23

girls to marry off, and precious little interest in provid-
ing them dowries. Aunt Estelle was bartered into an arranged marriage to the head of the Martin Shipbuilding
firm in Portsmouth, who wanted the noble connection
enough to come down handsomely for his bride. He
grew bitter when he realized his wellborn bride brought
him nothing but cuts, even from her own family. Dree
believed he shouted Aunt Estelle into an early grave.

Audrina's own mother refused to wed the man her father chose, instead running off with the young vicar.
She was happy, except for never seeing any of her family again. They disowned her as quickly as they repudi-
ated the daughter with a husband in trade. Mama had
died from exhaustion and lack of medical care, despite
unanswered pleas to the current marquis, her own
brother. Dree did not have much esteem for the nobility.

Not so Uncle Augustus, who was determined to have
his daughter rise where he could not, to show those
blasted in-laws of his. His birth couldn't open aristocra-
cy's door a crack; his fortune could. Dree didn't think
much of wealth either, if it could only buy the likes of
Lord Prendergast.

Prendergast was old, unwashed, and frog-eyed, with
protuberant white-rimmed orbs that stared and stared.
But he was a marquis, the same as Uncle's despised
brother-in-law. Mr. Martin didn't care that three wives
had predeceased Prendergast, nor that the man had gambled away all three of their dowries. That was why,
Dree surmised, he was now sniffing around Carrie and
her rich portion. His house was ancient and unim-
proved, sitting in the midst of an undrained swamp. It
looked more like something out of a Minerva Press
novel than the setting for delicate, sensitive Carinne,
who simply did not have the courage to be a heroine.
Which was why Carinne was upstairs weeping, and
Audrina was about to knock on her uncle's door.

"What is it, girl? Can't you see I'm busy?" Uncle
Augustus did not look up from his papers.

Dree smoothed the creases on her gown. She only hoped her cheeks didn't still appear reddened from the cold. "I only need a moment of your time, sir. It's about the house party at Briarwoods."

Augustus looked up from his desk and frowned, whether at her usual unkempt appearance, the interruption, or mention of an event that might entail an outlay of funds on his part, Audrina did not know.

"What is it to you, missy? If you've come to beg for a new gown or some gewgaw, save your breath. Swells like those ain't interested in vicars' daughters. Can't wed 'em or bed 'em, so they don't pay 'em no nevermind, no matter how fancy they're rigged out."

Now her face was red anyway. She could feel the heat in her cheeks. "Of course not, sir. I never thought otherwise. But they might be attracted to a beautiful, well-dowered girl like Carinne."

He raised his voice: "Carinne is as good as spoken for, missy. I told you both, and that's the end of it."

Dree put her hands behind her back so he couldn't see her wringing them. "But the banns have not been read, there's been no formal announcement. Why, Lord Prendergast hasn't even made Carrie an offer."

"That's because the silly twit won't come out of her room to see the man," he shouted. "And I won't have it, do you hear me? That gal is turning into a mealy-mouthed watering pot, just like her mother. And she said she'd feel better if you came to stay. Hah! Much good you've been." He pounded his fist on the desk. "Well, I've about reached the end of my patience with both of you, do you hear me?"

Since the end of her uncle's patience followed hard on the beginning of her uncle's patience, Dree hurried on: "But, sir, nothing has been signed yet and . . . and two of the houseguests are bachelors."

Mr. Martin grunted. He'd heard the news and made his own inquiries. "Podell's here to avoid the bill col-

"lectors at his door, and Blanford's giving advice about some horses. That's all."

"Oh, but that's not what I heard, sir. Mrs. Dodd's sister said she heard it directly from one of the maids at Briarwoods, that Lady Halbersham was happy as a grig, playing matchmaker."

"Hmm. Podell would be wise to get himself a wife. That's about all the basket-scrambler can do now to get out of dun territory."

Basket-scrambler? The on dit, from those who swore they'd seen the baron when he drove through the village on his way to Briarwoods, was that Lord Podell was a veritable Adonis. No one mentioned that he was a profligate. "The other gentleman is an earl," she ventured.

"And as well to pass as t'other is below hatches. Blanford's too proud to trade on his title besides."

"But he hasn't seen Carinne yet!" Audrina was sure no gentleman could resist her exquisite cousin.

"Bah, he's seen all the beauties of London without once throwing the handkerchief. That Podell, now, just might be in the market for a carefully reared wife. No, the flat's only a baron."

"But he's young, Uncle," Audrina almost pleaded.

"They both are. Either gentleman is bound to be a better husband for Carinne than Lord Prendergast. She's afraid of him, Uncle, and he smells!" Her own patience was wearing a trifle thin, due mostly to being left standing while her uncle sat behind his desk. She raised her chin. "She's your own daughter, sir. Surely you want her to be happy."

"With a London fribble?" But he was thinking, Dree could tell, about how Halbersham's friends had the entrée everywhere, right up to Carleton House. His daughter would be a fine London lady, instead of being immured in some dank castle with no one to appreciate her elevation in rank except the rats. He rubbed his chin.

"The Earl of Blanford is not such a young man. He'll be wanting a son. . . ."

"Stow your blather, girl. Blanford's too downy a cove to be caught by a pretty face. But Podell . . . I wonder how deep in debt the gudgeon is. Baroness, eh? I just might happen to have a word with the chap at the assembly this week. Suppose they'll be there, if he's serious about jumping into parson's mousetrap. Prendergast can wait."

Dree almost collapsed with relief, and from trying to keep her knees from knocking for so long. She felt confident enough to urge her uncle not to speak to Podell. "You'll ruin everything!"

Martin's jaws snapped shut. "What's that, missy?"

Audrina had just saved her cousin from an arranged marriage; she wasn't about to see her thrown into another one, with another fortune hunter. "Why don't you wait until they meet? After all, the earl is still unattached. He might fall in love with Carrie at first sight. Stranger things have been known to happen."

Augustus eyed her through slitted eyes. "What's it to you, missy, eh, pushing this earl on me? I've got it, you think he's the better catch so Carinne will have more pin money to toss to you and that feckless father of yours. Or are you hoping she'll find a place for you in his lordship's London household?"

In her usual honesty, Dree had to admit to herself that she'd always wanted to see London, the sights, the size of it. She'd even hoped once that her uncle would relent and send Carinne there for a Season. Dree would have gone along as her abigail if they'd let her. Now all she wanted was to see her cousin settled with a man who would treat her kindly.

"Whether you believe me or not, Uncle, I only wish Carinne's happiness." And Dree knew Carrie would only find it if her husband wanted *her*, not her dowry. Carrie deserved a love match, not some cold business transaction. She deserved better, and better than a down-at-heels fortune hunter. Dree vowed to herself that, having gone this far, she'd try to win the earl, the hero, the nonpareil, for Carinne. "So I can tell her there is no engagement to Prendergast?"

"Lord and Lady Habersham are giving a ball for Valentine's Day, eh? There's bound to be socializing sooner than that. I can hold Prendergast off till then without losing him entirely, if you can get Podell to come up to scratch. You'll have to get the chit to stop blubbering, and get her to show some spirit. A man wants a real woman for his wife, not some pretty doll. I'll make sure Podell knows the size of her dot."

Podell might know the size of Carrie's dowry, but Dree meant to make double sure it was the Earl of Blanford who'd collect it.

Chapter Four

Lords Blanford and Podell drove to Briarwoods in one day in Max's curricle. Max kept his hat on the entire drive.

The Halbershams came together into the foyer to greet them, with a butler and three footmen to collect their wraps. Max took a deep breath and cursed Thistlewaite to eternal damnation.

"Think of it as a dowager's turban," the valet had suggested. "Or a crown of state." Max thought of it as a small prehistoric rodent that had crawled to his forehead to die, its feet stuck in the tar pits of gum arabic. "You'll grow used to it," Thistlewaite swore. Max never had grown used to the fleas and lice in Spain, so why this vermin should be any different, he couldn't imagine, despite the valet's assurances that it was human hair. A dead human? A beggar selling his filthy mop for a cup of Blue Ruin? Sweepings from a barber's floor? Gads, it boggled the mind. And it itched. No matter, Max misdoubted he'd get used to looking like a billiard ball any time soon either. He took a deep breath and handed over his curly-brimmed beaver.

"Delighted you decided to come," his host said, enthusiastically shaking Max's hand. "Another male, don't you know. House is at sixes and sevens, what with preparations for the ball." He slapped Max's back to emphasize his welcome.

Blanford's fingers twitched, to reach up for reassurance or, barring that, to plant his doltish friend a facer. Instead he turned to his hostess, who was also in a dither, explaining to Franny that there would not be many other guests until the day of the ball, with so much to do. She was staring at Podell as he unwrapped his muffler, then divested himself of his greatcoat. Franny wore a puce waistcoat under a coat of lavender superfine with buttons as big as dinner plates, and a spotted Belcher neckcloth tied loosely around his neck. His blond curls were perfectly in place, even after a day in the carriage with a hat on. Viola clapped her hands.

"Oh, they'll just adore you!"

Franny was choking on a reply when Max addressed Viola. He still didn't trust a bow, so he took her hands and raised them to his lips.

Viola batted her eyelashes at him. "Why, Max, maybe there is hope for you after all." Gordie was glaring, so Max told her to save the flirting for her husband, at which she turned her attention back to Franny.

Max had started to breathe again when Gordie asked, "What, parting your hair different, Max?"

They all swiveled to stare at his new thatch. "Thistlewaite got carried away, is all," he said, vowing to see the valet carried away—in a pine box!

Viola was studying him, unsure. "Well, it's vastly becoming," she finally announced. "Let's hope you don't raise too many expectations, Max, if you don't mean to be accommodating."

"Let's hope your new style doesn't become the rage, rather," Gordie put in, "for the sake of us stodgy old unfashionables."

And for the sake of free-ranging rodents everywhere, Max amended. Then the moment was blessedly past. Viola took Franny's arm to lead him down the hall. Max and Gordie followed, grinning at the conversation. "Now, dearest," she was saying, as if she weren't ten years Franny's junior, "you must realize I couldn't invite only the heiresses, of course. I couldn't slight the squire or the other local families. But I have made a list of those females whose acquaintance you should particularly pursue. I mean, it wouldn't do for you to fall top over tree for some pretty chit, now that you've decided to take the plunge, if she cannot relieve your, ah, financial difficulties."

Max could see the perspiration dripping down Franny's neck, the poor sacrificial lamb. No way was Max going to let Lady Vi get a hint of his own intentions, but he just might peruse that list of the vicinity's wellborn females.

At dinner that evening the gentlemen were introduced to the rest of the small house party. Viola's younger brother Warden was there by mischance, having been sent down from school. The lad fancied himself a poet, and wore his hair in long, flowing locks to his shoulders. Max hated him on sight.

There were also two youngish females, bosom bows of Viola's, invited to even out the numbers. The Peckham sisters were a few years past their come-outs, if you counted years in dogs' ages, and they were everything Max didn't want in a wife. Oh, they were pretty enough and well mannered, dressed in the height of London fashion, albeit too gaudy for a simple country dinner. But they also giggled and simpered and lisped, and they fluttered their eyelashes at him so hard, Max feared for his toupee, caught in the crosswind. Their only interests seemed to be in gowns and gossip, with no willingness to be pleased with the usual country pastimes like walking or riding. They did not want to visit the local church or the nearby village, and were bored after one day at Briarwoods, to Viola's chagrin. If they thought Max was going to stay indoors all day entertaining them, they were more corkbrained than they seemed. And if they thought to attach his interest with pouting and striking poses, they were outright attics-to-let. He might offer for a female like that— when hell froze over.

"The pond might be frozen soon. Perhaps we can get up a skating party," Viola offered with a hint of desperation. Then she brightened. "And there is the assembly at Upper Throckton tomorrow night. You'll get to meet my neighbors."

Which was worse, trying to ensnare a gentleman with a lady's looks or with her father's pocketbook? Dree refused to acknowledge that prickling of guilt over what she was doing. She was *not* hoping to snabble an unsuspecting, unwilling *part* for Carinne; she just wanted to bring her cousin to the attention of the eligibles. Then they could discover Carrie's inner goodness for themselves.

"Perhaps a dab of rouge, Meg?" she asked her cousin's maid, biting her lip.

"Miss Audrina, and you a vicar's daughter! Face paint, indeed!"

"Yes, but my cousin looks as pale as her bedclothes. Carrie, can't you stop fidgeting?"

"How can I when . . . when . . ."

"When your whole life depends on tonight's assembly? Because of that, peagoose!" Meg was reaching for the hare's-foot brush. "And there is nothing to worry about. You look exquisite, as always." Dree twitched at the tiny puff sleeves of Carrie's pale pink gown, with its overdress of white net strewn with silk roses that matched the flowers woven through Carrie's golden hair. "Like a fairy princess."

"I wish you had a new gown, too, Dree. I could have—"

"No, you do enough. And I couldn't have used my allowance for such frippery, when Papa gives so much of his salary to the needy. What's new finery compared to enough firewood at the vicarage? My ivory gown is good enough."

Carrie looked doubtful and Meg clucked her tongue. The old satin gown hadn't been good enough for the year and a half Dree had been wearing it. It was once Audrina's mother's, and was once white. She'd dyed it with tea, but it was still out of style, ill fitting, and well known at the local assemblies. Audrina fingered the new blue ribbons she'd spent precious pennies on. Sometimes she wished things were different, too, but she wasn't one to lament over what couldn't be changed, so she flashed her cousin her best smile. "What good would a new gown do me anyway, silly, when everyone will be looking at you? You have enough beauty for the family. And no new frock is going to fix this"—she fussed with an errant orangy red curl, already escaping its matching blue ribbon—"or give me your elegant inches so much in style. Or a bosom."

"Dree!"

"Well, it's true, and made you laugh. See, you *can* enjoy yourself. Just think, you're not engaged to old frog-face. That should be enough to celebrate. And if none of the men there tonight pleases you, well, we'll think of something else."

"Like staying in my room so Prendergast couldn't make his offer in form? That was brilliant, Dree!"

"And it got us this time. So do not fret yourself, but *do* try to smile at all the rich, handsome, charming earls you meet. It shouldn't be too difficult. According to Mrs. Harribow at the inn, the gentlemen stopped there on their ride yesterday, and the earl was everything gracious." She didn't say how Mrs. Harribow only wanted to go on and on about the other gentleman, the one with blond hair and heavenly blue eyes, in the most elegant clothes that lady had ever seen. "Not high in the instep at all. And George at the livery said he was mounted on the finest bit of blood and bone in all England, and rode like the wind. 'A regular goer,' " she quoted.

"Oh dear. You know I can't . . . That is, I don't . . . They're so big, Dree." There went all the color from Carrie's cheeks, except the spots brushed on.

Dree cursed herself and patted her cousin's hand. "No gentleman expects a lady to ride neck or nothing, dearest. Just wait till he hears you at the pianoforte. That's what a man admires." She spoke authoritatively, to cover her total lack of knowledge, experience, or conviction. Carrie was trained in all the ladylike pursuits such as watercolors and needlework. They had to be worth something, hadn't they?

Carrie was still worried about the horses, Dree could tell. Her cousin was twisting the strings of her beaded reticule into knots. Dree took the bag from her to untangle. "No matter what else, you can be happy that Lord Prendergast won't be there tonight. He thinks himself above the common folk who can attend if they have the subscription fee."

"I heard he once had to partner the butcher's wife, and that was the last time he came to an assembly," Carrie's smile flickered. "Lord Blanford isn't like that, is he? I mean, he won't expect me to cut my friends dead, will he, like Mama's family did? What if he . . . He might . . ."

He'd better not, Dree swore to herself, but she told her cousin, "Of course not. He wouldn't be coming, else. And you know how the whole town was buzzing when Lady Habersham reserved all those extra tickets."

"Yes, for those London ladies in her house party. Oh, Dree, I know they'll put us all to shame with their fine manners and clothes and jewels!"

"No one can outshine you," Dree said firmly. "And the *on dit* is that those two friends of Lady Habersham's are firmly on the shelf. But if they try to capture all the gentlemen's attention, I'll . . . I'll . . ." She was sounding like her cousin now. "I'll spill punch on their gowns so they have to go home."

"Dree, you wouldn't!"

Meg clucked her tongue again. "Miss Audrina, your papa would be shamed, he would."

Papa would already be mortified if he knew his daughter was wondering what it would be like to wear diamonds and pearls and have an elegant gentleman flirt with her. Perhaps some handsome nobleman would ask her to ride? Dree had never been mounted on anything more exciting than her papa's old cob. Perhaps he'd sweep her off her feet and away to London, to countless balls and entertainments. Perhaps he'd offer Papa a fortune, for the honor of his daughter's hand.

Perhaps she'd get so excited if he even noticed her that she'd spill the punch on her own skirts.

Chapter Five

It was just a dance, like countless others the earl had attended, with the same overheated rooms, the same insipid refreshments, the same inane chatter. Unlike most parties Lord Blanford usually graced, here he would be expected to dance with the schoolmaster's sister, the drayman's daughter, and the not-so-prepossessing niece of the neighboring squire. He wouldn't have minded in the ordinary way of things. Didn't he always have a dance with his housekeeper at Public Day fetes? The mixed company reminded Max of his army days, which he hated, except for the men who'd likewise come from all walks of life. None of their sisters was a suitable Countess of Blanford either. And if he did take the floor, Max told himself, good manners dictated that he dance with his hostess and then the Peckham sisters, his fellow houseguests. Duty dances would take half the evening, with no opportunity to look about him for those females on Viola's list. He was determined to find his bride as expeditiously as possible.

What convinced him to look for her along the walls rather than on the dance floor, though, was the music. No graceful waltzes for this company; they were too

36

fast. Instead the small orchestra played country dances, mad jigs and boisterous reels. With all that hopping and capering about in this heat, he'd be wearing his hairpiece as a mustache next.

Max dared not chance it, so he made his excuses as soon as his party was settled in the assembly room. "You'll have to do the honors tonight, Gordie, Frances. You, too, Warden. My apologies, ladies, I can't dance. War wound, don't you know." He limped off, leaving at least one of his friends openmouthed.

"War wound? I thought he caught a fever, not a bu— Ouch!"

Lord Halbersham kicked Franny. "Not the thing to discuss in front of the ladies."

Max found the punch bowl, and a convenient post he could lean against, to watch the company. He made note of the females Lady Halbersham dragged Franny toward between dances, to put his name on their cards. From his vantage point, Max could see that Vi kept trying to head Franny toward two specific females, an absolutely stunning blonde and a little redheaded frump of a thing. The smaller chit kept taking the other's hand and dragging her off, into the arms of the innkeeper, the squire's son, and other local lads. All of the blonde's partners gazed worshipfully at the beauty, while the redheaded girl kept throwing glances in Max's direction, the forward baggage.

The little dowd in the dingy gown wasn't the only female trying to catch his eye, of course, but Max couldn't help watching the two girls, and wondering. One was so elegant, with a dress from one of Bond Street's priciest modistes, if he was any judge, and a diamond necklace that outshone anything in the room. The other was as shabby as the worn-out draperies pulled closed against the night air. She was just as popular as her friend, though, dancing every dance also. The young sprigs she chose as partners didn't just stare into her eyes, either, they laughed and chatted, and skipped merrily along. Max was feeling ancient again. Dash it, he thought, if he hadn't listened to Thistlewaite, he could have been on the dance floor having a high old time, too!

He asked Viola about the two females when the orchestra took a short intermission and his party gathered near the pillar he was supporting.

"The taller one is Miss Carinne Martin. I've been trying to introduce her to Franny all night, but the wretched girl keeps moving around and dancing. Her father is Augustus Martin."

"Of the shipbuilding company?" At Viola's nod, Max whistled. "Not even Franny could run through that fortune."

Viola nodded again. "Exactly. And her father is said to be holding out for a title, so it's perfect. The father is totally unacceptable, of course, but there's good blood on the mother's side. Miss Martin has been carefully raised, educated at a very proper young ladies' seminary in Bath. And she is certainly a beauty. That's why I've been trying to introduce her to Franny all night."

It sounded ideal, for Franny. "And the other?" he heard himself asking. He watched the redhead laughingly accept her blue ribbon from her last partner and try to tie back the wayward curls that tumbled about her shoulders. That fiery mane would look better spread out on a pillow, he found himself thinking.

"That hoyden?" one of the Peckham sisters asked, jealous of his interest. "She's naught but a poor relation, hanging on Miss Martin's sleeve."

Viola had also noticed Max's interest, and she read it correctly. "She might be a poor relation, but it's on the maternal side. One of the Dorset Kennleworths, don't you know. Besides, she's the vicar's daughter, Max, so don't get any untoward notions. You can take that gleam in your eye straight back to your fancy pieces in

London. I'll not have you working your wiles on such an innocent child as Audrina Rowe."

That innocent child was waving her fan at him in unmistakable invitation, unless Max missed his guess. He decided to stroll in that direction. For Franny's sake.

"Come on, old chap. Let's see if we have better luck scraping up an invitation to Miss Martin for you. Wealth and beauty, what more can a fellow ask?"

Conversation, for one. Miss Martin kept her eyes on the floor and her lips firmly closed. Luckily the cousin spoke up as soon as the squire's wife completed the introductions. Unfortunately, the vicar's daughter addressed all of her remarks to Max. Miss Audrina Rowe seemed determined to ignore Franny altogether, quickly asking about Max's journey, his first opinions of the neighborhood, even about his horse.

"For you must know the villagers are singing the praises of your mount. My cousin has a great appreciation of fine horseflesh. She rides out all the time, don't you, Carinne?"

Carinne blanched. She never rode anything but her ancient pony, and then only when no one was about to drive her in the carriage. Franny was squirming. Max crossed his arms over his chest, no help at all.

Audrina was not about to give up. "Do you enjoy music, Lord Blanford? We're thinking of having a musicale. Carinne has the loveliest voice. I swear, she's better than any I've heard." Since Dree had heard no trained voices at all, ever, that was not such a rapper as the horseback riding. Encouraged to be once again on the side of the truth, she rushed on: "And watercolors! How Carinne can paint! I only wish I was artistic, but she must have received all of the talent in the family. Have you viewed Somerset House, Lord Blanford? One of Carinne's instructors had a painting exhibited there. Perhaps you've seen it. What was the man's name, Carrie?"

"Mr. . . . Mr. . . ." The beauty raised her eyes in agony to her cousin, but caught Lord Podell's admiring gaze instead. Franny smiled.

"Not great on names m'self, Miss Martin."

Carinne smiled back. Dree looked from her beautiful cousin to the beautiful young man in his burgundy velvet coat crisscrossed by fob chains and ribbons. They were gazing at each other like mooncalves. Carrie hadn't spared a glance for Lord Blanford, keeping her eyes firmly on the toes of her shoes. How could Carrie prefer that dandy to the earl in his understated black with white unmentionables? Lord Blanford was elegant, refined, wearing his obviously expensive clothes with unstudied grace, instead of being worn by starched shirt collars and a cravat that could swaddle three infants. Why, the man was a fop, besides being a fortune hunter!

As the music started up again, Dree turned to the earl. "You don't dance, my lord?"

So she'd noticed. Max wasn't surprised. He was used to having females notice his actions. "War wound," was all he said. "Sorry."

"My cousin will be pleased to sit out with you, won't you, Carrie?"

"But I was . . . That is, Mr. Thatcher . . ."

"Why, Mr. Thatcher," the minx chirped, "here you are right on time for our dance."

As Max watched, Miss Rowe latched on to a gap-toothed lad in rough clothes who was as coherent as Miss Martin. Max would swear it was the first Mr. Thatcher knew of his promised dance with the little redhead. Before he or Max could protest, though, the chit grabbed the hand of a young female in yellow ruffles and had her partnered to Franny for the *contra danse* forming. They all left, leaving him with the tongue-tied heiress. Max was equally dumbfounded. Dashed if he hadn't been outmaneuvered by a flea-sized nobody as managing as a dowager duchess. But why?

Viola had said the chit was an innocent, but she'd

been casting out lures to him all evening. He'd caught enough in his time to know. The audacious female was a regular flirt who'd make a perfect Cyprian, if she wasn't a vicar's daughter. But why hand him, the biggest fish in the matrimonial waters, over to her cousin? What kind of female would do that? None he knew. Most young ladies he knew, in fact, wouldn't stand next to such a diamond as Miss Martin, much less befriend her. Miss Audrina Rowe was decidedly not an ordinary girl.

Just look at her dance, Max mused, curls tossed every which way, her laughter ringing out when her hair ribbon got lost and trampled. London females would be devastated. They'd be cringing if forced to appear in such an outmoded frock, hiding in the corners so no one saw the darned patches on their gloves. Not Miss Rowe. She was laughing and enjoying herself—and so was her partner. The farm lad had got over his disappointment quickly enough, Max saw, as the boy laughed with her and held her hand longer than the figures of the dance required. Max didn't like him. He was sure that Thatcher chap was a dirty dish. And hadn't there been a whiff of the stables still about him?

The earl's scowl had Carinne cowering at his side, which earned him a fierce look from the cousin, as she and Thatcher turned in the pattern of the dance. Miss Rowe's frown brought Max back to earth, and back to his manners. He was a gentleman, after all.

"Your cousin is an excellent dancer," Max put forth.

His conversational offering was the proper choice, for Miss Martin instantly agreed, without a hint of a stutter, even going so far as to add, "She is the finest cousin a girl could have."

Max's questions about her other relatives, her preferred dance, and comments on the neighboring scenery, anything he could think of, brought back the stammer. It took all of his charm to coax a complete sentence out of the beauty. And then it was: "Oh dear, I wish Dree were here."

"Dree? Miss Audrina?" At her nod he spoke his frustration at finding himself in a backwater with an awkward handful. "She can't always be around to entertain your dance partners, you know."

Those china-doll blue eyes glimmered. Tears? Good grief, Max thought, the chit was going to cry, right there in the assembly rooms. He knew without looking that the cousin would be shooting him dagger looks. Devil take managing females! He renewed his efforts with Miss Martin, fabricating a childhood as a shy, stuttering boy who hated being out among strangers. Miss Martin was actually smiling at his Banbury tale by the time Thatcher brought Miss Rowe back.

Dree flashed the earl a radiant smile to see her cousin looking so comfortable. She was right; they were a perfect pair. Her self-congratulations ended as the earl handed Carinne to Lord Podell for the next dance. There was no way Dree could prevent that dance, not without causing a scene that might give the earl a disgust of them altogether. Her smile faded even more when Lord Blanford turned to her again.

"Perhaps you'll take pity and sit out this set with a poor veteran, Miss Rowe, while your cousin does my friend the honor of dancing?" Max tried not to smirk, wondering how Miss Rowe appreciated being outflanked.

She didn't like it at all. "It's a pity indeed about your injury. How fortunate it doesn't interfere with your neck-or-nothing riding."

Max only smiled at the sarcasm, trying to remember to limp when he brought her a lemonade. She glared at him over the cup. What had the volatile chit in the boughs now?" he wondered. She had the most eligible man in the room fetching her drink, and all she could do was glower. Her ill temper wasn't directed at him, Max belatedly realized, but at her peahen of a cousin who was gliding serenely on Franny's arm, smiling into the eyes of her handsome partner without a hint of awkwardness. Franny was grinning back, relieved he didn't have to make conversation. Together they were a fairy-tale couple, and Miss Rowe was acting the evil stepsister.

"Bedfordshire is surprisingly full of charming young ladies," Max ventured, although why he thought to turn the vixen up sweet, he didn't know, except for a wish to see that carefree delight she'd shown the farmer.

Lukewarm and trite as it was, Max's compliment did restore Audrina's good humor. He'd been caught! Dree had to clutch her hands together to keep from clapping. "My cousin, you mean. Isn't Carrie the most beautiful girl in the world? And she's as good and kind as she is pretty. I just knew you'd like her if you got the chance to know her."

And Miss Rowe went on extolling her cousin's talents and traits, with a dazzling smile lighting up her face. The freckles that would sink a London deb's chances seemed to belong with that radiant glow, Max thought, like sunshine. She even had dimples. Max listened to her happy babble with half an ear while he admired the view, until her words and intent finally sunk in. Miss Audrina Rowe was matchmaking on her beautiful, wealthy cousin's behalf! He was astounded again at her unselfishness, and then he was chagrined. The vicar's daughter, a frumpy, flyaway little female, wasn't interested in the Earl of Blanford—except as a *parti* for her relation! And for this he was wearing the clippings from a shorn poodle?

Chapter Six

Gordon, Lord Halbersham, wasn't having any better time of it. He took up a position near Max's pillar after Miss Rowe skipped away on the arm of another bucolic beau. From there the viscount could watch his wife flirt with every man in the room from the septuagenarian squire to some spotted youth. Whilst Gordie listened to Viola tittering at some remark from an ill-clad country-man, Max listened to Gordie's teeth grinding. Fine, Max thought, he'd lose his hair; Gordie'd lose his chop-pers.

"Deuce take it, man, don't just stand there. Take the chit home and make her forget that any other man exists on this earth."

"You mean . . . ?"

"Yes, you clothhead, that's precisely what I mean. Go now before you can only gum at her earlobes. You can send the carriage back for Franny and me. We'll see the Peckham sisters home."

"What will I tell Viola to get her to leave so early?"

"You're the diplomat, Gordie. You can think of some reason. Or tell her you have the headache. Women use that excuse all the time."

"Only because they can't claim war wounds," Gordie

said with a wink as he moved off to cross the dance floor. He tapped his wife's partner on the shoulder and whispered something in Viola's ear that brought an instant blush to her cheeks. Max shook his head. For a politician, Halbersham had no subtlety. But Vi did agree to leave, so perhaps Gordon knew best after all. Who was Max to give advice about women, after tonight's fiasco?

Without Viola to choose his partners, Lord Podell was soon sharing Max's post instead of Halbersham. Together they watched the rest of the assembly.

"Did you meet all the females on Vi's list?" Max asked.

"Enough," Franny replied, grinning hugely. "Ain't she exquisite?"

There was no need to ask which *she* Franny meant. "A diamond of the first water indeed, but—"

"No buts. She's the one."

"How can you be sure? It's early days, man. You've only had one dance with the chit, and not a lot of conversation at that, I'd guess." He'd swear, in fact, that Miss Martin didn't have two bits of conversation to rub together.

Franny rocked on his heels, looking like the cat that got the canary. "A chap just knows. Miss Carinne is quiet, peaceful-like. She came right out and told me she didn't expect a fellow to keep thinking up things to say. You know, that humgudgeon the poetic types are always spouting at a pretty gal. Embarrass her, she said. Would embarrass me to say it. We suit."

"I still say it's early days to be calling the banns. You haven't met her father yet. I hear he's a rum go."

"According to Viola, all he cares about is snabbling a title and getting his daughter accepted in London society. You know I've got the entrée everywhere."

Max thought of that tongue-tied chit in the midst of Almack's patronesses. Might as well feed her to the lions at the Tower. "Do you think Miss Martin would like London? You said yourself she's quiet."

"And you said I should marry a rich girl and install her at m'country place. But I've half a mind to take Miss Martin to London anyway. Show her off, don't you know. She'll like the shops and the theater. And if she don't talk to anyone else, well, at least I won't have to worry myself to flinders like poor Gordon." Franny twirled his quizzing glass on its ribbon, satisfied. Then he raised it to his eye to examine Max more closely. "I say, you ain't trying to discourage me because you're interested yourself, are you? Beautiful girl and an heiress. I couldn't blame you."

"No, no, I've no intention of trying to cut you out with Miss Martin. I just think you should get to know her better before making such a momentous decision." Franny didn't hear anything but the denial. "Good. Her father'd toss me on my ear if he thought you were in the running. Stands to reason. Any father would. Mean to say, don't have much to offer. But I'll swear to make her happy. Mean it, too. That should win him over."

Not from what Max had heard about Augustus Martin. "Lud, just don't go plead your case too soon or he'll think you're a Bedlamite, or a fortune hunter. Once you get to know the chit, then you can swear undying devotion, not yet."

Franny sucked on the handle of the looking glass. "How long? Mean to say, all these other chaps won't let such a jewel go unclaimed. Do you think a week's enough time to convince Mr. Martin I'm sincere about Miss Carinne?"

"Wait a month at least. Then, once you know her better, you can put your luck to the test if you're of the same mind."

"Two weeks. And I will be."

* * *

Audrina was right: the party from Briarwoods did not attend services at her father's church the next morning, but not because the Halbershams felt themselves too grand for the humble village chapel. They overslept. Then they had to bundle their guests into carriages for the ride to Upper Throckton for the late service. After church the viscount and his lady disappeared upstairs again, which had the Peckham sisters tittering and Viola's brother Warden snickering over his mutton until Max fixed him with a stare.

"You'll have to take over as host for your brother-in-law this afternoon. Lord Podell and I have to make a call at Mr. Martin's White Oaks."

Franny had still felt the same the next morning. He was all for riding out to visit, to see if Miss Martin could be as lovely by daylight, until Max reminded him it was Sunday. He would have to wait till late afternoon, at least.

"You'll come along, won't you, Max? Mean to say, you know how to go on."

Max rather thought he would accompany Franny, and not only to oversee the other's courtship. Warden thought he might accompany them, too. "What, and leave our two charming fellow guests alone?"

Warden groaned. His Greek studies weren't half as boring as those two haughty Peckham females. "But I'd like to quiz Miss Rowe about her knowledge of the classics. With her father the vicar, and him giving lessons, perhaps she'd—"

"No," Max snapped. Warden had youth and hair. He didn't need the company of the only interesting female in the neighborhood.

The interesting female was shredding a roll. Uncle Augustus was taking his midday meal with associates in Throckton, so the two cousins had the dining room to themselves. Carinne wasn't eating her nuncheon either, but instead of fretting, Miss Martin was staring dream-

47

ily into space, her lips gently curved. Almost like an angel getting her first glimpse of heaven, Dree thought
impatiently. "What do you mean, you prefer Lord
Podell? I grant you, the man is as handsome as a Greek
god, but truly, Carrie, how can you? He's naught but a
man-milliner."

"So elegant, such a sense of style. And kind."

"Kind? The man is a fortune hunter! Why, you'd
never know if he cared for you or for your father's
gold."

"I'd never know with any man, but Lord Podell
seemed to like me."

"Perhaps he was just being polite. We might never
see any of the Briarwoods party again. They didn't attend church." And Carinne could be awkward at times,
Dree had to admit. Such a distinguished gentleman as
the Earl of Blanford was used to more sophisticated
company.

"He'll come." Carinne was positive. And pleased.

"But a Bond Street stutter, Carrie? You know you
never wanted to go to London."

"I never wanted a Season, rather. I'd enjoy the shops
and seeing the sights. And you were the one who tried
to convince me to go, for the cultural advantages. Besides, Lord Podell means to make his property in Warwick his home for most of the year."

"What, that starched and curled dandy means to set
up as a farmer?"

"He intends to try to bring his estates back into pros-
perity."

"He means to reclaim his acreage with your money,
you mean."

"I'd rather that than see Lord Prendergast gamble it
all away, wouldn't you?"

"Anything is better than Lord Prendergast," Audrina
conceded, finally taking a bite of her capon. She waited
till the footman brought the dessert pudding before she
tried again. "Don't you think you might consider Lord

Blanford?" She pictured the earl, tall and broad, with an air of command about him. He was strong, confident, capable. In short, everything manly. Dree knew her own experience of men was woefully short, but didn't doubt for a minute that his lordship would stand out in any gathering, noblemen or otherwise. "He's quick-witted and amusing, too."

"He frightens me."

"Spiders frighten you, goose. Do say you'll try to be friendly, if he should pay his addresses."

Carinne dropped her spoon. "Oh, I pray he won't! Papa will be sure to prefer him to Lord Podell."

And for once Audrina would agree with Uncle Augustus, but she'd keep her own counsel for now.

Miss Rowe might have kept a silent tongue in her mouth, but her actions spoke volumes—to Lord Blanford, at least—when he and Franny were shown into the ornately furnished drawing room that afternoon. Audrina jumped up and rang for tea after the initial greetings, and then tugged at Lord Podell's arm until he joined her on the crocodile-legged sofa, leaving Max to sit next to Miss Martin on the facing couch.

The others were oblivious to the machinations, however. After examining his saffron satin sleeve for hints of creases, Franny stared across the space into Miss Martin's eyes. She stared back, a tinge of rose on her creamy cheeks. The two could have been alone on the moon for all the attention they paid Dree and the earl. And they did look wondrous together, Dree had to admit, his lordship like a jonquil, and Carrie in a pale rose muslin that showed off her rounded form and elegant shoulders. A veritable garden of beauty.

Audrina frowned. Max grinned, as though he could read her thoughts, earning him another fierce look for not trying harder to engage her cousin in conversation. Dree couldn't fault the earl's appearance, in navy blue superfine and dove gray pantaloons. That was how a man ought to dress, she firmly believed. How could

Carrie not even glance in his direction? It was all Dree could do to keep from staring at the earl's firm legs, so well fitted were his trousers. And that devilish grin, lop-sided and boyish, with warm brown eyes that had a def-inite twinkle; how could Carrie ignore him?

It never once occurred to Dree that Lord Blanford was ignoring Carrie. Oh, he'd noticed how stunning she looked in the fashionable high-waisted gown with trail-ing ribbons—hell, a man would have to be turned to stone not to notice, not to appreciate. But he had a whole collection of beautiful artworks to admire. That wasn't what he wanted in a wife. Of course, a hobble-dehoy schoolgirl like Miss Rowe, in a shapeless sack of indeterminate color after so many washings and turn-ings, wasn't what he wanted either. The chit's red hair was all atumble again, and no, his fingers were not itch-ing to feel the silky fire; he only wanted to brush the curls off her satiny cheeks. Freckled cheeks, he amended. The chit had freckles. And she was devious and manipulative, everything he hated in a female. Wasn't she trying to hint Franny away with mention of her uncle's business connections, when asked Mr. Mar-tin's whereabouts? She managed to interject her uncle's sharp dealing, in case he missed the point that the man was in trade.

The only thing Franny missed was the opportunity to meet his future father-in-law and lay his heart at the man's feet. Miss Martin was an angel. Their fingers brushed over the tray of poppy-seed cakes. His day was complete.

Not so Audrina's. She was not ready to give up, even against admittedly overwhelming odds. "We're plan-ning a skating party for the next nice afternoon," she decided that instant. "There's a lovely pond behind the house that the gardeners have cleared of last week's snow. They say it is well frozen. We'll have a bonfire going alongside, and Cook can provide hot cider. We were hoping you would come, with the rest of Lady Halbersham's house party, of course."

What Dree was hoping, of course, was that Lord Podell would refuse. The popinjay wouldn't want to get his clothes mussed, she thought. Or he'd make a cake of himself on the ice, letting the earl's undoubtedly athletic prowess shine.

"Carrie's the most graceful skater in the village," she added for Blanford's sake when he accepted on the house party's behalf, and this time she told the truth. Carrie loved to skate and looked beautiful doing it. Surely the earl could not help but be entranced. And surely Carrie would finally see the overdressed Tulip Podell for a useless ornament.

Of course, Dree hadn't counted on the recent Frost Fair in London, when Lord Podell skated up and down the Thames for days. And she hadn't counted on Lord Blanford's war injury, which was going to keep him off the ice and away from Carinne.

Chapter Seven

"A war injury?" If that was what kept the Earl of Blanford at the side of the pond when all the others were gaily skating, how was he to explain to a neighbor lad eager for battle stories? That an enemy saber took off the top of his head and he had to keep a small bear-skin rug on it to keep his gray matter warm? That a cannon blast split his skull, so he couldn't bend over for fear of his brains spilling out?

He refused to lie about a shattered knee or such. That would dishonor the wounds his fellow soldiers suffered. He also refused to chance a fall on the ice. There hadn't been much opportunity for practice on the Peninsula, so Max was certain to go down at least once. He didn't mind looking like a jackanapes in front of his friends and their friends by losing his balance, or even losing his hat. His topknot was another story.

Hell and damnation, Max swore as he stomped around the edge of the pond in an effort to keep his toes from freezing, and to keep out of the reach of army-mad youths. What a cursed nuisance. He never should have come into the country where a man was expected to exert himself. He never should have let his valet convince him to don such an unreliable subterfuge. Just last night he'd feared he was going deaf in his dotage, besides, until he realized the blasted thing had slipped sideways, over his ear. Now he was forced to sit on the sidelines, weak-kneed. This was the first time Maxim Blanding had measured his courage and found it wanting. He was also wanting something stronger than the hot mulled cider the Martin servants were pouring out near the bonfire.

And, he had to admit, he was wanting to be out on the ice joining in the fun with an insufferable little female who was spinning madly, playing crack the whip with Warden and some of the local boys. He could pick her out by the red cape she wore—a hand-me-down, he supposed, which clashed horribly with her curls—or by her laughter that rang out even from the pond's farthest shores.

As Max watched, Audrina challenged the boys to a race, tearing across the ice in a mad scramble, all of them bareheaded, the harum-scarum lot. They didn't care if they fell or bumped into anyone, chancing some innocent skater's collapse. Max unconsciously tugged his beaver hat down tighter. He dragged his thoughts away from the hoyden in red before he did something foolish, and his eyes away from the childish fun, before they turned green with envy.

The cousin and Franny skated by, waving to him. Carinne was as graceful as promised, and stunning with her golden beauty framed by the sable lining of the hood of her maroon cape. Franny had a matching maroon muffler tied around his neck, as though they had planned it. Perhaps they had, for Franny hadn't left Miss Martin's side since helping tie on her skates. He even managed to guide their path around obstacles, all the while gazing into the Incomparable's eyes. They skated together as if they'd been doing it for years, and as if to violin music only they could hear. They glided effortlessly into magical turns, in perfect time.

Viola and Gordie were a perfect contrast. They darted

past in fits and starts, chuckling over mishaps, his hat gone flying, her muff skidding across the ice. But they were together, and laughing, Max was glad to see.

Even Mr. Martin made an appearance on the ice. Max thought he must have come to get a look at his prospective son-in-law, but the shipbuilder did lead both Peckham sisters across the frozen pond. He skated in slow, jerky steps, but at least their host was doing his duty by them . . . as Max wasn't.

So he was being discourteous, dishonorable, and deceitful, besides being depressed that he was missing what looked like a fine time. And all for the sake of a few strands of hair. No, a few strands were all he had left on the top. He was putting himself through this torture for his valet's sake. That and his vanity. He was almost of a mind to return to Briarwoods, give Thistlewaite the sack—and the hairpiece—then ride to London to face his future as a doomed, bare-domed bachelor. He'd leave this minute, damned if he wouldn't, before the hair on his chest froze off, too.

Then Miss Rowe skated to a stop in front of him. Her nose was red, adding to the offending color scheme. Max thought she looked adorable.

"I'm sorry about your wound, my lord. I should have thought of some other entertainment that you could enjoy with us."

"No, no. Not at all. I'm quite happy to watch. Very pleasant." Gads, her guilty apology was all he needed to make him feel even lower than the dirt beneath his feet—if he could still feel his feet. To change the subject, Max gestured toward Franny and Carinne, executing intricate figures in the middle of the pond. "They skate magnificently together, don't they?"

"They look like an artist's portrayal of winter bliss," Dree said with a sigh.

"And you don't approve?"

"Forgive me for speaking ill of your friend, but he's

a ne'er-do-well! I didn't want a basket-scrambler for Carrie. She deserves so much better!"

"Have you thought that Franny might see all of her fine qualities, too? Perhaps he likes her, the same as you do."

"He's not worthy of her!"

"Why, because his pockets are to let? It's not his fault, Miss Rowe, that his father gambled away his inheritance and left him with a mound of debts and a mortgaged estate. He's done his best to hold on to Podell Hall for his descendants. And you shouldn't fault a man for the cut of his coat." Or the length of his hair. "Franny can't participate in all the expensive pastimes of his cronies, so he indulges in his tailoring. He's entitled to some pleasure, isn't he?"

"I suppose I've judged him too harshly," Audrina conceded. "But a man's character doesn't show at first; his peacock's costume does."

"I can swear to his character, Miss Rowe. Frances Podell is a good friend, brave and loyal. He's not a gambler or a womanizer. He's just a terrible dresser."

"Carrie thinks he's elegant." Audrina shrugged. "At least he's better than Prendergast."

"Good grief, even a loveless marriage to Franny would be better than that. And I guarantee this isn't merely a match of convenience. Just look at them. You'd have to be blind not to see they are well suited."

Dree didn't have to look. She knew what she'd see: February lovebirds smelling of April and May. And she couldn't look over at the couple ice-dancing on clouds behind her, for she was too busy gathering a handful of the remains of last week's snowfall. She launched her hurriedly rounded missile with deadly accuracy at his lordship's high-crowned beaver hat. "It's too lovely a day to be so stuffy."

His lordship was not amused. He turned and dived after the hat—and his escaping hairpiece—while Dree was still giggling. Max slammed the hat back on before anyone could see what was inside it, instead of being on his head. He was sputtering with anger. Thistlewaite wasn't there for him to strangle, so he took his rage out on Audrina. "You . . . you brat! How dare you? Go play with the other children."

That hurt. Dree had been running her father's household for years, and taking on responsibilities for the parish long before most girls put their skirts down. She knew the earl could never see her as an equal, no matter how pleasantly he acted toward her, since their worlds were so far apart. Yet she thought they might be friends. She'd only meant to bring him some fun, not remind him she was naughty but a vicar's ragtag brat.

The others were taking up the game, the men tossing snowballs while the ladies squealed. Lady Halbersham snuck up behind her husband, who was aiming at Franny, and dumped a handful of snow down his collar. Lord Halbersham turned with a roar and scooped his wife up, to deposit her facedown in the bank of cleared snow at the edge of the pond.

Lord Blanford stalked off.

"Starched-up old sobersides," Dree muttered, brushing snowy mittens across suddenly damp eyes. "Lord Frances is a better choice for Carrie after all," she sniffed. "I'm glad she didn't pick any toplofty earl who is too full of himself and his dignity to have a good time. Go play with the children indeed." She couldn't resist one last toss, which landed squarely in the middle of Blanford's broad back. "And don't forget to limp this time," she shouted after him.

The next morning the earl sent a box of bonbons for Audrina, and she made her prettiest apology when he came to call with Franny that afternoon.

"Let's forget the unfortunate episode, shall we?" Max offered. "We mustn't be at odds, for it looks as if we'll be seeing a great deal of each other."

Carinne and Lord Podell were going through music at

the pianoforte, with more glances into each other's eyes than glances at the titles on the sheets. To give them some privacy while still protecting Carinne's reputation, Dree had to lead the earl aside and keep him entertained. She tried to be her most mature and demure, pouring out the tea with the airs of a duchess. Her good intentions lasted until the next morning when the gentlemen arrived with two mares in tow, begging the honor of a ride.

Carinne could do just fine at a walk, Lord Podell assured her. He wouldn't leave her side, the mare was perfectly behaved, and Miss Martin was exquisite in her sapphire blue riding habit.

Audrina was dowdier than ever in her cut-down, threadbare, washed-out brown relic of a riding outfit. It didn't matter. She threw her arms around the dainty mare, then almost embraced the earl in her delight. Instead of that outré behavior, she mounted and set off at a gallop, her bright curls streaming behind her. Max let her lead him and his stallion on a bruising ride through woods and over streams, content to listen to her merry laughter. The others could have been in the next county for all they knew or cared.

After that they rode out or drove—for Carinne's sake—every nice day, sometimes taking the rest of the Halbershams' guests along sightseeing, where Audrina's knowledge of the old abbeys and Roman fortresses impressed even young Warden. In the evenings they all often met at one neighbor's or another's for cards, music, charades, or dancing.

Carinne was in alt, floating on Lord Podell's arm. Audrina was resigned to the match, convinced it was more than cream-pot affection. And Uncle Augustus was so puffed up with success, he even gave Audrina a twenty-pound bonus, for matchmaking. The solicitors were already meeting, and the engagement would be announced at Lady Halbersham's Valentine's Day ball, two days hence.

"So buy yourself some gewgaw or other, missy. Maybe you can hook one of the blacksmith's boys."

With twenty pounds her papa could feed a lot of poor mouths. And she didn't want any of Jed Smith's hairy, dirty, illiterate sons. But Dree folded the note and smiled at her uncle.

"You'd do well to think on it, gal, for that's the last you'll have of me. My girl gets married and moves off, I'll not support you and that nodcock father of yours. Foxed yourself, you did, cutting out old Prendergast. If the chit had wed him, you could have moved in there and still been near your da. Old Prendergast would never have noticed. Now? My Lord and Lady Podell are going on a long bride trip to introduce Carinne to his fancy relatives. He'll see she makes her bows to royalty in the spring, too, see if he don't. I promised him another pile of blunt if it's done right. That leaves you out in the cold, missy."

Audrina straightened her back. "Carrie has invited me to London when they get there."

"What, you'd play dogsberry to a pair of newly-weds?" he goaded.

"And they do intend to settle at Podell Hall," she went on as if he hadn't spoken, or hadn't said anything she hadn't thought of for herself.

"After the place is renovated. My wedding present, don't you know. But aye, I suppose they'll be needing you when they start filling the nursery. Someone has to look after the brats, I suppose. Can't expect my daughter, the baroness, to change nappies. She'll be too busy entertaining the nobs at house parties and such. You still pleased with the match?"

"Carrie's happiness is the only thing that matters."

He snorted. "That and getting a grandson who'll be a baron. I hope that deuced caper-merchant Podell don't take as long about begetting me an heir as he does tying his neckcloths."

Chapter Eight

She could be a governess, Dree thought as she trudged back from the vicarage after giving her father ten of Uncle Augustus's pounds. Or a companion. Either would be preferable to being the perpetual poor relation. Dear Carric would never make her feel like a drudge, but Audrina was well aware that Lord Podell was already wishing her to the devil. Of course, he wanted privacy with his new betrothed; of course, Uncle Augustus ordered her to cling to them like sticking plaster. The only time Dree felt comfortable these days was when Lord Blanford was around. The earl was good company when he came down off his high horse.

Dree kicked a rock in her path. Who was she fooling? The earl wasn't a pleasant companion in her chaperoning duties. He was the most fascinating man she'd ever met, or was ever likely to. And he'd be leaving right after the Valentine's Day ball. He'd most likely come back for the wedding, but for his friend's sake, not hers. Then Carrie would ride off with her fair Lochinvar—and Dree would have to make some kind of life for herself.

Her future looked as bleak as this midwinter day. She supposed she could take Uncle Augustus's advice and find a husband. The Widower Allison needed a mother for his three young children. Tom Rush needed help in his butcher shop. Buck Sharfe needed strong sons to help work his farm. Without a dowry, without a Season in London or even Bath, that was the best she could hope for. But Papa needed the money her employment would bring, and Dree had needs of her own. She saw the stars in Carrie's eyes and wished for a love match, too. Besides, after knowing the Earl of Blanford, a lesser man just wouldn't do. And they were all lesser men, she feared, every male in the kingdom.

Audrina pulled her red cape closer, trying to warm the chill in her heart. How foolish, she chided herself, wishing for what she didn't have. What she did have, the saints be praised, was ten pounds, and the chance to attend her very first fancy ball. She turned her steps toward the little dry goods shop in the village. For once in her life Audrina Rowe was going to look like a lady. There were bound to be strangers at Lady Halbersham's do, perhaps a gentleman so strange he wouldn't notice he was partnering an impoverished vicar's daughter with flyaway red hair and managing ways. Perhaps he wouldn't mind that Papa's learning was her only dowry, and that her highborn relatives didn't acknowledge her. And perhaps, just perhaps, he wouldn't be a stranger after all.

Velvet as soft as kitten fur, the palest pink of sunset's reflection, that's what Audrina chose, and green ribbons for trim, to match her eyes. With the help of Carinne and her maid, she fashioned a simple gown with tiny puffed sleeves and a skirt that fell straight from the high waist just under her bosom. There were no flounces or lace overskirts or intricate embroidery—there was no time. There were brand-new white gloves, though, and silk stockings. And powder covering most of her freckles, and her hair done up in an intricate braid coiled atop her head, with just a few curls allowed to trail down her shoulder. The maid had pulled Dree's hair so tight, and set in so many hairpins, the arrangement wouldn't dare come undone.

Dree felt almost pretty, until she saw her cousin. Carinne looked like a princess in her silver sarcenet, with the diamond tiara her father presented her as an engagement present. She seemed even happier with the bouquet of flowers Lord Podell had delivered, and instantly demanded the maid weave them through the headpiece. Dree cut some ferns from the potted plant in the hallway and wove them into a wreath for her own hair, so it might look like someone sent her a posy, too.

There, Dree thought as she gathered her lamentably red cape, she'd done her best. It wouldn't be good enough for him, of course, who was so proud and proper, elegant and *à la mode*, but not even the Earl of Blanford could accuse her of looking like the parish brat tonight. That would have to be sufficient. She wasn't fool enough to hope for the sun and the moon.

Downstairs, however, a package waited for her, a nosegay of white rosebuds. The card read: *The supper dance? MB*. If not the sun and the moon, maybe she could hope for a few stars. There were certainly stars in her eyes as she dashed back up the stairs to pin the flowers to the neckline of her gown. Perfect! Except . . . except there was still something missing in her efforts to appear a mature, alluring woman: a bosom. Quickly Dree rolled up a pair of stockings and tucked them in the narrow bodice. *Now* she was ready.

The Earl of Blanford was torn. She was too young, too innocent. He was too old, too battle-scarred by life. But what future did she have without him? Not many men could afford to marry without a dowry; not many would look past the unfashionable clothes to see the charming young woman. The talk was of some menial position, or marriage to some local lout. Marriage to an old, tired rake had to be better.

And what future did he have without her? A cold

one. Oh, he'd find a willing bride, a proper female who
didn't like the wind in her hair and who didn't laugh
out loud, or tease. She'd give him sons, but she
wouldn't give him sunshine.

By Satan's smallclothes, he wasn't that blasted old!
And Miss Audrina Rowe wasn't anyone's little
charity-case cousin, not tonight. She was dazzling! Max
had to remind himself to shut his mouth. Why, in London she'd be called a Pocket Venus. She'd be a Toast,
with her lively sparkle and intelligent conversation. He
watched as she left Lady Halbersham's receiving line
and entered the pink-draped ballroom through an arch-
way of trailing vines and silk roses designed to look
like a heart. For a moment she stood there, the perfect
living valentine. She was searching the room—Max
could only hope she looked for him—before flocks of
men swooped down on her, and not just the neighborhood youngsters. Of course, every libertine in the place
would notice her, now that her light wasn't hidden
under a bushel of rags from the dustbin. And now that
the local beauty was spoken for, albeit the engagement
was not yet announced, Miss Rowe was even more in
demand.

The earl considered keeping his distance, letting the
young men discover her charms, letting one of them fall
top over trees in love with his fairy sprite. Then Max
wouldn't have to worry about her future or if he should
have a place in it.

Such noble restraint lasted halfway into the party. Viola had arranged a lottery for the first dance, with
various-colored hearts, cupids, and arrows cut in halves
with the parts put into a top hat or a straw bonnet. The
ladies and gentlemen each chose one, then had to find
their partners by matching halves. Max could have
rigged it. He thought about it, about having another
dance with her, but he decided not, for then Vi would
insist he rake the floor with every wallflower in the
room. So he stayed on the sidelines, watching Audrina

twirl and laugh and charm the pants off every partner she had. In their dreams, at least.

Max was tempted to call out one young buck who never raised his eyes off that bouquet of flowers nestled between her breasts. *My* flowers, Max growled to himself. One dastard kept plying her with champagne. Most likely the chit had never had any before; she should have had her first taste with him. Her next partner held her hand too long, drooling over her glove. That was it! The earl had had enough.

"My dance, I believe, Miss Rowe."

Dree stared up at the earl, taking in his elegant black and white formal attire, the ruby that glowed in his neckcloth, the commanding look on his chiseled countenance. She could have stared all night, if one of her beaus hadn't coughed. She fumbled for the dance card at her wrist. "Oh, but I thought we were to have the supper dance."

"That, too."

Dree was confused, but maybe that was the champagne. "But you don't dance," she insisted.

He held his gloved hand out. "It's Valentine's Day. Everyone dances."

"Oh." She took his hand, took two steps forward, then stopped. "They're playing a waltz."

"Vi thought it was too daring for a country ball, but I bribed the orchestra."

A waltz! Dree might have thought she'd died and gone to heaven, except . . . "I don't know how, my lord."

He just smiled. "I do. I'll show you. Just relax."

In his arms? Mere inches from the masculine scent of him, spices and lemons and . . . Dree shut her eyes, but the whole room started spinning. She giggled.

"You're foxed, minx. No more champagne for you. Now, listen to the count and let me guide your steps."

She did, and soon found herself floating on the strains of the music, in his embrace. Truly this was the

most glorious night of her life, she thought. It was going to be over all too soon, of course, but at least she
would have this memory.

At the end of the music, she curtsied, he bowed, and
they separated without saying a word.

Letting Audrina go off with her next partner was the
hardest thing Max had ever done. Avoiding Viola and
her platter-faced misses for the next half hour was almost as difficult.

Then came the supper dance. And it was a rollicking
country air, because Vi had threatened to dismiss the orchestra if they played another waltz. Max had always
intended to ask Audrina to sit out with him, to take a
stroll away from the stifling ballroom toward the hallway and the empty room whose key he held. Unfortunately he'd shown he could dance, without a hint of a
limp.

"But it's Valentine's Day," she reminded him. "Everyone dances. Please?"

Oh Lud. He knew she loved to dance. He did, too, for
that matter. And he desperately wanted to hold her
again, even if merely to twirl her lithe young body in
the figures of the dance. He reached up and patted his
pate. No slippage. If he was ready to put his fate to the
test, he may as well go all the way. Hell, if he was too
old to dance with her, he was surely too old to wed with
her!

Everyone in their set was laughing and hopping
about, dancing with joyous abandon, even the Earl of
Blanding. In the face of Audrina's pleasure, he was able
to forget his own worries. Then disaster struck.

It was a calamity so unexpected, so catastrophic, that
for a moment all of Max's battle-hardened responses
fled. He stood stock-still, staring, as a stocking popped
out of his partner's bodice, sailed through the air, and
unrolled itself at his feet. He shouldn't laugh. Oh Lud,
he couldn't laugh, not once Max saw the stricken look
on Audrina's face. He'd seen less pitiable expressions

on trapped hares. Gathering his wits, he scooped the silk garment into his fist, having pretended to stumble in the dance steps. He whisked the stocking into his pocket and gave Audrina a wink.

She was still standing rigidly, though, color by turns flooding her cheeks and draining away to leave a few freckles in stark relief. Max had seen enough panicked raw recruits to know she wasn't going to budge, not in her mortification. The other couples in their set were already starting to lose their places in the figures, bumping into each other. It was only a matter of time before someone noticed that Miss Rowe wasn't moving, that she was, in fact, listing to starboard as it were. The poor puss couldn't replace the stocking here, nor could she remove the other one with all eyes turning in her direction.

With cries of "For the honor of the regiment" echoing in his mind, Max did the only thing possible. He snatched off his hairpiece, tossed it toward a row of dozing dowagers, and yelled, "Rat! Rat!"

Chapter Nine

Iola Halbersham was never going to forgive him. She might even urge Gordie to call him out for ruining her party—if Gordie stopped laughing long enough to issue a challenge. No matter, Max thought, it was worth it. In the ensuing pandemonium, he'd been able to tug Audrina out of the ballroom with no one giving her a second glance. Everyone was too busy rushing for the exits or tending to swooning ladies.

Max bustled Dree into a small room and locked the door behind him, blocking out the screams and shouts in the hallway. Dree turned her back to him, her shoulders shaking.

"Ah, sweetheart, it's not worth crying about. No one saw."

But she wasn't crying, he saw as she turned to him, the second stocking in her hand. She was laughing and pointing at his bald head!

"I should have left you out there, brat!" But he looked down at the stocking, and had to laugh, too.

"The look on your face . . ."

"And yours!" She gasped and wiped tears out of her eyes. "You did that, for me?"

Max stopped laughing. "I'd do anything for you, Miss Audrina Rowe."

Then she was in his arms. No, Max told himself, it was only gratitude. Besides, she was too small. He'd get a crick in his neck. But Miss Rowe must have stood on tiptoe, and raised her face along with her arms, pulling his mouth down to hers, for now she felt just right. He was tasting the champagne on her soft, willing lips, and feeling her sweet body pressed against his. And that felt just right, too.

Alas, Max was a gentleman. He set her a bit apart. "Do you mind?"

"Mind? It was the most beautiful kiss I could ever imagine!"

"Not the kiss, sweetheart. Do you mind, you know, about my hair?"

"Mind what?"

"Deuce take it, that I am going bald!"

There, he'd said it. Max half expected her to burst into giggles again, but Dree wasn't laughing. Suddenly shy, she took a step farther away. "It's not for me to mind one way or another, my lord."

"My name is Max, and blast it, of course it is. I know I'm making mice feet of this—I've never done it before, you know—but I am asking you to be my wife."

"Your wife?" Audrina couldn't believe her ears. Her imagination must be running away with her again.

Not precisely thrilled with her reaction, Max repeated, "My wife. Will you do me the great honor of bestowing your hand in marriage?"

"But, but, I'm only a vicar's brat, remember?"

"No, you're everything I want in a wife."

"But I'll never be a grand lady. I'll never know how to go on in your world. Why, look what happened at my very first ball."

"London will adore you, as I do."

Dree could only sigh and say, "Oh, Max." This was what she wanted more than anything in the world, but she knew in her heart she wasn't worthy of him. She twisted the stocking she still held in her hand. "You deserve so much better."

Max took her hesitancy for rejection. "It's me. I'm too old for you. I should have realized."

"Never! Why, someone would think you were in your dotage, to hear you speak, or that I was still in the schoolroom. You're just the right age to keep me from falling into scrapes, is all."

"And you don't mind, about the hair?"

"What, did you think I wanted a beau whose hair was longer than mine like that rattlepate Warden? Or who spent an hour each day putting every curl in place like your friend Podell? But you, do you mind that I'm not . . ." Blushing, she held out the stocking.

"That's nothing a babe or two won't cure, but no, I don't mind. To me, you are perfect." And he closed the gap between them, and showed her how much he didn't mind. "I love you, Miss Audrina Rowe, just the way you are."

"And I do love you, Max, and have forever. But . . ."

He groaned. "Have pity, sweetheart. Just say that you'll make me the happiest of men."

She smiled, but said, "But you haven't asked my father."

"What? You never cease to amaze me. For such an independent little thing, I wouldn't have thought you'd be such a high stickler."

"I could never marry a man my father didn't approve, Max. And you've never even met him."

"I'm sorry, puss. I know you and your father are close. And you mustn't worry about him, you know, after we are married, for he'll be welcome to make his home with us or at any of my estates. Or we'll find him a curate to help here. Whatever you want."

"What I want is for you to meet Papa first. I always said I'd only marry a man just like him."

"Good grief, Dree, you're asking the impossible. By

all accounts your father is nearly a saint. I go to church and all, and try to support a great many charities. You don't expect me to give up the earldom and my fortune, do you?"

"Of course not, silly. Papa is everything good, but that's not what I meant about wedding a man like the one my mother did. She gave up her world for him."

"I swear I'll make you the same kind of loyal, devoted husband. And you won't have to give up anything."

"Just go meet Papa, then decide if you can be the man I always wanted."

Max whistled the whole way back to Dree's uncle's house from the vicarage. His heart was lighter than it had been in years, as he rode his great stallion through the wintery woods to claim his bride. Reverend Rowe had given his permission, finally, for Max to pay his addresses in form. Max had enumerated his titles and holdings, then the contents of his bank accounts. It wasn't until he revealed the contents of his heart, though, that the vicar had relented.

"Can't live without her, eh?" he'd asked, his eyes twinkling behind the lenses of his spectacles. "Aye, I felt the same way about her mother. Well, you've my blessing, if she'll have you."

"She'll have me, sir. She wants a man just like her father."

And they both laughed over a glass of sherry, the earl with less hair by the day, the vicar whose last hair had kissed his pillow good night some twenty years ago.

The Last Valentine

Friday

Mrs. Barrett was a late sleeper.

George the cat was an early riser.

As usual, George prevailed. Thus Martine, the Widow Barrett, groped for her black shawl in the cold February dawn and draped it over the shoulders of her flannel gown. Without candle, without slippers, and without coming fully awake, Martine stumbled down the stairs of her modest home on the outskirts of Chelmstead village and fumbled at the lock on her front door.

George complained at the delay.

"Oh, shush. I'm hurrying as fast as I can. And don't you dare awaken Mrs. Arbuthnot." Mrs. Arbuthnot was the elderly lady hired by Martine's father to act as her companion. Watchdog was more like it, though, Martine thought, or spy. The crotchety old dragon hated George. She wasn't particularly fond of Martine either. The only thing that made the woman at all bearable, besides knowing she had no choice in the matter, was the fact that Mrs. Arbuthnot never rose above the ground floor. Her ankles were too swollen and sore, from too many sweet rolls and sugarplums. She had taken over the morning room and a small parlor at the rear of the house, which was why Martine was trying to get her cold-numbed fingers around the latch at the front of the house. Martine did not wish to discuss having animals in the house, appearing downstairs in one's undress, or showing consideration and respect for one's elders—not at six o'clock in the morning. Not ever.

Not for the first time did Martine consider that her life wasn't precisely as she wished it either. The door open and George gone, she stared out at the barren winter landscape. Gray, everything was gray. The cloud-covered dawn, the shriveled bushes in her front yard, the stark, square houses of the village, her days and nights. No, this was not how Miss Martine Penbarton, privileged daughter of the Earl of Halpen, had planned to spend her life. Parties, travels, gowns, servants, and handsome gentlemen, those were the things she had dreamt on as a girl, not making her own clothes, doing her own baking and wash, growing her own vegetables, or helping Chelmstead's frail old vicar tend to his needy flock. She'd thought to have a houseful of infants. Instead, she got to teach a handful of farm children their letters when their families could spare them. She also taught Sunday school, mended altar cloths, and took tea with the matrons of Chelmstead village. Her only friend was George the cat, and sometimes she wondered about him.

Things could be worse. Oh, they could be a great deal worse, Martine reminded herself. Mrs. Arbuthnot never lost an opportunity to remind her either, of the sights they'd seen in London on their way to Chelmstead, four years earlier. Martine's father had directed the driver to take the hired coach through the worst of London's stews and slums, so she could see the women half-naked in the streets, begging or plying their miserable trade to filthy lechers and foulmouthed soldiers and falling-down drunks. Yes, things could be worse without the earl's grudging generosity. They could also be a great deal better, if he showed some mercy to his once-cherished daughter.

It seemed he'd cherished his own dreams of her marrying his heir more than he'd cherished Martine. When she refused, and disgraced herself in her rejection of Cousin Elger, the scandal was quickly covered up. Martine was bundled away to obscurity with Mrs. Arbuthnot to see she brought no further shame on the family. Meager provision was made for her welfare, but there were no luxuries, few comforts, and less forgiveness from her father. And now, four years later, Martine thought she could never forgive him for telling the world he had no daughter. What he had was no heart.

George was long gone about his own business of terrorizing the birds. Bess would let the cat back in when she came up from the village to cook and clean. She'd also start the fires, thank goodness, for Martine's bare toes were turning blue. She turned to shut the door and go back upstairs to bed. Her days were long enough without starting them at the crack of dawn.

As she turned, a scrap of white caught her eye. A folded note was wedged under the brass door knocker. Martine removed the paper and went inside. How odd, she thought, turning the note over as she made her way upstairs. It had no direction and no return address. The seal on the back was unidentifiable, to Martine at least.

Shrugging, she broke the seal and held the page closer to the window in her bedroom.

There is one week until Valentine's Day, she read. *I have waited this long to ask you to be mine. I will try to be patient until then.*

There was no salutation and no signature. Martine shrugged. The note was romantic, mysterious, and a mistake. The sender must have directed a messenger to the wrong house, for Martine had no beaux at all, much less one waiting any amount of time. Why would he wait, this unknown admirer? Mrs. Barrett was a poor but respectable widow, still wearing mourning for her soldier husband, who, of course, had never existed. That is, George Barrett had once lived, and died, but not in Martine's vicinity. Her father had simply borrowed the fallen cavalryman's name for his fallen daughter. She'd named her cat after him; it was the least she could do.

At any rate, no other man had approached her in her tenure at Chelmstead. Perhaps that was Mrs. Arbuthnot's sneering influence, for she would be out of a position should Martine find a husband. Or perhaps it was Martine's aloofness that discouraged the local merchants and tenant farmers. She was attractive enough, and only two and twenty, but she truly wasn't interested. Her life might be easier with a prosperous husband, but she doubted she could ever love again, and she could have married Cousin Elger if she wanted a loveless marriage.

No, the note had to be a mistake, or someone's idea of a joke. But the paper was too rich and thick for any local apothecary or haberdasher, and the writing was too well formed for the farmers and sheepherders. Martine doubted that even the neighboring squires had such fine, educated hands.

Perhaps the note was meant for Mrs. Arbuthnot, she thought, and had to stifle a giggle at the idea. 'Twould take a brave man indeed to get his courage to the sticking point to approach that formidable misanthrope. No wonder he needed another week.

Was it truly just a week until Valentine's Day? Martine supposed so, although she'd need to look at a calendar, since all her days seemed to melt together. And Valentine's Day, well, that was for starry-eyed lovers and young dreamers, not for ones such as she. No, never again.

She tossed the note onto her desk, climbed into bed, and pulled the covers over her head. She didn't even think of her own, long-lost love. Not once, not after four years.

Saturday

It has been four years, the new note said. *I can wait another six days to ask you to be mine, but oh, how impatient I grow, knowing you are so near. I think of knocking on your door, sweeping you up into my eager arms and riding off with you, but no, this time I shall do the thing properly. Sweethearts' Day it shall be, dearest, the day the birds select their life mates. And yet I find I must ask, am I waiting in vain? Are you spoken for? If there is someone else in your life, if you would rather I left, please, sweeting, put me out of my misery now. I swear your happiness means all to me. Here is a rose as a token of my affection. If you accept it, I can keep on waiting, keep on hoping.*

She should take that rose and snap its stem, shred its petals, scatter them to the ground, then stamp on them. Instead Martine clasped the note and the flower under her shawl and fled back inside and up the dawn-lit stairs, like a thief in the night. She told herself that such a perfect red rose was too precious to destroy. Not even Squire's succession houses boasted such prize blooms.

Of course, Martine knew she couldn't place it in a vase in the drawing room, not without facing an interrogation that would put the Spanish Inquisition to shame.

Even in Martine's own bedroom, Bess was liable to notice and wonder where the widow came by such a flower in the dead of winter. It would be a shame, but Martine would just have to press the rose in her Bible, where no one could see it. For now, though, she climbed into her bed, the flower still clutched in her hand. Thank goodness the thorns had been removed.

This morning Mrs. Barrett was not going right back to sleep.

Four years, the note had said. Four years. It had to be him, then, not some prankster or bashful beau or mistake in the note's delivery. In fact, he must have been watching the house, to know Martine was the one to put the cat out at dawn each day. There'd been no names again either, so he must be aware of Mrs. Arbuthnot, too. This way, if the letter blew away or got into the wrong hands, there was nothing to point in Martine's direction. Lud, if the old besom caught a whiff of the rose's perfume, Martine would be locked in her room, if she didn't get tossed out in the streets. And Digby would be hung up to dry on the clothesline. Oh God, Digby.

Four years. They had been four long years for Martine. She'd stopped crying over him ages ago, telling herself he was not worth her tears, until she was convinced. It didn't take long. The dastard had left her in the middle of their elopement. He'd taken the money her father had offered and then decamped, leaving her disgraced and devastated. Lord Halpen still wished her to marry his heir. Cousin Elger still had damp hands and rotten teeth. She refused. Her father refused to have her in his home, declaring that his honor forbade him to offer any other gentleman such soiled goods in marriage. While she was still numb with heartbreak and disillusionment, the earl packed her off, in hastily fashioned widow's weeds, to this little backwater village, where she could rot for eternity in genteel poverty or marry some schoolmaster. He cared not which, so long as she lived a virtuous life. The threat of being cut off entirely was there, with no resources, no recommendations for employment, no capabilities beyond a smattering of education. She had been reared for marriage, by heaven. How could she make her own way in the world?

Her home, her family, her future, all gone with Digby Hines. Now here he was, sending her valentines! Martine wiped a treacherous tear from her eye and stroked the velvety petals of the rose. She should take it outside right now, before Mrs. Arbuthnot arose, before she had to watch it wither and die like her love had done at Digby's betrayal.

Of course, she didn't love Digby anymore. Why, she couldn't recollect what he looked like, except for his fair hair and blue eyes. And what did an eighteen-year-old know of love anyway? she wondered now at twenty-two. Perhaps it was just infatuation, perhaps the thrill of a forbidden romance, perhaps merely an escape from her father's rigid demands.

She hardly remembered Digby, but she did remember love. There in her solitary bed without even the cat to keep her warm, Martine recalled how it felt to be in love, believing one was loved in return. As sweet as the scent of the rose, it was, and as short-lived. But she did not take the flower back outside.

Sunday

My precious, how relieved I am not to find my flower left out in the cold, with my dreams. And now there are only five more days to be got through, although it still seems an eternity. Each day brings a new agony to me. I swore not to rush my fences, not to ask for your hand until Valentine's Day, the perfect day for lovers, but now I live in fear that you'll turn me down out of hand, that you've never forgiven me for leaving you. I find I've turned craven overnight, but I'd rather face another four years of French cannons than see the look you gave me that last day.

How can I explain? I loved you. You must believe me, for I have never stopped loving you. But I had nothing to offer, my dearest, only the most uncertain of futures. I couldn't live on the outskirts of society like so many other men without fortunes, gambling to pay the rent, outrunning the bailiffs every few months. And I could not ask you to live that way. Nor could I face being supported by my wife's income, whatever it was. Blame my pride for leaving you, not the depth of my affection. I was determined to make a success of myself in the army, to prove my worth, but how could I ask you to follow the drum, such a tender bud that you were? And *how could I marry you, knowing I was leaving, perhaps never to return? I could not, in good faith, so much as ask you to wait for me, not such a young and beautiful woman, so full of life. A soldier's fate is too uncertain. At least I do not have that on my conscience.*

I leave you this box of ribbons, paltry stuff, I know, except they might help to prove that I am not a coward, not entirely, anyway. Can you accept this token, and my poor excuses for whatever unhappiness I may have caused you?

Digby a soldier? Martine thought her memory must be faulty indeed. He'd been everything he said, when she met him in London at her come-out, a regular Bond Street beau. His shirt collars were up to his ears, and his debts were up to his eyeballs, but so were all the other young men's. Digby was the most handsome, the most elegant, with the most practiced charm, she realized later. And she was the wealthiest heiress Out that Season.

Yes, she'd thought Digby a coward for not standing up to her father when the earl rejected his suit, and again, when Lord Halpen found them at that inn halfway to Gretna. Digby had cowered before her father's wrath, and fled with his gold.

But here was a carved wooden box full of medals, ribbons and such, a hero's horde. Martine lit a candle in her room, to spread them out on her bedstead as she reread that letter again and again. What did they represent? An act of valor, a battle won, an injury, a promotion? There were so many, he must have been in constant danger, trying to prove himself worthy of her. Oh, how she had misjudged him!

He must have taken her father's money, she realized now, and bought himself a commission. She knew nothing of his ambition before that, Martine reasoned, because he would have been too proud to confess his dream, knowing he couldn't afford it.

The woman she was now would have followed him

to the ends of the earth, but he was right: the pampered debutante she was then could not have cooked hares over campfires or washed his uniforms. She would not have exchanged her gay London life for the squalor of a barracks, not by half. He was right, but not in leaving her, not in going away without an explanation, not in leaving her heart so bruised she could never love again. Could she forgive him? Loyalty to king and country demanded it. Digby must have become one of England's bravest soldiers, risking his life countless times. The least Martine could do was hear him out. She put the ribbons under her mattress, to think about what she should do.

Martine had never been ready for church so early before. Her hair was neatly combed under her lace cap, and her black wool gown was freshly pressed, twice. She spent the opening hymn searching for him through the pews of the little church, her eyes seeking any fair-haired man, in case she hadn't recognized him on the first glance. There were no soldiers in uniform, no well-muscled, weathered gentlemen, no strangers whatsoever. Mrs. Arbuthnot pinched her arm and hissed at Martine to stop acting like a long-necked goose. Martine had to be content with adding his name to her prayers, thanking God for his safe return.

That night when she called George in after his last foray, Martine left a token of her own outside the door. She should return the ribbons, she told herself, and not get involved. No, she should return the ribbons and add a ha'penny, to show what she thought of him for leaving her for her father's money. He'd been bought off, for goodness' sake! Instead she carefully placed one of her old hair ribbons from when she wore colors next to the front step. The pretty blue ribbon with pink roses embroidered on it would seem to have been dropped by accident, or windblown there, in case he didn't come. Then she had to pry it out of George's claws. "It's not a toy, confound you." She shrugged and tied the bow to the door knocker. She'd be up with George long before Mrs. Arbuthnot saw this evidence of her depravity.

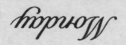

Monday

What noble forgiveness, my precious. Thank you from the bottom of my aching, anxious heart. I could only think of buying you these bonbons, in return for your sweet generosity of spirit.

Martine opened the parcel she'd found on the stoop that morning, along with the letter. The box contained chocolate bonbons, sugared walnuts, pink marzipan hearts with iced flowers on top. Such delicacies hadn't come Martine's way in ages. She popped one in her mouth. Chocolates before breakfast; now, wasn't that decadent! Mrs. Arbuthnot would have apoplexy. Martine had another candy, then returned to the letter.

But I prayed you could forgive me, being so warm and loving. You are what we were fighting for in Spain, you know, cara mia. And you are what I dream of day and night, in those wretched tents and blood-soaked fields. I think the image of you was all that kept me sane amid the horrors of war. I wrote to you almost every day, you know. No, how could you, for I never mailed the letters. I couldn't, when I didn't know if I was ever to return, or if I'd come back less of a man, maimed beyond recognition like so many of my fellows. But I did write, whenever there was a pause in the shooting, when we were back at headquarters, when I was recuperating in the hospital tent from my, thankfully, minor wounds. I told you a hundred times that I should not have left; that I should have stood by you no matter what, that war was a fool's gamble. I was such a green youth. I didn't know what I held until it was lost. Youth lasts but moments on a battlefield, and now I have come back, all of me in working order, to claim what should have been mine.

There are only four more days to suffer through until Valentine's Day. I can do it, hold to my resolve, sweeting, because you deserve the most romantic valentine I can conjure.

Martine dabbed at her eyes with the corner of her bedsheet and ate another bonbon. That dear man. How proud she was of him, her hero, and how guilty she felt for having to struggle to remember the tone of his voice or the smell of his cologne. She hadn't thought of him in months, and then only for the what-might-have-been, not the who it might have been with. She hadn't read the war news for his name on casualty lists or recommendations. She hadn't prayed for his safe delivery. Instead she'd cursed his very existence, as the self-serving villain who ruined her and deserted her.

"Oh, my love, can you ever forgive me?" Martine sobbed. But obviously he had; he was sending her letters and flowers and promises. And candy. She sat up and wiped her eyes. What was she going to do with the candy? Pigs would fly before she shared them with Mrs. Arbuthnot, even if Martine could explain them away as a Valentine treat she'd purchased. If she left them here, Bess would find them, or George. There was nothing for it but to eat the candies, every last one of them.

"You ain't coming down with something, are you, gel?" Mrs. Arbuthnot demanded over lunch.

"No, ma'am. I'm just not very hungry today."

"Well, eat anyway. I can't abide finicky chits, you know, so don't you go putting on airs."

"No, ma'am. In fact, my mind has been distracted. I have been thinking of putting off my blacks. It has been four years, and I am sick of these dreary, depressing rags."

"Twenty-two years I've been in mourning for Mr. Arbuthnot. It shows respect. For you, it shows your respectability."

Martine put down her napkin. "Our neighbors know me for a decent, proper widow. There is no need to keep up this charade."

"No!" Mrs. Arbuthnot hissed, making sure Bess had returned to the kitchen. "You'll keep on pretending to be a devoted, grieving widow all your days, gel. Keep you from tossing your bonnet over the windmill again."

She went back to her mutton.

Martine could feel her cheeks grow warm, but she insisted: "Mrs. Arbuthnot, if I wished to toss my bonnet, it would not matter what color it was, black or red with purple ostrich feathers. I have saved some of my housekeeping money, and I am going to purchase material for a new gown this afternoon."

"I shall write to the earl immediately after lunch!"

"And say what, that I am sinking into a life of sin because I wish a new gown?" Martine sat up straighter. "Go ahead. But be sure to ask yourself where your next meal is coming from, after he cuts me off without a farthing." She stared pointedly at the mounds of food on Mrs. Arbuthnot's plate, then rose from the table. "Forgive me, I find I am not feeling quite the thing after all."

She was feeling just fine when she walked to the village shops that afternoon. Even Miss Fletcher at the Emporium noticed the roses in her cheeks, the sunshine in her smile, the bounce in her step. "It's a man, I wager," she whispered to her sister while Martine inspected the bolts of cloth.

"And about time, too, I swear."

The sisters were so pleased for the gracious young widow who'd added so much to their little community that they wrapped a few bits and scraps of ribbon and lace along with the rose velvet dress length Martine chose, in case she wanted to make a valentine for her sweetheart. Martine thought she just might.

Meantime she purchased a bunch of dried rosemary with her hoarded pennies. For a new recipe she wanted to try, she told the Fletcher sisters and Mrs. Arbuthnot, who intercepted Martine in the hall before she could make her way upstairs with her parcels.

"Can't taste any rosemary in this chicken," the old woman complained at dinner.

"Perhaps I didn't use enough." And perhaps she didn't use any, preferring to braid the rosemary into a small heart-shaped wreath she'd hidden in the bushes. Rosemary was for remembrance; everyone knew that.

After the meal Martine cut and pinned her new gown while Mrs. Arbuthnot muttered dire warnings about the wages of sin. At nine o'clock, Martine went to the kitchen to make their tea. Mrs. Arbuthnot had hers with a tot of rum every night, to help her sleep, she said. She never seemed to have any problems with that, declaring it bedtime as soon as the tea things were put away. So Martine put on her cape and put out the cat. She stayed outside, the door partly open so she could find her wreath, then find a place where Digby would notice it, but not think it was a decoration for the door. Then she stayed out, wondering if he was near, trying to feel his presence.

"What maggot have you got in your brainbox now, missy?" Mrs. Arbuthnot shouted from the parlor. "Leaving the door open and standing outside in the middle of winter!"

"Someone in the village today said a storm was coming. I'm just trying to see if it feels like snow."

It didn't. It felt like springtime in her heart.

Tuesday

*M*artine was up before George. Considering that she'd stayed up half the night basting the gown—and looking out her bedroom window—that was quite a feat. She hadn't got much sewing done, and she hadn't seen or heard a thing, so she couldn't sleep for hours even when she blew out the candles, wondering if he was coming back at all.

He had come, though. The wreath was gone, and in its place were two packages tied in silver paper, atop a sealed letter. She opened the letter first.

I remember, my precious darling. I never forgot. Three more days, and we can share the memories and make new ones.

I want to buy you the sun and the stars, but I cannot, so I had to be content with these trifles for now. The combs are from Spain, for I thought of you so often there, and how your silky hair would look in the señoritas' style. And the book is because you deserve sonnets written to your beauty, but I am just a soldier, not a poet.

I must tell you that I do not intend to stay a soldier, if you will have me. I do not intend for you to follow the drum any more today than I did four years ago, and now there is no reason. I have proved myself in my own eyes, if not the eyes of the world, and I have prospered. I might not afford to buy you the moon, but I can purchase a small estate for us somewhere, with a few acres to farm. No more paltry cottages. My saved-up pay, a tidy competence I receive, and an unforeseen inheritance make me a man of substance, if not wealth. Yes, I am puffing off my prospects, sweeting, in hopes that you will look more favorably on my suit.

Other officers spoke of their futures, of travels and Town life. I have had enough excitement to last the century. I want nothing more than to settle down, to put roots into the land, to see things grow finally, instead of the death and destruction of war. I want to watch our children run and play where the air is clean and good, with you by my side. I would take you to London if you yearn for the glamour—I would take you anywhere, dearest—but oh, how I have dreamt of the peace and quiet and contentment of a country home, a family. In three days I'll ask you to share that with me.

A home, a family, a loving husband—and two presents! What more could a woman want? Martine swore she would not weep, not again. But she hadn't received a single present since she'd been in Chelmstead, except for the occasional dead mouse from George. Now here was Digby Hines, the man from her past, offering her a golden future, showering her with gifts.

The combs were intricately carved ivory masterpieces that demanded she unbraid her long auburn hair and try them in different styles. The book was Shakespeare's love sonnets, in hand-tooled leather with gilded pages.

Martine's resources hadn't extended to books, so this was even more precious. She'd even had to let her subscription to the lending library expire, because Mrs. Arbuthnot declared novels to be the devil's own handiwork. Oh, the old dragon would love this! "Shall I compare thee to a summer's day" indeed!

Of course, Mrs. Arbuthnot must never see the book.

Martine could leave it here in her bedroom, among her old volumes on the shelf, for Bess couldn't read and wasn't interested in learning. But the combs had to be hidden. Even if Martine swore they were hers from before, Mrs. Arbuthnot would instantly recognize them as something foreign and heathen, therefore improper. With sore regrets, Martine buried the beautiful ornaments under the velvet lining of her jewelry box. She went back to sewing on her dress, a smile on her lips. She had to have Bess's help pinning the hem that afternoon.

"Oh, you do look a treat, Mrs. Barrett," her house-keeper cooed. "Will you be going to Friday's assembly up in Wolford then? They're having a special do for Valentine's Day, don't you know. You're sure to take some handsome gentleman's fancy, I swear."

"No, we won't," Mrs. Arbuthnot answered for Martine with a thump of her cane. "It's not fitting. Any-one with a few pence can attend the assemblies. A lady could find herself dancing with turnip pickers and plow-men. That's whose eye she'd catch in that indecent gown anyway. No, we shall not attend." She glared at Martine, daring her to challenge the decision.

Martine loved to dance, but no, the festivities in Wolford were not part of her Valentine's Day plans. She was more concerned with the style of her gown. Inde-cent? The dress was velvet, not some filmy, near trans-parent gauze, and it had long sleeves and a high neckline. There were no flounces or scallops at the hem, no embellishment at all beyond a darker pink ribbon at the high waist.

Even Bess was taken aback. "Why, I seen Squire's wife wear a lot less fabric, with a lot more to put in it, iffen you catch my drift. Even her daughters as is just out of the schoolroom wear their thin muslins cut down to there, with less to show off than Mrs. Barrett. Noth-ing improper as I can see."

Mrs. Arbuthnot snorted. "It's pink! Pink is for debutantes—or harlots."

That night Martine put a folded paper outside the front door and hoped the snow would hold off another day, or that Digby would come soon to fetch it. Her efforts at watercolors were never quite successful, but today, in her haste—well, a dampening could not improve the picture. She'd wanted to leave him something, to give something back to the one who was giving her so much, in tokens and in joy. Even if her finances permitted, though, and Chelmstead's shops provided, she wouldn't know what to purchase for him, to show she shared his hopes and dreams. So she'd painted a landscape of a white house on a hill, with six, no, ten chimneys, surrounded by fields and cows. At least she'd meant them as cows, but they ended up looking more like trees, so she'd put apples in them. Yes, an orchard would be lovely. The sky was blue, with no clouds; the grass was new-green, except for one corner where the colors ran together, so she made a pond. And flowers everywhere, dabs of bright colors, at any rate. She'd put a tiny couple in the doorway, watching even tinier children who were chasing a dog, a ball, and a water drop. They all wore pink.

Wednesday

We'd left her a music box. The music was unfamiliar, but two porcelain doves turned on the base when
she wound the key. *You make my heart sing,* the note
read. Oh, how I wanted to hold you close to me when I
saw the painting, but I have wanted to hold you, touch
you, kiss you, ever since we parted. I can wait the two
more days, my dear heart.

Was that your light I saw late into the night? I
watched from outside, wondering if you were lying
abed, reading the poems, thinking of your humble,
hopeful suitor. We should have been together in your
white house, reading aloud by the fireside, sharing a
cushioned sofa. But I fear my imaginings wandered, and
I confess we would not stay long on that sofa, reading.
Too well do I remember your exquisite body. How I
ache to hold your rosy softness against me. There was
no softness in Spain, querida, only you in my dreams.
Let there be no untruths between us: there were other
women. I am just a man. But none were you, none
moved me to my soul, with none did I feel the love in
lovemaking. Two more days, my darling. Two more
nights.

Martine's cheeks were flushed, even under the bedcovers. Goodness, she thought, Mr. Shakespeare was not half so stirring as Digby Hines. Her rosy softness? Oh my. Yes, her bones were turning to mush at the very thought of . . . of what he was thinking. She must be a fallen woman indeed, to become overheated by a letter.

Martine was a bit surprised at Digby's ardor. They'd only made love twice before her father found them. The first time was messy, awkward, painful, and uncomfortable. The second time was simply uncomfortable. Just when she was beginning to feel there might be something appealing about this act, it was over. And messy. From the giggles and snatches of conversation at the ladies' sewing circles, she gathered not every woman felt that way. She was willing to try to enjoy herself. From her reaction to Digby's warmish letter, Martine doubted she'd have to try very hard. At the very least, she vowed, if he got so much delight from the act, she could gain her own pleasure from giving him his.

That night she left out a valentine. Two pink velvet hearts, scraps from her new gown, trimmed with lace bits and ribbon roses, were firmly joined by enough glue to hold together a piano.

When Martine broke the seal on the letter, a gold heart on a chain fell out.

Please wear this, until I can lay my own heart at your feet tomorrow.

When shall I come? Must it be a proper morning call lasting a proper twenty minutes, or shall I come for tea with you and your duenna? I am wishing you can be rid of her, so I can take you in my arms, but I want no blot on your reputation, my dearest. Should I meet you at the assembly in Wolford then, and greet you among strangers? Tomorrow would be the longest day of the year in that case. Tell me your wishes, cara, I'll make them mine.

Tomorrow was going to be the longest day in history if Martine had her way, but only because it was going to start the earliest. She was not about to meet him for the first time in four years in full view of the population of Chelmstead or Wolford, or under the gimlet stare of Mrs. Arbuthnot. That harridan would never leave them alone long enough to pledge their love, much less seal the pledge. Martine fully intended to give Digby the only valentine she had left to offer, herself in her new pink gown.

Martine put an extra measure of medicinal rum in Mrs. Arbuthnot's tea that night. Then she let George in, but didn't lock the door, and didn't snuff the candle in the upstairs hall. Outside was an old, broken clock, as if left for the trash. The hands were set to a minute past twelve. She wrote "midnight" above the twelve, to make sure he understood. Then she went upstairs to change.

The pink gown whispered around her hips, the gold heart nestled between her breasts, the combs pulled her auburn curls back off her forehead before letting them tumble down her back. Would he still think she was beautiful? Her figure was fuller now and her face thinner, paler, except for the spot on her chin from eating all that candy. She blew out another candle.

The fire burned low in her sitting room, a bottle of wine and two goblets waited nearby. George was snoring. Martine was pacing. The ormolu clock on the mantel must have stopped running, so she shook it to make the hands move faster.

Then she heard what she'd been waiting for, the sound of the door handle turning. She waited at the head of the stairs, in the shadows, merely whispering "Shh" when he appeared. She could just make out the scarlet uniform as she beckoned him up the steps and into her sitting room. Then she turned and threw herself into his waiting arms. His lips came down on hers as his hands pressed her against his firm length. Her hands wove through his hair, pulling him even closer, and the earth shook.

"Oh, Digby," she sighed against his chest some minutes later, just as he murmured, "Rosalyn, my Rosalyn," into her hair.

Martine's eyes snapped open. "Rosalyn?"

His arms dropped to his sides. "Who the hell is Digby?"

"D-digby Hines," she sputtered uncertainly, "the man

who has been sending me valentines and presents," She fingered the chain around her neck.

"I've been sending the blasted valentines!" he shot back in a harsh whisper. "But who the deuce are you? They told me in the village that the Widow Farrell still owns this place."

"She does; I lease it from her."

The look on his face was so comical, Martine had to laugh. It was either that or cry. She crossed to the mantel and brought him the glass of wine. "Here, sir, I think you are in need of this."

He took a swallow, then ran his hand through his hair, making even more of a mess than Martine had. It was dark hair, and curly, nothing like Digby's, she realized as she studied him while he drank the rest of his wine. He was taller, too, broader-shouldered and more muscular, with a bronzed complexion from his years on the Peninsula. Digby had always appeared pale, colorless from his hours in drawing rooms and gaming parlors.

The officer put down the glass and gave her a tentative smile. "I'm afraid it will take a deal more than a glass of wine to fix this argle-bargle. I've really made a deuced mull of it, haven't I?"

Martine shook her head. "Not by yourself, sir."

"You are too kind, Miss . . . ?"

"Barrett, Mrs. Barrett."

"And Mr. Barrett? No one in the village mentioned him. Is he going to come bursting through the door at any minute demanding I name my seconds? It needs only that."

"No, Lieutenant Barrett won't be coming, Captain." She figured out his insignia.

"My apologies, ma'am, for being so clumsy. I should have known, for everyone spoke of the pretty widow lady at the edge of town. I just assumed they meant . . ."

"Rosalyn."

He nodded "Do you know where Mrs. Farrell is now?"

The poor man was already so devastated, Martine hated to give him more bad news, but she had to tell him that Mrs Farrell had married a wealthy merchant from Wolford "All of Chelmstead was still talking about the wedding when I moved in, four years ago in April."

"April! I just left in February!" He moved toward the window to stare out at the night. "She hardly waited for my ship to sail "

"I'm so sorry" And Martine was, seeing his shoulders droop "You must have loved her very much."

He gave a hollow laugh. "I loved a dream. I was miserable, lonely, and afraid, so I found a memory to cherish, that was all Do you know, I should have realized something was wrong when I overheard those men in the pub singing your praises They said the young widow at Farrell's place was kind to everyone despite her own hardships, full of goodness to those less blessed. A real lady, they called her—you I was thrilled, you may be sure, thinking that Rosalyn had changed for the better, for that was precisely what I wanted in a wife Rosalyn was a selfish, greedy minx. She made no secret of the fact that she married her first husband for his money "

"Then you are well out of it "

He turned back to Martine, where she had taken a seat next to the fireplace When she nodded toward the matching chair the captain sat and asked, "But what about you, ma'am, waiting so patiently for your Digby? This must have been a crushing blow By God, I am sorry What, was he missing in action, that you thought he'd been returned to you?"

"Digby, missing in action?" Martine was confused.

"Lieutenant Barrett, your husband "

"Oh, that wasn't Digby, that was George I never knew him " Hearing his name, the cat jumped into Martine's lap. "Good George," she crooned. George purred, the officer stared.

He got up and brought the other wineglass over to Martine, along with the bottle. "I think you need this. The shock and all."

She shook her head, blinking away a tear. "No, it does make sense. And like you, I should have known better than to think Digby was suddenly so caring and thoughtful. Digby Hines was the man who ruined me. We were eloping, but my father caught up with us half-way to Gretna. Digby let him, I think. I was an heiress, you see. Papa told Digby he'd never see a brass farthing of his blunt, if we married. So Digby let my father buy him off. I haven't seen him since."

"The bastard ought to be drawn and quartered."

Martine shrugged. "George Barrett was a dead soldier my father chose from the casualty lists to give me some respectability—and a name that wasn't his—when he established me here."

Before taking his seat again the officer looked around at the skimpy furnishings, the meager fire. "In grand style, too. You haven't been very fortunate in your menfolk, have you, Mrs. . . . Miss . . . ?"

"Miss Penbarton, I was, Martine." She chuckled.

"Anything but Rosalyn."

He smiled back, flashing even, white teeth. "You're a regular trump, Miss Martine Penbarton Barrett. Any other female would be swooning or weeping or throwing things at me."

"Oh no, I'm made of sterner stuff."

Now that his shock was wearing off, the officer was taking note of precisely what she was made of. Martine could feel his eyes travel from her head to her toes, with a long stop at the gold heart between her breasts. They were very nice eyes, a soft brown, with laugh lines at the corners. Still, Martine blushed and made to remove the necklace. "No, no. You must keep it for your trouble. Besides,

I could never give it to anyone else. But that's a minor point. Miss, ah, Martine, we have to decide what we're going to do."

"Do? There is nothing to do. I'll go fetch your ribbons—you really should be wearing them with pride—and you'll go off to find your cozy nest in the country. Hopeful mamas will be trotting their daughters past your gates before the cat can lick his ear."

He frowned at the prospect. "But what about you? I've seen how you live." He waved his hand at the room, the house.

"Oh, I'll get by. Perhaps I'll start getting out more."

"And perhaps you'll be ruined."

She had to laugh. "I am already ruined."

"Not here in Chelmstead, you're not. Everyone admires you. But what if someone saw me come in? I was careful, but you never know. What if some late-night reveler sees me leaving? Or if your dragon wakes before I'm gone? What would your fond parent do then?"

Martine gasped and clutched the gold heart in her hand. "He'd cast me off without a shilling. Oh dear, please leave now. Take your gifts lest someone find them. Here—" She pulled the combs out of her hair, letting the silky curls fall to her shoulders.

He drew a deep breath at the sight of the reddish tresses in the fire's glow. "No, there is another way. We could get married."

"Married?" she squawked, then clamped her hand over her mouth. "I . . . I don't even know your name!"

"Damn and blast," he muttered. "Cursed barracks manners. My apologies." He stood and snapped to attention. "Captain Aden Kirkendale of His Majesty's Cavalry, ma'am, at your service." He bowed, then dropped to his knees next to her chair and reached for one of her hands. "Martine, hear me out. I realize we don't know each other very well." At her raised eyebrows he corrected himself: "All right, we know each other hardly at all, but arranged marriages are made all the time between strangers, strangers with less in common than we have. We've both been disappointed, and we've both been alone too long, I know you share my dreams. Your painting—"

"Was a mess, a childish effort."

Aden patted his jacket pocket. "A masterpiece which I wear next to my heart. Don't you see? I fell in love all over again, but with the woman the villagers talked about, the one who was honest and loyal and kind, everything a woman should be, everything the mother of my children should be."

"No, no, you are just being honorable, in case my reputation is destroyed." Martine tried to reclaim her hand, but he held fast and stroked it, still kneeling at her side, sending shivers up her arm.

"Silly puss, have you looked in the mirror? Any man would be thrilled to have you across the breakfast table for the rest of his life. I would count myself the most fortunate of men if you accepted my offer, and I'd spend eternity trying to make you happy. I'd understand, of course, if you don't feel that you could come to care for me."

Now Martine patted his hand and laughed softly. "I have to admit that I fell halfway in love with your letters. You were so noble and so gentle, someone to trust and lean on."

"So lean on me, Martine. The rest will come, I swear." He brought her hand to his mouth and kissed her fingers, then the palm. "You felt that kiss when we first met, I know you did. It was perfect."

The earth shook.

"No, I'd stepped on the cat. But there was a spark. We can build on that, too. Trust me, Martine. We'll make each other happy. And if not, if we find we don't suit after all, I'll just go back to the army. There's always a war going on somewhere. You'd be provided for no matter what."

This was insane! And very, very tempting. "But . . . how?"

Aden grinned. He could tell she was weakening. He touched his pocket again. "I have a special license right here. We can call on your vicar first thing in the morning and be on our way by noon unless you have a lot to pack."

Martine shook her head no. "I don't have much, and most of my clothes are for mourning, not a honeymoon."

"Good, then we'll stop off in London and buy us both new wardrobes, since I have only my uniforms. We could take in the theater and the opera while we consult some land agents about property and I arrange with the War Office to resign my commission. Would you like that?"

"I love the opera."

"Me, too," he lied with his fingers crossed behind his back. "See how well we're matched? Are you convinced?"

"You're sure this is what you want?"

For answer Captain Kirkendale reached inside his uniform and brought out a small box. He opened it to reveal a gold ring with a square-cut diamond in the center, surrounded by a cluster of rubies in a heart shape. He put it on her finger. "Will you make me the happiest of men, dear Martine, and be my valentine, now and forever?"

"Now and forever," she repeated, then met his lips in a kiss that seared their souls together. "Just don't step on the cat."

Love and Tenderness

Chapter One

$\mathcal{A}$ girl expected some degree of anxiety on her wedding night. Senta Tarlowe, abruptly and henceforth Senta Morville, Viscountess Maitland, had anticipated the butterflies in her stomach spawned by awkwardness and inexperience. After all, she hardly knew this stranger who now held her future and the hem of her first lacy nightgown in his large hands. Senta was even prepared for the pain her scarlet-faced mama had stammered about, before disappearing into the carriage on her way home this afternoon. What the new Lady Maitland hadn't expected, not in her most vivid imagination or most horrific bad dream, was the sight, over her husband's shoulder, of a specter at the foot of the bed.

Senta knew the figure wasn't real flesh and blood because she could see the flickering flames of the fireplace behind him, right through his cloth-of-gold suit, wide belt, and high boots. Whereas she'd convinced herself to suffer silently through the indignities and uncertainties of the marriage bed, ghosts, ghouls, or heavenly visitations did not count.

Since her husband, Henley, Viscount Maitland, had been pleasantly absorbed in nibbling at his young

bride's tender earlobe, nuzzling at her silky neck, nudg-
ing her neckline lower, his ear was in close proximity to
Senta's open mouth. Just as he was murmuring, "Oh,
Senta, how I want you. I need you. I—" she shrieked.
The sound could have shattered the crystal chandelier
at the Royal Opera, much less the eardrums of one
slightly befuddled bridegroom. Henley, Lee to his
friends, clamped his hands over his ears. "What the
deuce—"

The apparition also clamped his hands over his ears.
"What the hell—"

He was no angel, then, which was less than reassur-
ing to Senta. "Wh-what do you want?" she managed to
gasp out.

The glimmering figure merely shook his head in a
confused manner, but Viscount Maitland was either less
rattled or more aggrieved. "What do I want? That
should be obvious even to a blasted vir—gently bred
female. I want to make love to my wife!"

Senta had taken the moment of Maitland's distraction
to pull the covers back up to her chin, both for modes-
ty's sake and the sudden chill in the room. Now she
stared from the viscount's scowl to the phantasm's be-
fuddlement, back to Maitland's expectant "Senta?"

Maitland didn't see the ghost. He was right beside
her, and he didn't see a flickery gold-suited gentleman
with rings on his fingers and a huge diamond in his belt
buckle. Somehow that made Senta's panic worse, that
she was alone in this nightmare. She pulled the covers
over her head and cried, "Go away!"

Lee pried the sheets out of his wife's trembling fingers and drew them away from her face. "You'll suffo-
cate, goose. Now listen, Senta, I know you aren't used
to any of this, and it's natural to be frightened."

Frightened? She was staring at him in abject terror,
her eyes so round she looked like his aunt's pug.
"Come on, Senta, you seemed to be enjoying yourself."
Lee knew he was. "We'll go nice and slow." Any

slower and he'd embarrass himself for the first time since he was sixteen. The viscount gritted his teeth, reminding himself for the thousandth time that night that she was young and innocent. "And tomorrow we'll laugh about the whole thing."

He might laugh, Senta was thinking, but by tomorrow she could be an empty corpse, her soul sucked out of her by this demon who was staring around the room. Too scared to speak now, she could only shake her head, no. Oh, great heaven, no.

"Then you really want me to leave? I'll go if you want me to, Senta, for I would never force any woman, especially not my wife. But you are my wife, and you'll have to face this sooner or later. You know I want an heir."

Her husband might be a near stranger, but he was big and strong and alive. Oh Lord, don't let him leave! All she could croak, though, was, "Not you. Him."

"Him?" The viscount jerked himself upright, pulling Senta's covers every which way. While she scrabbled to shield herself from the fiend's now-interested view and the cold draft, Lord Maitland tore at his hair. "I knew there had to be another man! I just knew it! Why would such a beautiful young woman still be unmarried after two Seasons in Town? And why would she give herself to a man twelve years her senior? I should have known it was too good to be true." The viscount got out of the high bed and reached for his robe on the floor. "What, was he unacceptable to your family, or was I simply the bigger prize with the title and Maitland fortune? Lud, don't tell me they forced you into the marriage. No, I don't think I could face that tonight. Hysterics are bad enough."

Lee crammed his arms into the robe without looking back at his gasping bride, whose own arms were held out beseeching him not to leave. He wrestled the sash at his waist into a knot. "You're in no state to discuss this tonight, and I'm afraid I'm not either. We'll have to

107

straighten it all out in the morning. Until then, my lady, my sincerest regrets." And he slammed out of the room, barefoot, stomping right through the dark-haired, broad-shouldered wraith.

Senta passed out.

When Senta awoke, the room was in darkness, the fire having burned down to a few embers. What a terrible dream she'd had! As she lay there, though, shaking her head to clear it, Senta recalled that it hadn't all been just a bad dream. She'd actually made a shambles of her wedding night, sending her bridegroom fleeing in high dudgeon and disgust, all on account of her foolish wedding jitters. Bridal nerves, that was it, and too many toasts at the small wedding breakfast, with too little food in her stomach.

She'd made a proper mull of it, Senta reflected, wiping a tear from the corner of her eye. Now Lord Maitland—she really had to start thinking of him as Lee—must think she was a ninnyhammer or, worse, an unwilling bride. Of course he was insulted, although how he could think her dear parents would force her to marry a man of their choice was beyond her. Mama and Papa loved her. They would have given her another Season if she hadn't settled on the viscount this year, and even another, if it meant a happy marriage for their only child. They had never even pressured Senta to accept the viscount, despite Lord Maitland's standing as one of the premier prizes in the Marriage Mart. They didn't have to. Senta had fallen top over trees for the quiet gentleman, as soon as she got over her awe that Lord Maitland had singled her out for his attentions.

The viscount was rich and titled, yes, and handsome enough that when they danced she was the envy of every female in the room. The other gentlemen—those not already wearing corsets—tried to hold in their stomachs, such a fine figure did he present. But none of that would have mattered to Senta. Lord Maitland was a favorite of the ladies without being a dissolute rakehell, a favorite of the gentlemen without being a profligate wastrel. He was a Nonpareil in her eyes. And he was kind.

He was much too kind to let suffer through the rest of the night thinking that his silly bride didn't like his touch. She'd liked it very well indeed. Tomorrow's talk would be embarrassing for both of them, having to discuss bedroom matters in the harsh glare of day. 'Twould be far better to get the explanations over with tonight, while darkness could hide her blushes. And while she still had the courage.

Senta reached for the candle by her bedside and struck the flint. She tossed back the covers, put one foot out into the cold air—and there he was. Not Lord Maitland, but the see-through shade.

She was *not* going to scream, Senta told herself, stuffing her hand in her mouth to make positive. She'd disturbed the servants once this night, she was sure. Heaven only knew what they were already thinking, or how she was to face them in the morning. By comparison, facing this ... this spirit had to be easier. Senta took her hand out of her mouth, put her chilled foot back under the covers, and studied her visitor as it—no, definitely he—slept in the nearby chair. The seat's upholstery stripes wavered through his outline.

His long legs were casually stretched in front of him, tightly encased in the gold unmentionables. Heavy dark hair had fallen onto his forehead, giving him a much younger look. He had high cheekbones, a perfect nose, thick eyelashes, and a mouth a Greek sculptor would have cried for. He was, in fact, quite, quite beautiful, like a fallen angel. Asleep, he seemed too innocent to be any minion of Hell, though. Besides, Senta was still alive and unharmed. Therefore he had to be a mere ghost, which was not to say a gently bred female liked to find that her new home was haunted, but a peripatetic predecessor was preferable to a demon. Senta couldn't begin to imagine from which century this Maitland ancestor hailed. And she'd made a careful study of the portrait gallery this past month. Most of the gentlemen were sandy-haired, like her husband. None of them remotely resembled her somnolent specter. Furthermore, Senta firmly believed that the Morville clan, dead or alive, was too mannerly to cut up a lady's peace.

"Sir?" she called softly, determined to direct this lost soul on his way.

He came awake with a start, blinked, and brushed the hair out of his eyes. He noticed Senta sitting up in her bed, the candlelight reflected off her ivory skin through the lacy gown she wore. One side of his mouth curled up in a smile. Definitely no angel, Senta thought, pulling the bedcovers up.

"Sorry 'bout that, ma'am." He shook his head. "Sorry 'bout the whole thing."

So he did have some manners. Maybe he was a Maitland ancestor after all. Senta couldn't place the accent. The long sideburns were somewhat in the military mode, though, and there had been a lot of Morville officers. "Who . . . ?" she began. "What . . . ?"

Now he scratched his head. "Don't rightly know, ma'am. I just kind of show up places. Sometimes I remember bits and pieces of stuff. Other times something sounds familiar, but I can't quite put my finger on it."

"Surely you know your own name."

He curled his lip again. This time it looked more like a sneer than a smile. "You'd come as far as I have, you'd be all shook up, too."

He cocked his head, as if hearing distant music instead of Senta's correction: "All shaken up."

He said, "I've been racking my brains all night."

"Could you be a Lord Maitland?"

"Maitland? No, that doesn't sound right. It's more like a turnip. Parsnip?"

"Your name is a vegetable?" Senta pinched herself under the covers. Unfortunately, it hurt. She was awake.

"Uh, maybe it would help if we discovered *what* you are. You know, ghost? Guardian angel?" She had to add, "Devil?"

"You mean a ghoul? Like me?"

"I," she corrected automatically. "A ghoul such as I."

He stood up, looking confused. "No, ma'am, I'm no bogeyman. I'm a legend. That's it, a legend that never dies."

"A legend? Like King Arthur?" Now Senta dredged her mind. Parsnip? Parsley? Sage? "I know! You must be Father Time. You know, t-h-y-m-e."

"No, that don't sound right either."

She thought some more. "Saint George? How about Parcival? That sounds somewhat alike. Could you be Sir Parcival who went after the Holy Grail?" She'd always thought the story was fiction, but she supposed such a hero could take on a life of his own, more or less.

His brows were furrowed. "It sounds close. You know, like a name on the tip of your tongue. I think what happened is my memory got left somewhere else, and just hasn't caught up yet. Hell, sometimes I feel as though if I could just remember a few more details, I could go on home."

Senta made a silent toast to that. But her visitor was obviously distressed, so she asked, "Why don't we just call you Sir Parcival for now?"

"I don't know about that Holy Grail stuff, and the 'sir' don't sound right either."

"Then you aren't a knight?" she asked in disappointment.

"Not even a Pip."

Senta bit her lip. With all those jewels, he was certainly of the upper classes. "Then are you an earl? A duke?"

He raised his perfect chin. "Ma'am, I'm the King."

Senta was fairly certain no King of England ever looked like this. "King of what country?"

"More like rock, ma'am."

"You're the King of Gibraltar?" Senta didn't think there was such a thing. Then again, history had never been her favorite study. "Did you actually sit on a throne?"

He put his head in his hands. "Don't ask."

She took a deep breath. Here it was, her wedding night, and she was entertaining a ghost, and a crazy one, to boot. Well, the mad King of England thought he was the palace cook or some such, so Senta supposed her ghost—legend—could be as balmy as he wanted. If he just left. "Ah, besides seeking your lost memory, was there some particular reason you arrived here?"

He looked around. "Reason?"

"You know, like vengeance, or to right an old wrong." Senta thought back over ghost stories she used to hear at school. "If you weren't buried properly, or didn't receive last rites. A mission."

"I don't rightly recall, ma'am. I suppose I'm here to make things right for you."

"Nothing was *wrong* for me until you got here!"

"Didn't look that way to me."

"You were watching?" Senta gasped. Thank goodness he couldn't see her flaming cheeks.

He shrugged. "Nothing much else to do. You were a-lying there like a sacrificial virgin. And what about this forced marriage and some other guy? You got someone else's bun in the oven, sister?"

"That's Senta. And what do you mean, someone else's—Oh." She figured it out. "Of course not. And my marriage was no such thing. It wasn't even an arranged match, like that of many of my friends."

"Arranged?"

"You know, where the parents decide to join two estates or two fortunes. The brides have to hope their fathers make the right choices for them."

"The fathers get to choose? Hmm."

"Yes, but mine wasn't that way at all," Lord Maitland

even asked me if it was all right to ask my papa for permission to pay his addresses. He thought I might be pushed into accepting him, once he made his formal offer. But I wanted to marry Viscount Maitland, very much."

"He don't seem to know that."

Senta chewed on her thumbnail, which she hadn't done in ages. "No, he thinks it was a marriage of convenience, I suppose." Sir Parcival, for want of a better name, was looking more confused than ever. Senta didn't know why she was telling her troubles to a transparent Bedlamite, but she continued anyway: "A marriage of convenience is when a titled gentleman, for instance, marries a girl with no family connections, but a large dowry. He gets the money; she gets the title."

Sir Parcival's lip curled. "We don't call that convenience; we call it commerce. They don't have to love each other at all?"

"They don't even have to like each other. There are many matches in the ton like that, where both partners go their separate ways. I'd never have a marriage like that."

"But your bridegroom would?"

Senta chewed on her fingernail some more. "He started attending debutante balls and Almack's for the first time in memory, and everyone said it was because he needed an heir after his younger brother's death. He is two and thirty, you see. It was time to start his nursery."

"So he wanted a broodmare. What was he offering as stud fee?"

Senta ignored the vulgarity. It was all too true that any unattached female would have tossed her bonnet over the viscount's windmill. She sighed. "He has everything. Wealth, title, lands, influence, looks, intelligence, honor. He could have had any woman he wished." ⋅

"But he chose you."

She smiled, and hugged that thought to herself. Lord Maitland had chosen her, with merely passable looks, undistinguished family, and average portion. And she was delighted. She'd wanted to dance and shout and sing, but there he was, so serious in Papa's library, telling her that he would not announce any understanding yet, in case she changed her mind. In fact, he didn't want her to decide until after the end of the fall Little Season. If she was still willing, she and her family could spend the Christmas holidays at his country property, to see if she might be happy there. He was no absentee landlord, he carefully warned her, and the place was somewhat of a moldery old pile sorely in need of a woman's touch. He'd asked again on Christmas eve, and again she'd said yes, and he'd given her the family betrothal ring, finally.

"He must have thought I'd make him the most biddable wife." Senta fumbled for a handkerchief so she could blow her nose. "And I meant to be, I swear. Now look at the mess I've made!" she wailed.

Sir Percival was scowling. "You stop that blubbering, sister. I hate when women cry. Did you ever tell the man you loved him?"

She sniffed. "My name is Senta. And . . . and I don't love him. I hardly know him. My parents approved, and he was everything kind."

His lip curled again. "Sure, you don't love him and I'm Prince Charming."

Senta didn't think so, not with that sneer. "How could I tell him such a thing? He's so proper, he made sure we were never alone. But he should have known! When he asked if I wanted to wait till his year of mourning was up in the spring to have the wedding, so I could have a big affair at St. George's, I said no. I told him I'd rather get married right now, right here at his home, before Mama and Papa left after New Year's, rather than wait. That should have told him I wasn't just interested in all his grand connections. He should have known!"

Sir Parcival was up and pacing. "I reckon that's my mission then, to tell him you love him."

"You can't do that! I'd die if he thought I loved him when he ... he only wants a mother for his sons."

"So what I have to do is get him to love you back, right, and make this a real marriage?" He moved toward the door.

Senta gave a watery laugh. "You? You don't even know your own name, and he can't see you. Oh, it's all such a mess." She started weeping again for her lost dreams.

"Doubts, huh? I've had a few." Sir Parcival stepped through the closed door. Before he disappeared, he called back, "Little sis— Senta, don't you do ... Don't you do that ... Don't you cry."

Chapter Two

"Damn and blast," the viscount muttered. "I knew it would never work!" Lord Maitland was in his library, in his undress, in despair. He poured himself another cognac from the cut-glass decanter on the cherrywood desk and tossed it down. "How could I ever expect a jewel like Senta to fall for a dry old stick like me?"

She was a diamond, his new bride, beautiful to look at, beautiful on the inside, too. When he first came up to Town in the fall, determined to find himself a wife and fulfil the responsibilities of the succession, Miss Senta Tarlowe caught Lee's eye immediately. She was such a gay, spirited young thing, always smiling, pleased with whatever entertainment the day offered, from lavish balls to simple country picnics. She didn't blush, simper, or bat her eyelashes, nor did she put on the airs and affectations so many of her peers wore in pretend sophistication.

Lee had watched her at various functions before even seeking an introduction. He noted how, as often as she was the center of a knot of admiring beaux, just so often she was like to be found in a gaggle of female companions, belles as well as wallflowers. Other times she seemed content to sit quietly with her parents.

Her reputation was spotless. He'd made inquiries, as far as he could without seeming obvious. No one had the slightest ill to speak of Miss Tarlowe, except a few disappointed suitors who found her too particular in her notions. Maitland couldn't fault her for that: getting legshackled was a serious enterprise. He'd allowed himself a year for the business.

It wouldn't be the grandest match of the Season. The Tarlowes were solid country gentry, while the Maitlands were used to running the country. Nor would the gal bring any great riches or vast estates, which suited Lee to a cow's thumb. He had more than he could do handling his own properties and investments. Any dowry Miss Tarlowe brought would only be settled on her children. His children.

For the first time since his brother Michael's death, the idea of becoming a tenant for life grew more appealing. As he watched her swirl through the paces of a *contra danse* with some spotted youth, Lee was convinced Miss Tarlowe would make him an excellent wife.

He approached cautiously at first, a dance here, a not-so-chanced meeting in the park there. Lee knew what a storm of gossip his least interest would produce, and wished to spare Miss Tarlowe that discomfort. But there were so many other, younger, men trailing at her skirts, men with no greater needs than to sit at her feet and write poems to her golden locks. Lee sat on two Parliamentary councils and wrote briefs for the Foreign Office. Nor could he dally on in London, worshiping her eyebrows like those sprigs, not when the Corn Laws were wreaking havoc in the countryside.

But what if she accepted one of them? Suddenly all those other fishes in the matrimonial seas were blowfish or barracudas or big-mouthed bass. It had to be Miss Tarlowe.

And she seemed to favor his suit. The viscount wasn't naive enough to be surprised, yet he was delighted and relieved nevertheless. He moved slowly, quietly, not about to frighten her off with protestations of devotion and endless passion. And he gave her every opportunity to retreat without dishonor. He was even willing to wait six months to give her another Season to look around, to decide if he was the best she could do. It might have killed him, but he gave her the chance.

She hadn't taken it. She'd taken him instead.

Lee poured out another glassful and this time sipped it slowly. No, he thought now, she'd taken his title and fortune and social standing, not the man. Not the man she'd just thrown out of her bed.

That man's feet were getting cold, so he tugged on the bellpull. He knew the household was up, for he could hear scurrying and whispers beyond the library door. Hell, he'd be glad if Senta's shrieks hadn't awakened the sleeping Morvilles in the family crypt.

When he heard a scratch on the door, Lee's heart leaped up, but it was only a footman with an armload of firewood. Then his valet came in, handing over a pair of slippers without meeting his master's eyes. Even the butler, Wheatley, who was as much a fixture at the Meadows as the suits of armor in the hall, entered silently. He made room on the desk for a pot of coffee and a cup, not too subtly moving the cognac decanter aside.

Lud, what the staff must think of him now! Lee shook his head. Years of being a fair and generous employer, earning their respect, were wiped out in one night. What kind of beast brutalizes his sweet young wife into hysterics on their wedding night? Lee couldn't imagine. But he was sure his servants could. By tomorrow the tale would be all over the countryside, too. Trying to stop the gossip would be like holding the ocean from the shore. He shoved the coffee aside and reached for the cognac. "Hell and damnation, is it possible to make more of a mess of this night's work?" he asked himself.

Lee didn't see the gold-clad figure glide through the wall, nor did he hear Sir Parcival's answer: "Un-uh, reckon it's impossible." The spirit had drifted through the vast mansion looking for the viscount, catching giggling maids and leering footmen. "Man, this place is bigger than ... bigger than ..." He shook his head. "By the grace of God, I wish I could remember."

Lord Maitland, meanwhile, decided on the coffee after all, to warm him. He shoved the cognac back and filled a cup of the strong, hot brew. He'd had too much to drink already today, perhaps enough that he could blame some of the night's fiasco on the devil in the bottle. He wasn't one to overindulge in the usual course, so perhaps all the toasts at the wedding breakfast had him a trifle disguised. If his head had been clearer, maybe he wouldn't have frightened poor Senta so much.

Sir Parcival gazed longingly at the decanter, but shrugged and strolled about, admiring the rows upon rows of leather-bound volumes. He was even more impressed with the tiger-skin rug in front of the fireplace. Lee didn't notice.

Thunderation, the viscount cursed to himself, he'd known Senta was frightened. Hell, he'd been quaking in his boots himself, or out of them, as it were, nervous about making the first time pleasant for her. He wasn't inexperienced, not by a long shot, but the women he was used to were usually even more experienced. Most assuredly Viscount Maitland was not in the practice of deflowering virgins. He'd even had a cold bath before knocking on the door of her bedchamber, to dampen some of his ardor. It hadn't worked a bit.

He couldn't wait to make her his, to tie her to him with bonds of passion, to express his love in a way his fumbling words never could, to make her forget every other man who ever existed. Maybe she'd even get to like him, just a little. But no, he'd rushed his fences. His head hadn't been clear enough to exert control over his wayward body. Lee blamed himself for the whole debacle, for having too much on his mind to pay attention to Senta's anxieties. Then he told himself it wouldn't have mattered at all, if she had another man on her mind.

Lee sighed and pulled open the top drawer of his desk. Reaching toward the back, he pulled a hidden lever and another, secret drawer opened. The viscount withdrew two folded notes. "I didn't make her happy," he lamented aloud. "Didn't make her like me. Now I can't even protect her from scandal."

Sir Percival stood behind Maitland's chair to see what was bothering this jackass so much he didn't get back upstairs and make love to his wife. "Hell," Sir Percival muttered, "you wouldn't find me down here catching my death, if I got a woman waiting upstairs." He cocked his head. "Nah."

Lee was studying the two notes. Fine, he thought, his wife had two lovers; he had two blackmailers.

Sir Percival leaned over his lordship's shoulder to peer at the notes. He read one and whistled through his teeth, causing the viscount to tug at the collar of his satin dressing gown to avoid the draft. He couldn't, for Sir Percival whistled again, after he read the second message. "Those ain't no love letters," he drawled. "No wonder your hand's shaking like a leaf on a tree."

The first letter, written in bold but elegant script on fine-quality paper, advised: *If you do not wish your bride and the public to hear the true facts concerning the death of Lieutenant Michael Morville, send five hundred pounds to the Seven Swans posting inn, in London, attention, Mr. Browne.*

The missive had arrived at the Meadows right after Christmas, via the troubled hands of Lee's London secretary, John Calley. Lee hadn't paid the demand, of course. Once you paid an extortionist, he became your pensioner for life. Besides, you could pay and pay, and still have no guarantee that your family skeletons would stay in the closet. Lee wouldn't put his trust in finding any honor among such thieves as would steal a dead man's integrity.

Instead he'd sent back with his trusted secretary a thick letter to Mr. Browne, three pages folded and sealed with the distinctive Maitland crest. Let the dastard think his blood money was inside.

The pages were blank, while Calley had enough blunt to bribe everyone at the inn from the porter to the potboy. Someone ought to be able to identify Mr. Browne when he retrieved the letter, quickly enough for the men Calley was hiring to follow him. If Lee had to spend more than the five hundred pounds in rewards and bribes, it would be money well spent, to defang the viper. Let Calley just find the snake's name and direction, then let Mr. Browne see how he liked the payment Lee was planning to give him.

So far, there had been no report back from London. Nor any gossip.

The other note was on common stock, and had arrived today before the wedding. No, 'twas past midnight. Lee's wedding day had come and gone. It was already yesterday now. He could only shake his head at the waste, and look back at the second message. This one was written in ill-formed letters, which could have disguised a gentleman's handwriting, even a woman's, but Lee didn't think so, from the caliber of the threat: *I know what really happened to your little brother. I'm at the inn. We need to talk.*

This villain was a fool, thinking to get away with extortion in Maitland's own home village of Mariwaite, where every stranger was immediately suspect. The townspeople had been loyal to the Maitland family for centuries. If the fellow dared breathe a word against Michael, he'd be lynched before Lee could get to him, which would be a deuced shame.

Not that the viscount meant to pay off this gallowsbait, any more than he would the muckworm in London. And he didn't need to talk to anyone about his brother, for he already knew more details than he wished. Details that he thought—prayed—he could carry alone to his own grave. It was not to be.

Maitland stood and carried his coffee to the mantel, over which hung a picture of the late viscountess, his mother. She was wearing a rose-colored gown in the style of twenty years ago, and she was smiling down at the child at her feet. Another boy, himself, stood rigidly at her side, already serious and solemn at ten. The baby frolicked with a ball at his mother's skirts. Lee remembered the nursemaids endlessly chasing after toddling Michael to return him to the sitting, while the artist scowled. Lee had stayed put, hating every minute of it, because the heir to Maitland knew his duties. Mama just smiled.

Oh yes, Lee knew how Michael had died in Portugal. Thank goodness their mother had passed on before she had to know.

The official version, because of Maitland's money and influence, and because the army couldn't afford another scandal right now, was that Lieutenant Morville was accidentally killed when his rifle discharged while he was cleaning it. It was just one of those quirks of war, they said, that a young man could serve with distinction through all those bloody battles and retreats, even survive the fevers and fatigues of the occupying army, then succumb to a misfired bullet. Frightful loss and all that. There were even rumblings among the condolence-callers of shoddy weapons, misspent appropriations. Lee had nodded, accepting the sympathy, because the heir to Maitland still knew his duties.

The story was a lie. The generals knew it; Lee knew it. They thought they were the only ones, that they could get away with the fabrication, so Lee could bring the body back and bury Michael next to their parents in the family plot with some degree of honor. It wasn't a hero's burial, but neither was it a traitor's hanging, or a suicide's ostracism.

For in truth Michael, that little cherub playing so sweetly at their mother's feet, had done them all the courtesy of blowing his own brains out before the army got a chance to court-martial him. He'd led his own men into an ambush after selling information about their movements to the French.

Lee still couldn't believe it. He had a hard enough time believing dashing, daring Michael was never coming back, much less that he was a turncoat. But the evidence was there, laid out by Michael's commanding officer: the French script found in his bunk, the gambling chits he'd signed, the casualty reports of a supposedly secret mission. Most damning of all was the general's own report of the bullet to the temple. Innocent men don't kill themselves.

Why hadn't he sent home for money if he found himself up River Tick? Lee had asked himself a hundred times. He'd never refused Michael anything, not even the commission the young hellion begged him to purchase. All the young officers gambled; that was no great failing. No, Michael knew his sins were so great that suicide was the only solution.

But it hadn't been a solution at all, not one the army or Lord Maitland could live with, so they'd devised a death by misadventure. Lee could hold his head up, with his family name still untarnished, while he searched for a woman to give him heirs to replace his fallen brother. That was his duty now.

He went courting and found a pure, innocent girl, he thought, with the light of heaven in her blue eyes. Well, they'd both cheated on their wedding vows.

Senta's soul wasn't quite so unsullied, although he still believed her body was. So far. On the other hand, he'd offered his fine old name, which was in reality as tarnished as a pinchbeck teapot. If she'd married him for the exalted social position, she was in for a disappointment as bad as this wedding night was to him.

The truth was bound to get out now, even if he paid.

If two men knew the truth, there would be others. It would be a scandal of epic proportions, and a blot on Lee's own honor, that he lied and laid out donations to the war effort to get Michael a decent burial.

No matter, Lee had no intention of paying. But he did intend to do what he could to repay the blackmailers for his anguish.

"I'm not going to let this night be a total waste," he vowed out loud as he left the library, calling for his clothes, his pistol, and his carriage, in that order.

Wheatley protested from his position of aged family retainer. "But, milord, there's flurries starting. Who knows, but we could have a blizzard by morning. You can't go out in this, and on your wed—"

"I'm going," Lee snapped back before Wheatley could finish that thought. "I'm only going as far as the inn in the village, old man." Let the whole staff think he was going to drown his sorrows in local ale or in the arms of a willing tavern wench. Lee didn't care. He was going to get some satisfaction out of this evening.

Sir Parcival, his brow furrowed, long fingers tapping out a silent tune on the desktop, stood staring at the two notes. He didn't know what he was doing here, or how to get back to something familiar. He figured that since Senta could see him and no one else could, he must be here to help her. He hunched his shoulders. How? He didn't even know what her husband intended to do out there in the night.

He stared at the letters as if the answer lay in their words. If he could just figure out the meanings and motives behind these two notes, he'd know better how to help. Then maybe he'd get his memory back and go home.

He tapped the London missive. "Number one's for the money. And number two"—he looked down at his fancy high-heeled, pointy-toed boots—"is for the snow."

Chapter Three

"But, my lord, it's the middle of the night. Your wedding night." The landlord of the village inn was practically in tears as he tried to seat Viscount Maitland in his one private parlor.

"I bloody well know what night it is. Everyone seems bent on reminding me!" Lee was having none of the landlord's hospitality as he stood in the hallway brushing the snow from his greatcoat's shoulders and stomping his frozen feet. "What room?"

"But . . . but you can't go wake up the paying customers!" The landlord dropped a plaintive "My lord" at the end.

"Can't I? Just watch! Either you tell me which room holds the man who sent a note up to the Meadows yesterday, or I'll go kicking down every door upstairs until I find him. And I wager whoever's paying Bessie to warm his bed tonight won't be half pleased."

Nor would that other couple who stopped here on account of the snow. Cousins, they said. The kissing kind, the innkeeper swore.

"What room?" the viscount demanded again, snapping his coiled driving whip against his thigh. His lordship wasn't known for his temper, but the innkeeper wasn't known for his foolhardiness either. "The second door on the right."

Lee took the stairs two at a time, calling back over his shoulder, "See that my horses don't take a chill. I won't be long."

Sir Percival was still outside in the snow, staring up at the wood sign swaying above the doorway of the inn. As usual, there were no words, from the days when almost no one could read, just the carved and painted outlines of a hart and a drake. "The Deer and the Duck?" He curled his lip. "Man, these folks have no imagination."

It didn't take much imagination to figure what Lord Maitland had in mind when he pounded on the second door to the right with the handle of his horsewhip.

"It's Maitland."

A scratchy voice answered: "I need a minute, m'lord, to put on my—"

A minute was too long for Lee. He pushed the door in, rushed toward the bed, and grabbed for the figure sitting there wiping his eyes.

Lee lifted the man in one hand by the collar of his flannel nightshirt. "If you say one word," he warned, brandishing the whip in his other hand, "I'll kill you. Do you understand?"

What was not to understand? The man nodded as vigorously as he could dangling from the viscount's fist. That was when Lee realized his captive had almost no weight to him. "What the deuce?"

He dragged the fellow toward the open door and the hall lamp. What he saw did not make him happy. The mawworm was missing most of his hair, a few of his teeth, one of his legs, and part of his ear. Besides that, he was half Lee's weight and twice his age. "Damn and blast, I can't kill an old cripple."

"I never thought I'd thank them Frogs for what they done to me," the old man croaked.

Lee shook him once and dragged him back to the

bed. "Shut up, I said." He lit a candle, then slammed the door on the innkeeper's anxious face. Sir Parcival came in anyway, but no one noticed, except for the sudden chill. There were some noises in the hall as the landlord reassured his other guests that the inn wasn't on fire or under attack. A dog was barking out in the stable, but soon even that sound died, until all that was left was the viscount's whip tapping against his breeches, the old man's raspy breathing, and Sir Parcival humming "Cherry Ripe," which he'd heard a maid singing.

"Thunderation!" Lord Maitland swore, shivering with the cold. "What else can go wrong in one night?"

"With you? Anything, if you keep going off half-cocked," Sir Parcival commented with that half-arrogant look as he leaned against the window ledge, staring out at the falling snow.

Lee wasn't looking, or listening. He was searching the room's meager contents for weapons. The chest of drawers contained a comb and a razor, a change of linen, and two handkerchiefs. The peg behind the door held a suit of rough but serviceable clothing. Lee patted the pants pockets to make sure they were empty, then tossed the worn breeches to the oldster, who had taken the opportunity to strap on his wooden leg.

"It's like this, m'lord," he began.

Lord Maitland was checking under the mattress. He tossed a thin purse he'd found there onto the bed and took a threatening step closer to the graybeard. "I told you to keep your mouth shut!"

"Then how you going to find out about—"

Lee's whip snapped inches away from his nose. "I can take a fly off my leader's ear at a full gallop. Do you have anything else you'd like to lose?"

The man buttoned his lip, and his woolen pants.

"Now, listen," the viscount ground out after opening a frayed carpetbag to feel among the folded shirts and pants. "I don't want to hear any of your filth except the answers to the questions I'm going to ask. Is that clear?"

The old man spit between the gap in his teeth, peril-ously close to the viscount's feet. "Clear as the mud on your boots, m'lord."

"Don't push your luck, granfer. It's your years keep-ing you alive, not my patience. That's in short supply tonight. Now, what's your name?"

"Waters, m'lord, Private Jacob Waters, late of His Majesty's Army."

"Too late, it looks like."

"Aye, but they wasn't handing out pensions, and I never had nothing to come home to. So I stayed on." He knocked on the wooden leg. "Till they tossed me out when I wasn't fit to be cannon fodder no more. Shipped me home with a pocketful of silver and a coach ticket."

It was a common enough story, and not one to make decent Englishmen proud, how the country treated its returning veterans. Nor was it an excuse to turn to a life of crime.

Waters went on, now that the viscount seemed to be listening: "It weren't so bad when we wasn't seeing ac-tion. I got to make extra money taking care of some of the younger officers' weapons and uniforms and such. Them as didn't have a batman of their own. That was how I got to know Lieutenant Morville. Kept his billet for him, I did. Your brother was—"

Waters found himself dangling above the ground once more.

"Don't you even mention my brother's name again, do you hear me?"

"I bet they can hear you clear 'cross town," Sir Percival put in, for no one's benefit but his own. "If you'd just listen to the old warhorse, we could all go home and get into warm beds."

Oblivious, Maitland had lowered the soldier back to the ground. "Who else knows?"

"That I took care of Lieu— the young officers? Everyone in the company, I'd guess. Weren't no secret."

"Damn you, who else knows how he died?"

Sir Parcival nodded. "Now, that's more like it, man."

Private Waters must have thought so, too, for he let out a deep breath. "Well, there's this señorita, Mona."

"The devil take it, I don't want to hear about your lightskirt."

"You got it wrong. She was your bro—" The look on Maitland's face made the private's voice trail off. "Mona's nó lightskirt."

"Stubble it. I want to know who you told in London."

"London? I called at your place there, but they said as how you were in the country. I didn't talk to nobbut the butler."

"My own butler's not blackmailing me, by Jupiter!"

"Blackmail, is it?" The man rubbed his stubbly chin. "That why you're so prickly? You think I—"

"I think that if you don't have an accomplice, you have a competitor. I'll see both of you rot in hell before I give either of you one shilling. Now, who else knew the truth about my brother's death? Someone who might be in London now?"

"I guess it must be one of those toffs Mona saw. They come out to headquarters to fetch home a relative as got wounded. An officer. She didn't get their names, and I was on maneuvers. But they was the ones what rigged that card game what made the lieutenant—"

"Not anther word!"

"But we come all this way to tell you the story. We figure one of those nobs was the—"

"I've heard enough." Lee waved his fist under the smaller man's chin. "You'll never tell your story to anyone, do you understand? I've managed to give my brother more honor than he deserves, and I mean him to keep it. Why, if I had my way, I'd put you on a ship to

New South Wales along with the other scum of the earth."

"Here now, gov'nor, you can't do that!"

"Of course I can. I'm the magistrate."

"But I didn't do nothing!" Private Waters wailed.

Lee was sick of the whole thing by now. "You threatened a peer of the realm. That's enough to get you transported." He started throwing the man's things into the carpetbag. "Be happy I'm only sending you to my plantation in Honduras. You can tell your story there till you are blue in the face."

Sir Parcival was shaking his head. "Blue Honduras? Nah."

Waters, meanwhile, was hobbling around, trying to keep his belongings away from this madman. "Honduras? Threat? I only wanted to make sure you knew the truth about your brother."

The viscount tossed the old man his coat. "I know all there is to know about my brother," he said through gritted teeth.

"You don't neither of you know nothing about t'other. He thought you was a fair, intelligent man, and you believe he could be a trai—!"

Lee stuffed the fellow's nightcap in his mouth, bundled him into a blanket, and tossed him over one shoulder. He picked up his whip and the satchel with his other hand, and stormed out of the room, down the stairs.

The landlord was standing there, mouth agape. Lee tossed him the carpetbag while he reached into his pocket for some coins. He put a golden boy into the man's hand. "This should settle Private Waters's bill and any other questions you might be thinking of asking."

"Nary a one, my lord, nary a one. Good evening and . . . and my felicitations on your wedding."

Lee just grunted as he threw Waters and his valise onto the seat of his curricle when the stableboy brought it around. He gave the boy the nod and tossed him another coin. Then he cracked his whip, this time well over his horses' heads, sending them off at a trot through the snow-covered lanes.

Sir Parcival was perched behind, where the tiger would ride. He was staring back through the swirling snow at the inn sign while it was still visible in the light of the lanterns kept burning to either side of the door. "The Stag and the Scoter? The Buck and Wing? Yeah, that must be it. The Buck and Wing. Not bad."

The village had a tiny gaol, a shed behind the livery where prisoners could await trial. The viscount didn't take Waters there, not to spew his filth into any passing ear. Instead he drove through the village, then down the hill to the shallow valley where some of his tenants had their cottages. Beyond that he turned the curricle onto a side path that took a shortcut through the home woods. The snow was falling softly, but the geldings were surefooted and the moonlight was sufficient. The only sounds were the jingle of harness and the horses' breathing.

In fact, Lee couldn't help thinking that this could be a lovely drive if it were his wife tucked cozily at his side to share the carriage blanket. Instead he had a footless ex-foot soldier next to him. And a chill down his spine as if the Devil rode at his back.

He drove through one of the clearings that gave the Meadows its name and reined in the horses at an empty gamekeeper's cottage. The windowless back room had a padlock, to keep out mischief-makers and poachers. Here was where the viscount deposited his prisoner and his bag.

"There's a pallet and some blankets. I'll start the fire in the other room so you'll get some warmth, and someone will be out in the morning to bring food. Take off the leg. You aren't going anywhere." Lee looked around at the neat little cottage while Waters, protesting the order, protesting his kidnapping, and protesting his innocence, removed his peg leg.

"You had only to ask." His lordship put the wood and leather contraption on top of the mantel, in the outer room. "If you were in need, I would have found you a cottage like this, just because you took care of Michael."

"I didn't come begging for no charity. I got some blunt put by. I only wanted to see justice done."

"At what cost? And how many lives ruined?" Lee shut the back door on the old man's ragings. "Go to sleep, Private Waters. If I find your friends in London and put them out of the extortion business, too, who knows? Maybe I'll reconsider and just send you to Ireland."

"But what about Mona?" Waters shouted as he heard the lock click shut.

"Mona? Oh, your Spanish whore. If she wants to go to Ireland, she can go, too."

"Mona ain't no whore. She's a lady, and your brother was going to . . ."

Maitland drove off. When he got home, Wheatley was waiting in the hall to remove his master's greatcoat, as if it were two in the afternoon, not two in the morning.

"Dash it, I can let myself into my own house and see myself to bed, Wheatley," the viscount complained as he handed over his gloves and hat, feeling guilty about keeping the man from his rest. "I've told you a hundred times."

"Yes, milord. But that's what you hired me to do."

Maitland nodded. "Well, as long as you're up, I'll need you to locate our most trustworthy footman. He'll be bringing food and supplies out to a prisoner at the old gamekeeper's cottage in the morning. I don't want him talking to the man, and I particularly don't want him talking about the man."

"Our people do not gossip, my lord."

"I did not mean to disparage your staff, Wheatley. Whoever you select will need to keep watch over the cottage until I can get to London and take care of a bit of business."

"Is he a, ah, desperate criminal, my lord? Should the footman be armed?"

"He's older than dirt, and only has one leg, dash it, or I'd have beaten him to a pulp. He'll be gone from here as soon as I can arrange passage out of the country for the dirty dish. Notify the stable I'll want the closed carriage first thing in the morning."

"In the morning." Wheatley stared somewhere over Lord Maitland's shoulder. "And Lady Maitland?"

Lady Maitland. He'd forgotten he was a married man. What an insult his leaving would be to a new bride! And how embarrassing she'd find the household's pretending nothing was wrong. But there was nothing for it. He had to go to London. The War Office was bound to know what young officer was fetched home the week Michael ... died. If not, they could dashed well find out. Besides, he couldn't trust himself with Senta. While he was here, while she was his wife, he was going to keep wanting her.

"Lady Maitland must be asleep by now. I'll leave her a letter. She'll understand."

Sir Parcival fell off the pedestal where he'd been making the acquaintance of a long-dead Sir Morville slumbering in his suit of armor. Understand? When cow's milk turned blue!

Chapter Four

She was leaving her. The letter had been brought up with Senta's chocolate and toast. She'd asked for break-fast in her room rather than confront Lord Maitland over his kippers and eggs this morning. After the mor-tification of last night, she needed more than a fresh dress to face him.

Her husband had gone out last night. Senta's bed-room overlooked the carriage drive. He'd returned sometime before daybreak, while she huddled miserably awake in her cold bed. Lord Maitland had been so dis-appointed in her, he'd had to leave the house in the middle of a snowstorm.

Senta had spent the entire night thinking of how she was ever going to make things right. How could she ex-plain to such a serious-minded, rational man like her husband that she'd been frightened by a ghost? Or whatever that figment of her imagination and indiges-tion called himself. Maitland was sure to hurry home for that—to see her locked away in Bedlam! Fairy tales come to life, by George! Next thing she knew, Beowulf would be chasing Grendel through the corridors of her dreams.

Well, now she wouldn't have to think of another excuse for her skitter-witted behavior. He was gone.

His letter spoke of urgent business in London. While he was supposedly on honeymoon? And oh yes, he'd added a brief personal message: While he was in London, Lord Maitland intended to speak to his solicitor about obtaining an annulment. Personal indeed! He did not believe, the viscount wrote, that nonconsummation on its own was grounds enough to negate a marriage; it was bound to be a consideration, though, when he sought the annulment because their vows were already forsworn. If the fact that she loved another man didn't sway the courts and the clerics, he wrote, a few generous donations would. It seemed to Senta, as her teardrops made blurry tracks down Maitland's letter, that whereas money couldn't buy love or happiness, it could surely purchase his freedom.

Lord Maitland hadn't put it quite that way, of course. No, what he wrote was that he wanted what was best for her, with no discredit to her name. Whatever gossip arose would be a nine days' wonder, especially since most of society's gable-grinders were away from London in the dead of winter. Her speedy remarriage to a man she chose for herself would put paid to any scandalbroth. She wasn't to think of what effect an annulment might have on his, Maitland's, reputation. Her happiness was all that mattered.

How kind, how honorable, how thickheaded could one man be? If Lee Maitland were here right now, Senta swore she'd throw something at him! Herself. She would force him to see that *he* was the man she wanted, and none other.

Unless he was just looking for an excuse to get out of a misalliance. Miss Nobody from Nowhere was no match for the noble scion of the Morville dynasty. Why, she knew nothing about running a grand household or holding a man's interest. She couldn't even keep her own husband for one night.

And now what was she supposed to do? Wait around for him to toss her back, like a fish too small to keep? She didn't feel she had the right to begin her reign as mistress of the Meadows, not when it was to be one of the shorter tenancies in history. Nor did Senta feel like facing the stares and sympathy of his lordship's staff. Already this morning her own maid was clucking her tongue. For all Senta knew, the rest of the servants, from the stately butler to the saucy parlor maids, were blaming her for his lordship's sudden flight. Most likely none of them thought she was good enough for their beloved master either.

So Senta escaped to the little family chapel where she had been married just yesterday. The flowers had been removed to the public rooms and the slate floor had been scrubbed after the guests left. No one would bother her here.

It was quite beautiful, besides, with the stained-glass windows letting in a flood of gem-colored light. The thin layer of snow on the ground outside must have magnified the effect, for rainbows patterned the walls and floor and benches. Senta took a seat in a clear crimson sunbeam that streamed through some ancient Morville's robes.

Yesterday she'd been too excited to notice more than the sea of faces, neighbors and family and friends, with retainers standing in the back behind the last filled row of carved wooden pews. After that, she'd only had eyes for her magnificent groom, in his white satin breeches and midnight blue tailed coat. He had a single white rosebud in his lapel, to match the bouquet Senta carried. She did remember now how the chapel was filled with flowers, their scent everywhere. Someone, Wheatley, she thought, had proudly informed her the blooms were all from the estate's own forcing houses. The man in the back who wept throughout the service must have been the Meadows' gardener. Senta reminded herself to thank him later, to tell him how happy his great sacrifice had made her.

And she had been happy, facing her new life with all the hopes and dreams of innocence. She was going to make Henley Morville the best wife there had ever been. She'd keep his house, entertain his guests, bear his children. She practically had the infants named. There would be no babies now, no chance to make him love her.

"What, are you weeping again? Dang, I hate that."

Senta looked up at the sudden draft and wiped at her eyes. "I thought even the ghosts had deserted me." No such luck.

Sir Parcival was standing in a patch of blue reflected from the stained-glass sky above a cherubic Morville who had died too young. Everything about him was blue, right down to his shoes. As he stepped closer, though, through other colored rays of light, Senta realized he was dressed all in white, with sequins sewn all over his coat. Senta was almost blinded by the rainbows bouncing back from the tiny mirrors. "Are you sure you aren't an angel?"

"I've been called a lot of things in my time, sweetheart, but never that, if I recall."

"No, and you haven't exactly brought me any blessings," she concluded sadly. As a matter of fact, she blamed most of her troubles on this phantom's appearance, but she was too polite to say so. He had enough trouble searching for his missing memory without assuming a burden of guilt for her misery.

On the other hand, he might just be a hallucination and she really was ready for the lunatic asylum. In which case, his feelings wouldn't be hurt. "Oh, go away, do. You've been nothing but a headache."

"Now, *that,* I've been called." He sat next to her, and Senta couldn't resist the urge to touch him, to see if he was real. She nudged her hand along the cushioned seat of the pew, to his sleeve. Her hand passed right through, with a tingling feeling that sent chills up her spine.

"Yeah, it was always like that." He gave her a slow smile that instantly explained to Senta why he always had that effect on the girls.

"So what are you going to do," he was saying, "sit here all day in a river of tears or something?"

"What am I supposed to do, go back to my parents?" Her lip trembling, she waved Maitland's letter, crumpled now and waterlogged. "He doesn't want me."

"Oh, he wants you, all right, sister. A blind man could see that. Of course, he thinks he's too old for you to love him back, but what are twelve years or so? Nah, he's just upset over his brother's death."

"I know. That's why he married me. With his brother gone, he needed an heir."

"No way. He couldn't help falling in love with you. Trust me, I mightn't know my name, but I know about these things. Some loves are just meant to be."

"Thank you." She sniffed into her handkerchief. "But he's still gone."

"So that leaves you to find out what really happened to this brother Michael."

"It was a terrible accident."

"No, that's what they told everyone, but your man knows that just ain't true. He thinks Michael killed himself after making a deal with the enemy that got his own men killed."

"Oh no, not Maitland's brother! I can't believe it."

"But he does. That's what has him chasing his tail like a dog with fleas."

"You mean he's not just angry at me?" Senta permitted a little hope to creep back into her heart.

"He's just trying to protect you, it looks like. Only he's going at it hind end first, begging your pardon, ma'am. Seems there's this old army retiree who might have the real facts, only your boy wouldn't listen. He shut the old guy up in some abandoned cellblock in the woods. We've got to go see the codger and find out what he knows."

"But I can't interfere."

"Well, you can't just sit here, crying in the . . . What did you call this place?"

Chapter Five

What happened to Lord Maitland's sweet and docile bride? If Wheatley the butler was wondering, at least he kept his thoughts to himself. He sent to the stables for the gig—one horse, no groom—as his new mistress had ordered. Her unfamiliarity with the surroundings, the fog setting in over the thin layer of snow, the general unsuitability of Viscountess Maitland going abroad unaccompanied, none of Wheatley's respectful protests were heeded.

"Begging your pardon, my lady, but I am sure the master would not approve."

"Then the master should be here to drive me himself."

Senta got the gig. And she was not going without a companion, for Sir Parcival sat on the bench next to her, directing her to direct the horse, Lulu.

"She was a Christmas present from Lord Maitland," Senta said when Sir Parcival admired the bay mare. "I call her Lou."

"Lou Christmas?"

He really was attics-to-let, her ethereal guest. "No, that's Father Christmas. Goodness, will he be showing up here, too?" He'd be more useful, she thought with just a touch of regret.

They drove up the hill, still within the Meadows' boundaries, and down into the hollow where the viscount maintained a cluster of homes for his tenants and workers. The fog was so bad there, Senta could barely make out the lane to follow.

"It's like pea soup, in the valley."

They had to backtrack a bit on the other side of the valley to find the trail that led through the home woods. At last they reached the clearing.

Senta got down, tied the horse, and said, "This isn't any gaol; it's just a house."

"But the back room has a lock on it."

Sir Parcival followed slowly, his head cocked to one side. "Jailhouse lock?"

Senta picked up a likely-looking rock for smashing the padlock, in case Maitland had taken the key with him.

"Jailhouse stone?" He shook his head. "Nah. That ain't it either."

The key was on a hook beside the door. Private Waters was thrilled to see them, to see Lady Maitland, at least, Sir Parcival being invisible to him.

"Fellow from up at the Meadows brung me food and got the fire going again, but he wouldn't listen to nothing I said about the lieutenant, or Mona, or anything. It was like I didn't exist."

"I can relate to that," Sir Parcival muttered.

"I even tried to slip some coins under the door here, for him to go tell Mona where I'd got to, but he wouldn't touch a groat of it. It's that worrited I am. So if you can just reach me down my wooden leg, I'll say what I come to say and be on my way afore his lordship has a change of heart."

Senta started to say, "His lordship didn't—" but Sir Parcival pinched her. It wasn't exactly a pinch, more a frosty blast, but she got the message. "That is, his lordship truly wants to know what really happened to his brother. Lieutenant Morville could not have been a traitor, could he?"

"Not on your life, my lady, and I'll take on any man who dares say different. He was a good officer, and took right good care of his men. He wouldn't of done nothing to put them in danger, least of all lead them into an ambush."

"And he was loyal to the Crown? He didn't have any Populist leanings?"

"He was an Englishman, ma'am. No offense."

Senta nodded. "Then what happened? How could they accuse him of trafficking with the enemy?"

"Well, I don't know about trafficking, but someone sold the information, that's for sure. We marched right into a company of Frenchies. The lieutenant, he managed to regroup the rear columns and take them around to come behind the Frogs, to save what was left of our troops. He was a regular hero, and none of the men who made it out of there alive could figure why he didn't get a chestful of ribbons. Instead, they shipped him home, quiet like, saying he had an accident."

"But he didn't?"

"The lieutenant could clean and load that rifle in his sleep, ma'am."

"And you don't think he killed himself?"

"No way. He and Mona was going to get married as soon as he could get leave. It was all he talked about. Fellow getting legshackled don't up and shoot hisself."

Senta thought of Lord Maitland and wondered if that was true. If he was desperate enough to end a marriage ... "You say Lieutenant Morville loved this Mona?"

"As God is my witness. And then there was the Frenchy blunt they found in his billet. Well, it wasn't there in the morning when I made up the bunk. They made me swear not to talk about it ... and then they made sure I was shipped off so I couldn't ask any more questions."

"So what do you think happened?" Senta asked.

Waters scratched his bald head. "Well, some turncoat gave away our position, that's a pure fact. Then the rat framed Lieutenant Morville."

"And . . . killed him?"

"He would of defended hisself, otherwise. Dead heroes don't tell no tales. There were two fine London gents in camp the week of the battle, gambling and drinking with all the officers. My guess is one or both of them was the traitor. Now they're out to blackmail Lord Maitland, on account of the brass letting him claim an accident with the gun."

"Is that why Lord Maitland went to London, because someone was blackmailing him?" No wonder he was distracted!

Private Waters eyed her narrowly. "Didn't he tell you what he was doing?"

"He, ah, didn't want to worry me."

"Well, you best worry. Iffen I miss my guess, one of those lying, cheating toffs is a murderer asides."

Dear heaven, Lee was in danger! Senta looked toward Sir Parcival for help, but he was combing his hair in the little washstand mirror.

"Do you have any proof? Do you know their names? Their direction?"

"No, but Mona saw them and heard them talking about someone named Antoine. That's a Frenchy name for sure. She was serving in the cantina at the time, and they didn't know she could speak English. Don't go thinking Mona's just a tavern wench, like the colonel said, when she went to him with her suspicions. She was a right proper lady, but the war killed her family and she had to make her own way. She was working there just until she and the lieutenant could get hitched, so as they could have proper digs, not a tent in a muddy field."

"I see, I think. But Mona doesn't know the men's names? Can she recognize them?"

"She could of, if his high-and-mighty lordship hadn't gone off in a rant, begging your pardon, ma'am. Now he's liable to stir up a real hornet's nest, leading right back to Mona and me. So I'll just go fetch her from that inn in your village, and we'll be on our way."

Private Waters quickly learned that Lady Maitland was nearly as hardheaded as her husband. She didn't lock him up, but she took his wooden leg with her in the gig, to go fetch Mona.

"Then we'll find you a safe place to stay until his lordship gets back and can listen."

Waters spit out the door. "And pigs'll fly."

Mona was happy to leave the inn with Senta once she saw the peg leg. She'd been nervous there by herself, even with Private Waters's wallet and pistol. She pulled the latter out of her wide black skirts, to Senta's discomfort. In her imperfect English she made it quite plain that she would do anything she could to clear her lost love's name and hold his murderers to account.

"I, Ramona Consuela las Flores y Vegas, I shall tear their hearts out with my bare hands," the small, dark-haired woman swore, "the way they stole my *corazón.*"

Then she started to cry.

"Another weeping willow," complained Sir Percival. "Man, I can't stand this." He tried to put his arms around her. "That's all right, Mona." His arms went right through her, and she kept crying and shivering, until Senta suggested she go upstairs and gather her belongings.

When Mona returned, she wasn't carrying bags and boxes; she had a baby in her arms.

Oh Lud, Senta was thinking, and the private said she was a lady. Lord Maitland wasn't going to be happy about this. Wheatley wasn't going to be happy about this. Her own mother would have kitten fits, if she ever found out. Senta turned to Sir Parcival for some guidance. He was as happy as a grig, entranced by the infant who was gurgling up at him and reaching for his gold necklace. The babe seemed confused when her little hands couldn't touch the glittery object. Senta was confused, too.

Sir Parcival shrugged. "It's a female thing. And innocence."

Innocence, which seemed to be in short suppy on the Peninsula.

Mona raised her chin. "We were, *cómo se dice*, promised? We were going to be married, my Miguel and I." Shifting the baby to her shoulder, Mona reached into the bodice of her heavy black dress. She pulled out a chain. "Miguel, he said, '*Cara*, until we can wed, wear my ring around your neck.' "

Senta recognized the Maitland family crest on the gold ring, a match to the one her husband wore constantly. Michael would not have parted lightly with his. Sir Parcival nodded.

Mona tucked the chain back out of sight. "But to wait, with the battles, the danger . . ." She shrugged. "Things are different with the army."

"You can say that again, ma'am."

The Spanish girl turned the baby in her arms. "He never got to see his daughter, but Miguel, he would have loved her very much. I named her Vida, for life. Vida Miguela las Flores y Vegas."

"Vida las Flores? Vida las Vegas? Man, that almost sounds familiar."

Mona smiled tenderly at the infant, while Senta scowled at Sir Parcival for fussing with his lost memory now. Unfortunately, Mona caught Senta's look of disgust. She stared back defiantly. "If you cannot accept my *niña*, me and my Miguel's love child, I will understand. This is not the thing for grand señoras, this I know. We can wait here for Private Waters. He is a good friend."

"I'm sure he is, but my husband will want to make provision for his brother's child." Senta crossed her fingers behind her back. Maitland was so very proper. He already believed Mona was a mere camp follower. Heaven knew what he'd think if she sprang a baby from the wrong side of the blanket on him. "Besides, until we find the real traitors, you are not safe here alone."

"But I am not alone. Private Waters left his dog here to guard me and Vida." She handed the infant to Senta and went to fetch the animal.

"I had a dog once," Sir Percival reminisced while Senta jiggled the baby. "I'm sure of it."

"Will you forget about remembering what you forgot!" Senta hissed. "We have to figure what to do with all of them."

An old brindle bitch plodded at Mona's side. "Her name is Sheba," Mona told them.

"Old Sheba? Nah, that wasn't it."

There was a problem when they returned to fetch Private Waters. Senta had thought getting Maitland to accept Mona and Vida, and listen to Private Waters, was her big hurdle. She didn't even consider what she was going to tell the staff at the Meadows to explain the unlikely trio. Quartet if you included Sheba, who was nothing like the sleek, well-fed foxhounds in his lordship's kennels.

That wasn't the problem, however. After a hurried conversation with the old soldier in Spanish, Mona refused to go to the Meadows.

"*Su esposo,* your husband, he believes my Miguel was a traitor."

"That's what the army told him. We have to help him prove otherwise. That's why you came, isn't it?"

"He called me *puta.* I will not sleep under his roof. We will stay here, in this little house."

Senta didn't bother saying that the cottage was as much Maitland's as the Meadows was. "But the man he sent to guard Private Waters will be back. He'll lock him up and toss you out."

Mona was adamant. "Me, I have slept on the ground before. We will camp in this forest until he begs my forgiveness, your so proud viscount."

"But it's cold!" Senta feared it might be a cold day in hell before Maitland took in a baseborn child and its unwed mother. "And you must think of the baby! January in England is not what you are used to in Spain."

Private Waters scratched at his chin. "She's right, and there are game wardens prowling about, and poachers, too. It ain't safe. We can't go back to that inn neither; the keep's wife weren't none too keen on babies, or foreigners, or young girls with no wedding ring, even if I did say you was my daughter-in-law. And getting hauled out of there oncet was enough, thankee."

Senta did some quick thinking. "I know. There used to be a hermit living in a cave by the ornamental lake. It was all the rage in Lord Maitland's mother's time, he told me. But they couldn't get anyone to take the position, to look picturesque, you know, until they built a snug dwelling at the back of the cave, with a fireplace and all. It's still habitable. His lordship took me there before Christmas."

Senta pretended to fuss with the baby's blanket, to hide her blushes. They were supposed to be gathering holly and ivy to decorate the hall under the watchful chaperonage of Mama, two cousins, and an old aunt. Instead, the viscount had tugged her inside the cave for a quick kiss, their first.

"No one goes near there in winter, and it's close enough to the house that I can come visit and bring whatever you need, just until Lord Maitland gets home and straightens everything out. You'll be warm and safe from prying eyes in the grotto."

Sir Parcival looked up from making the baby coo with his humming. "In the grotto? You're going to stash them in the grotto?"

* * *

Now all Senta had to do was explain to Wheatley how the footman's visits to the cottage in the forest were no longer necessary. She did not want the stable hands and gardeners scouring the home woods for a one-legged soldier.

"About that small difficulty at the gamekeeper's cottage," Senta informed Wheatley, trying her hardest to imitate Lady Drummond-Burrell's haughtiest tones. "I have taken care of matters myself."

"And that troublesome report of a young foreign person in the village, with an infant?"

"Lud, nothing got past Wheatley." "I have seen to that also. They have all left the countryside."

Wheatley was relieved. Such havey-cavey goings-on at the cottage were not what he was used to, and that other situation boded no good for anyone. With no directions from Lord Maitland, Wheatley had been at a stand: leave the young person in the village to generate heaven knew what rumors or insults, or incarcerate her with that other fellow, quite illegally. Let the young mistress deal with it. Lord Maitland would never have her pretty young head on a platter.

"I am going to want some baskets of food," Senta told him, so he could notify the kitchens. "I noticed some of the tenants appeared to be in need."

Wheatley nodded, as if Lord Maitland would ever let any of his people go hungry. He'd guess she had the ragtag group in the boathouse or the grotto. He'd have to warn the staff to keep their distance. Welladay, she'd make a viscountess yet.

So Senta saw her guests settled in, and sat back to wait for Lord Maitland's return so she could surprise him with proof that his brother wasn't a loose screw, just a tad impatient. What a surprise that would be! She waited for him, and waited . . . and cried herself to sleep.

Sir Parcival walked the halls of the Meadows night after night, echoes of Senta's fallen teardrops jumbled in his head with all the confusion of places, people, poetry. He had no one to talk to when Senta slept. Out in the grotto the baby would gurgle for him, but she wasn't much of a conversationalist, and her mama cried. He had no way to make things right for her, either. He was no closer to promoting anyone's happiness or regaining his own memory.

With heavy heart, Sir Parcival went back to the slumbering soul in the suit of armor in the entry hall. "Are you lonesome too, knight?"

Chapter Six

Lord Maitland did not come home that week. He was not going to come home the following week. Senta knew it in her heart, the same as she knew that if she wanted to save her marriage, she had to go to London. He couldn't very well claim irreconcilable differences if they were living in the same house, could he? On the other hand, he would be so furious that she'd followed him to Town like a lost puppy that he might pack her up, bag and baggage, and ship her to her parents in Yorkshire, or some one of his far-flung holdings. Then she'd never get to prove to him that she hadn't married him for his wealth and title.

But if she did travel to London, Lord Maitland might think she merely craved the parties and entertainments of Town life, that she couldn't be content in the country. He'd think she'd spun her love of the rural life out of whole cloth, just to meet his requirements in a bride. When she'd told him how much she enjoyed small-town living and bucolic pastimes like riding and gardening and observing nature, she hadn't meant all by herself!

She also recalled blushing when the viscount had asked if she liked children. What did it matter that she adored babies, if she was never to have one of her own? Tiny Vida was precious, but she was Mona's baby. Maitland wasn't about to beget his heir by wishful thinking . . . if he still considered Senta a fit mother to his children. How could she stand his telling her not, face-to-face? No, she'd better wait here and hope he came to his senses. Perhaps a letter?

But there was the problem of his brother's death. Lee hadn't taken Senta into his confidence, which the meanest intelligence could assume meant that he wouldn't like her knowing about the accident/suicide, much less her putting her nose into his affairs. But if it was murder, then he had to know. Senta couldn't bear sitting over her embroidery while her husband's life might be in danger.

Besides, everyone for miles must already know about Mona and the baby, with all the supplies Senta had been toting out to the grotto. She'd even raided the attic for infant clothes and a small cradle. Wheatley and his staff were very good about turning their backs when she piled load after load onto the gig, but they must know. And Private Waters's dog begged at the kitchen door no matter how many scraps Senta put into the baskets of food. So their presence was no secret, and they could be in danger, too. In London, Mona could dress up as a lady's maid so she wouldn't be recognized as a foreigner. No one noticed servants or spoke to them anyway. And in London they could all help in the investigation into Michael's death.

But Senta had promised to obey her husband. He hadn't exactly ordered her to stay put, but he'd meant it. He wanted to be in London alone, to see about the blackmailers, and his business interests, and his Parliament responsibilities . . . and his old flirts. Senta had to go.

She put it to Sir Parcival. "Should I go to London or stay here?"

"Did I ever play there?" he wanted to know.

"How should I know where you played? I don't even know what century you lived!" Today Sir Parcival was dressed in a loose plaid jacket, but she could not identify the tartan. His trousers were somewhat in the cossack style, with extra fabric everywhere. No, she doubted he'd set out after the Holy Grail in that outfit. His feelings were obviously hurt, so she added, "That is, many little boys sail their boats on the Serpentine, so it's possible. I know they love to visit Astley's Amphitheatre and the menagerie at the Tower. My little cousins were in alt when they visited last spring. They rolled their hoops in Grosvenor Square for hours. Does any of that sound familiar?"

"Just the square part."

"But shall I go? Would it be a ninnyish thing to do?"

He listened carefully to all her reasoning, pro and con, then said, "Well, wise men say . . ."

"Yes? What do they say?" Perhaps her gudgeon of a ghost really knew some wiser heads.

"I can't remember."

Senta decided to go. Then she had to convince her entourage.

"I ain't going," Private Waters crossed his arms over his scrawny chest. "The man'd as soon send me to the Antipodes as give me the time of day. He wouldn't listen afore; he ain't going to listen now."

"But he won't have to listen to you. That is, he'll have to listen to me. I'll explain the whole thing, you'll see. And you never meant to extort money from him, so he really cannot charge you with anything. I rather think he'll be grateful to you"—and to herself—"for bringing this matter to his attention."

She prayed it was so. She needed Private Waters with her as her excuse for coming to London in the first place. The evidence she could present, showing that his brother was a loyal officer, ought to outweigh Maitland's anger at her presence. *Ought* was the pivotal word here. Senta couldn't begin to fathom the viscount's mind.

"What'll I do there? Can't go on living on his charity, especially how his lordship thinks I crawled out from under a rock, just to queer his game."

"You won't be dependent on his goodwill at all, Mr. Waters. I have an enormous household account and a generous allowance." She wanted this old soldier to think better of her husband, so she added, "Lord Maitland really is quite open-handed."

Waters's only comment was to spit between the gap in his teeth. Senta stepped back. "Yes, well, I can pay your wages myself. You can be my personal footman."

"You having a footman with one foot, tagging behind carrying your parcels and delivering your notes, is sure to sit fine with his high-and-mighty lordship. I'll do it."

Mona wasn't as easy to convince. London, in that *perm* Maitland's house? Never. Besides, it wasn't fitting for Lady Maitland to have an unwed mother in her home. She knew how things were in the *beau monde*. Mona was grateful enough for this time to rest from the journey; she would not ruin Senta's good name.

Senta's name would be mud if Maitland went through with the annulment, but she was not about to discuss that with Mona. Instead she reasoned that no one would have to know. They would simply call her a widow, Señora Vegas, who was acting as Lady Maitland's companion. That way Mona could go about with Senta in society, looking for the two men who played cards with Michael Morville, then framed him for treason and killed him.

"It's the only way we are going to clear Michael's name," Senta told her. "And think of the baby. You can't keep little Vida living in a cave, for heaven's sake!"

"But you will tell your husband who we are?"

"Of course. He has to know, in order to make his investigation, and to make some arrangement for your future. I know you are proud, and I know you would do your best to find work, but again, what about the baby? That kind of life is not what Michael would have intended for his child. Further, you would be dishonoring his memory, making him into a libertine who used women in the basest manner without taking responsibility for the outcome."

"Not my Miguel! Never!"

"Then let his brother fulfil Michael's obligations. Let Maitland look after you and Vida. It's the only way."

Mona nodded. "But what if this grand nobleman of yours rejects us? What if he says Miguel would never have promised to marry so far beneath him? What if he does not believe my precious *hija* is Miguel's baby at all?"

"Then you and Vida and Private Waters, if he wishes, will always have a home at my parents' house in Yorkshire. With me."

That left Wheatley to win over.

"But, my lady, his lordship left very specific instructions that you were to remain here until his return."

"Were those my husband's only instructions?" Senta asked in her sweetest tones.

"No, my lady," poor Wheatley had to confess, having said as much to Lady Maitland when she was first abandoned here. He'd been trying to make the master seem less of a blackguard, more fool he. "The master directed the staff to see that you had everything you wanted."

"Thank you, Wheatley, I want to go to London."

"But Maitland House is not up to our standards at this time. His lordship uses only a small portion of the rooms. The rest are in Holland covers or a state of deterioration."

"I've driven past Lord Maitland's London residence."

The outside is quite grand. Do you mean to tell me that it is a hovel inside?"

The butler cleared his throat. "Not precisely. The late viscountess did not often visit the city once she started filling her nursery. Her husband, the previous Lord Maitland, took no interest in domestic affairs like seat covers and wall hangings, less so when his lady passed on. His lordship, the current viscount, also prefers the Meadows as his residence; he frequently patronizes his clubs when in the city, so never saw the need to refurbish the town house. Therefore, the Portman Square property has been without a woman's touch for a long while."

"Too long. That's all the more reason for me to go, don't you agree? Someone should see about restoring the place to its former glory, to do the family name proud. Why, his lordship is very involved in governmental affairs. How can he entertain his political friends in a ramshackle old barn of a place?"

Wheatley took a deep breath. "But there is almost no staff to speak of: his lordship's man, the cook-housekeeper, a few maids, and perhaps two footmen. Not nearly enough to see Maitland House set to rights. I could send a staff ahead to ready it for your ladyship's arrival if you wish."

And warn the viscount so he could forbid her to come. "I'm sure a few days of discomfort without an army of servants around will not give me a disgust of the place. And they do have employment agencies in London, you know."

The butler blotted beads of perspiration from his forehead. "Take on strangers at Maitland House?"

"No? Then you'll come, too?"

Wheatley made one last try: "But his lordship had important business to transact in London. He will not appreciate the commotion of moving the household or renovating the premises."

"Oh, we shan't interfere with his lordship's business

at all. We'll be so quiet, he won't even know we are there."

Senta was to ride in the crested carriage with her maid, led by outriders and postilions. A hired coach for Mona and her baby, Private Waters, his dog, and the new nursemaid followed. Another three carriages were required for the staff Wheatley insisted they needed. One fourgon held Senta's trousseau. She'd bought the gowns, bonnets, and negligees for Lord Maitland to see; by heaven, he was going to see them. Of course, she could buy new clothes while in London, but Senta was determined to look fashionable while shopping, at least as fashionable as the demireps who would be hanging on her husband's sleeve. Senta was *not* some dowdy matron come up from the country; she'd had two London Seasons and meant to look the part. Maitland would have nothing to complain about in her appearance.

Another coach held the china and linens Wheatley deemed necessary for civilized living, until the house was in order. Three wagons were following with enough produce from their own farms to feed an army on the march. Hams, chickens, mutton, smoked fish, sacks of vegetables, flour from the local mill, cheeses from the dairy, oranges from the conservatory, carefully preserved herbs, and Cook's special spices. London could not provide anything near the quality of their own harvest. Cook had a carriage of his own, with his precious pots and pans.

"I thought you didn't want to draw any attention," Sir Parcival commented with that half sneer as they got ready to leave. "How you're going to keep sixteen coaches a secret is a mystery to me."

Senta looked over the crowded courtyard. "I count eleven."

She couldn't worry over her addled apparition. Not today. Today she was going to London, to her husband.

She got in the lead coach, leaving Sir Parcival shaking his head. He hunched his shoulders. "Then again, life's a train of mysteries to me these days."

Chapter Seven

"Bloody hell!"

Lord Maitland was drawn to the entry of his Portman Square residence by the sounds of commotion in the street. Only the commotion was not in the street, it was in his own hallway. Now he stood in his shirtsleeves, as his previously tranquil household was turned into a circus. There were footmen performing acrobatics with trunks, maids juggling parcels. There was even an animal act, an old dog most likely with a flea circus of its own.

"What the deuce?"

His cook, his own personal chef, whom he'd ransomed out of a prison ship, was shouting hysterically at a squad of helpers. He was shouting in French, naturally, which not a one of them understood. "Do not excite yourself over the unpacking, Jacques," Lee told the man, "for you'll be returning to the Meadows on the instant."

"Non, non, monsieur, the food, it must be unloading before it spoils. Ice, I need ice," he shouted. "*Tout de suite.*"

Amid the turmoil Lee's butler was issuing orders, directing traffic, overseeing the unloading of an entire

158

caravan of coaches parked up and down the street. The neighbors must be getting an eyeful.

"You don't have to worry about the foodstuffs," Lee told the cook in a controlled fury, "for you'll be serving Wheatley's liver and lights unless this whole mingle-mangle is straighted out and you are on your way back to the Meadows within the hour."

Wheatley bowed. "I am sorry, my lord, but that will be impossible, with all due respect. The horses are tired, for one, and the staff at the Meadows has been given a holiday while the premises are being treated with a solution of turpentine and a bit of arsenic. Termites, my lord, I regret to say."

"Termites!" Lee exploded. "There are no termites at the Meadows! Who gave that bloody order?"

"Why, I did, of course," Senta told him in her most dulcet tones, hoping her voice wouldn't quaver and betray that she was shaking in her half boots. She took her hand out of her ermine muff and held it toward him.

In front of the hordes of servants there was nothing Lee could do but bow over the offered hand and kiss her fingers. "Lady Maitland, what a pleasant surprise." Under his breath, he muttered, "You better have a deuced good explanation for this."

He'd never looked so dear to Senta, with his shirt collar open and his sandy hair mussed, nor so intimidating. She wanted to throw herself into his arms and beg him to let her stay, but that wasn't the way to win him over, she knew. She had to prove her loyalty. Well, she shouldn't *have* to, she thought with a twinge of resentment. She was his wife, by all the saints. Still, given his unfortunate opinion of her, she had to earn his trust. Of course, disobeying his orders wasn't the best way to start.

She pretended to survey the hallway while the servants swirled around them. Wheatley was right: the hangings were dingy, the wood railings were dull, the carpets were faded underfoot and threadbare in places.

"It's a good thing I arrived when I did. This place certainly needs a woman's touch."

"You are not staying," he uttered through clenched teeth. She could see the muscles of his jaw spasm.

Just then another long line of footmen, all in Maitland's blue-and-gold livery, entered the hall. One short fellow was hidden behind a tall pile of parcels, but there was no hiding the man's wooden leg.

"What the devil?"

"Oh, we knew how you wanted to keep an eye on the man, so we brought him along."

Keep an eye on him? Lee wanted the fellow bound and gagged. He started forward, but felt an arm at his elbow.

"He's given his parole not to escape, and really, you'll find him quite useful."

Lee was about to tell her how he could use the old trooper as bait when he went fishing next, when a woman entered through the open doors. She was dressed in black from head to toe, with a veil hiding her face, so all Lee could tell was that she was of average height. She curtsied in his direction, then followed a maid up the stairs.

"Who the blazes was that?"

"Oh, that was my new companion," Senta gaily replied. "You wouldn't want me traveling alone, would you? It's not at all the thing."

He didn't want her traveling, period, but before he could utter the words, a maid in a gray uniform with a gray cape entered, with a blanket-draped bundle in her arms. Wheatley had a footman escort her above.

"And that? That . . . ?"

"We'll discuss that later, my lord, when you're feeling more the thing."

"We'll talk about it now." He took her arm in a none-too-gentle hold and half dragged Senta down the hall. She could only be glad he hadn't seen Sir Parcival, who'd gotten hold of a medieval lute somewhere in the ether and was trying to fix its strings. He was dressed today in some iridescent silver suit, with ruffles on his shirt collar. And his legs were twitching.

"What's wrong with you?" she mouthed at him behind Lee's back. Did ghosts get rabies?

"Well, bless my soul," he replied with a wink, kissing the instrument. "I'm in love." He disappeared through the wall, leaving Senta feeling somewhat bereft, somewhat relieved.

And more than somewhat nervous as she faced her angry husband in his library. She was pleased to see that this room, at least, was in excellent repair, with a fire going in the grate. She started toward the warming flames, but her husband took her arm again and swung her to face him.

"What is the meaning of this, madam?" he shouted. "Don't you know this will make it twice as hard to get an annulment?"

Of course she knew. Senta's heart rejoiced that he hadn't seen the deed done already.

Just then someone cleared his throat. They both turned to find Mr. Calley, his lordship's secretary, standing red-faced behind his desk.

Senta nodded to him, having met the man when he came to the Meadows to help with the wedding arrangements. He was quite the tallest man of her acquaintance, taller than the viscount, taller than Sir Parcival, who had entered the room through the ceiling and was studying the secretary's long frame. He was wearing that remembering look Senta was beginning to know quite well, half-hopeful, half-confused. Trying to see if a name could jar his memory, Senta began, "Good day to you, Mr. Cal—"

But his lordship interrupted. "That will be all for today, John."

"Very well, my lord, Lady Maitland. And may I take this opportunity to welcome you to—"

161

"No, you may not. Her ladyship is not staying. You are excused, John."

Senta had taken the opportunity to remove her fur-lined cloak and seat herself near the fire. Let the viscount shout across the room if he wanted; Senta was not going to budge.

To which end she informed her husband, "I am not leaving."

Lee took three deep breaths to calm himself. Then he started pacing. "What happened to the sweet young thing I married? In two weeks you've turned into the most hardheaded of women."

Sir Percival's legs started having tics again. Senta couldn't watch the poor man's palsy anymore. She turned back to her husband in time to hear: "I could have you picked up and carried home bodily, you know. A wife is a husband's property, to do with as he will. But I am not a tyrant. If you are so determined to be here, say your piece now, before I move to one of my clubs."

"What, and make a laughingstock of both of us? Is that why you married me?"

Things were bad enough already, Lee knew. He was well aware that they were the butt of every kind of malicious gossip going the rounds. The bridegroom appearing in London within days of his wedding, sans bride, was a natural target for conjecture, if not outright insult. As a matter of fact, he had not been going to his clubs for that very reason. Nor Gentleman Jackson's Boxing Parlor, Manton's Gallery, or any other of his usual haunts. He hadn't brought himself to seek out his solicitor yet either.

So he wouldn't move out. Rather than concede, however, he growled, "That's better than why you married me, I swear."

Senta wanted to tell him that she'd married him be-cause she loved him and wanted desperately to make him love her. Instead she quietly told him, "I married you because I thought we could be happy together."

Lee ran his fingers through his hair. "Well, now you can see that we don't suit. You'd be better out of the marriage."

The best offense being a good defense, Senta went on the attack. "You wouldn't betray your country, would you?"

"Of course not. What's that to the purpose?"

"The purpose is that your brother would no more commit treason than you would!"

"My brother? What do you know about my brother? Oh, you've been talking to the old gaffer with the wooden leg."

"No, I've been listening to Private Waters. There's a difference, you know."

"And what did that mawworm try to get out of you, to insure his silence?"

"All he wants is to clear your brother's name, my lord. Why can you not accept that?"

Lee turned from his pacing and pounded his fist into the mantel. "Because it's impossible, that's why. Dash it, do you think I could accept that my brother was a traitor without proof? They showed me, his general, his field officer, his major, the colonel who treated Michael like his own son. The man had tears in his eyes, by Jupiter."

Sir Parcival had tears in his eyes now, too.

"But what if they were wrong?" Senta asked quietly.

"If they were wrong, then Michael would be alive."

"Unless someone killed him in such a fashion to make him look more guilty."

"Killed him? You and that . . . relic have concocted a murder out of this?" He finally took a seat in the chair facing Senta's, with his head thrown back.

"Would you rather believe your brother was a traitor or a murder victim?"

For the first time, Lee began to doubt what he'd been

given as truth. "Do you have proof? Damn, just a shred
of evidence would give me hope."

"You'll have to speak to Private Waters for yourself.
I was convinced, I admit."

"And that's what brought you to London?"

Senta didn't answer. She just asked how far he'd gotten with his search for the two wellborn civilians who
were at army headquarters at the right time, who won
Michael's gambling chits the night before the ambush.

"Half the War Office staff is away on holiday still,
but I've managed to get a list of what wounded officers
were sent home on leave that sennight. I have men
making inquiries as to how they were transported, who
met them, et cetera."

"If they were Londoners, Mona could recognize them
for you."

"Mona? Wasn't Mona the name of Waters's Spanish,
ah, convenient? Please tell me that the woman who entered my house dressed in black, your new companion,
is not a common camp follower."

"She was no such thing. She was Michael's fiancée."

Now he reached across the space between their chairs
and took her hands in his. "Senta, you have a kind
heart, but people will tell you what they want you to believe. That doesn't make it so. Michael would have
written to me if he was betrothed."

Squeezing his hand, trying to make him see, Senta
asked, "Would you have approved? Was Michael a frequent correspondent? Were the mails from Portugal always reliable?"

"No. No. And no. But that doesn't prove this female
even knew Michael. She and Waters could have cobbled
this hubble-bubble for your sake. They want your sympathy, don't you see, so you will come down heavy
with conscience money. Or convince me to."

Senta touched the heavy gold signet ring that never
left his hand. "She has Michael's ring. And no, don't
even think of saying that she could have stolen it. Ac-

cording to Private Waters, some of the evidence against Michael was that he was found with a great deal of money. That would have been easier to take, easier to get rid of, than his distinctive ring. I really believe she loved your brother. She wants to help find his murderer." Reluctantly she removed her hands from his. "We all want to help."

"What, get another female involved in this? Never. It was bad enough trying to shield you from possible scandal, Senta, but now . . . If there really is a murderer loose, I don't want you or any other woman anywhere near. No, you and your, ah, companion are going home in the morning." Lud, how could he keep her here, when just the touch of her hand had him yearning to make her his?

"Without anyone to protect us? You wouldn't."

Deuce take it, he wouldn't. He couldn't let her go again. Bad enough there were highwaymen and bands of unemployed soldiers on the roads, now he'd have to worry about murderous traitors, too. Besides, he could see that Senta was struggling to hide her yawns and drooping eyelids. The journey must have been wearisome. "We'll speak of this again in a day or two, when you have rested."

That was more than she'd hoped for. Senta hurried to her feet before he could mention the two words she wanted least to hear.

"But this changes nothing between us, you know. I still intend to seek an annulment."

There was one of them.

"Oh, and perhaps you might spare me a last moment to explain that other item you thought we'd discuss later."

"Item? I don't recall anything else that we needed to discuss, as long as you agree to speak to Private Waters and Mona." She scurried toward the door, knowing that a footman would be on the other side waiting to show her to her room, where she'd be safe. If Lord Maitland was going to have the marriage set aside, he certainly was not going to be visiting her this evening.

"The baby, Senta."

There was the second word. "The, ah, baby?" She turned at the door and took a deep breath. "The baby. Yes, well, she has your smile. When you smile, that is."

"What?" Lee bellowed. He was not smiling now. "Are you accusing me of leaving my butter stamp around the countryside?"

"Of course not. That is, I hope you shan't be bringing baseborn children home, except if you do not intend to make our marriage a true one, and you do still wish heirs, I suppose—"

"Senta?"

"Very well. She is Mona's baby, and Michael's. The sweetest, dearest infant you can imagine. Her name is Vida."

Lee shook his head. "You did say fiancée, didn't you, in reference to Michael's inamorata? Not wife?"

"These things happen, my lord."

"Oh, I am well aware that they happen. They just don't usually happen in noble households in the middle of London, where gossip is as pervasive as the fog. Your so-called companion is no better than she ought to be, and her child is a bastard."

"And your niece."

He ignored that for now. "Just what kind of acceptance do you think you'll find in London, or anywhere in the whole country for that matter, if it's spread about that you associate with soiled doves and their illegitimate offspring?"

"About as friendly a reception, my lord, as I would get if your brother is named a traitor, which he might be without Mona's help. And as cordial a greeting as I would receive if you cast me aside like an old shoe. Good night, my lord."

With that, she made good her exit, before her husband could issue any orders.

"Bloody hell," Lee muttered to himself as he poured a glass of brandy. "Does a man ever win one of these arguments?"

"Once in a blue moon," Sir Parcival answered. "Once in a blue, blue moon."

Chapter Eight

*I*t was even more important to find the blackmailer now, Lord Maitland thought. If there really was a murder, then the blackhearted extortionist might lead him to Michael's killer. He might even *be* Michael's killer, so confident that he'd gotten away with his heinous crime.

Lee *would* find him, and make him pay.

But it made no difference, he thought, sitting by the fire, whether Michael was exposed as a traitor or exonerated as a victim of foul play. Senta would still be better off with the man of her dreams.

The man of her dreams—fuddled nightmare, more like—was having girl trouble of his own. Sir Parcival was in the nursery playing with little Vida, but she wanted to be picked up. The infant could not understand why her friend with all the glittery rings and gem-studded belts would not lift her out of the prison of her cradle.

"I'd rock you if I could, buttercup, all night long," he told the unhappy child, "but my rocking won't work any better'n my memory. Now, roll over and go to sleep."

Instead, Vida started crying. She set up such a racket that the nursemaid was there, Mona was there, and Private Waters was there with his pistol and his dog. But the baby didn't need a clean nappy, a midnight snack, or protecting. She wanted Sir Parcival, now.

The wailing got louder. Senta arrived and took her hand at cuddling, patting, walking the halls with Vida, for Mona was exhausted from their trip. The nursemaid decided Vida was teething, and went off to find the coral ring somewhere in their unpacked baggage.

Still Vida screamed, turning all red and overheated. Now Sheba added her howls. Senta kept walking, Sir Parcival kept dangling shiny things in front of her, but Vida wasn't falling for that trick again. There was never anything there when she reached out, nothing to clasp, nothing to chew on, only cold air. She screamed some more.

"What the devil is going on?" Lord Maitland demanded from the doorway.

Private Waters swung his pistol around, in the viscount's direction. Sheba growled.

"Oh, put that away, old man, before you shoot someone by accident. And tell your mutt that this is *my* home. It seems I may owe you an apology. We'll talk in the morning." When Waters still didn't lower the weapon, Lee told him, "But don't think that means I've decided to keep you on, you insolent antique."

"Nor I ain't decided I want to be in the employ of anyone so hot to hand." But the gun was tucked in the waistband of Waters's trousers.

"Fair enough. But what did you think I was going to do anyway, run amok among all these women and children?" There seemed to be only one child, but the noise level was such that Lee wondered if his wife had any other surprises tucked in the old nursery's odd corners. There were any number of ill-gotten children and stray dogs in the streets of London for her to drag home.

The females were eyeing him suspiciously, except the infant, who was howling like a banshee. Lee nodded to the nursemaid, then bowed slightly to the dark-haired woman who was still dressed in black, although some of the gown's buttons were undone, as if she'd dressed hurriedly. "Welcome to my home, doña. I share your grief."

Mona nodded, but did not say anything. She was just too tired to fight with this toplofty aristocrat, and she was too embarrassed that her child was creating such a fuss in his house.

Lee bent his head toward where Senta was still jiggling the infant, to no avail. "May I?"

Mona bit her lip but gave her permission, since he'd asked so politely. Senta carefully transferred the furious bundle into his arms. Lee held the squalling infant gingerly at first, as if she were made of spun sugar that could crumple at his lightest touch. "So much noise from such a small person." He tried to keep the child's hands from thrashing around. "There, there, little one, shush." Vida didn't shush. Sheba started howling again.

"Thunderation!" Lee was about to hand the child back. Lud, his head was aching from the caterwauling. Besides, this scrap was nothing to him. He could tell. There was no resemblance in this dark-haired, dark-eyed foreigner, no bond, no affection. He felt nothing for her but the urge to have her gone. And quiet.

Then Lee reached into his pocket for his fob watch and dangled it in front of the baby's eyes.

Now, this was more like it! The watch hand moved, the casing glittered, the chain was a fascinating pattern, and the whole thing ticked loudly! Vida stopped screeching and reached for the watch, her tiny brows furrowed in concentration to see if this new toy would slip through her fingers. It didn't. She hiccuped and tried to put it in her mouth. Three women came running, but Lee said, "It's only a watch." And it had only been in his family for generations.

Then Sir Parcival started singing, some "Hey Nonny Nonny" air from the parlor maids. Vida spat out the watch, keeping it firmly in her little fists, and she grinned. If the direction of Vida's gummy grin was somewhere over Lord Maitland's right shoulder, he never noticed.

"You're right," he told Senta. "That's Michael's smile. He was always laughing. And thank you," he said to Mona, even begrudgingly jerking his head toward Private Waters, "for bringing my niece home."

There was no more talk of sending them all back to the Meadows. There were five new footmen and armed guards whenever Senta and Mona were abroad, which was often. Senta was determined to establish herself as Lee's wife in society, to make it harder for the viscount to discard her. So she accepted invitations, paid morning visits, and held at-homes. Mona was equally determined to help unmask the criminals, so she entrusted Vida to the nursemaid and trailed Lady Maitland's skirts, keeping a watchful eye for familiar faces, from behind her black veil.

Senta also decided to make herself indispensable to her husband. He wouldn't come to her bedchamber, and she couldn't go to his uninvited, but she could certainly make his home a more pleasant place. She threw herself into refurbishing Maitland House with a zeal that could have gotten Hannibal's elephants back across those mountains, twice.

Surprisingly, Sir Parcival was a big help, better than Mona, to whom the English styles were overstuffed and overcrowded. Sir Parcival, on the other hand, liked everything and thought she should have it all.

"See? This parlor looks empty and bare. Needs more chairs."

"Yes, and I can hang a picture right . . . over the mantel."

When in doubt, Senta asked the viscount, then she took Wheatley's advice.

* * *

Town was beginning to fill as the ton trickled back, especially the more conscientious members of Parliament and their wives. There were no grand parties as yet where Senta felt the chances of Mona recognizing anyone were better, but there were the theater and the opera.

One night toward the end of January, they sat in the Maitland box, Mona to Senta's left, with her opera glasses scanning the audience. Senta was wearing her diamonds and a new gown of silver tulle over a satin underskirt, with brilliants strewn across the bodice. She caught her husband's frequent bemused glances. No, the décolletage wasn't too low, as she'd feared. It was just right. For tonight she would be content to bask in his clear admiration, even if he wouldn't let her any closer. For tonight she could imagine herself happily married, and escorted by the two most handsome men in all of London. So what if one of them was invisible to everyone else? He liked her dress, too.

Lee was not happy with this evening. His wife was exposing herself to danger. Hell, another half inch and she'd be exposing herself altogether. But she seemed so happy. Even Mona, whom they were calling Señora Vegas, looked more relaxed, although she did keep scanning the boxes. Lee's contacts at the War Office and his own inquiries had brought him no new leads, so there was no other choice but to put his womenfolk at risk, much as it galled him. In truth, he couldn't have stopped them.

At least the opera was good, the tenors in voice, the soprano dying gracefully to thunderous applause. Private Waters, who'd seen the performance from the pit, sniveled, "Now, that is art," when he joined them at the carriage.

"I don't care how great the art," sneered Sir Parcival into Senta's ear. "You can't dance to it."

* * *

Lord Maitland called a council of war. They were getting nowhere. His house was overrun with carpenters and upholsterers and painters, and his wife had him escorting her and Mona to some social function or other almost daily, but they were no closer to finding the blackmailer or the murderer.

The War Office list of wounded officers sent home at the right time was shrinking considerably as Maitland's paid investigators tracked them down. Most were crossed off as having returned to England via troop ship or, if by private means, in the company of brother officers. Some had long since returned to the Peninsula; a few had died of their injuries. Either way, they were not available to be interviewed.

Lee read aloud the few names that remained under consideration. When he got to one Theodore Sayre, Private Waters spoke up: "That'd be Lieutenant Sayre. They called him Steady Teddy on account of he was so cool under fire. Never left his post, he didn't, that last time, even with a bullet in the ribs. The general had to order him to surgery afore he'd leave his men. He couldn't be no traitor, I'd swear on it."

"He was Miguel's *amigo*," Mona added. "We shared our food and our fires. He would not have betrayed Miguel."

"Still," the viscount said, "I'd like to see your Teddy Sayre."

Sir Parcival stopped humming to Vida to listen. He shrugged and went back to his nonsense rhymes.

Lord Maitland ordered another log on the fire and went on: "The lieutenant may be a pattern card of an officer and a gentleman, but his brother is something of a dirty dish. Sir Randolph Sayre associates with a rackety crowd, gamblers and wastrels mostly. Unfortunately, the lieutenant, by all reports, is still in Bath recovering from his wounds. Sir Randolph could be anywhere. We don't move in the same circles."

Senta was all for throwing a grand party as soon as

the ton started returning to Town and her house was in order. "If it's big enough, we can invite everyone on your list, even Sir Randolph, without being obvious. Mona can sit on the sidelines and watch."

"It's too chancy. And I don't want every loose screw in London in my home." Especially if one was the basket-scrambler Senta might have married. "No, we'll wait. Now that we are so visibly on the town, I think the blackmailer will make his move."

Lord Maitland was right, for a few days later another extortion note was received. This one wanted twice the amount as the previous, and no tricks, or else Lord Maitland's pretty young bride would be reading a nasty tale in the newspapers.

With his pretty young bride not knowing a thing about it, this time Lee was going to make sure the blackguard didn't get away. The last time, the dastard managed to outfox all of the viscount's spies and informants at the inn. A false cry of fire out near the stables had everyone running. The packet was missing when they got back.

Maitland would take the money himself tomorrow to the address on Olney Street, just over London Bridge. It was a commercial district, sure to be crowded at three o'clock, the designated hour. The blackmailer could be hiding anywhere, but so could the viscount, after he made the delivery. And Waters would keep watch.

"You, old man? You can't even run after your hat, much less an escaping criminal."

"Aye, but I can fit in with the ragtag street beggars. Or was you planning on stationing a squad of your footmen, in livery and wigs, at the street corners? Asides, Sheba can track what I can't catch. And I reckon I'm a better shot than any of your staff. Mona's a dab hand with a pistol, too. Had to be, at the front."

"No! I am not putting a woman in danger. Why, that neighborhood wouldn't be safe for her at the best of times. Furthermore, she'd tell Senta, and I'd have another argument on my hands."

So it was decided, without Mona or Senta's knowledge. Sir Parcival would have told her, but he was busy learning the words to "Greensleeves" from an upstairs maid making the beds.

Before the viscount left, he gave orders to both Wheatley and his secretary, Calley, that if Lady Maitland was permitted out of the house, they'd both be dismissed. Or boiled in oil.

At the appointed time, Lord Maitland, in his caped greatcoat, dismissed the hackney at the foot of Olney Street and walked up the block, which was little more than a crowded alley. He tossed a coin to a bald, one-legged beggar and his mongrel, and kept going.

The others, footmen and grooms in disguise who had been stationed in the vicinity beforehand, were waiting nearer the bridge for Waters's call to give chase.

The call never came.

The blackmailer wasn't taking chances this time. He was waiting in a recessed doorway when the viscount went past, seeking the right number. He struck Lee on the back of the head with a lead weight, then dragged him inside before anyone could see what happened, not that anyone much cared, in this neighborhood. He searched the unconscious viscount's pockets for his payment. Making sure the envelope held real money this time, he then emptied the viscount's wallet, to make up for the previous fakery. After dragging his bleeding victim outside again, behind some barrels, the villain re-entered that back door on Olney Street and went through the run-down building to its front entry, on another street altogether, where he mingled with the clerks and costermongers.

Waters waited. And waited some more. Then he began to get a real bad feeling, like he was in battle and the enemy was behind him, not in his sights. He and Sheba moved into the alley.

Urchins playing in the dirt. Passed-out drunks. Mounds of trash. No viscount. Waters cocked his pistol. The ragamuffins disappeared. Sheba started nosing at some garbage, but the trooper called her back.

"No time for scraps, girl. We got to find his nibs."

They found him, by Sheba's nose and the viscount's groans. He was only half-conscious, with a huge gaping wound in his head that bled through the soldier's handkerchief in seconds.

Lord Maitland did manage to open his eyes a fraction and recognize the old soldier. He feebly grabbed for Waters's hand. "Got to . . . get home, old man. Got to . . . return to Senta."

Chapter Nine

*W*aters shouted for help. "Maitland's down! To me, men!" No one came. He fired his pistol. No one came. There was so much traffic over the bridge and under the bridge, no one was going to hear him over the din. He couldn't leave the viscount to go for aid; those young alley rats would have his lordship stripped and bare, if not sold to anatomy class, before Waters could say jackrabbit. In fact, he made sure to reload his gun before unwinding the viscount's neckcloth to use as another bandage.

Waters couldn't drag the much heavier man as far as the main road, even if moving him wasn't likely to finish the nobleman off. Besides, looking at the viscount's absolute stillness and pallor, Waters misdoubted as there was time. He did the only thing possible: he sent Sheba home. "Go on, girl, go home. Get Mona. Her ladyship. Wheatley. Get Cook who's been feeding you. Go on, Sheba. Home, girl."

Senta thought she heard a dog barking. "Could that be Sheba?"

She was seated at the pianoforte, playing for Sir Parcival. He was positive that familiar music would jar

177

his memory better than anything they'd tried so far. He liked the hymns well enough, but kept urging Senta to play them faster, despite the lowering temperature that stiffened her fingers. The Irish ballads were his favorites. He could hear Senta play them through once, then be able to join her in the vocal parts. But none of them struck a chord, so to speak. Neither did the dog's frantic yipping.

"Nah, that ain't nothing but a hound d—Well, maybe it is old Sheba."

It was, and a shaken Wheatley soon came to find Lady Maitland. "I'm afraid this means Private Waters is in difficulty, along with the viscount. I have sent for the carriage, a surgeon, blankets, hot bricks."

Senta was already reaching for her ermine-lined cape.

"Those gudgeons tried to find the blackmailer by themselves, didn't they?" She didn't wait for an answer, just headed for the door. "Do you know where they were?"

"Yes, they were meeting the blackmailer on a side street, just over the bridge."

Sir Percival got into the carriage with Senta. He was shaking his head. "Waters in trouble over the bridge? Troubled Waters over the bridge?"

"Oh, shut up, do," Senta demanded, which had Mr. Calley, who was ducking his head to enter the coach, decide to ride up with the driver.

After a harrowing ride, with the heavy coach careening around turns and barreling through traffic, they crossed the bridge. The carriage couldn't fit up the narrow side street where a mob had gathered. Waters had promised one of the street urchins a coin if he ran around gathering the viscount's men, so they were all there, trying to decide the quickest and least jarring way to get his lordship out of this filthy alley.

Senta jumped out of the coach before the steps were down and ran toward the knot of men. Sir Percival was right behind her, but he kept going. "Got to see if there's a hotel down at the end of this Olney Street."

"We don't need a hotel! His head is broken! We need a hospital!" She was at her husband's side, trying not to faint at the sight of all the blood. Mr. Calley was right there, with the extra footmen and enough blankets to make a workable litter. They got Lord Maitland back to the coach, his head cushioned on Senta's lap so she could hold a towel to the wound. "So much blood," she fretted, her tears dribbling on the poor man. She couldn't wipe them away, for she was holding Lee with her other hand, to keep him from falling off the seat on the mad dash back to Portman Square. "How can he lose so much blood?"

Sir Parcival looked over at the unconscious peer. "Stop crying. He ain't going to die."

"Are you sure?" Senta asked eagerly, figuring maybe her haunt had a connection at the Pearly Gates after all.

"Of course I'm sure. I don't do sad endings."

"You don't . . . ? Never mind."

Wheatley and a crew of servants were waiting when they finally reached Maitland House. So was the doctor, who wasn't nearly as optimistic as Sir Parcival. "Such a blow to the head can mean anything, my dear," he told Senta. "We won't know if he's left paralyzed or addled until he wakes up, if he wakes up. Then again, the fever might take him. I cleaned the wound as best I could, but all that filth . . ." He shrugged. "It's in the Lord's hands, my dear."

And Senta's. She wasn't going to let Lord Maitland die on her, she just wasn't. Not when he was beginning to care for her. Not when she couldn't live without him.

She sat there with him through the evening, holding his cold hand, willing him to live, for her. Then, when his hand got warmer late at night, and finally hot toward morning, she bathed his brow and helped his man change the damp nightshirt and linens. Mona came and sat with her, then Private Waters and Calley, and still she sat, pouring out her love for him into ears that couldn't hear.

The doctor came again and shook his head. He put on fresh bandages, left some powders, and patted Senta on the shoulder. "You must be brave, my dear."

She was brave enough to tell the man good riddance.

"For it's a wonder any of your patients recover if you have them dead and buried before they've stopped breathing. Get out. And any of the others of you who don't believe he'll recover, get out. The rest of you can at least be praying."

So they left her for the most part, except the servants in to fix the fire, to bring her meals on a tray, to carry fresh bedclothes. Mona and Waters did convince Senta to have a nap in the afternoon, while they kept watch. She woke in a panic, that Lee had died without ever knowing how much she loved him. She rushed through the connecting door to his bedchamber.

"There's no change, my lady," Private Waters told her. "I'm thinking that's a good thing. His brain is resting, like. It's the fever that has me worried. Can't get none of the sawbones's powders down him, more's the pity."

"Here, let me try." The medicine just dripped out of the viscount's mouth.

"Don't want to go and drown him neither."

So Senta dipped her clean handkerchief in the potion and dabbed at his parched lips, his dry mouth. She kept at it, dribbling bit by bit onto his tongue until the viscount finally swallowed. They all cheered.

"That's the ticket, my lady, get as much into him as you can," Private Waters advised, handing over a fresh hanky while Mona mixed up another glassful of the healing drug before leaving to feed her daughter.

Senta went back to work, wetting her cloth and squeezing droplets between his lips. "Swallow, my love."

He did, but he also began moving his arms. "No, darling, lie still. It's just Senta, just a hanky. This will help your burning, love."

Sir Parcival got up from his seat in the corner. "Hanky? Hanky, burning love?"

While Private Waters's back was turned, Senta hissed at Sir Parcival to get out, too, if his only contribution was more of his nonsense. "Can't you do something? He's got the fever!"

"I can see he's got the fever, little sister, but I don't know what you expect me to do about it. All I'm any good at is singing."

"So sing, dash it all."

So he did, all those hymns Senta had played on the pianoforte. Their composers mightn't have recognized the old church music, and the viscount couldn't hear them, but Sir Parcival's strong voice made Senta feel better. She kept dripping the medicine into her wounded husband's mouth and whispering words of love into his ear.

It may have been the prayers, or the powders, or even Senta's impassioned pleas for him to recover. More likely it was the chill draft kicked up by a spirit's singing. Either way, Lord Maitland's fever broke and he fell into a sounder sleep.

He was going to recover, Senta rejoiced, if only he'd wake up!

Toward morning on the longest day of Senta's life, Lord Maitland's eyelids fluttered. "If only half of what you said to me was true," he told his wife, who was lying beside him on the bed, "then I can't die yet. Heaven wouldn't be this sweet."

Senta sat up and felt his hand, his forehead, his cheek. "You're alive! And awake. Do you know me?"

Lee struggled to bring one of his hands to the side of her face. "No, precious Senta, I don't think I ever knew you, but I swear to learn."

Lord Maitland was mending, but slowly. He was weak and dizzy, with frequent headaches, no appetite, and an irascible temper at being kept in his bed. Alone.

Only Senta's presence—reading the newspapers to him, playing chess or backgammon or cards, telling him about her childhood while she did her needlework by the window in his bedroom—made the hours bearable. Lee was coming to know Senta, and to appreciate her all the more. How could he have been such a gudgeon as to suspect her innocence?

Easily, since she was plotting behind his back. A few days after the episode at the bridge, Senta brought up the topic of the attack on him. She closed the book she was reading aloud at the end of a chapter.

"I have been thinking, Lee, about how we are going to find the man who did this to you. I mean, we cannot permit a cold-blooded killer to lurk about London. He wouldn't have cared if you died." She shivered at the very thought. "At the very least, he's prepared to spread scurrilous gossip about your brother."

The viscount patted her knee, where her chair was drawn next to his bed so they could share Sir Walter Scott's latest offering. "Don't worry, love, Calley's brought in Bow Street, and we've offered rewards to all the denizens of that rabbit warren of an alley. Someone must have seen something. For the blunt, they'll sell their own mothers." He didn't remove his hand, but slowly started to stroke her leg along her silken skirts.

"That's all very well and good," Senta stated, trying to keep her mind on the matter at hand, and not on his hand on her thigh. "But it is taking too long, with you in danger the whole time. I decided on another plan while you were unconscious." His hand stopped its delicious course. Senta cleared her throat. "This time we are going to do it the easy way, all together."

His brows raised, his hand back on his own all-too-uninteresting thigh, Lee asked, "Which is?"

"We are going to hold that Valentine's Day ball I spoke about before."

"Valentine's Day is just two weeks off, isn't it? You can't get a ball together in such a short time."

"We'll be a trifle late, but no one will mind."

"No one will come, Senta. It's too early in the Season. The roads might be impassable."

"They'll come to see Maitland House reopened for the first time in decades. And they'll come to see why the great Lord Maitland married his bride in such a hole-in-corner affair. I intend to wear a very revealing gown."

Lee had the grace to blush. "I owe you an apology for that, for the whole thing. We should have had a proper wedding with all the tattlemongers in the front pew so no tongues would wag."

"No, no. I had precisely the wedding I would have wished. But then there is that, ah, interrupted honeymoon. You must be aware of the gossip. The ball should put an end to it once and for all."

He stared up at her, as if trying to read her soul. "You know that it will be nearly impossible to annul the marriage once we put on a show for all the rabbles."

Senta was counting on it. "I know."

There was a wealth of meaning in those words, and a world of promises. Unfortunately, Lee couldn't think about the implications. He still had to talk Senta out of this skimble-skamble ball. "It's too much work. You must be exhausted after staying up nursing me."

"Most of the work is already done. Between Wheatley, Cook, and Mr. Calley, there's hardly anything for me to do."

"It doesn't matter. We're not having a ball. It's too damned dangerous."

"As opposed to walking down a dark alley with a known criminal waiting at the other end?"

"Touché. All right, treat me like the fool I was, but dash it, it's too risky."

Senta stood up and put the book on his nightstand. "That's too bad, for the invitations went out this morning." She very properly ignored the blasphemies coming from her husband at this pronouncement. When he seemed in danger of repeating himself, Senta interrupted: "Besides, the danger is mostly to Mona, that she might be recognized as someone who could identify the miscreants, but she is anxious to do this. Mr. Calley had the list of those officers whose connections might be suspect. We invited them all. I am counting on you and your Bow Street officers to guard Mona ever so carefully."

"Bloody hell." The viscount's fists were clenched at his sides.

Senta decided it was time to make a tactical retreat. "It's time for you to rest now. I have to go see about the decorations."

Luckily she could not hear Lee's comments about the decorations and their ultimate destination, since she was heading out the door. She did, however, hear his plaintive: "But I counted on you to stay and bathe my fevered brow."

Senta rushed back to his huge four-poster bed and put her hand to his forehead, which was cool and dry. Lee took her hand, turned it over, and placed a kiss on the palm. "Please stay, darling."

Senta snatched her burning hand back. "I think it's a different kind of fever you're suffering, my lord."

"Well, how can you blame a fellow?" he asked with a boyish grin. "If there is to be no annulment, when does the marriage start?"

"When you are recovered," Senta answered primly, hoping her cheeks weren't as red as they felt. "The doctor said you were to have no strenuous activity. Besides, you'll need all your strength for the ball. Now, I really must go."

"What, and leave me here all alone, Senta? Don't be cruel!"

Chapter Ten

"*That* was mean, sister, teasing the poor man like that. Why didn't you stay, anyway? I even left you alone so you'd have privacy. Isn't that what you wanted?"

They were in the grand ballroom so Senta could decide about the decorations. How could she concentrate on wall hangings, though, and floral arrangements, when her mind kept having untoward thoughts of her husband upstairs in bed?

"Well, yes, I did—I do—want a real marriage. But he didn't really want me. That is, that's all he wanted. Oh, how can I be talking about this to a . . . to a . . ."

"Friend?" Sir Parcival offered.

"I suppose, in a way." Senta was used to the spirit's odd appearance. Now, for instance, he was dressed in black leather, with fringes. She thought she'd seen something like his outfit at a masquerade, complete with bow and arrow. She was sympathetic of his faulty memory, and had even learned to ignore the awful tic he was afflicted with that made one side of his upper lip twitch. And no one else understood at all.

"He never said he loved me," she confessed now.

"He is lonely and bored, most likely grateful for my nursing. That's all."

Sir Percival did that thing with his lip again. "He was worried sick about you. He cares about your safety and wants you with him all the time. If that's not loving you, I don't know what is."

"He still needs an heir, and I seem to be the only woman to hand."

"I've seen the way he looks at you. No man looks at a broodmare that way. Well, at least you're not crying all the time anymore."

"No, he . . . he does like me, I think. I'll learn to be content with that. Besides, there's too much to do to fall into the doldrums today. I need to figure how many yards of lace to order, and how much satin ribbon."

"Blue," was all he said.

"No, I told you, I refuse to be blue-deviled today. I have to make this ball perfect so Lord Maitland will see I'm no harum-scarum female. I want his respect, in addition to his . . . his carnal desires."

Senta was afraid her companion would be sneering again at her girlish dreams, but Sir Percival was smiling, making him look so astonishingly handsome that Senta almost wished she were better with her paints, so she could do his portrait for when he was gone. Perhaps on black velvet, which was all the crack now. She caught herself having nearly carnal thoughts about a man—or wraith—not her husband, and blushed. She quickly amended: "And at the ball we'll catch the scoundrel who's been causing such trouble. I just know it."

"All I meant was you should do the ribbons and fluff up in blue. Looks good. This old barn of a place will look prettier'n that grand old opera place we went."

"I know blue is your favorite color, but this is a Valentine's Day ball! We have to have red hearts and flowers, pink streamers, and, yes, pink candles in all the chandeliers and wall sconces. Cook has already ordered raspberry ices from Gunter's. Why, whoever heard of a blue Valentine's Day?"

"Whoever heard of a blue Chr— Nah, you're right."

A few days after the invitations to the ball went out, Senta had an unexpected visitor. Most of her friends in Town knew she'd be too busy for morning calls, so they just sent notes asking after the viscount's welfare. Many wrote that they were dismayed at the dreadful state of society when a peer of the realm could be cut down in broad daylight for his pocket change. What was the world coming to? As for Society, they all wrote that they were coming to her party, with eager anticipation.

Lieutenant Theodore Sayre sent in his card with the corner folded down to show that he had called in person, and asked for a moment of Lady Maitland's time. Senta dropped her sewing—the thousandth satin heart, it seemed—and hurried to the morning room, where Wheatley had left the young officer.

The lieutenant was a good-looking young man, scarcely older than Senta, with reddish blond hair and military sideburns that earned Sir Parcival's approval. He was quite dashing in his scarlet regimentals, his arm in a sling, but Senta thought he seemed terribly ill at ease. Suspiciously so.

She invited Sayre to be seated and rang for tea. "Or would you prefer something stronger, Lieutenant?" She was hoping to calm his nerves—and loosen his tongue.

He sat, awkwardly, at the edge of his chair. "Tea is fine, ma'am, that is, Lady Maitland. I wouldn't be bothering you, never been introduced and all. Not the thing, with you planning a ball and his lordship knocked cock-a-hoop. That is, everyone's talking about the attack on Lord Maitland. And here I thought the Peninsula was dangerous." He tried to smile at her, but the light never reached his shadowed eyes. "The thing is, I hoped to see Lord Maitland."

Senta busied herself pouring out the tea and fixing a

plate of Cook's delicacies. She placed both on a pie-crust table so the lieutenant wouldn't have to juggle them with his one good arm. Meanwhile she was wondering if Lee would murder her for sticking her nose into his business. Well, her husband getting his brain split open *was* her business, she reasoned. "I left his lordship asleep, but he should be awake shortly. The doctor says he is recovering nicely, thank you, and I know he will be pleased to see a new face if you could wait a bit. We could become acquainted in the meantime."

Teddy felt the urge to loosen his collar. Instead he took a deep swallow of his tea, which was too hot, and burned his tongue. "Agh, ah, that would be my pleasure, ma'am."

Senta was beginning to suspect that the poor boy's nervousness was due more to shyness than to guilt, especially when he sat numbchance after that. Senta asked if he'd received her invitation.

He patted his pocket and turned nearly as red as his coat. "Meant to thank you right off. Honored to attend, my lady."

Another silence. "Are you well acquainted with my husband?" Senta asked.

"Not as well as with . . . That is, never got a chance to pay my respects to him, about Michael and all, being wounded at the time. Then when I got your invite"—he patted the pocket again—"and saw you were in Town, I came right up from Bath. Need to ask his lordship about . . . about . . ."

"He has a great deal to ask you about, too. You were a good friend of his brother's, then?"

"Best friends, ma'am, and proud of it. Michael saved my life when I took this hit and got thrown. He got down in the middle of a pitched battle, dragged me across his own horse, and led me out. Then he went back and finished off a few more of Boney's men."

"So you don't think he could have sold information to the French?"

Teddy's cup rattled on its saucer. "Michael a traitor? Never. He was as loyal as they come. I'd stake my life on it. Did, in fact."

Senta crumpled a macaroon, thinking how angry her husband was going to be. "The reason I ask is that some nasty rumors are going around that someone did betray Michael's unit to the enemy. Lord Maitland is very upset over these rumors."

"I heard something about that before I came home. Headquarters was pretty sure there was a spy at first, but then they dropped the investigation. It couldn't have been Michael anyway, not in a million years."

"But who else knew about the troop movements? I assume they're always supposed to be secret. There's no sense in telling the enemy where you're going to march. The general trusts his staff implicitly, I'd guess."

"I should say so. If there was a turncoat at headquarters, we'd never push those Frogs back."

"But there were other men who had to know, to lead the troops. Michael knew."

"Of course he did. That doesn't make him a traitor. I knew, for that matter. Michael came to the hospital to tell me before they moved out."

Senta just looked at the lieutenant over her teacup.

Sayre jumped to his feet, spilling tea onto his trousers. "You're not thinking that *I* sold out the men! Dash it, Lady Maitland, that's not the thing to say to a chap." He dabbed at his pants with the napkin she handed him. "It's no wonder your husband got coshed, if you go around accusing honest Englishmen that way. I wouldn't be surprised if he finds himself challenged to duels every afternoon. Illegal and all, but to cast doubt on a fellow's honor . . . Not the thing."

Ignoring his indignation, Senta asked, "Could anyone have overheard your conversation, yours and Michael's?"

"I don't know. I was too delirious at the time." The lieutenant thought a moment while he chewed a biscuit. "But no, Michael would have kept an eye out."

"You were in a fever?" Senta remembered Lee's disordered babbling before his fever broke. Some of his rambling made sense, as when he called her name, or Michael's, or shouted for his horse and pistol. "Could you have repeated Michael's orders, in your delirium?"

"I suppose I could have, ma'am, but there are no spies at the field hospital. Wounded French prisoners are kept separate, and the sawbones don't need the additional work they'd get, sending our men into ambushes."

"Of course not," Senta changed the subject. "You didn't have to sail home on the hospital ship, did you? I hear they are appalling."

"No, my brother and his friend came to fetch me in Northcote's yacht." He shook his head. "Oh, no, you don't. My brother's a rattle, always under the hatches. He's a gambler, don't you know, not even a good one. But he wouldn't sell out his country."

"And this Lord Northcote"—whose invitation to the ball was even then being inscribed in Senta's mind—"did he visit you in hospital, perhaps while you were speaking in your sleep?"

"Lud, I suppose so. Randy kept popping in to see when we could leave. He was that anxious to be gone before the sawbones gave my release." Teddy took up a poppy-seed cake. "Never understood what my brother saw in Northcote. He's a gambler, even worse than Randy, older, too. Northcote likes to play with green 'uns, johnny raws who are easier to fleece. His dibs were in tune on the ride home, though. We had the best accommodations, the highest-quality horseflesh at the changes. No breakdowns for Baron Northcote. I appreciated it at the time, ma'am, but I do remember being surprised a cold care-for-naught like Northcote would go to so much trouble. Do you think . . . That is . . .

could I have been the one who gave the information that cost all those lives?" Gone was his soldier's erect bearing. Lieutenant Sayre was slumped into his chair, almost swallowed in its depths.

"Not intentionally, I'm sure, Lieutenant. Never that. You'd better talk to my husband, hear what he has to say. Someone was a traitor, and someone tried to blame Michael for the crime. We think they might have killed him."

The officer whistled. "I never bought that faradiddle about Michael's rifle misfiring."

"What the army believes is that he killed himself over his dishonor. Now someone is trying to get my husband to pay silence money to keep that quiet. That's what the attack on his lordship was about, you see, although we are not revealing the truth to anyone."

"You can trust me, ma'am. I'm not delirious anymore. I wouldn't let Michael down again, I swear."

"And I believe you." How could she not, when he'd already put his life on the line for his country?

"What can I do to help find the dastard who caused all the trouble? I'll see him hanged, even if it's my own brother. Lud, I hope it don't come to that. How could I explain to my mother?"

"We do have a plan, Lieutenant, and it involves the ball. I'm sure Lord Maitland will be happy to assign you a part in the trap we're setting. I'll just go see if he is awake yet."

The young man stood when she did, but stared down at his highly polished Hessians. "Before you go, ma'am, I need to ask a favor."

"Of course, Wheatley will show you where to go."

His face went scarlet again. "Not that. I, ah, did come to pay my respects and all, and I knew it was a bad time with his lordship laid up and a ball to plan, but there's something I just have to know. I'm sorry, but I can't find out anywhere. Michael had a . . . a friend."

"Mona?"

"You know about Mona? Do you know how she is? Where she is? Did she have the baby? I've been worried sick. Couldn't get word of her from anyone, and the mails are so slow. I know it's not at all the thing to ask you, you being a lady and all, but I had to try."

"Yes, Mona said you were friends. I'll put you out of your misery. She is here with her baby, a darling little girl who we all adore. Mona is acting as my companion until we get this matter resolved and make other arrangements. She calls herself Señora Vegas."

Senta found her hand being shaken so vehemently, she was afraid she wouldn't be able to write out those last invitations. "You're a Trojan, Lady Maitland. Not every woman would take in a female like that with a baby and all. My own mother wouldn't. I asked, in case I could find Mona and get her to come to me in England. Not that Mona isn't a lady, 'cause she is and I'll take on anyone who says otherwise. She's good and kind, and properly reared. Michael was all set to marry her as soon as he had time to find a willing priest, the lucky dog. It was the war that got in the way."

And it was Michael who got in Lieutenant Sayre's way, Senta guessed. With the wind in that quarter, she'd have something else to work on after the ball. Lieutenant Sayre could be the answer to another big problem if his intentions were as honorable as Senta thought. "Private Waters looks after her," she told the young officer, so he would know Mona was not to be treated lightly, just in case.

"Waters is here, too? Capital! I should have known he'd see Mona to safe harbor. Do you think I could . . . That is . . ."

"I'll take you up to the nursery as soon as you've spoken to my husband. I'm sure you'll be even more eager to help with our plans for the ball when you hear that Mona stands ready to identify the traitors if they show up there. She overheard two men speaking after the ambush, speaking of a Frenchman and counting French money."

"Mona is involved? Just tell me what to do. I'm ready. Why, I'd walk to the moon and back, for her."

Sir Parcival got off the sofa and winced. "Man, that gives me a headache." He grimaced at Senta's quizzical look. "The wonders of youth."

Chapter Eleven

A heavy rain was falling the day of the ball. A cold, unlucky rain, Sir Parcival felt.

"Nonsense. Rain is only unlucky for weddings. I'm just happy it's not snowing."

Sir Parcival still had mixed feelings about this evening. "Doesn't sound like my kind of party," was all he could say in explanation. He raised his lip at his own formal attire, black fitted coat and trousers, ruffles at his neck.

Senta thought he looked stunning. With his hair pomaded back, her strange guest could almost pass muster as a member of the ton tonight, unless you looked too closely at the cut of his jacket, the style of his neckcloth. For a moment Senta wished she could introduce him to some of the lady guests. What a stir he'd make with that sultry, brooding look of his, or that slow smile that could light up an entire ballroom, she swore. Then again, he'd most likely forget his dance partners' names and insult any number of influential dowagers or tongue-tied debutantes. Just as well he was invisible. Besides, this ball wasn't being thrown to raise hopes in the hearts of every unmarried female; it was being held to catch a vicious criminal.

Their plan had to work. With the blackmailer loose, with the threat of Michael's disgrace hanging over them, and his brother's murderer at large, Lord Maitland was not going to permit himself to be the husband Senta so desperately wanted.

They were waiting—Senta was waiting anxiously; Sir Parcival was just lounging about, as usual—downstairs for the first of her dinner guests to arrive, before the ball itself. Senta straightened a leaning rosebud in the Sèvres vase on the mantel. Some of Sir Parcival's uncertainty had rubbed off on her.

"What if Lieutenant Sayre's brother and his friend don't come?"

"Yeah, they could all get cold feet, with this rain in their shoes."

"No, Wheatley's had the men erect an awning from the carriage drive right to the front portal. And planks were laid, then carpeted. In addition, we've had fires going all day in the ballroom, to take the chill off."

"Well, you said it was the promise of high-stakes gambling that would draw the men you wanted, not a hot meal."

"Yes, and Teddy made sure to tell his brother that there would be a lot of wealthy younger men here, too, some of Michael's friends from the Home Guard."

"They'll come then if they've got the gambling fever. There's none such dumber, none such prone to taking risks."

Senta still needed her husband's reassurance, which he was happy to give after he caught his breath at the first sight of his exquisite bride. Senta was wearing a gown made of layer upon layer of chiffon in shades from the palest pink to the deepest scarlet, falling from a minuscule bodice of rose-blush silk.

"Worried?" Lee answered her query. "Why, no. Tonight I feel like the luckiest man on earth."

Combined with the smile he gave her, Lee's words

would have melted her soul if they'd stood in a blizzard. As it was, Senta felt the heat rising from her mid-
section. And how could she have thought Sir Parcival
handsome, when her husband outshone any man she'd
ever seen?

Lee was opening a box he'd taken out of his pocket.
"But just to make sure, I've bought you a good-luck
charm. Happy Valentine's Day, darling." He took out a
magnificent diamond necklace, embellished with an
enormous ruby pendant. While Senta dabbed at her
eyes, speechless, Lee unfastened her pearls and affixed
the diamonds.

"There, now you look perfect," he said, standing
back to admire his handiwork. The ruby hung just
above the low neckline of Senta's gown, in the cleavage
of her breasts. He frowned. "Perhaps too perfect. Don't
you have a fichu or something? Maybe a scarf or a
shawl or a burlap sack, so no other man can get a look
at you."

Senta giggled. "The necklace is absolutely too stunning to hide, Lee. Thank you, but . . . but I don't have
anything to give you for Valentine's Day."

"Don't you, Senta? We'll talk about it tonight, after
the ball." Lee stared into her eyes, telling her without
words that they'd do a lot more than talk.

Senta would have pursued the matter then and
there—to perdition with spies and supper guests—but
Sir Parcival cleared his throat from the window seat.
Wheatley cleared his throat from the doorway. Their
guests had arrived.

Dinner was a success, of course. Cook and Wheatley
would have permitted no less. The few handpicked
guests were excellent company even if they were
mostly War Office minions or Bow Street officials and
their wives. And Lieutenant Sayre at Mona's right had
that young woman laughing and smiling for the first
time in Senta's memory. The only fault Lady Maitland

found with her first dinner as hostess, in fact, was that her husband was so far away from her down the long stretches of linen-covered table. When he did glance her way, around the floral centerpieces, the serving dishes, and candelabra, his eyes seemed to drift to her necklace.

"My, it's toasty in here," she told her dinner partner, to excuse the warmth rising in her cheeks.

The gentlemen took their port and cigars in a hurry, then they all took their places. Senta and Maitland, of course, stood at the entrance to the ballroom to greet their guests. Some of the men went immediately to the rooms set aside for cards, while others took up positions along the ballroom's fringes. Mona sat on a gilded chair in the space reserved for chaperones, dowagers, and wallflowers, with Teddy Sayre right beside her, his sling giving him excuse enough not to leave her for the dance floor.

"You have some interesting guests," Sally Jersey commented as she passed through the receiving line and noted the preponderance of sober-sided gentlemen.

Senta quickly looked around for Sir Parcival. He was sitting up on the raised platform with the orchestra, behind a screen of potted ferns. "Amen to that," she murmured as she greeted the next guest.

After most of those invited had arrived, Lord and Lady Maitland left their post, signaled to the orchestra, and opened the dance. The ball was on.

The music was lively, the refreshments were lavish, the gentlemen for the most part did their duty by the ladies before disappearing to the cardrooms. The quizzes could find no fault either with Senta's marriage or her ability to manage a grand household. Only one old crow was heard to squawk about how the flighty chit was like to beggar the viscount, with all her redecorating and entertaining. No one even listened; Maitland's pockets were some of the deepest in the land, and he obviously doted on his young bride. No, there was no complaint, no criticism from any of the guests. Senta's party was declared a sad crush, therefore a triumph.

Except for Senta. After that first dance with Lee, she'd been too busy to accept any other partners. There were all those scarlet-coated officers to introduce to the debs in white. The mamas and matrons and beturbanned grande dames had to be settled and served. Until Wheatley could leave the door where he was announcing latecomers, the servants needed direction about refilling platters and glasses. There was Private Waters, for instance, manning the punch bowl ladle in Maitland livery, his bald head covered by a powdered wig and his peg leg hidden by the tablecloth. Senta thought no one would recognize him; she hoped no one noticed him take the occasional sip.

"Just making sure of the quality, my lady," he said with a wink.

And then there was Sir Parcival, humming along with the orchestra so loudly that he was creating a cold draft that had the music sheets fluttering and the musicians' fingers faltering. That, in turn, had the dancers stumbling. Senta jerked her head in his direction to get him to move toward the dowagers' corner, where clacking tongues were raising the temperature by a few degrees. This wasn't what Senta wanted. She wanted to be dancing with Lee again, to be held in his arms instead of being held in thrall by Lord Conovan's boring narrative. She wanted to be whispering in his ear, instead of shouting into Lady Malverne's ear trumpet.

And the suspects hadn't arrived.

The very worst was that, while Senta was on tenterhooks over the absent evildoers, and on trial as a gracious hostess, her husband was on the dance floor. Lee seemed to be having the time of his life with every winsome widow and wayward wife in the *beau monde*. Now Senta was on her uppers. She made her way toward where Sir Parcival was leaning against a pillar.

"Do something," she whispered at him, meanwhile smiling at Admiral Rathbone and his wife.

"Sister, if I could do something, no one would be sitting still."

"This isn't the time to speak about your problems. It's Lee. He's danced twice with that woman."

Sir Parcival craned his neck to see. He whistled. Mrs. Admiral Rathbone shivered. Senta fumed.

The stunning redheaded widow was draped over the viscount like a fur stole, and he didn't seem to be minding one little bit. In fact, his mind seemed intent on memorizing every inch of the lush female. Since her gown, what there was of it, was nearly transparent, his task was that much easier.

"Her name is Marie de Flandreau," Senta told Sir Parcival when no one was nearby, through lips that were about to crack with the effort of maintaining her smile. "But they call her Marie Flambeau, for obvious reasons. She and Lord Maitland were close not too long ago."

"Marie the Flame? His last year's dame? Nah."

"Yes, and she's good ton, more's the pity. Her husband was a *comte* who managed to send his much younger wife and the family coffers to safety before he lost his life."

"She doesn't look like a grieving widow to me."

Senta tapped her foot. "And he doesn't look like a happily married man to me. You have to do something."

"Me?"

"You said you were here to help. So help."

"Why don't you go on over there? She's a stunner, all right, but he married you."

"What, and act like a jealous wife? Never."

So Sir Parcival looked around until he spotted a woman hovering near Lord Maitland and his former *chérie amour*. A refined but impoverished gentlewoman of a certain age, Miss Evelina Cadwaller was the *comtesse*'s companion, a sop to convention and a romantic to the core of her flat-chested, knock-kneed body. She was also as chaste as a nun, not necessarily out of choice. Miss Cadwaller, of course, could see Sir Parcival. Or she would have, if she hadn't been too vain to wear her spectacles.

"Ma'am," he said, bowing in front of her, seemingly out of nowhere, "I can't help but notice you've got the prettiest green eyes I've ever seen."

Miss Cadwaller squinted in his direction.

"Yes, they remind me of the green grass of home."

"Oh, are you from Sussex, too?"

Now Sir Parcival squinted. "I don't think so."

While Miss Cadwaller was trying to decipher that cryptic remark, Sir Parcival asked her to dance. "I know we haven't been properly introduced, ma'am, but would you do me the honor?"

Well, Miss Cadwaller hadn't been asked to dance in more years than she cared to remember, and here was such an attractive gentleman. With a cautious glance to see that her employer was still occupied with the viscount, she batted her colorless eyelashes and said yes. She placed her gloved hand in his. But his didn't seem to be there. She scrunched up her eyes and tried again. This time her trembling hand went right through his.

Miss Cadwaller did the only thing possible for a spinster lady who'd just been opportuned by a ghost. She fainted into the arms of the nearest gentleman, with a smile on her face.

In the ensuing commotion, Senta was there to direct the footmen to carry Miss Cadwaller to a small side chamber. Madame de Flandreau would naturally wish to go along to see to her ailing companion, wouldn't she? When hell froze over, but Senta was already leading her husband away, to discuss whether they should have some of the windows opened. Did he not think it was growing a trifle warm in the ballroom if ladies started swooning? Should the footmen stop pouring wine for the royal duke who was becoming castaway? And where the deuce were Sir Randolph Sayre and his friend Baron Northcote?

"Don't fret, darling. It's early yet. Creatures of the night like those two don't crawl out from under their rocks until the night is half gone. Come, we have time for another dance."

"I really shouldn't. Supper is going to be served soon, and I need to be ready to hand out the valentines. And Miss Thurston-Jones has hardly danced all night. Really, you should—"

"Miss Thurston-Jones can find her own partners whose feet she can step on. I'm tired of doing the pretty with all of these boring, bothersome women when all I want to do is dance with my own wife."

"Really, Lee? Marie Flambeau is boring?"

He grinned and swept her into the waltz just beginning. "She's not you."

Chapter Twelve

Sir Percival was wrong, Senta decided. He must be an angel after all, for this surely felt like heaven. She drifted in her husband's arms and didn't even notice when he signaled the orchestra to play the waltz again without intermission. She didn't notice, either, how many high-strung young girls in white gowns were swooning as Sir Percival moved among the ranks of those debutantes not permitted the waltz. Wheatley did, having left his post by the door to announce supper as soon as his lord and lady ceased acting like moon-calves. He ordered the windows opened onto the balcony. Sir Percival went to see if the rain had stopped.

When the waltz was over, Lord and Lady Maitland led their company into the supper room, which was, in fact, two parlors thrown open and filled with small tables and huge buffets. Every delicacy imaginable was offered, mounded into heart shapes, colored with cherry or raspberry sauce, decorated with spun-sugar cupids. Numbered lace valentines were handed out to all the young people as they entered, the youths from Lord Maitland's red basket, the girls from Senta's. Matching numbers denoted partners for the dance following supper. By some odd coincidence, the viscount pulled the same number as his wife.

There was teasing and laughter and a few good-natured groans as when Lord Hathaway discovered he'd been partnered to his sister. The chaperones smiled indulgently, pleased with Lady Maitland for guaranteeing at least one dance for the least favored chits. There would be no wallflowers at Senta's ball, she'd vowed.

But she'd saved the best partner for herself.

The dance was the quadrille, whose intricacies required concentration and precision. Senta was tripping along gaily, pleased with how well Lee's steps and hers matched, when he whispered in her ear, "Don't look now, but Teddy's brother and the baron have arrived." She stumbled; he stepped on one of the chiffon panels of her gown; there was a loud tearing noise.

"You did that on purpose," Senta accused, holding her skirts up as he led her off the dance floor. "You didn't want me near those men, so you made sure I'd have to go pin my hem up instead."

Lee just smiled and kissed her hand. As soon as she was out of the ballroom, Senta raced to the ladies' retiring chamber, where her own maid would be waiting to assist any of the guests in need of just such repairs. She didn't notice the inordinate number of young chits having smelling salts waved under their noses, but she did smile when a few of their friends asked why they hadn't been introduced to Lady Maitland's most attractive guest.

"Oh, your mamas would not see the wisdom of it." They would not see Sir Parcival at all. "He's not suitable company for unattached females. Too dangerous by half," she told them, increasing by fourfold their desire to meet the mysterious stranger.

While Senta was having her gown mended, Lord Maitland was playing host.

"Sorry you missed my wife, Sir Randolph, Baron. She's gone upstairs for a moment. I'm sure she'd bid me welcome you to our home and direct you to the dining room. Supper is over, but refreshments are laid out there."

The two men protested that they'd just come from dinner.

"The musician's are in fine form this evening if you care to take the floor. No? Cannot say as I blame you—I usually find it excruciatingly tedious myself—but with the proper partner . . ." He let his words trail off like some besotted newlywed. Let them think he had nothing on his mind but his pretty young bride.

"If I cannot interest you in the food or the dancing, I suppose it's the cardrooms. We have two chambers set up. One's for silver loo and chicken stakes, and the other is for more serious gaming. I hate trying to play my hand when ladies are chatting over their cards, don't you?"

Lee was leading them out of the ballroom as he spoke. Sayre was quick to agree, but Northcote held back. "Odd to find such arrangements at a ball," he noted.

"Yes, but my wife is a remarkably understanding woman. Besides," the viscount added confidentially, "she'd rather see me enjoying myself with the pasteboards than with another female."

They laughed, buying his explanation, so he went on: "Truth to tell, I aim to get there as soon as Lady Maitland returns to oversee things in the ballroom. Be honored if you save me a seat."

The two men nodded, happily calculating how much blunt they could extract from the viscount's deep pockets. With all the extravagance they saw around them, he'd never notice. Lee was just about to steer them into the hall when he stopped abruptly. "Oh, but you'll want to greet your brother first, Sayre. He tells me he's been recuperating in Bath. The waters must have finally done someone good, for he seems right as a trivet to me. Except for the sling, of course. I'm sure you'll be delighted to see how he's come along."

Lord Maitland held Sir Randolph's arm so the baronet couldn't demur as Lee led him back through the ballroom. "I'm sure you'll want to see young Teddy, too, Northcote. He told us what great service you did in seeing him home."

Northcote tried to shrug off the praise, but Lee was having none of it. "I only wish I'd been able to do as much for my young brother." A shadow passed across his face, but then he smiled when they reached the rows of gilded chairs. "Here we are. Doesn't our lieutenant look fit? Oh, and may I make you known to Señora Vegas, my wife's companion?"

The two men made their bows, asked after Teddy's health, and made a beeline for the cardrooms as if the pigeons would all fly away before they could be plucked. Behind their backs, Mona nodded.

A middle-aged dandy who appeared to be half in his cups called out to Sayre to join his table in the more private cardroom. Lord Dunbarton hailed the baron. "I say, Northcote, good timing. We need a fourth over here. Cantwell lost his purse and went back to try his hand with the heiresses."

The two men's eyes locked in silent communication, then they split up and took their seats. There were only four deal tables in the paneled room, and a well-filled sideboard of liquid refreshments presided over by two liveried footmen. Play was quiet and deep. Occasionally a gentleman would throw in his hand and leave in disgust, or check his watch and mutter about returning to the ballroom to escort his wife home. Empty seats were quickly filled, as were empty glasses.

The two men were not to know that Wheatley himself stood at attention outside that room, directing the casual gamblers toward the much larger cardroom. Only a select group of well-informed, well-prepared gentlemen were permitted to enter this particular chamber.

Neither were Sayre and Northcote to know that they

were being allowed to win in order that they might grow overconfident, that they were being deliberately separated, or that Sayre, whose penchant for the bottle matched his pursuit of the baize, was being deliberately plied with spirits. The baronet's eyes took on a feral gleam, from the piles of coins and counters in front of him and from the alcohol inside him. He kept licking his lips, like a snake flicking its forked tongue in and out. He barely acknowledged Viscount Maitland when Lee finally slipped into a seat at the table, and paid no attention to the crowd of spectators who had gathered round to witness the play, or the additional servants carrying trays, fresh decks, and cigars. Sayre certainly never noticed Sir Parcival drift through the room and out to the terrace.

The stakes went higher; likewise the pile of coins and notes and markers in the center of the table. And then the real wagering began.

Lee raised the ante and pushed his bid to the middle. The man to his right, the foppish, inebriated Honorable Mr. Bradford, made a great show of deliberating over his move. Lee took the opportunity to say, "Señora Vegas recalled meeting you in Spain." He spoke softly, so as not to be heard at the other tables. Only three were in play now, Maitland's, Northcote's, and one other, the members of the fourth having abandoned their game to watch this higher-stakes contest.

His eyes shifting from the pot to the cards in his hand, Sayre snickered. "I met a lot of señoras there. And señoritas, too." A few of the men around them chuckled.

Lord Maitland went on: "Mrs. Vegas was a friend of your brother's over there."

"They still are, from the looks of things," Mr. Brad-ford volunteered, slurring his words. "He hasn't left her side all night."

The baronet was getting impatient. "Your play, Bradford. My brother is old enough to keep his own company."

Bradford made his wager, but Lord Maitland wasn't finished. "Mona was a better friend of my brother's."

"That the way of it, eh?" Sayre managed to get a leer into his tone. "Surprised you let her companion your wife."

"The lady"—Lee emphasized the *lady*—"has been a great help to us in our time of sorrow."

Some of the other gentlemen murmured words of condolence, and the play continued around the table. When it got to Maitland's turn, the viscount spoke again. "You must be proud of your brother, Sayre. Getting decorated on the field, mentioned in the dispatches."

"Yes, yes, he was a bloody hero. Are you going to blather all night or are you going to bet?"

Lee ignored Sayre's vexation. "I was proud of my brother, too."

Mr. Bradford, half falling out of his chair, mumbled, "Thought he shot himself cleaning his gun. Doesn't take a lot of courage, I'd say." He was immediately hushed by Lord Sinclaire in the seat across from him.

"I don't believe that's what happened," Lee said. "Neither does Mona, that is, Señora Vegas. What do you think, Sayre?"

"I hadn't thought about it. Dash it, are you going to play? My cards are growing cold."

Lee just stared down at his own hand. "Oh, but you must have thought about Michael's death. You were with the army at the time. There had to be talk."

Sayre's tongue darted in and out. He finally lifted his eyes from the table to look at Maitland. He obviously didn't like what he saw there, for he was quick to utter: "I didn't listen. Didn't concern me."

"Oh, but I think you did. I think you know a lot more about my brother's murder than anyone."

"Murder?" Sayre's voice rose. "No one said anything about murder."

"Did they mention treason then?"

Sayre looked from side to side. All the men were avoiding his eyes. "I heard something, yes."

"And blackmail. Did you hear about that, too, or was the extortion all your idea?"

The baronet's tongue was doing double time. He looked longingly at the fortune in the middle of the table. "I don't know anything about blackmail."

"A man fitting your description was seen in Olney Street the day I was attacked while attempting to deliver the payoff. Attacked from behind, too."

"That's absurd. No one saw— That is, no one could have seen me, for I wasn't there."

"No, but you were at Mother Natick's bordello that afternoon, which just happens to have a rear exit on Olney Street."

Sayre tried to laugh. It came out as a croak. "A chap has certain needs. Not all of us are so lucky as to have a pretty young bride." He looked around for understanding. There wasn't a friendly face in the crowd.

Maitland was on his feet. "You will leave my wife out of this, you scum." He nodded to Mr. Bradford, who was no longer slouched in his seat.

The dandy, currently attached to the Lord High Magistrate's office, pulled a legal document out of his pocket. "I hereby arrest you in the name of the Crown for the crimes of extortion, bodily assault, and treason. You are under arrest."

Lord Sinclaire on Sayre's other side made to grab his arm, but the baronet pulled away, still eyeing the booty on the table. "What, go from a jackpot to a king's warrant? I'm hurt," he claimed, one last bluff. "Yes, that's it. I'm hurt that . . . that suspicious minds could accuse me of such heinous acts on the flimsiest of circumstantial evidence from an abbess and a Spanish whore."

Major Lord Sinclaire, currently out of uniform, threatened. "Just give the Home Guards one night with you and you'll be singing a different tune."

"And the last refrain from my fists," claimed Maitland, pushing the others aside to land Sayre a facer, then another. "That's one for the money, and two for the blow to my head." He was about to start enumerating the other crimes on Sayre's hapless body, with none of the others the least bit interested in interfering.

Sayre held his hand up. "You're right, but I'm not going to be left holding the bag. Northcote was the traitor. He killed your brother."

"And he's gone!" one of the men at the other table yelled, shoving his chair aside.

From the circle around Maitland and Sayre, Mr. Calley shouted. Taller than the rest, he looked over their heads. "He's headed for the door!"

Where Wheatley was positioned with Teddy and three other young officers from his and Michael's unit. Senta was hovering nervously nearby, awaiting the outcome of their machinations.

Northcote saw the soldiers ready to pounce on him or give chase. They had dress swords and pistols, and twenty years less of dissolute living. No escape there. So he pulled a pistol out of his pocket, snatched Lady Maitland against his chest, and dragged her back with him to the cardroom, warning her that he'd bash her over the head if she made so much as a peep.

"I'm going out the back door," he declared. "And no one is going to try to stop me. One move from any of you and I'll shoot the wench."

"Take me with you," Sir Randolph begged, but his erstwhile companion merely sneered.

"If you hadn't gone greedy and tried to bleed Maitland, you'd never have been a suspect, you fool." He sidled toward the rear of the room.

"Surrender!" shouted Dunbarton, the king's man.

"It's now or never," yelled Major Sinclaire, training his own pistol on the baron, along with at least ten others in the room. "Make your move."

209

"We're playing for keeps, Northcote," warned Bow Street's assistant director.

"But I've got a woman," snarled the baron.

"Hiding behind a woman's skirts." Private Waters, still in his footman's garb, lowered his weapon and spit. "And they said you was high class."

But it was Lord Maitland who gave the order. "Let him go, men. He's finished here anyway."

The baron inched his way across the room, trying to watch his back and keep Senta between him and any of the fools with hair-trigger pistols in their hands.

The viscount watched, venom in his stare. "Know this, Northcote," he said. "If you harm my wife in any way, the merest scratch, I'll track you down to the ends of the earth. Men, money, whatever it takes, I'll see you hanged for this."

Northcote kept going. There was no noise in the room but Sayre's occasional whimper. At last Northcote reached the glass doors to the patio. If he could make it out there, he could drop the female, jump the garden fence, and be gone before a shot was fired.

"Unlatch the door," he ordered Senta. She looked at her husband in despair.

"Do it, darling. There's no choice."

So she did, and Northcote dragged her out the doors onto the stone terrace, where Sir Parcival had been practicing all the new songs he'd heard that night. As usual, his spectral voice had created quite a draft. As it mingled with the cold rain, a sheet of ice had formed. Lord Northcote took two hurried steps and skidded. The gun went flying and Senta rolled behind a concrete bench. Five soldiers sprang up from behind the potted yew trees and tackled the baron where he lay sprawled on the ice.

Sir Parcival looked under the bench at Senta and shrugged. "Well, I did it my way."

Chapter Thirteen

Lord Northcote was going to be tried, and most likely hanged. Randolph Sayre was being permitted to leave the country, with stipulations, after testifying against Northcote, the actual traitor and murderer. The conditions were that he never return, and that he relinquish his title and holdings in favor of Teddy.

The new Sir Theodore Sayre, bart., lost no time in calling at Maitland House to ask the viscount's permission to pay his addresses to Mona. "I'm not sure if she considers you her guardian, but she is living in your house, so I thought I should approach you to make my offer in form."

Lee wasn't sure of the protocol involved either, and he was positive that Mona and Teddy, Sir Theodore, had already come to terms, but he nodded. Senta, who refused to leave the library during such an interesting discussion, said she thought Teddy was behaving just as he ought, which had that young man blushing.

"I mean to resign my army commission," he told them, "and take up the reins of the family property in Durham. I aim to make the estate succeed for once, rather than bleeding it dry. I know you would do something for Mona, find her a cottage somewhere at one of your estates, my lord, but I can offer her a real home and a life of her own. I can give her my name, which you never can."

"But you told me your mother wouldn't have taken her in," Senta reminded him. "Mona doesn't deserve to be treated like a, um . . ."

"Soiled dove?" her husband suggested, and she agreed.

Teddy nodded. "But now the manor house is mine. If Mama cannot accept my wife, she does not have to make her home with us. It's that simple. My mother is happier in Bath anyway."

"And will Mona be happy?" Lee asked. Senta thought she already knew the answer.

"I will spend my life trying to see that she is, my lord," Teddy assured the viscount in great earnestness. "I believe that she'll accept my offer because it's the right thing to do for her and the baby. Having lived through the hell she has, she's too practical for anything else. But I like to think she would marry me anyway."

Senta smiled her agreement.

"And you're not afraid she'll still be mourning Michael?" Lee wanted to know.

"I don't expect her to forget him, if that's what you mean. But I hope in time she'll grow to love me, too, maybe in a different way. I know she likes me, and if that's all I ever have, it will be enough." He reached inside his coat pocket and extracted a signet ring, Michael's ring that Mona had worn on a chain around her neck. "She asked me to give this back to you. That's a good sign, isn't it?"

"Are you sure she wants to part with it?"

"I think perhaps she wants to start with unchained memories, too. Besides, you'll be needing it for your firstborn son."

Now it was Senta's turn to blush. Lee put his hand over hers where it rested on the sofa.

"And what about Mona's baby?"

"I would be proud to raise Michael's daughter as my own. We could claim a secret marriage in Spain or a premature birth, anything so that Vida never has to be stigmatized as a bastard. We'll be living quietly in the country, far from the London gossip mills. No one ever needs to know."

The viscount pretended to think a moment while Teddy wiped beads of perspiration from his forehead. Senta squeezed her husband's hand. "Well, yes, that sounds like the perfect arrangement, except . . ."

"Yes?" Teddy asked.

"Except I shall have to insist on being Vida's godfather, and frequent visits, and that you take Private Waters and his dog with you, too."

After Teddy left to find Mona, Lee and Senta stayed on in the library, her head resting on his shoulder.

"Teddy is a brave man," Senta said.

"Of course he is. Did you see all his medals?"

"No, I meant about Mona. I thought I could be content with your liking me, when I thought you just married me to get an heir. But I couldn't. That wouldn't have been enough for me."

"And I tore myself apart when I feared I was second in your heart, second in your dreams, always worrying that you preferred another."

"But now you know there never has been another, never could be another." Senta cuddled a little closer. "And I think that I could not be like Mona, loving again, for I have only one heart to give."

"When I saw you in that villain's arms, and thought I might lose you after all, I knew my life wouldn't be worth living without you."

So Lord and Lady Maitland had their wedding night after all. It was a bit late in the marriage, and a bit tardy even for Valentine's Day, but no less wondrous or romantic for all that.

Senta was in her husband's arms, in his bed, as close as two lovers could be, when she felt a cool draft on her bare skin. Sir Parcival was standing at the foot of the bed. "I think I'm getting my memory back!" he mouthed.

"Good, now go!" She made shooing motions with her hand.

"What's that, dear heart?" Lee asked.

"Nothing, my love, I just thought I heard the dog barking."

Lee went back to what he was doing, which was turning his innocent bride into a remarkably content wife. "Oh, my darling Senta," he whispered, "I love you."

Senta sighed, but Sir Parcival said, "And?"

"And?" Senta turned a perplexed look on the specter.

"And?" asked Lee, even more confused.

Sir Parcival was waving his hands around, twitching his legs, all the while growing dimmer and more transparent to Senta's eyes. "And?" he demanded.

So she shrugged and repeated, "Oh, my darling Senta, I love you' and . . . ?"

To his credit, Lee hesitated only an instant. "And I always will."

"Yes!" shouted Sir Parcival, fading completely, leaving only a cool breeze behind.

And "Oh, yes," Senta sighed, before losing herself to her husband's passion.

The last thing she remembered hearing, or maybe she said it, was, "Thank you. Thank you very much."

His wife—how wonderful that sounded—was nearly asleep, arms and legs all tangled with his. When Lee made sure she was covered, Senta gave a sleepy "Hm?"

"Nothing, darling, just that you have made me the happiest man on earth. Now go to sleep; we have a lifetime ahead of us, dear heart."

Someone nearby cleared her throat and said, "Ah, excuse me?"

Lee looked over Senta's tousled curls to see a woman standing at the foot of his bed. She was wearing some kind of leather headcovering, goggles like the ones jockeys wore, and a white silk scarf around her neck. "Excuse me," she repeated. "Did you say dear heart, or Earhart?"

Lee could see the firelight flickering in the grate right through the bizarre figure. Obviously he was seeing things because he was exhausted. "Get lost."

"I think that was the problem in the first place. . . ."

Road to Ruin

Now go we in content
To liberty and not to banishment

—Shakespeare,
AS YOU LIKE IT, I, iii

Prologue

THE SCRATCH OF a quill pen upon paper was amplified by the quiet of the wood-panelled library, where a lady sat at a writing desk, her dark head bent as she wrote. The sombre grey of her gown, which suggested a recent bereavement, did not conceal her charms. She was strikingly lovely, with a pair of indigo eyes accentuated by bold, arching brows. Nature had cleverly placed a beauty mark near her generously shaped mouth, drawing attention to its pleasing shape.

The room was still, lit only by the fading afternoon sun, and golden motes of dust danced in the rays that slanted in through the windows. The chairs were shrouded in hollandcloth, and the table tops were bare of any ornament. Several paintings leaned sadly against the wainscoting, and although the grate gleamed from a recent and thorough blacking, there was no fire in it. Even the long-case clock was silent, for it had not been wound this day.

That Nerissa Newby had been busy at her task for some time was evident from the small pile of folded notes that had accumulated at her elbow. Suddenly her swiftly moving hand stilled, and while she searched her mind for a word or phrase, she stared out of the nearest window, left open to admit the fresh air. October was not yet a week old; the weather was pleasantly dry and mild, and with the leaves of the trees on the turn, the landscape was a pleasing mix of green and golden tints. In the distance, Nerissa could see the tall, narrow spire of the local church, which pointed skyward as if to pierce the bright blue heavens.

In its time, the Buckinghamshire village had withstood flame, flood, and enclosures. It had also been immortalised in the verses of the poet Cowper. But Nerissa, who much preferred the architectural varieties of London, had never been fond of Olney. The high street, though broad, was lined with stone buildings that had always seemed to her to be as stern and unlovely as their inhabitants. Nearly all the roofs were tiled now, but the cottages that sheltered the less affluent were still covered with thatch, which had contributed to the spread of a great fire many years ago. The flames had ravaged the town, consuming forty-eight dwellings, as well as numerous barns and outbuildings. Nerissa had been a child at the time, and she would never forget the alarming spectacle of gutted houses, and the pall of acrid smoke that had lain over the neighbourhood for days after.

She transferred her gaze from the church steeple to a small cottage just visible through the trees. No plume of smoke wafted from the chimney today, and its absence was a painful reminder of yet another loss. Catching her lower lip between her teeth, she resumed her writing. But her industry was short-lived, for she heard the sound of hoofbeats in the lane, and put down her quill again. The rider, a fair-haired gentleman, was approaching her house, but she sat perfectly still until she heard the heavy, ominous pounding of the door-knocker. Then she rose, almost reluctantly, with a slow, languorous grace, and made her way to the dark hallway, carefully stepping around a pair of corded trunks.

When she opened the front door to her visitor, his handsome face revealed his surprise. ''But where is Mary?'' he asked.

"She is much occupied just now," Nerissa replied. "Do come in, Andrew."

He entered, his eyes widening when she led him past the trunks into the hall. The state of the library affected him powerfully, and he looked about in consternation. "Nerissa, what is going on here?"

Before answering she smoothed a tendril of mahogany hair which had escaped the coil atop her head. In a firm, clear voice she replied, "I am closing up my house, Andrew. I summoned you here to tell you so. And also to ask what the *devil* you've done with Lucy Roberts—and the child."

"I thought I forbade you to go to that cottage again," Andrew said severely.

During the twenty-three years of her life, Nerissa Newby had heeded one person only, and he was six months dead. "I am not some child to be ordered about, nor have I yet taken any vow to obey you," she said pithily. "As for my visit to Lucy, I had a purpose in going—I owed her a quarter's wages at Michaelmas."

"She was paid." He avoided the smouldering blue eyes she had turned upon him.

"You sent them away, didn't you?"

Andrew Hudgins drew himself up to his full height. "Nerissa, I could hardly stand by and let the common folk gossip about my future wife. And I have four unmarried sisters to think of. Not only you, but my whole family have suffered from your association with that low woman and her ill-gotten brat."

"Don't call her that!" Nerissa struggled to control her rising temper, and succeeded well enough to say in a less volatile manner, "He is called Samuel. I named him myself."

"That may be, but it's hardly a boasting matter."

"Neither is bustling the pair of them off in that furtive way—it only confirms the rumours flying thick and fast from Olney to Weston Underwood to Clifton Reynes.

''I did what had to be done, and I refuse to justify my action beyond that. The girl has gone to live with her mother, and there's an end to it.''

His stubborn certainty that he had acted correctly vexed Nerissa beyond the limits of her endurance. ''But you've done the worst possible thing, don't you see?'' she cried. ''You might just as well have printed a placard with the most damning version of the story and hung it in the marketplace for all to read.'' Lifting her chin, she continued in a declamatory voice. '' 'Miss Newby, while living with her father in London, gave birth to a love-child. The captain, an unconventional fellow, let her keep it, and together they passed it off as the washer-woman's brat.' ''

Andrew said repressively, ''I find this conversation in very poor taste, Nerissa.''

''Well, you brought it upon yourself,'' she told him bluntly.

''The possibility that you are the mother of that infant is quite absurd,'' he said. ''There may be some slight resemblance, enough to arouse comment, but you need not fear that I would ever condemn you on such flimsy evidence.''

''And what of your mother?'' she retorted. ''No fortune, not even mine, is great enough to induce her to swallow scandal-broth so hot and rich and spicy!''

Nerissa took an agitated turn about the room, her skirts rustling with each energetic step. Suddenly coming to a halt, she said wearily, ''What's done is done. With Lucy and Samuel gone, at least I can console myself with the fact that they are well out of this coil. And I mean to be as soon as I possibly can, otherwise the talk will never die down.''

''When may I expect you to return?''

''I don't know that I will ever return.'' Seeing how

disturbed he was by her candid and unequivocal reply, Nerissa said more gently, "I'm sorry to pain you, Andrew, truly, but I think upon reflexion you will agree that it is for the best. As fond of you as I have always been, I am not—I will never be the wife you deserve."

She walked over to the desk and picked up the fine sapphire ring which had formerly graced her left hand. When she held it out to him, her face wore a faint, self-mocking smile. "You stand too much upon good form to ever cry off, especially now I'm in a scrape. My reputation is already so tarnished that being called a jilt will hardly make a difference. Or perhaps they will say you jilted me—for I well know I've given you a good enough cause to do so."

He drew a deep breath, expelling it in a long, regretful sigh, but he did take the ring from her. "Will you go to your cousins in London?" he asked quietly.

She was thankful for his calm, unemotional acceptance of the blow she had dealt him. But that was to be expected; he was a gentleman and as such would make it easy for her, whatever he felt inside. Maybe he had known, deep down, that this rift was inevitable, and had prepared himself for it. "Never London," she said, shaking her head. "I couldn't face all the necessary explanations, not just now." Her shoulders sagged, but she squared them almost at once. "And without Papa, I think I would have a hard time of it, living in town. No, I have decided to pay a long visit to my friend Mrs. Sedgewick, who lives in Staffordshire. I leave tomorrow."

There was very little more to be said. Nerissa gave him her letters, asking if he would be so kind as to post them for her. One was to her trustees in London, informing them of the termination of her engagement. Another was for Andrew's mother and sisters, thanking them for their many kindnesses to her after her father's death. Although neither their attentions nor her gratitude had been completely heartfelt, Nerissa knew her duty to his family.

''I am writing a reference for Mary,'' she continued. ''And if you should hear of anyone in need of a groom, perhaps you could recommend Alfred. One of the maidservants has already found a new place, and the other will go to Northampton to work for a wool-comber. And speaking of Northampton, I have decided to hire a post-chaise there, to avoid notice.''

''I shall convey you there at whatever hour you please.''

Politely but firmly she refused this offer. ''John has already offered to drive me in the gig.''

''You have discussed this with my brother?''

She nodded, and saw that this distressed him as much as the return of the sapphire ring. ''I couldn't tell you of my plan to leave,'' she explained, ''because I didn't want to worry you any more than I've done already. For pride's sake I'm determined to be far away before it becomes generally known. And before you begin to regret ever knowing me.''

Staring down at the ring he held, Andrew said, ''I don't believe I do know you, Nerissa. Not really, not as I've always wished I might. It's to be farewell, then?''

''It must be,'' she replied, striving to keep her voice steady, for this part was far more difficult than she had anticipated. He was a good man, he had always been her friend, but he would never be her husband. To hold out false hope would be too cruel, and her father had always taught her to be fair in all her dealings.

His attempt to smile was not entirely successful.

''After all this time, I don't quite know how to say good-bye—until a few moments ago, I believed we would be spending the rest of our lives together. It is what I always dreamed of, you know, even when you were a wild little girl—the delight of your papa and the despair of your aunt. Good-bye, Nerissa.'' He kissed her cheek in the same tentative, brotherly way she had grown used to, and left her standing in the middle of the darkening room, surrounded by the ghostly, cloth-covered chairs.

She crossed to the window to watch her erstwhile fiancé ride off towards the village. A chapter in her life was forever closed—several chapters, in fact, and she ought to be glad of it, for none of the more recent ones had been very pleasant. It was not her way to repine, yet she couldn't help wishing for her father's comforting presence, though she knew what he would tell her, in his bracing, salt-laced language. Determined not to give way to despair, she whispered the oft-spoken creed: "A calm sea makes for a dull voyage.''

But oh, how smooth and easy her passage through life would have been if she had been born dull and plain, like Andrew's older sisters, Ruth and Judith, for then her good name would never have been sullied by suspicion. And even if she had possessed the common prettiness and flirtatious ways of Sarah and Rebecca Hudgins, not a soul would have whispered that she had borne a bastard child. But Nerissa Newby's face was neither plain nor pretty, but something else altogether, and it had damned her.

HIGH ABOVE THE vast, busy city, the black velvet canopy of sky was adorned with numberless, diamond-like stars. The evening was several hours old, but the fashionable part of London had only just come alive. Faint strains of music and bursts of muted laughter from Mayfair's most notable residences drifted into the night, mingling with the cry of the watchman and the clatter of hooves on pavement.

Clifford Street, to the east of Berkeley Square, was less busy on this October night when so many of London's elite were abroad. Although Number Seven had received its share of visitors when it was the principal residence of a political giant, now it was shuttered and silent. Lord Sidmouth, formerly His Majesty's chief minister, was no longer in power; Mr. Pitt, his abler predecessor, had retained the royal favour. Because his lordship lived retired at White Lodge at Richmond, a gift to him from a grateful sovereign, he seldom visited Number Seven. Clifford Street was poorer for his neglect.

Most of the residences lining the street were quiet, but several doors down from Sidmouth's celebrated address an evening party was in progress, to the delight of the children living in the house across the way. Three boys had gathered at an upper window to observe the comings and goings, but because these occurred at uncertain intervals, they were growing bored

and were on the point of giving up the vigil. Their
interest revived when a town carriage came into view,
drawn by four horses, their satiny coats gleaming in
the diffuse light of the street lamps. The proud bearing
of the liveried coachman on the box and the swift ef-
ficiency of the bewigged footman who climbed down
from his perch to open the door were similarly impressive. The possessor of this handsome turn-out,
whoever he might be, was no commoner: a family crest
was visible on the door of the coach. The children
waited breathlessly for the bearer of these arms to
emerge.

When a tall, cloaked figure climbed out of the carriage and turned to address his footman, the boys
leaned even more precariously over the sill. There was
no mistaking the servant's reply, a respectful, "Yes,
milord."

The resulting babble of excited voices overhead
reached the ears of this lordly gentleman, who immediately glanced up. Seeing that row of nightshirted
urchins framed by the window, Dominic Sebastian
Charles Blythe, second Baron Blythe, was forcibly reminded of the long-ago nights when he had stood at
his bedroom window to observe the evening traffic in
Grosvenor Square. Prompted by this sharp stab of nos-
talgia, and with a beautiful disregard for the butler
who had opened the front door to him, he raised his
arm in salutation.

His youthful admirers, overwhelmed by this splendid act of condescension, gleefully returned the compliment.

His lordship, now fully caught in the game, waved
back. To his sorrow, a shadowy figure—unmistakably
female—bustled the lads out of sight and followed this
act of cruelty by slamming the window shut. Dominic
turned towards the house, and when he entered it he
grinned shamelessly at his host's butler, a witness to

his indiscretion. Removing his long cape, he handed it to the footman who stood at the bottom of the staircase. At the top stood the couple whose recent marriage was being celebrated this night.

Although his felicitations would be genuine, a certain irony attended them. Dominic had known Sir Algernon Titus all his life, but he was more intimately acquainted with the baronet's bride, with whom he'd spent a riotous fortnight at Brighton some six years ago. The workings of fate were curious indeed: his own former mistress—if that term was applicable, given the brevity of their association—was now the wedded wife of one of his closest friends.

The lady herself was not unaware of the irony. Lady Titus, watching as the baron ascended the staircase, smiled upon him in a way that would have given her elderly husband pause, had his attention not also been on the newcomer. In evening attire, Lord Blythe was a study in stark contrasts, for he wore a black coat over a snowy shirt, black satin knee breeches, white silk hose that fitted and flattered his long legs, and a pair of glossy black pumps. His colouring, too, was all black and white, the thick, straight hair was as dark as midnight, his fine-boned face as pale and luminous as the moon. But even if he had been as ugly as a gargoyle, Lady Titus would have received him thankfully. For the past hour, too few had entered her house, far too many had left it, and she was desperate for the sight of a new face.

She had been born Miss Georgiana Symonds, and in her seventeenth year had eloped with a dashing young lieutenant. Three years later, the war with France made her a widow, but already her reputation was such that none of the numerous gentlemen so eager to console her offered anything more than *carte blanche*—which she had occasionally accepted. After a campaign of two years, she had finally lured a baronet to the altar, no mean achievement for a humbly born lady of twenty-seven years. But this, her first evening party since becoming Lady Titus, had attracted very few of the fashionable persons to whom she had wished to display her matrimonial triumph, and her new husband's curling lip and satirical eye were provoking in the extreme. She had given dozens of parties during her first marriage, and even more during her dashing widowhood, and all had been successful. To be sure, some had also been attended by a measure of notoriety, but it wasn't kind of Algy to remind her of that, not now that she was respectably married again. She glanced at the greying head of the gentleman standing at her side, thinking pettishly that the worst thing about older men, apart form their inordinate jealousy and an outsized sensitivity about their age, was that air of insufferable superiority.

When the handsome nobleman bowed over her hand, Georgiana sucked in her breath, thereby increasing the swell of bosom that was barely concealed by her low décolletage. "Why, Blythe, how good of you to come," she murmured, surreptitiously squeezing his fingers. But despite the warmth of this welcome, she received only an impersonal nod before Lord Blythe moved on to shake hands with her husband.

"Dominic, my dear boy," Sir Algernon Titus greeted the newcomer. "I warned Georgie not to count on seeing you tonight, but I must say I've never been happier to be proved wrong. Finally returned to town, eh?"

"As you see, sir," Lord Blythe replied. His voice was low, with a slight huskiness that enhanced rather than detracted from its appeal. "Some trifling business with the settlement of my father's estate brought me back to town sooner than I wished. But not soon enough—I would have liked to offer my toast at your nuptials." His grey eyes flickered towards the opulent

blonde, whose satin gown matched the warm, creamy
tones of her overexposed flesh.

The baronet shrugged. ''It was a simple affair. I
persuaded Georgie that the spectacle of a man my age
taking a wife was absurd enough without the attendant
pomp and ceremony.''

''What Algy means is,'' the bride announced un-
blushingly and with a saucy toss of her head, ''he was
afraid of gossip. But it's not as though he's the first
man to marry his mistress.''

''Nor will I be the last,'' her husband declared before turning his attention back to their guest. ''The
young Marquis of Elston is here, with some cousin of
yours in tow. Says he's Cavender's brother.''

''What? Not Justin?'' Dominic asked in surprise.
''I must ask him how Lincoln's Inn suits him after the
rigours of Oxford.''

Sir Algernon chuckled. ''Oh, aye, these young men
do wear their brains out at university, don't they? I tell
you, Dominic, I see something of your father in the
boy, and don't doubt that he'll be lording it over some
ministry office before many years have passed. I hope
I live to see it. But what title will our king find for
him, I wonder? Your father was rewarded with a barony, but Justin might go higher yet. And with his
brother a viscount in his own right, I predict you
Blythes will hold a monopoly on titles someday.''

His lordship laughed. ''It may well come to pass,
sir, but Justin has a long way to go yet. My father's
honours came late in life, and after many years of service to the Crown.''

After he and his host exchanged a few remarks of a
less personal nature, Dominic went to the saloon, so
sparsely populated that he sighted his quarry with no
difficulty. Two well-favoured young men in their early
twenties stood side by side, the brown head of one
bent close to the bright gold one of the other. He ap-

proached this pair from behind, clapped his cousin on the shoulder, and intoned, "Justin Richard Blythe, for the crime of dereliction of duty I arrest you in the name of the law."

The young man so named whirled around, clearly shocked, but when he saw who had accosted him, he cried out in delight. "Nick! What the devil are you doing here?"

"I might ask the same of you, stripling. Have you deserted your law studies so soon after beginning them?"

"You're taking the wrong man to task. The blame rests entirely with this fellow," said the Honourable Justin Blythe, indicating his companion. His leaf-brown eyes twinkled with mischief as he explained, "Cousin Damon forced me to accompany him, you see, and I am here very much against my will."

Damon Lovell, Marquis of Elston, exhibited a lazy smile. "My dear Nick, do not begrudge Justin this night on the town. We poor mortals must cram what pleasures we can into our brief time on this earth."

Dominic shook his head. "Clearly you are bent on corrupting my cousin."

"*My* cousin, too," the marquis reminded him. "Through our mothers."

"And yet," Justin interposed, "despite our tie of blood, I never met Cousin Damon till our paths crossed at Oxford. What an odd family we are!"

Said Dominic, with mock gravity, "You acknowledge the connexion? But I warn you, this cousin of yours is quite notorious—the most shocking example of hedonism to be found among all the noble houses of this land." The two younger men laughed, and he continued. "What brings you to Sir Algernon's house tonight, Damon?"

"Curiosity," drawled the marquis.

Dominic lifted his black brows quizzically. "Oh?

but the lovely Georgiana's reputation is really no worse than that of any other society lady, however common her origins.'' He swiftly inspected the assembled company, and added, ''When she sent out her cards, she certainly gave the preference to peahens and peacocks.'' He added, ''Have you noticed how all the ladies are so shrill and charmless and unlovely, and their mates so very ornamental?''

The truth of the latter part of his observation was borne out by the three gentlemen themselves. Both the baron and the marquis were dressed in the height of the mode, with an elegance that surpassed the efforts of other men. But in every other respect, they were perfect foils: Lord Blythe's black hair found its opposite in Lord Elston's gilt locks. And his lean, aristocratic face resembled polished marble, while his friend's features looked as if they had been sculpted from alabaster. Although Justin Blythe presented a less dramatic appearance than either of their lordships, he was memorable in his own right with his chestnut crop, merry eyes, and air of quiet assurance. They made a most attractive grouping.

The ladies present, however, would have preferred to divide that arresting trio and draw lots for the individual components. Each of the two noblemen had his own set of devotees, ranged on opposite sides of the question of whether the baron or the marquis was the more worthy of admiration. Now that another promising member of the family had arrived on the social scene in the pleasing person of Justin, a third faction was forming. Many a member of the fair sex, wearied of a husband or bored with her paramour, would happily overlook his status as a younger son, since position and wealth, so indispensable in a mate, were negligible qualities in a lover.

But it was war, not love which occupied the three gentlemen, who were discussing Lord Nelson's inef-

fectual pursuit of Villeneuve and the French fleet. Said the marquis, shaking his bright head, ''He chased the Frogs all the way to the West Indies, and to no avail. The great confrontation we've hoped for is still before us, rather than a settled thing.''

''The Lords of Admiralty appear to be satisfied with Nelson's abilities,'' Dominic commented. ''He only sailed from Portsmouth a mere three weeks ago, so we need not despair about his present campaign quite yet.''

His friend's reply was drowned out by a sudden cry from Justin. ''Look there, it's my brother—see, he's standing by the door.''

''So he is,'' Dominic observed. ''Cousin Ramsey's presence at this gathering is even more of a surprise than yours, Damon.''

Lord Elston concurred, saying grimly, ''One would expect to find Ram in the shires at this season. Can it be that he lacks the funds to keep up his hunting?''

''I would advise against raising that question,'' Dominic warned him.

The Twelfth Viscount Cavender was a thickset, stocky gentleman, whose athletic build, tanned complexion and gold-streaked brown hair attested to many hours spent in the saddle. He was greeted warmly by Justin, with less enthusiasm by his fellow peers, and he, in turn, was no more than coolly civil to them.

''So, Nick, you've returned from Wiltshire,'' he remarked. ''Surely you haven't wearied of playing farmer?''

''Never that,'' Dominic replied imperturbably. ''Blythe was looking its best, and I hated to tear myself away. By the by, while I was in the neighbourhood I took it upon myself to look in at Cavender Chase. Your tenant appears to be well satisfied, and so should you be with his management.''

Viscount Cavender's sun-bronzed face clouded over

sends regular reports, you know.''

"I do know, but your agent isn't a member of the family," Dominic pointed out. "That reminds me," he said, turning to the marquis, "I chanced to meet your bailiff on the Bath Road one day, Damon. Without saying it directly, he left me with the impression that you've neglected to visit Elston Towers since you came of age—three years now, isn't it?"

Lord Elston's blue eyes were suddenly as hard and cold as ice, but his voice was as languid as ever when he replied. "True, but so long as the estate continues to return a profit, I care nothing for it. The place has never been a home to me."

Justin Blythe, conscious of the tension around him, tried to ease it with a laugh and a jest. "Admit it, Damon, you're a Sussex man at heart and by habit. Even so, you were born in Wiltshire and your lands march with ours, and thus we have a greater claim upon your loyalties."

The sudden burst of masculine laughter reached the ears of Lady Titus, who had given up her post on the staircase to glide in and out among her guests. When she reached the quartet in the corner, she favoured Mr. Blythe with a smile and expressed the hope that he had enjoyed himself since his arrival in London.

Justin, politely averting his eyes from her low neck-line, assured her that he had. "Cousin Damon persists in telling me how tiresome the city is at this time of year, and even Dominic agrees. But if this is their notion of dullness, they must be sadly spoiled."

Georgiana beamed her pleasure at what she deemed a compliment to her party, and she added in a confi-dential tone, "My dear sir, I believe they are." Trans-ferring her melting gaze to Dominic, she murmured, "Lord Blythe, you must be tutoring your young cousin

in gallantry. I vow, he could not wish for a more practiced instructor in the art of pleasing the ladies."

Her words sparked a flash of fury in Viscount Cavender's brown eyes. It was fleeting, but Georgiana saw
it. She knew she'd made a mistake by raising his ire,
however inadvertently, for he was a vengeful man.
Thinking it best to efface herself, she said, "I really
must go warn my butler that we won't be needing *quite*
all of the champagne we ordered for tonight. Pray excuse me, gentlemen."

Her silent prayer that Lord Cavender would not take
her to task went unanswered. A little while later he
accosted her, and his expression caused her to say nervously, "Enact no scenes here, my lord. Remember
whose house this is—whose guest you are."

"You failed me last night," he growled.

"I couldn't help it. Algy didn't go to his club after
all."

"You're lying, Georgie. I saw him there with my
own eyes, and when he settled down to a game of
whist, I dashed back to my lodgings. Where were
you?"

She shrugged one bare shoulder, and the gesture was
eloquent of nonchalance. "I can't arrange our meetings so easily as I did before my marriage," she told
him. "How many times must I remind you? It's imperative that we be discreet."

"Discreet?" he repeated under his breath. "And I
suppose that's what you were being just now, when
you were flirting with Blythe!"

Georgiana reflected, not for the first time, that her
lover was much less attractive in anger than when he
was in one of his rare good moods. To appease him,
she trilled a disclaimer. "Flirting with Lord Blythe?
What an absurd accusation!"

"Is it? You fancied him once, and it's my suspicion

you mean to have him back again—now that you've secured your baronet." He ground his teeth savagely.

"He already has a mistress, as you know very well. Oh, *how* you bore me with your passions and jealous pets," she cried, momentarily forgetting how her disdain might be received by this volatile gentleman. "My *affaire* with Nick Blythe is ancient history, so brief and so long ago that even Algy, who knows the worst about me, never heard of it. Honestly, Ram, your rivalry with your cousin is too tedious for words. Sometimes I think it's the only reason you sought me out in the first place."

"Come to me tomorrow night," he replied, "and give me the chance to prove otherwise."

She shook her head, and the golden ringlets bobbed.

"Damn you, Georgie—"

"I promise I'll contrive another meeting soon, but only if you leave now. Algy is no fool, and more observant than you may think. He's also quite a good shot, and we wouldn't want to put him in the position of defending my honour, however tattered it may be."

Ramsey made no move to go. "Meet me tomorrow, in Carrington Street." But Georgiana only smiled wearily and walked away from him without giving him the answer he'd demanded of her. He glared after her retreating figure, oblivious to his watchful host's approach.

When he heard Sir Algernon say reflectively, "Poor Georgie, she is all aflutter tonight," he turned around to find the baronet standing near.

Uncertain of how much, if anything, Georgiana's husband had overheard, Ramsey said diffidently, "So I perceive. Why should that be, I wonder?"

"Oh, several possibilities leap to mind. She is preoccupied with her duties as hostess, perhaps, or too conscious of being on view at her first public appearance as Lady Titus."

Ramsey regarded the baronet through hostile eyes. "Or could she, perchance, be discomfitted by the presence of someone from her past?"

Sir Algernon smiled, but in a decidedly unpleasant fashion. "To the best of my knowledge, I am the only gentleman who matches that description."

"You are much mistaken in that assumption, sir," Ramsey told him harshly.

The older man maintained his composure, although the strain of it showed in his face. "I listen to no tales about my wife. And by God, Cavender, you'll keep your distance from her—or answer for it!"

"Fling your threats at my cousin Dominic's head, not mine," the viscount retorted.

"What the devil are you implying?" the baronet thundered.

"Merely that you would do better to investigate the questionable nature of Lord Blythe's relations with Lady Titus –past *and* present!" On that wrathful note, Ramsey stalked off.

A few hours later, when the birds were first beginning to stir, a solemn cavalcade of two riders and a horse-drawn carriage arrived at Chalk Farm. The sun had not yet shown its face; its advent was heralded by a pink haze in the eastern sky, which threw Primrose Hill into the dark, ominous silhouette. Lord Elston, Mr. Justin Blythe, and a pale young man who clutched a small black bag climbed out of the coach. These three conversed in controlled, clipped voices, but the two horsemen, who had dismounted, said nothing.

Bred though Dominic Blythe had been to revere and uphold the honourable code, he now found himself questioning its validity for the first time. He was about to exchange pistol shots with a man old enough to be his father, who had, in fact, been his own father's good friend. And a good friend to him as well, until last night.

When Sir Algernon, his face red with fury, had cornered him and flung an insupportable insult to his head, he'd believed his host had partaken too freely of champagne. It would have been within his rights to demand satisfaction, but instead he had apologised for whatever fault he had committed, all unwitting. The older gentleman, even more incensed, had called him a lying blackguard and had insisted that they meet at dawn to settle their differences. Dominic, knowing that a refusal would cast doubt upon his honour, which Sir Algernon had called into question, could do nothing else but accept the challenge. Whereupon he had left the soirée, never fearing that Justin and Damon would somehow mediate the bizarre, unprovoked quarrel. He returned to his house in Grosvenor Square, expecting that he would soon receive a letter of apology from the baronet, but the only note delivered into his hand came from Damon's pen, specifying the time and place of the meeting. Experienced in these matters, Dominic had resigned himself to the inevitable. He knew the chance for a reconciliation between two parties was directly proportionate to the length of time that elapsed between the challenge and the duel itself. This one would not be averted.

Now, as the morning breeze whipped at his hair, he cursed himself for attending that party. And he wished he were still in bed, asleep, and that this was truly the nightmare it seemed.

He watched Justin and Damon load the weapons and heard the metallic click-click as each one was cocked. The fearsome sound echoed in the silence of the new day. When Justin stepped forward to present the object, Dominic made his selection swiftly, fatalistically, submitting his chosen weapon to a cursory examination. The pistols were his own, and had belonged to his father.

"Damon is as perplexed about this as you and I," Justin said, his breath hanging visibly in the frigid morning air. "Sir Algernon has hardly spoken a word to him—and Damon is his second! His forcing this duel upon you makes no sense."

"No," Dominic agreed, "but he left me no choice but to meet his challenge. I hope to heaven he doesn't mean this to be a killing affair, for I should hate to die without knowing the cause."

"Oh, there's no possibility of that," Justin replied, a little too heartily. "Depend upon it, he knows he's in the wrong, but daren't cry off for fear of being thought craven."

The twelve paces were duly marked out by the seconds, and the principals took their positions. Dominic, standing stiffly at attention, reflected that only yesterday he would have described himself as the most fortunate of fellows. He possessed a respected name, a title, a large fortune, a prosperous estate, good friends, and a cosy little mistress who adored him. But at that moment all of those advantages were as worthless as the dirt beneath his boots. On a duelling ground, all men met as equals.

"Take your marks!" Damon called out sharply, and the men raised their weapons.

Dominic, knowing that to fire into the air would be a confession of guilt, pointed the barrel of his pistol slightly to the left of the man who faced him.

"Fire!"

He heard the simultaneous, ear-splitting reports, then a sickening hiss when a bullet flew past his ear, coming so close that he felt the heat of it. The smell of singed powder filled his nostrils, and he knew he would relive that moment in his dreams for the remainder of his days. He was so surprised to find him-

self on his feet for a moment he failed to realise
that his antagonist had fallen, but as the clouds of grey
smoke dissipated, he saw Sir Algernon seated on the
grass, holding a balled-up handkerchief against his
right thigh.

"Your father taught you to shoot better than that,
boy," the baronet grunted when Dominic joined the
others kneeling beside him.

"Yours taught you a damned sight too well," Dominic retorted grimly, fingering the cheek that might
have been shattered a moment ago. "I swear I saw my
life pass before me."

Lord Elston turned to the whey-faced surgeon hovering nearby and snapped, "Come here, damn you,
and take a look."

As the young doctor fumbled with the clasp on his
leather bag, his hand shook so badly that Justin Blythe
asked in a rallying tone, "What, Master Sawbones, is
this your first duel?"

To everyone's astonishment, the man nodded, and
in a chilling dumb-show, he held his case open wide.
It contained nothing more than a bandage or two, and
a single probe. "Medical student," he choked.

"Damn you, Damon," Dominic thundered, "why
didn't you engage an experienced surgeon?"

His friend's blue eyes blazed back at him. "How the
devil was I to know the difference? He *told* me he was
fully qualified." Wasting no more time on words, Lord
Elston shrugged out of his fashionable, tight-fitting
coat and fashioned a makeshift pillow, which he placed
beneath Sir Algernon's head.

Dominic, eyeing the charred rent in the baronet's
breeches, asked the nervous medical man if the ball
could be extracted, and received a helpless look in
reply. "Then we must return to town as quickly as
possible. I trust he can sustain the journey?"

The medical student swallowed convulsively, his

prominent Adam's apple rising and falling. "Not if the artery was hit," he said in a voice of doom. "But if that were the case, he'd be nearly dead by now."

Dominic gave a snort of disgust.

As the young man bound his leg, Sir Algernon closed his eyes and murmured, "Best see to your safety, Nick, before the authorities hear about this."

"Nonsense, sir. You've got a scratch, nothing more, so how could I be in any danger?" he replied, with a certainty that was far from genuine.

The baronet squinted up at him. "I suspected she had a lover. Married her anyway, the more fool I, never guessing that you—Charles's son—would be the one to serve me such a trick." His face contorted in a spasm of pain that was as much mental as physical.

"Is *that* what this was all about?" Dominic asked in amazement. "Why didn't you say so? I swear, upon the honour you were so quick to doubt, that I never betrayed you. Why, you had only to ask Lady Titus, and you could have believed her denial."

"I dared not confront her—didn't want to hear lies, and couldn't bear to hear her say it was true."

Justin Blythe, his face filled with outrage, said staunchly, "Well, it's *not!* And anyone who said otherwise told you a base lie!"

"Base—yes, he is that indeed, if he knew of your innocence, Nick," the wounded man muttered cryptically. Looking up, he smiled and said, "This position is not only uncomfortable, but most undignified for someone of my advanced age. I'll thank you to get me home, lads."

The baron and the marquis made a chair of their crossed arms, and shifted Sir Algernon to the waiting coach. The drive to London was accomplished swiftly, and the baronet spoke only once, to ask Dominic, also riding in the carriage, if he knew any prayers. " 'I am the resurrection and the life, saith the Lord—' How goes the rest of it?''

'' 'And whosoever liveth and believeth in me shall never die,' '' Dominic recited woodenly.

''You should've been a parson,'' the older man said. ''Just now I rather wish I were a surgeon,'' he replied, and he was relieved when his friend gave a weak chuckle.

Immediately upon their arrival in Clifford Street, Sir Algernon was borne upstairs to his bed, to await the arrival of his personal physician. This gentleman answered the summons promptly, and Dominic, Justin, and Lord Elston remained on the premises to learn his opinion of the patient's condition. An hour passed with no word from the sickroom, and their optimism began to wane.

When Lady Titus herself entered the saloon, her face streaked with tears, it vanished altogether. Moving as stiffly as an old woman, she walked up to Dominic.

''*Why* did the doctor insist upon his being bled,'' she asked desperately, ''when he had lost so much blood already?'' Georgiana continued to gaze up at him, her eyes wide and blank with shock, and he sought in vain for something to say, some word of comfort—of apology. ''At least he did not die thinking that we—you and I—'' He put his arms around her, and she wept upon his shoulder, murmuring self-recriminations, all of which indicated that her husband's suspicions about her infidelity had not been unfounded. Dominic, conscious of the presence of Justin and Lord Elston, asked no questions, although he was curious about the identity of her lover.

It was his duty to prepare her for what lay ahead. Leading her to the sofa, he said gently, ''You must steel yourself for the ordeal of an inquest, Georgiana. There were witnesses to the duel, and they will be called in to give evidence. We cannot hope to hush up the truth of how Sir Algernon received his wound.''

''I think he was more concerned for your welfare than his own,'' she whispered, dabbing at her streaming eyes with her handkerchief. ''He was so very careful to say nothing that might incriminate you. But you are not to blame—it was the doctor who killed him, Nick. The ball had to be extracted, but Algy ought never to have been bled—but for that, he would be alive still, and laughing with us now.''

Georgiana and Dominic, united by a shared grief and guilt, clasped hands, and silence fell in the very room where, only hours before, the whole tragedy had been set in motion.

2

IT WAS MIDNIGHT when Dominic reached St. Albans, some twenty miles to the north of London. Over the long, barren stretches of road he had spurred Lord Elston's horse as though the devil followed him, but he'd been careful to pass through villages at a leisurely, sedate pace to avoid attracting notice. Dead tired from lack of sleep and hours in the saddle, he cared not how this endless day ended, so long as it ended soon.

From force of habit he stopped at the White Hart, one of the several posting inns in the town. "You'll have no luck here, your honour," the ostler called out to him, "and none at the Woolpack, nor the Peahen either. 'Tis fair-day tomorrow, and not a bed to be had anywhere I know of."

"No matter," Dominic replied, "I merely require stabling for my horse." He dismounted and slung his saddlebags across his shoulder. Addressing the ostler once more, he said, "I hope your barn is not as full as your inn."

The fellow gave him a gap-toothed grin. "Nay, we've accommodation aplenty for beasts. 'Twill cost you five shillings."

Dominic handed over the requested sum with a curt reminder to rub the horse down properly. "One of Lord Elston's grooms will collect him tomorrow or the next day," he said before leaving the inn yard on foot.

Most of the houses on Holywell Hill were dark and silent, so he was surprised to see a light shining in an upstairs window of the one he sought. The maidservant who answered his knock gasped to find him on the doorstep, but he merely said, "Is your mistress yet awake?"

"Oh, aye." The girl continued to stare at him.

"Will you fetch her?"

But this lady, having heard the slight commotion, was already coming down the stairs, clad in her dressing gown. When the servant stepped aside to reveal the late-night visitor, she hurried down the last few steps and said briskly, "Find the decanter, Molly, and then go up and ready the spare bedchamber. Don't stand there gaping, now, but be quick about your business!"

As the girl scurried off, Dominic smiled fondly down at the diminutive, decisive mistress of the house. "What presumption, Cat Durham! I haven't yet asked you if I might spend the night."

"I should hope you know it isn't necessary for you to ask," she answered. "Come and sit down, my lord. You look ready to drop." Her hasty, all-encompassing glance at his pale, unshaven face took in the volumes of trouble writ there, and when she took the dark cloak from him, she noted the wealth of road dust upon it.

Dominic followed the lady into the parlour, and while she was busy lighting candles and stirring up the fire, he collapsed into an armchair, his every muscle throbbing with fatigue. When she asked if he had ridden all the way from London, he looked up at her curiously, blankly. He closed his eyes a moment to clear them, then rasped, "I had to. I fought a duel yesterday morning. Only yesterday?" he wondered aloud.

"Dear heaven," the lady whispered.

"Fortune did not favour my opponent. Nor me, though I still live."

Only a flutter of Cat Durham's eyelashes betrayed her distress over this chilling announcement. With seemingly unruffled composure she went to take the tray from Molly and reiterated her earlier command about preparing a room for his lordship. When the girl was gone, Cat poured out the wine and asked Dominic if he desired any food.

"Thank you, no." He accepted the glass she held out to him and leaned his head against the back of the chair. "It was Sir Algernon Titus who called me out," he told her. "We met at Chalk Farm, at dawn. But I never meant to kill him."

"Of course you didn't." Cat sat down, folding her hands in her lap. "And you needn't say another word about it if you'd rather not."

"I *must* talk of it, or go mad. He meant to kill me and missed—I wanted to miss him but didn't. I aimed well to the right of him, I'm sure of it, but the damned pistol threw left and I wounded him in the leg. Dear God, Cat, how he bled." He set his glass down and placed his black head between his hands.

"Why would Sir Algernon want to kill you?"

"Someone, I know not who, told him I was Georgiana's lover. I have no enemy, none that I know of, and I can't think why someone would wish to blacken my name. Unless it was the guilty party himself, seeking to put Algy off the scent. Or out of the way," he added grimly. "I daresay I'll never know the truth of it." He paused for another swallow of wine, then went on with his tale. "The attending surgeon was no surgeon at all, and Algy's physician was no better."

"But if *you* did not kill him," Cat said softly, "why should you have to flee?"

"Because there was an inquest this morning, and the damned medical man—the one who witnessed the duel—gave his evidence. It must have been damning indeed, for the jury returned a verdict of murder, Cat— willful murder!''

"But a score of duels are fought every year, some of them fatal, and the whole world looks the other way,'' she protested. "Mr. Best was never prosecuted after his affair with poor Lord Camelford, and even though Captain Macnamara was tried for killing Colonel Montgomery, he was acquitted. Why should your case be any different?''

"I don't know,'' he said. "But Damon took the precaution of hurrying me into hiding, and I spent the night at my cousin's rooms near Lincoln's Inn. Well before noon today the street-criers were shouting the inquest verdict for the whole world to hear. After sundown I left Justin's lodging house by a back way, and Damon, plucky lad, let me have one of his best horses and accompanied me to the edge of town. I trust he'll get some sort of message to Ellen. I felt rather like Charles the Second, begging him to look after her. 'Let not poor Nelly starve.' '' Dominic's mouth twisted. "That sort of gallantry seems to run in our family. My father said much the same thing to me, before he died. About you.''

He was silenced by the thought that he might never see Ellen Cleary again. It was impossible not to think of her in the presence of the lady seated across from him, for all his mistresses had been chosen for their resemblance to Cat Durham—small, cuddly women, with dark hair and good sense and impeccable manners. Ellen, formerly a milliner's apprentice, was a merry, bright-eyed little thing, who had proved surprisingly loyal in the face of numerous rival propositions. He'd set her up in a modest house just off Picadilly, where he visited her regularly whenever he was in town. She'd have no difficulty finding a new protector, for if she wasn't exactly a beauty, she possessed qualities that were far more lasting, and which would serve her much better in the years ahead.

''However did you escape London undetected?'' Cat wanted to know. ''The keepers must have been on the watch at the Hyde Park gate, and beyond.''

''It was the easiest thing in the world. My dear Cat, don't you know that Baron Blythe is 'a great rich fellow what drives about in a shiny coach with a crest on the door'? I heard him described to me in those very words.'' He ran his hand across a cheek shadowed with stubble and gave her a crooked grin. ''Tonight, at each of the five toll gates between London and here, not a one of the keepers recognised his lordship. Would you have done?''

''No, and I certainly don't now,'' said Cat, smiling faintly. ''In the morning I'll have to send Molly out to acquire a razor for you, and I hope she and I can manage to brush that coat into a semblance of its former self. But for now, if you will pardon my saying so, you ought to go up to bed, my lord.''

Dominic, more than willing to heed this practical suggestion, made his way to the chamber allotted to him. A nightshirt had been laid out—he supposed it had belonged to his father, whose portrait stared down at him from the wall. Hoping it was merely a trick of the light that was responsible for that uncharacteristically stern expression in the painted eyes, he shed his clothes, slid the crisp shirt over his head, and climbed into bed. It had been forever since he'd slept. The night before the duel he had been wakeful, his nerves on edge, and last night had been even worse. But weary though he was, he still found it difficult to drop off to sleep, for whenever he closed his eyes, he saw the painful visions that had lingered in his mind for so many desperate hours: Sir Algernon lying on the grass, Justin's worried eyes, Damon's frown of concern, Georgiana's tear-streaked face. To banish these shades, Dominic stared up at the tester above his head, tried to conjure up Ellen Cleary's image, but it was even more elusive than slumber.

He woke several hours later, feeling somewhat refreshed. Upon discovering that his garments had been spirited away in the night, he covered himself with the dressing gown left in their place. The girl Molly brought him some shaving water and a shiny new razor, along with the news that her mistress had left the house on an errand. Then she hurried downstairs to fetch his breakfast, which came in the welcome form of sausages, fresh buns, and strong coffee. His long sleep, more or less restful, and the comfort of hot food combined to raise his spirits. As he ate, he wondered if perhaps his flight from London had been premature.

But when he said as much to his hostess upon her return, she was violently opposed to his plan to return to town. "You *can't* go back! Why, you might be taken up and put into prison!" Cat cried, her tiny hands fluttering in agitation. "It would be folly- only wait till I tell you what I've heard this morning."

Guessing a great deal from her face, so puckered with worry, he heaved a sigh. "It's hardly likely that pleasant news would have travelled so swiftly. What is being said?"

"That Lord Blythe will be sought by the law officers in a case of willful murder," Cat reported, holding out a folded newssheet. "I had this from the White Hart, a traveller up from London left it behind yesterday."

Dominic glanced at the column indicated by her trembling finger, which told him—and anyone else who chose to read it—the results of the inquest into the death of Sir Algernon Titus. It was a shock to see his own name in print, and to read of his alleged connexion with a vile crime of passion, as the duel was described. He laid the paper aside with a sinking heart,

but he said with tolerable unconcern, ''If these printers mean to whip the public into a frenzy by sensa-
tionalising what has happened, I suppose I must
remain here indefinitely.''

Cat shook her head in protest. ''That would be just
as dangerous as returning to town. Not that I wouldn't
be most happy to keep you,'' she faltered when he
turned surprised eyes upon her. ''But St. Albans lies
directly on the London Road, so you'd hardly be safe
for very long. Why, the landlord at the inn told me
Bow Street Runners may be on the case already, and
I daresay they'll be watching for you at the ports as
well.''

''If I must be wary of both land and sea, where can
I go?''

''To Ireland.''

''Ireland?'' he said incredulously.

''Consider for a moment—you require no passport
to get there, yet you'd be well beyond the reach of the
London authorities. You may take my valise, and
Molly has already gone to purchase some shirts for
you. Now do listen carefully, Nick, for if you but—''

Suddenly she broke off, flushing, and said in a subdued voice, ''Your pardon, my lord.''

He reached for one of her plump hands and squeezed
it. ''Don't be a goose, Cat. Hearing you call me Nick
makes me feel a youth again.'' Her eyes darted towards the portrait of the first Baron Blythe, and he
asked softly, ''Haven't been pining for him, have you?
He wouldn't approve of that, you know.''

Cat crossed to the window to draw back the curtains. ''Not pining,'' she said, ''though I still miss
him, and always shall. In London, during those first
months without him, I was quite miserable. But last
winter, after I came to St. Albans, I managed to find
a sort of peace. I pass for a respectable widow, you

see, and not a soul would ever guess quiet Mrs. Durham was once a nobleman's fancy-piece.''

Dominic regarded her bowed head, dappled with sunlight, and saw that the dark, neat chignon was beginning to show streaks of grey. It had been a dozen years since his father had introduced him to Cat, when she had been thirty, his present age. Now she was all of two-and-forty, and suddenly he felt even older than that.

''I have a favour to ask of you,'' he said, and she looked around. ''Before I went into hiding, I did as Damon suggested and withdrew a substantial sum from my bank. I have it with me now, in large notes, and I want to leave—'' he thought for a moment. ''—a thousand pounds with you.''

Her eyes flashed as she said, ''Your father provided for me, and I lack nothing.''

Laughing, Dominic shook his head at her. ''Pull in your claws, dear Cat, the money isn't for you. But I do want you to put it with your own bankers against the time I have need of it. Will you?'' After she nodded, he returned to the subject of his impending journey. ''Now tell me, where do I pick up the Irish Road?''

''At Northampton. It's a busy enough place, so nobody will much notice a plain-dressed man. How will you travel?''

''It will be wiser, to say nothing of more comfortable, to go to Holyhead by post-chaise, and in slow stages. The longer I take to reach the port, the more relaxed the watches will be by the time I arrive there. It shouldn't be too difficult to engage a private fishing vessel to carry me across the channel to Ireland.''

When this and other details of his trip had been settled, Cat told Dominic she would be sorry to see him go, although she knew he must, and soon. ''When will you depart?''

"That depends entirely upon you, my dear Mrs. Durham," his lordship declared, "for until you return my breeches to me, I can go no farther than this room!"

Worried as she was, Cat was not immune to the charm of his smile, and she gave him one in exchange before rushing out of the room to do his bidding.

Dominic shifted on the hard, wooden seat, wincing as his stiffened muscles protested. He had chosen this bench not from a desire to torture his aching body any further, but because it commanded a view of the main road connecting Northampton to London. Thus far he had recognised none of the private carriages passing by, nor had he heard any report of Bow Street Runners in the neighborhood. Still, it was troubling, the fact that the only chaise available for hire was damaged, but not, he hoped, beyond repair. Even now the wheelwright was busy with what he trusted were the finishing touches to the rim.

Fortunately for him the Angel was all but deserted, and thus far only two other persons had stopped there, a young couple in a gig. Although the lady wore a white veil pinned to her bonnet, they were not newlyweds, as Dominic had originally supposed, for they were now bidding each other farewell. All he could see of the young woman was her slim, straight back, but he could hear her pleasant voice; it was neither shrinking nor shrill, the two things he most deplored in females. And his ear caught the warm undercurrent of humour when she told her friend, "You leave me in good hands, John, for Papa always used to say Mr. Gudgeon keeps the best cellar in Northampton. Now do not make such a disapproving face—I give you my word that I won't set foot in the taproom, or talk to strangers, or do anything shocking. I shall behave like a *proper young* lady."

Her companion threw back his head and laughed out loud. "Now *that* I should like to see!" He turned to climb the gig, but the lady placed a hand on his arm to stay him.

"Wait, John." Dominic saw her reach into her reticule, from which she extracted a banknote. "It's ten pounds," he heard her say, "and I wish it were ten times that. Will you send it to Lucy for me? She's at her mother's house, in Chelsea—Andrew can give you the precise direction." She bowed her head, and Dominic leaned forward, listening even more intently. "Samuel grows so fast now that he's rising two, and I must do what I can to keep him in dresses. I daresay he is too young to miss me much, but that's cold comfort."

"There now," the young man said, "did you not tell me, but a little while ago, that everything has happened for the best?" He clasped her hand, then took his place in the gig. As she looked up at him, the lace veil rippled and danced on the breeze. "Have a safe journey, my dear, and may God be with you."

The young woman stood in the yard, watching until he was gone, and as soon as she turned towards the inn, she reached up to adjust her veil. In the instant before that lacy curtain fell, Dominic received a brief, tantalising glimpse of her face, and climbed to his feet in polite acknowledgement of a female presence. She gave him a perfunctory nod in return as she swept past him to enter the building.

He concluded that she must be a married lady who had been unfaithful to her husband, and the child she'd mentioned had to be the result of her indiscretions. No doubt her spouse was unwilling to accept it as his, so she had been obliged to place little Samuel in the care of another woman, the Lucy who lived in Chelsea. Thinking over all he had observed and overheard, Dominic doubted that the fair-haired young man was her lover; he had seen nothing of illicit passion in their exchange, but friendship and brotherly concern.

The lady's sorrow over the separation from her young son haunted him. Ironic, he thought, as darkness fell upon the inn yard, that her shame was bringing a new life into the world, while his had been contributing to the loss of a life. He felt a strange bond with her, his fellow traveller on the road of adversity, for she was apparently as much a victim of cruel fate as he was.

At last the wheelwright put aside his tools, and a bow-legged ostler stumped towards the stables to ready the horses. Dominic, still curious about the lady, called him over and asked if he knew her. ''Aye,'' the man replied, bobbing his head, ''I've seen her often. Her father, the Captain, did abide over to Olney-way. So fond of her he was, she being his only chick. Miss was going to be wed next month, but from the looks of things, summat went awry.'' The ostler's mouth twisted to one side as he surmised, '' 'Tis likely she shied off at the thought of the widow Hudgins as her mother-in-law. That one has a face could curdle new milk.''

A single lady, Dominic sighed to himself, drawing his cloak around him to ward off the chill, and yet she was a mother. Had her shameful past driven her from her home? If so, she, too, was an outcast—hard enough for a man to bear, but for a woman even worse.

As Dominic considered her plight, his sympathy for her increased.

''I'm sorry, miss,'' the proprietor of the Angel told the young woman when she expressed her wish to hire a post-chaise for her journey to Staffordshire. ''I've but one on the premises, with a broken wheel, and 'tis spoken for already. And though I'm expecting another back from Daventry, there's no saying when it will arrive. Or in what condition,'' he concluded gloomily.

Mr. Gudgeon, who so proudly advertised his neat carriages, fast horses, and experienced postilions, disliked turning people away, but owing to a sudden and unexpected demand, his coach house was nearly empty.

Unwelcome as these tidings were to her, the lady in the blue pelisse accepted them stoically. "So be it," she said. "I will not take my custom elsewhere—my father would turn in his grave, he was that loyal to the Angel. I'll await the chaise from Daventry and hope for the best."

He ushered her into a private parlour, where a cheerful coal fire leaped and crackled in the grate. Pulling off her gloves, Nerissa warmed her hands, and the rest of her; her pelisse was more fashionable than serviceable, and the drive in the open gig had chilled her to the bone. When she asked the landlord if he could recommend an inn at Lutterworth, where she expected to pass the night, he gave a favourable account of the Denbigh Arms there. "And where might you be bound, Miss Newby?" he asked.

"For a village called Leek, in Staffordshire. I daresay you've never heard of it."

Mr. Gudgeon showed every sign of being hurt by her lack of faith. "I fancy I knows most towns along the great roads, miss, being as how my postboys always return with some sad tale: a wheel come off at Ashborn, the traces broke at Towcester." He shook his head dolefully.

Nerissa's laugh was muffled by her veil, and she said gaily, "I hope you receive no such dire report of my journey!"

The landlord made no reply, being distracted by the presence of the ostler, who stood in the hall. "What is it, Ned?" he asked impatiently.

"Begging your pardon, sir," said the man, "but I've come to deliver a message from the gentleman outside. He bid me tell you he's giving up the chaise to the miss—says he'll stop here for the night and take up his journey to Ireland on the morrow."

It was the best of all outcomes for Mr. Gudgeon: Miss Newby, whose late parent had been a valued customer, would not suffer a delay, and he had acquired a paying guest, who would need a bed, a meal or two, and plenty of drink before continuing on his way.

Nerissa, who had heard this exchange, instantly forgot her promise to John Hudgins about not speaking to strangers. "How very kind, to be sure. Ned, will you ask the gentleman to come in? I'd like to thank him."

Her veil distorted her vision, but when her benefactor entered the parlour a few minutes later, she could see he was tall and well-formed, with dark hair. He carried a triangular cocked hat, many years out of the mode, and wore a long black cloak flecked with mud and road dust.

"You are most generous, sir," she said, going to meet him, "but I'm sorry to be the cause of so much inconvenience to you."

"A good night's sleep is hardly an inconvenience, ma'am, and that is what I gain by letting you take the chaise."

His hoarseness instantly roused Nerissa's compassion. He was ill, and she was depriving him of the only available conveyance. "Perhaps I can repay your kindness in kind," she said, as the thought came to her. "Ned mentioned that you are bound for Ireland, and Lutterworth, where I will stop the night, lies on the Irish Road. It appears that we are travelling in the same direction, so we might as well share the chaise, don't you agree?"

"You are asking me to accompany you?" he asked, surprise making his still voice more uneven.

Nerissa had acted impulsively, and, she now feared,

unwisely. Mortified, she murmured, "I've shocked you."

"Not at all," he said politely.

"Well, I've rather shocked myself," she confessed, "but it would be foolish—and selfish—to be constrained by convention when I may be of some assistance to you."

The gentleman's face, so pale and strained, relaxed in a smile. "During our journey to Lutterworth, I'll strive not to give you any cause to regret your magnanimity," he said, thereby making plain his acceptance of her invitation.

AS THE CHAISE rolled out of the inn yard and into the night, Nerissa wondered if she had not made a grave mistake in so recklessly suggesting that the gentleman travel with her. She had thrust herself into a situation fraught with impropriety, and now she sat in a dark-ened carriage bound for an unknown town on an un-familiar road, a stranger at her side—and a male one at that—and she had no one to blame for it but herself. But for twenty-three years impulse had been an in-grained habit, so that her father had often teased her about her fatal tendency to tumble headlong into trouble. Except that lately the troubles had not been very amusing ones, and at the present moment they lay heavy on her heart and mind.

It had been a long time since she had covered any distance greater than that between London and Olney, and never before had she gone anywhere by herself. But after the indignity and disgrace she had suffered in recent weeks, she doubted that travelling without a chaperone could further damage her reputation. At least, Nerissa told herself, she could take comfort from the fact that her travelling companion knew nothing about her other than her destination, and that she was paying a visit to a friend from her boarding school days.

Initially their discourse consisted of each enquiring whether the other was tolerably comfortable. He ex-

hibited the sort of quiet good manners that would have
soothed her alarms, had she been of a nervous disposition. Inevitably an awkward silence fell, with every
sign of becoming a lasting one. Frantically, Nerissa
searched her mind for some unexceptionable remark
that would serve to inaugurate a dialogue between
them. Before she could utter a syllable, the gentleman
said quietly, in that curiously rough-edged voice, "You
needn't be afraid of me."

Her head swerved in his direction. "I'm not."

"Yet you keep your face concealed." He sighed, as
though disappointed. "I do understand, however, if
our paths should ever cross again, you wouldn't want
me to recognise you as the lady I escorted to Lutterworth in a closed carriage at night."

Behind her veil, Nerissa smiled. "No, I certainly
would not."

"Do not feel you must tell me your name," he went
on, "for your safety is ensured by your anonymity. As
is mine," he added grimly, under his breath.

She suspected him of jesting with her, perhaps to
put her at ease, so she asked merrily, "Are you in such
grave danger, then?"

"If you only knew . . . the tales of my exploits
might alarm even so intrepid a lady as you appear to
be," he replied in a lighter tone.

"Now I don't know what to believe, for a moment
ago you said I need not fear you," she reminded him.

"Well, I've only recently become a reformed character."

Laughing softly, Nerissa made a slight adjustment
to the lap robe. At that moment the wheels met with
an uneven patch of the road, and both passengers
reached up to take hold of the leather straps provided
for just such an occurrence. Although Nerissa gripped
hers tightly, she couldn't avoid jostling the gentleman.
"I'm sorry," she murmured, blushing in the darkness.

Once they were past the rough spot, he said, ``I'd forgotten how tiresome night travel can be.''

Although Nerissa agreed with him, she ventured the opinion that daytime travel was not much different. ``For even if the postilions can see the ruts in their path, they don't always manage to circumvent them.''

They fell into an easy discussion of the many perils of travel. The gentleman described a particularly wild drive from Bath to London, attended by such mishaps as a drunken coachman, a broken wheel, and a tumble into the road. When he reached the end of his tale, he laughed, which made him look much younger, and even more handsome. Nerissa regretted that it was so dark inside the coach, and her vision was so impaired by her veil.

He offered no explanation whatever for his journey to Ireland. She assumed that he had property there, or family. Or, she thought, eyeing the old-fashioned cocked hat that lay on the seat between them, he might have suffered financial reverses and could be escaping his creditors. His dark cloak and the doeskin riding breeches were well-made, although somewhat the worse for travel stains. And the black boots, though sadly dulled by dust, were the most expensive kind. She knew, because her father had owned just such a pair.

The memory of that similarly tall, dark gentleman was always with her; his loss was an unhealed slash upon her heart. As a child, she had been accustomed to his extended but temporary absences, and yet as a grown woman she was quite unable to accept the permanence of his death. She had never admitted to her intrepid parent that old fear from her childhood, that he might not return from one of his voyages. That he could die of a fever in the prime of his life, in a sick-room with a doctor in attendance, had seemed such a remote possibility that she had never even considered it. She missed his hearty embrace and lively discourse, spiced with tales of the exotic places where he had traded—Madras and Calcutta, China and the islands of the West Indies. But most of all she missed the way his eyes, the same deep blue as her own, had filled with pride whenever they had gazed at her.

People had frequently commented upon how closely she resembled him. But one of Nerissa's treasures was a miniature portrait of her mother, a beauty from the island of Jersey, which showed quite plainly the origins of her milky complexion and the reddish tints in her unruly chestnut mane. Still, her papa's legacies were the more obvious ones: the indigo eyes and slanting dark brows, the humourous curve of her lips, and her low, rich laugh. The beauty mark hovering near her mouth came from neither parent and it was entirely her own.

Six months had passed since Captain Richard Newby had been laid to rest in Olney churchyard, beside his wife and sister. Not long ago Nerissa had believed herself incapable of straying very far from that grassy, well-tended grave, or the fields she and her papa had roamed. He had left her in Olney, and there she had intended to remain, almost as if he might return to her, and her reluctance to uproot herself had been so strong that she had not discouraged Andrew Hudgins when he'd hinted that he hoped to marry her when the prescribed period of her strictest mourning ran its course. But her hopes for a happy future at his side, one that would be ordered and ordinary, had been shattered by the gossip linking her to little Samuel. Less than a month after her father's demise, when the people of Olney had begun to whisper about her relationship to the baseborn child, she'd believed the talk would die down in time. Unchecked, it had spread like some evil, destructive disease, touching and tainting everyone connected with her, especially poor Andrew.

Nerissa hadn't lacked a safe haven from the tempest that had forced her from her home. Her mother's family, the de Tourzels, still lived on that remote isle so uncomfortably close to the Continent. But they were complete strangers, only names to her, so in the end she had struck them off her list. Her father's cousin, a wealthy and powerful duke, was someone she knew very well indeed, quite well enough to know what would happen if she should seek shelter in his elegant mansion in Mayfair. She would be obliged to submit to a tediously formal introduction to society, at her relation's expense; even worse, everyone would expect her to apologise for her father's mercantile interests and activities, and that she could never do. There were times, and this was one of them, when the comfort and commiseration of a friend would be preferable to any kindness from a relative, however well meaning. And she had therefore dispatched a letter to Laura Sedgewick, *née* Greene, announcing her impending visit.

As the chaise lumbered on towards she knew not what, Nerissa began to feel the first faint stirrings of optimism. She was strong and healthy, she had money enough, and she was leaving her past and her troubles farther behind with every milepost she passed.

The yard of the many-gabled Denbigh Arms in Lutterworth, the inn so highly recommended by Mr. Gudgeon of the Angel, was cluttered with coaches, ostlers, and postboys, which seemed to prove its popularity with travellers along the Holyhead Road. As the gentleman handed her out of the carriage, Nerissa prayed it had rooms enough to accommodate two more.

When her companion turned away to supervise the removal of their baggage from the rear of the vehicle, she pondered how best to raise the sensitive subject of who should pay the posting charges. The notion of being beholden to a stranger was abhorrent to her, yet she hesitated to press money upon him for fear of offending him. His single, battered valise more than hinted that he could be short of cash.

Her uncertainty must have been apparent to him, because he said firmly, "You may go inside, ma'am. I shall settle with the postboy."

"Might we not share the expense?" She received no reply, for he was staring beyond her, and his expression of grave concern made her glance over her shoulder. The object of his scrutiny was a short, burly man in a frieze coat who stood in the side-yard talking to one of the ostlers. His accent and mode of speech, barely audible to her, proclaimed him a resident of one of London's less refined boroughs.

The gentleman grasped Nerissa's wrist, and said, in a wild, rough whisper, "I need your help. A matter of life or death—my life, or my death!"

His urgency startled her, but her response was immediate. "Yes, of course, what shall I do?"

"Keep your veil lowered, and remain silent, no matter what I might say," he instructed. "I swear no harm will come to you."

He flung one arm around her waist, and she stifled the sharp protest that rose instinctively to her lips. He hurried to the door, and the moment they crossed the threshold, he began shouting for the landlord at the top of his voice. This was puzzling; a moment before he'd been so anxious to avoid attracting notice. The common room was filled with men, all staring curiously at the noisy intruder, and Nerissa was thankful her face was still hidden by the veil.

A neatly dressed man stepped forward. "How may I be of service to you, sir?" he asked.

With a harsh laugh, the gentleman tightened his hold on Nerissa and said, "Is it not obvious? Show us to a bedchamber, man, and let it be your best!"

The landlord hesitated before replying, ''I've but one room left, by no means my finest.''

''Twill suffice—so long as it has a bed.''

Although Nerissa was willing to lend him the assistance he required, she felt this was going too far. But he had told her to keep quiet, so she indicated her objection by tugging upon his sleeve.

''So impatient, sweetheart?'' he cried, grinning down at her. ''But soon we'll be alone, and you'll have me all to yourself!''

An expression of distaste crossed the landlord's face and he said stiffly, ''Follow me, sir, if it please you.''

Nerissa's companion let him precede them up the narrow staircase, and when the man's back was turned, he whispered in her ear, ''Good girl! Don't fail me now, I beg you.'' He pretended to stumble on the stairs, recovering just in time to prevent a fall, and smiled sheepishly up at the landlord. ''I fear I've had an overabundance of spirits this night. But how could one avoid it, with such a lovely bride to toast?'' He pinched Nerissa's waist, and she let out a horrified gasp.

''My felicitations, sir,'' said the landlord at his most wooden, from the upper landing. With a nod in Nerissa's direction he added, ''And madam.''

He ushered the amorous bridegroom and his veiled wife into the one available chamber, which was dominated by an enormous fourposter. It's other furnishings included a gate-legged table flanked by Windsor chairs and another pair of armchairs on opposite sides of the fireplace. Two servants carried the baggage into the room, and their master stirred the fire. He inquired politely whether Madam desired the maid's services.

''I can send Nan up to you, if you wish.''

Nerissa, who caught the trace of pity in his tone, had never needed it more. ''Thank you, no, but I could fancy some supper,'' she announced in a shrinking voice that she hardly recognised as belonging to herself.

To her great surprise and relief, her escort endorsed this request. "An excellent notion, my love. We will dine. My good man, pray send up a bottle of your best vintage at once." He tossed his cape onto the bed, and the landlord bowed himself out of the room.

Nerissa removed her bonnet and veil while the gentleman crossed to the window and drew the curtains. "I *do* hope," she said with what she hoped was withering disdain, "you mean to tell me why we are playing this ridiculous May-game."

Dominic turned around, but his intended reply was a thing forgotten.

She was much younger than he had originally supposed, for the composure she had displayed throughout the journey had led him to estimate her age at something nearer his own. Her charming countenance, now clearly visible for the first time, caught him unawares. The lady's hair was a rich mahogany in colour, and she was gazing back at him with the largest, bluest eyes he'd ever seen, and she had a pair of full, rosy lips accentuated by a tiny black mole as dramatic and alluring as a courtesan's beauty patch. He understood perfectly why she'd been so careful to keep her face covered; having once seen it, no man could forget it.

"I'm not mad," he told her, never guessing that his bemused expression might encourage her to think otherwise. "Indeed, I am in grave danger."

"Who was that man outside?" she demanded. "Do you know him?"

"Not exactly. I've never seen him before, but he must know me. I will have been described to him." She was, he noted, taller than the average for her sex, and in addition to possessing a wanton's face, she had a superb figure, lithe and lush. Belatedly recalling her question, he said, "The man is a Bow Street Runner."

''Good heavens,'' she breathed and her eyes grew even larger, a thing he had not believed possible.

Drawing a chair forward, he indicated she should sit, which she did as swiftly as if her legs had suddenly given way. ''We haven't much time to speak in private, I'm afraid, for they'll be bringing our dinner soon. I'm glad you thought of food—I'm hungry as the devil.''

''I, too. But, sir, we cannot continue in this charade—''

''My name is Nick,'' he proceeded as though she hadn't spoken, ''and because I cannot be forever calling you 'sweetheart' and 'my love' and so on, may I know yours?''

''Nerissa Newby. But, sir—''

''Forgive my boorishness on the staircase just now, Miss Newby, but you can understand why it was necessary. While we are alone together, I will refrain from crudities of that kind.''

''You cannot expect to go on any further with this— this *hoax*,'' she persisted, with ill-concealed impatience.

''But I must,'' he said evenly. ''The moment we arrived here you became indispensable to me, for I am safe only as long as the Runner believes me to be an overeager bridegroom. Until he is gone, which may not be till morning, I have no intention of leaving this room—at least, not for any considerable period of time.''

She gripped her hands together tightly, and her reply emerged as a nervous whisper. ''You must know I will be ruined if I spend the night here with you.''

''And I may die if you do not.'' Dominic added more gently, ''All I'm asking is your permission to sleep on the floor. I will not otherwise impose upon you, on my word of honour.''

''But there must be other inns in the town, other

towns on this road," she said desperately, not yet giving up her attempt to dissuade him.

"I prefer to remain beneath the same roof as the Runner, for to travel ahead of him would be to risk his catching up with me. I had much rather keep my eye on him for the present, and try to discover where he is bound."

Nerissa bounded up from her seat. "What have you done that he should be chasing after you?" Perhaps, she thought desperately, she had reason to be more frightened than she actually was.

A sharp knock sounded upon the door, and the gentleman took a single, swift step towards her. "I will tell you everything by and by."

Nerissa had divined the purpose of his advance, but she was not quick enough to evade him. His arms imprisoned her, and had he not held her so tightly, she believed she would have fallen to the floor from the shock of it. Firm, insistent lips smothered her startled gasp, and she was further alarmed to discover that his kiss sparked something more than outrage in her breast.

Suddenly, without warning, her captor released her. Vaguely aware that another person had entered the room, Nerissa looked towards the door, blushing furiously.

A pimply serving boy righted his tray just in time to prevent the full decanter and a pair of glasses from tipping to the floor. He deposited his burden on the table and mumbled, "Master says tell you dinner'll be brought in half an hour, sir."

Nerissa was grateful for his ill-concealed grin, because as soon as she recognised the humour of the situation, her fears about it subsided.

When she and the man she knew only as Nick were alone again, he poured the wine. "To a successful deception," he said, raising his glass.

Still somewhat ruffled by what had just transpired, she said tartly, ''I wish you will not take my compliance for granted, sir—it's bad enough that you broke your word to me only seconds after giving it.'' He looked back at her curiously and she reminded him, ''You promised not to impose yourself upon me, and if that display just now was not an imposition, then I don't know what is.''

''It won't happen again. I understand your concerns, but—''

''Do you indeed?'' she flared. ''How *can* you, when I don't even know myself whether I'm on the point of being murdered, molested, or robbed by you, Mr.—Mr. whatever-your-name!''

''Oh, I'm not so fearsome as all that. Nor is it my habit to prey upon defenceless females, so you are quite safe from attack, Miss Newby. Besides, not even the most *ruthless* criminal would risk an outcry with a Bow Street Runner so near.''

''You don't look like a criminal,'' she admitted, ''although you've already proved that you are rather more than ruthless.''

The ghost of a smile flickered across his pale face. ''True, but I mean no harm, neither to your person nor your property.''

''That's all very well,'' she retorted, ''but you've already destroyed something less tangible, but no less valuable—my reputation.''

''My dear girl, you aren't acquainted with a single soul in this inn, and no one but ourselves will ever know what does—or does not occur—in this room.'' Pausing, Dominic ran one hand through his black hair, then asked, ''Do you truly believe the reputation of a lady is of greater value than the *life* of a gentleman?''

Nerissa, finding no answer to that question, sat down before the fire and submitted her wine glass to a close inspection.

"Yesterday, I fought a duel near London," he said, his voice flat, devoid of all expression. "You already know I am sought by the authorities, so you can guess the outcome."

She looked up. "You killed a man?"

"That point is open to dispute," he sighed. "Still, however you look at it, I am responsible for his death. But what makes it so much harder for me is that he was my friend."

It was a dreadful burden, and Nerissa, who had been so absorbed by her own problems that she hadn't even guessed his might be worse, suddenly felt ashamed.

"Miss Newby," he continued, "if you were as concerned about your reputation as you make out, you'd have a chaperone, or at the very least, a maidservant at your side."

The fire dancing in the grate was nothing compared to the sudden flame in Nerissa's cheek. She had to accept that it was useless to prose on about her good name, for her own words and actions had given him no reason to believe her. At some cost to her pride, she acknowledged, "You are perfectly correct, I have no respectability to sacrifice on your behalf. I am not a proper young woman, I never was. Or could be," she added softly, staring down at the fire. "And that is why I, too, am a fugitive. Neither am I a stranger to scandal, for we are old friends, indeed."

This time when he approached her, she didn't back away. After hours of sitting beside him in the carriage, and now that he had kissed her, his nearness was familiar to her, even comforting. She looked up at him without fear. His eyes, she noted, were grey, and the white skin surrounding them was etched with faint lines of weariness.

"Neither are you and I strangers, Nerissa," he said, and the husky, whisper-like words sent a shiver along her spine. "Despite the fact that we've been acquainted only a few hours, and though I know nothing about you but your name. I don't seek to uncover your secrets, and you already know the worst of mine. By revealing it, I have placed my very life in your hands. Can you guess why I did?"

She continued to gaze mutely back at him, and he explained, "My every instinct tells me that I can trust you. Twice tonight your generosity of spirit has outweighed your concern for the finer points of convention. Otherwise you would not have offered me a place in the chaise, nor would you have accompanied me to this room. Be generous with me again, and I swear by all I hold dear that you will not suffer for it."

His voice was curiously rough and smooth all at once, and so very persuasive. A strong current of communion surged through Nerissa, for she could accept the truth of his assertion that they were alike. If he was a strange creature, well, then, so was she. And what he said was quite true, no one in the world would ever know of this night's adventure. That being so, what danger could there be in it?

Even before she gave him her answer, he said softly, "I thank you, Miss Newby, with all my heart."

His uncanny ability to trace her thoughts even as they began to take shape in her mind confused and disturbed her, just as he did when, with infinite tenderness, he reached down to brush a stray lock of hair from her brow.

4

FULLY COMMITTED TO helping the gentleman, Nerissa abandoned her chair and knelt down before the small sea chest that still bore her father's initials in brass. "If I am to pass as your wife," she said over her shoulder, "I think I had better put on my mother's wedding band." She lifted the lid and took out the ivory box containing her valuables: a pearl necklet, a garnet set, and several rings.

When he asked if he might look at the box, she gave it to him, and he turned it this way and that, examining the intricate carving. "Very pretty," he said, returning it to her.

"Don't you mean to have a look inside?" she quizzed him.

"Thievery is not my crime, I told you that. Is it Chinese?"

"Yes. Papa had a habit of purchasing pretty trifles for me on his voyages—bits of ivory and jade from China, and sandalwood from India. He was captain of a merchant ship," she explained.

Dominic offered to refill her glass, but Nerissa declined, lest an excess of wine make her lose her reserve entirely. Not knowing what else to do with herself, she continued to unpack, a flush decorating her cheek as she removed such items of apparel as a bedgown and a lace-edged nightcap. She wished she could match her companion's easy acceptance of this unusual situation, but he was a man, she thought resentfully, and therefore could have no notion of how his very presence might discomfit a female.

She was arranging her silver-backed brush and mirror on the mantel when she heard footsteps in the passage.

"That will be our dinner," he said.

And so it was. This time the serving boy was accompanied by an older waiter, and after the two had opened up the gate-legged table, they proceeded to lay out a modest repast. The sight and aroma of roast duckling was most welcome; suddenly Nerissa was very hungry. She took the chair opposite her bridegroom-for-a-night, smiling at him in a spirit of camaraderie, and he smiled back. The lad snickered audibly and received a sharp rebuke from his superior. Throughout the ensuing meal, conversation was general, in part because of the presence of the servants, but also from Nerissa's fear that she might inadvertently slip out of her role.

When the covers were removed, the waiter placed a bottle of port on the table and asked if the gentleman required anything more. "Why, yes," he replied, "you may send my compliments to all the gentlemen in the taproom, and bid them enjoy a round at my expense."

The youth's eyes bulged upon hearing this, and his comrade said respectfully, "Aye, your worship."

Then the bridegroom pressed a handsome gratuity upon each of the servers, and the boy was emboldened to announce, "To be sure, sir, it's a famous night for the Denbigh Arms. There's a Bow Street Runner below, wishful of stopping the night here. It's my belief he's on a case, though he will not say outright."

"Cease your chatter, lad," the waiter warned him sharply. "New-wedded folk care naught for Runners."

"Oh, but we do." Dominic smiled at Nerissa, who nearly choked on her wine. "So, my love," he said brightly, "our wedding night will be memorable in at least one respect—we have the honour of sleeping at the same inn as a Bow Street Runner! My good man, let him have as many bottles as he pleases this night, and tell the tapster to add his charges to my reckoning."

The two servers exited, and when the cheerful sound of their laughter faded along the passage, Nerissa discovered that her own merry mood had vanished with them. Now that she was once more alone with the man named Nick, she felt as nervous as any true bride. Perched uncertainly on the edge of her chair, she fidgeted with a bowl of nuts and sweetmeats, picking out the almonds, and avoided his eye. She wondered what she would do if he tried to force himself upon her during the night. Would the servants, believing her to be his lawful wife, respond to her cries for help?

She wished she could believe he was no threat to her, but whenever she let herself remember the intensity of his kiss, and her own mad desire to respond, she was troubled. She conjured up the image of her mild, gentle suitor, who had never given her cause for alarm. How shocked Andrew would be if he ever knew she had spent a night with a stranger—and when she heard the stranger laugh softly, she realised she had spoken her thought aloud.

"You mustn't mention another fellow's name on your wedding night," he jested. "It will make your husband jealous. Is Andrew the unhappy swain you left behind, the one with a dragon of a mother?"

Nerissa's head jerked up. "Was Gudgeon gossiping about me this afternoon?"

"Not he. I had that tidbit from the ostler."

"Well," she said matter-of-factly, "I had several reasons for terminating my engagement to Mr. Hudgins, and his mother was but one of them. If I ever *do* marry, I think it will have to be to a gentleman who has no mother. Or sisters," she added darkly, remembering how spiteful the four Hudgins girls had sometimes been.

"We are well matched, you and I," he said with mock gravity. "Apart from an aunt I seldom see, I am quite unencumbered by female relations. As we are on the subject of family, how does it happen that yours permits you to jaunter about the country alone?"

"I haven't any family," she answered bluntly. "Which is why I must depend upon my friend to give me a home, for the present. She is wed to a solicitor, a very fine man, and they have three children."

When her lovely face clouded over, Dominic supposed she must be thinking about another child—her own little Samuel. By way of a diversion, he said, "Have you always lived in Olney?"

"Only for the past two years, and during my childhood. I was at school for a time, and then with Papa in his house in the Adelphi Terrace. He liked to live as near to the water as he could, so we had a fine view of the Thames, but I was never partial to the situation—the stench at low tide!" She wrinkled her nose expressively.

Dominic, aware that the Adelphi was no longer inhabited by persons of fashion, was now able to make an informed guess as to Miss Newby's precise social standing. She had more than hinted that her father had been involved in trade, which meant she sprang from merchant stock. Her origins must be respectable, but no more than that, and given the strict code of morality of the middle class, her relations had probably cast her off when she had gotten herself into trouble.

It was yet too early for bed. Remembering Cat Durham's insistence that an occasional game of patience would relieve the tedium of his lonely nights at remote, wayside inns, he asked Nerissa if she liked to play cards.

"Have you some?"

"I do." He went to fetch the pack Cat had put in his valise, and returned to the table. "Piquet is my preference. Shall I teach you?"

"My papa did so years ago," Nerissa replied. "But if you think me a pigeon ripe for plucking, you are much mistaken, sir. I have no intention of gaming away my funds."

"It's not your money I want, but a much higher stake." Dominic shuffled the pack expertly, leaving her to wonder at his meaning. When he had finished dealing the cards, he looked up to say, "I covet one of the feather pillows from your bed—the floor is cold and hard, you know!"

She joined in his laughter, and a moment later the contest began.

Although Nerissa's was the more comfortable accommodation that night, she was the wakeful one. Lying in the vast fourposter, listening to the deep breathing of the gentleman who reclined on a makeshift bed of blankets—and a pillow—she knew that he'd had no difficulty dropping off to sleep. She had to smile, remembering her fear that he might try to slip under her covers and have his way with her. He was too weary to attempt her seduction, and knowing what she now did about his recent history, she could understand it.

But she had also seen his face in that moment when she had revealed her face to him. His reaction hadn't surprised her, nor had it pleased her. Instead, it had reminded her that nearly all of her present sorrows could be traced to the one thing about herself that was beyond remedy or change—her appearance.

Even as a child she had been aware of being different. Not due to any excess of beauty, not in those days, but from what she had deemed a hopeless lack of it. As a result, she had developed an early rapport with adults; unlike her chief playmates, Ruth and Judith Hudgins, they didn't ridicule her too-large eyes, disfiguring black mole, and thick, unruly hair. Her greatest friend was her father, who fondly referred to her as his little gypsy girl, and she had dearly loved her Aunt Portia.

The gentle spinster, following her brother's instructions, had placed her spirited, precocious charge in a seminary for gentlemen's daughters. Happily incarcerated at her school, content with her lessons and her new friends, Nerissa quickly outgrew her self-consciousness. The uneventful years flew by, and one day she looked up from her books long enough to discover that many of her contemporaries were suffering the agonies of puppy fat and spots and crooked teeth. Miraculously, she was passing through adolescence unscathed. That dread sense of being different came rushing back, only this time, she was surprised to find that the difference was to her advantage. In her thirteenth year she was considered one of the two prettiest girls in her form, an honour that had followed with regularity during the succeeding terms. She found an ally and a friend in the other beauty, Laura Greene, an ethereal blonde. The two girls admired each other fervently; that they were also perfect foils physically did not occur to them until several years later. Nerissa, so tall and dark and wild, was a splendid contrast to Laura, who was small and fair and ladylike.

At about the time his daughter emerged from the schoolroom, Captain Newby abandoned the high seas and settled in London to manage his business affairs. Nerissa, suitably chaperoned by her aunt, met the many gentlemen who made up her father's curious and varied collection of friends: seamen and scholars, lords and lawyers, poets and priests. His reputation as an excellent host and raconteur, coupled with her provocative beauty, lured many a male visitor to the handsome house in the Adelphi Terrace.

Nerissa's figure, which had matured early and fully enough to make her the envy of her schoolmates, began to attract scrutiny of another kind. As a girl she had deplored her long legs, thinking them coltish, but as a young woman she learned to like the way they enabled her to keep up with a gentleman's stride. Her rippling chestnut hair would, if coaxed, hold a curl to perfection, and even the beauty mark, previously the bane of her existence, turned out to be an asset. She was not vain of her looks, merely conscious of them, like any handsome animal that knows itself to be remarkable and is frequently pointed out as such. This awareness showed in her gait, in the proud tilt of her dark head, and in the perceptive glint in her blue eyes.

In her father's drawing-room she met with startled, admiring glances; on the streets of London, she was the recipient of sly, sidewise stares. And it wasn't long before Miss Portia Newby began making noises about the necessity of presenting Nerissa to society in the proper fashion. Their cousin, the Duke of Solway, might lend his assistance—the happy fact that the heir to the dukedom was very near her niece's age had occurred to the good lady. But before any of her grandiose schemes for Nerissa's advancement could be put into action, she suffered a fatal heart spasm. Within the year, her brother the captain was also dead.

Nerissa, valiantly striving to shift her thoughts from the unhappy events of the past, rearranged her covers and turned on her side. Eventually she slept, fitfully but dreamlessly.

In the morning, she was roused by a knock upon the door. Lifting her head from her pillow, she discovered that the gentleman was gone, but his valise still stood in the corner and his coat hung from a peg on the wall. The insistent rap sounded once more, and although she would have preferred to tell the intruder to go away, she mumbled, ''Come in.''

It was a chambermaid, an ugly, gawking girl who bobbed an execrable curtsey, spilling a little of the water from the brass pitcher she carried. Nerissa watched her pour the rest of it into the washbasin, and the wispy curls of steam rose from the bowl so invitingly that she thrust the covers aside. ''Where is Mr.— where is my husband?'' she asked.

''Bein' shaved,'' the girl replied. ''Should I iron somethin' out while you're washin'?''

This was not necessary, for Nerissa had packed her trunks carefully, guarding her garments against creases with paper. She changed into a fawn-coloured muslin gown, and when she sat down at the table and held up her silver-backed hand mirror, she decided that the snowy ruffle at her throat lent her an appropriately matronly appearance.

''Let me arrange your hair for you, ma'am,'' the girl offered.

It was soon evident to Nerissa that her eager hand-maid had little experience in the art of hairdressing. She suffered the pulling and tugging of her tresses without a murmur, but when the brush hit her temple for the second time, she thanked the girl with more politeness than was warranted, saying, ''You may fetch the bottle of scent I left on the washstand.''

Even this simple task was too much for the clumsy maid. She dropped the delicate crystal vial, shattering it and spilling the contents on the floor. Nerissa, barely keeping a rein on her impatience, bade her clean up the shards of glass. When this was accomplished, she said dismissively, ''Thank you, that will be all,'' and the red-faced servant girl fled, nearly colliding with the gentleman.

He was clad in shirt, waistcoat, and breeches, with his cravat neatly tied and his cuffs buttoned. "Good morning, Madam Wife." He sniffed the air, now oppressively scented with roses. "A heady perfume."

"And an expensive one," she said mournfully. "Now I shall have to make do with lavender water." As she pinned the final coil of hair into place, she asked if it was safe for him to be wandering about the inn.

"Oh, the Bow Street Runner is long gone," he said, shrugging into his coat. "I was a joyful witness to his departure, and the moment he was out of the way, I made the arrangements for our journey to Leek."

Startled, she asked, "What do you mean, *our* journey?"

"I'm escorting you there, of course." Nerissa opened her mouth to protest, but he forestalled her, saying, "Now let's not begin this day as we ended the last one, with a catalogue of objections. The landlord tells me that Leek is on the road to Holyhead and as I happen to be bound for Ireland, your destination lies directly in my path."

Nerissa, sadly out of temper after her restless night and the annoyances of the morning, said sharply, "Is this offer prompted by chivalry—or convenience?"

"Both," he answered imperturbably. "I did hope I might continue to pose as your bridegroom for the distance of sixty or seventy miles."

Although she frowned, it was not in response to what he had said. "You've a cut on your cheek," she told him, and handed him her mirror.

"So I have," he agreed. "I'm afraid the barber who attended me is not the most skilled I've ever encountered." After she had recounted the whole of her experience with the hapless chambermaid, he smiled at her and said, "Poor Miss Newby, no wonder you're out of sorts! Now tell me, may I accompany you for the remainder of your journey?"

"Only if you will tell me your surname," she said spiritedly, "for you still have the advantage of me in that respect."

"It is Blythe." Dominic's trust in her was such that he would have admitted the existence of his title as well, had he not been afraid of endangering her. If the Runner did succeed in tracing him, his lovely accomplice would be placed in a precarious position; only by leaving her in ignorance of his exact identity could he ensure her safety. So he invented an alias for himself, albeit one that was founded upon truth, and rechristened himself when he announced, "I am Nick Blythe, Esquire."

The chaise into which he duly handed his supposed bride was not so new as the one Mr. Gudgeon of the Angel had provided, but it was no less comfortable. The postboy was a stunted, stupid fellow, but apparently he understood his passengers' desire to make short work of their journey; he spurred his horses indefatigably along the miles of open road, past fields and towns and the occasional manufactory. As the day wore on, Nick grew more and more optimistic about his chances of eluding the authorities.

Nerissa Newby, whom Providence had placed in his hands, was an entertaining companion, and easily entertained; his gratitude warmed into genuine liking. He encouraged her to talk about herself, and by careful questioning he was able to learn something of her history—her early years with her aunt in Olney, her days at school, and her later life in London. Knowing the shame of her past as he already did, he could see that her fall from grace had been inevitable, even inescapable. He sympathised with her, for with that sea-dog of a father, and no mother to guide and rear her properly, how could she have avoided being the prey of some unscrupulous gentleman? And what a tempting piece she was altogether, with her provocative face and that voluptuous figure. Sitting so near to her, in such a confined space, he was inclined to regret that a man of honour must not trifle with a damsel in distress, however beautiful and available and unprotected.

Although she never once alluded to her disgrace, or her baby son, everything she said confirmed his belief that these were responsible for her rift with her Mr. Hudgins. The more he knew of her, the more he believed she had confessed the truth to her fiance, only to be rewarded for her honesty by repudiation and banishment. Nick supposed he would never discover exactly what had happened in Olney, and it was not something he could ask; he had to respect her reserve as she respected his.

The late Captain Newby had taught his daughter far more than the surprising proficiency at piquet she had displayed the previous night. She was knowledgeable about current political events and was particularly well versed in the various naval campaigns of recent years. But as much as he enjoyed her lively style of conversation, such heavy topics as politics and war grew burdensome after a while.

She must have felt the same, because at one point she said, "Mr. Blythe, last night you bested me in a game of skill. I wonder if you are brave enough to put sheer luck to the test, and join in a game of travelling piquet?"

Nick hadn't played since his childhood, so he prevailed upon her to refresh his memory. With painstaking care she explained the various point values, and when she was done he observed that since it was such a blustery day, he placed no dependence on seeing a person riding a grey horse, or an old woman under a hedge.

"Craven," she murmured.

"Yet a few miles back I saw a gig carrying a man and a woman and a child, so that nets me forty points at the start."

"Unfair! We hadn't yet begun to play," she protested. "The game will commence as soon as we reach the next mile-post."

For the next two hours they kept their noses pressed to their respective windows, each crying out with delight when some meaningful object came into view. They had no paper and pencil and thus had to add their scores in their heads; the sport was enlivened by disputes over the accuracy of the total.

"Three hundred and sixty-five," Nerissa announced, when at last they called a halt.

"Two hundred ninety-seven," was Nick's grudging admission. "How came you to do so well at the last? I demand a strict account, ma'am, and a refusal will confirm my belief that I've been cheated."

"Sixteen flocks of sheep at twenty points, two flocks of geese at ten, nine men on horseback for a total of eighteen points, and seven persons walking along the road at one point apiece. That's the tally and I stand by it."

"Are you quite certain about the sixteen flocks of sheep?"

"I am," she stated firmly. "There's an advantage to sitting on this side of the carriage, you know. Being on the traffic side, you will have seen more post-chaises and horsemen."

"Six chaises, eleven men on horseback. Perhaps we should continue," he said hopefully, but the lady shook her head.

"You must accept your defeat, Mr. Blythe, for I've won fair and square. And I only wish we'd set a very high stake before we began playing."

"Never mind, I'll pay for your dinner," he declared handsomely.

She gave him a saucy smile. "You would have done anyway—I'm your wife, remember?"

It was much colder now than when they had started the journey, and at the next posting-house they descended from the chaise to await the change of horses indoors. Nerissa drank a cup of tea by the fireplace and Nick stood at the window, warming his insides with brandy, when he saw their postboy stump out of the stable on his short bowed legs, his creased face set in ominous lines. Excusing himself, Nick went out to consult with the man.

"Is there a problem?" she asked when he rejoined her.

"With the harness," he replied. "One of the metal links has snapped—the one that holds the breeching strap to the collar. But happily there's an ironmonger in the village, and the postboy has gone to fetch him. We may as well dine here, for I should think it will be some time before the repair is completed."

He was amused when his companion vented her frustration by kicking out at the fender like an impatient child. "Oh, of *all* the misfortunes!" she cried. "I've never undertaken a journey so fraught with difficulties at every turn!"

"If you consider this a difficult journey, then you haven't travelled very much," said Nick, and after delivering this friendly scold, he went to order their dinner.

That night, much later than either of them expected, the weary travellers reached the Staffordshire town of Leek. Nerissa accepted the fact that she would have to put up at an inn for the night; it was a most unsuitable hour for descending upon even the closest of friends. As she told Nick Blythe, a household with three young children would have retired many hours ago, and he agreed that it was very likely.

"If only that stupid man hadn't taken so long with the harness," she fumed. "What a miserable little village that was! We never did learn the name of it, did we? So much time lost—but I suppose it's useless to cavil over that now."

"It is," Nick agreed.

She sighed. "Just as well that I don't go to Laura's house, for I'm in no fit company after such a day as we've had." Looking over at him, she smiled and said, "You are very patient with me, Mr. Blythe. Forgive me for being so tiresome."

"I expect a glass of wine, a warm fire, and a good night's rest will set you to rights." He reached for her hand, saying, "Only think how far we have travelled together in these twenty-four hours, a journey I will always measure in friendship more than mere miles."

The carriage began to slow down. Nerissa was saddened to think that soon they would part and go their separate ways, never to meet again. She would be safe and secure in the midst of a loving family, while he journeyed on alone towards the port at Holyhead. His crossing to Ireland might be a treacherous one; the autumn gales in the Irish Channel were notoriously fierce. And when he did reach the opposite shore, he would enter into a lonely, solitary exile. Whatever his crime, he did not deserve so dismal a fate.

During the course of the long day, she had come to loathe the sight of any roadside establishment, but the George at Leek was far pleasanter than many they'd visited. A plump, efficient landlady conducted her to an upstairs room and made her perfectly comfortable there. A little while later, a maidservant delivered a verbal message from Mr. Blythe, who invited her to join him in his private parlour. Nerissa declined, pleading weariness, a convenient excuse as well as being a true one. Now that she'd resumed the style of a single lady, she was reluctant to arouse comment by doing anything unusual—she had learned that lesson all too well. But she spent the hour or so before going to bed regretting her decision, and hoping he hadn't felt slighted by her refusal.

The next morning she took pains with her toilette, for although she knew Laura would rejoice to see her even if her clothes were undistinguished and her coiffure less than fashionable, she well remembered her friend's elegance. While she washed and dressed, she was aware of the bustle of the inn. Doors opened and closed, and she could hear the frantic footsteps of the servants in the passage and the stamping of hooves beneath her window. It seemed that everyone was departing all at once.

Fearful that Nick Blythe might be of their number, she speedily finished her preparations and hurried downstairs. She found him in a small private parlour, reading a newspaper. At her entrance he laid it aside and came forward to greet her, looking much as he had when she'd first met him—deeply troubled.

"Good morning, Miss Newby," he said gravely. "I was on the point of sending a message to you."

Had he planned to depart without bidding her a personal farewell, after all she'd done for him? "I came down to—to say good-bye," she faltered, "before you leave."

"I will certainly not do so before I've broken my fast. And definitely not until I've seen you safely settled with your friends."

Vastly relieved, Nerissa sat down in the chair he pulled out for her. Soon a waiter brought them hot rolls and steaming coffee, and she readily partook of both. Mr. Blythe picked up his paper, and Nerissa knew better than to disturb him; her father had been no fit companion until he had gleaned every scrap of war news from his favourite journal. She didn't mind his abstraction, which permitted her to observe him closely without his being aware. The dark coat looked all the better for a good brushing, and his ebony locks had been coaxed into neat waves. He looked every inch the gentleman, and she would not be the least bit ashamed to introduce him to the Sedgewicks.

When he folded up his newspaper, his face was still grim, and she asked if he had been reading the war dispatches. "No," he replied, "it was the London news that caught my eye." From the way he had said this, she surmised that it hadn't pleased him very much.

They received directions to Mr. Sedgewick's house from their waiter, and within an hour they set out. After passing a spacious marketplace, they turned down a broad street banked by uniform brick houses and stopped at one situated midway down the row. Mr. Blythe beat a tattoo with the brass knocker, and he smiled at her as they waited.

An enormously fat woman opened the door to them. Her scowling face was composed of bulges of flesh in the place of cheeks, chin, mouth, and jowls. "What is it?" she asked, in less than welcoming accents.

"I am Miss Newby," Nerissa announced. "Mrs. Sedgewick is expecting me."

The woman's expression became more hostile. "Are you sure?" When Nerissa nodded, she heaved an exasperated, alcohol-flavoured sigh. "Oh, very well, I suppose you'd best come in, then, but the mistress made no mention of visitors to me!" This omission was clearly a sore point.

Nerissa cast an uncertain glance at Mr. Blythe before accepting the woman's curt invitation.

The house was deathly silent. Where, she wondered, was the happy laughter of the children, and the scampering of their small feet up and down the stairs? And search though she might, she could find nothing of Laura's quiet dignity in the decoration of the drawing-room to which she and the gentleman were led—and where they were abandoned. The burgundy damask that covered the walls and the chairs was too dark, and the arrangement of the several pictures was neither artful nor pleasing. She had a wealth of time to ponder these inconsistencies before another female arrived on the scene.

This one was as angular as the other had been rotund, and her voice was a near-whisper when she said, "You wished to see me?"

Nerissa, now completely bewildered, barely refrained from staring. "There must be some mistake— I asked for Mrs. Sedgewick. I wrote to tell her I was coming here."

"I *am* Mrs. Sedgewick, and I've had no letters this week. Who are you?"

A swift glance at Mr. Blythe's impassive face bolstered Nerissa's courage. "I am so sorry, we must have intruded upon you in error. Foolish of me not to guess there might be more than one Sedgewick family in Stockwell Street! Can you tell me if Mr. Henry Sedgewick, the lawyer, is one of your neighbours? The lady I am seeking is his wife."

All of a sudden the woman's bony face was transformed into a mask of fury. "You have indeed come here in error if you expected to find *that* hussy under my roof!" she declared with considerable heat. "Who are you? One of madam's fancy London friends, I'll be bound." Her pale eyes darted towards the gentleman, and she spat, "It's just like that wretched Laura to run off without informing me that she was expecting company!"

"Do you mean to say that she does live here?" Nerissa asked.

"Not for a fortnight past," was the venomous reply. "She's gone now. With her abigail, the children, Nurse—*and* my Henry. My only, my dearest boy! She lured him away, the spiteful thing, from the very mother that bore him!"

When Mrs. Sedgewick, senior, dropped into a chair and gave way to sobs, Nerissa's only desire was to beat a hasty retreat. She waited for the woman's means to subside before saying, "I regret causing you any further distress, ma'am, but could you possibly tell me where Laura went?"

"I don't know, nor do I care! My Henry had no reason to leave Leek—he had respectable clients, his business here was prospering. But she took it into her head that he could do better for himself—in London, I daresay. I don't know what she said to convince him, and I can only guess how she must have maligned me. To be sure," Mrs. Sedgewick said bitterly, "*some* people consider her a beauty, but I never saw it myself. My servants didn't suit her fine notions, and when Henry accused poor Mrs. Grant of cheating me in the household accounts she took his part, the sly thing. Spent too much time in the nursery, too, and so I told her, again and again."

"Perhaps, but—"

"And my poor Henry, to be taken in by those quiet ways of hers. Well, still waters run deep, and I don't doubt she's been hatching her plot to wrest him away from me since the moment he slipped the ring on her finger. She was always jealous of me!"

Nerissa did not doubt that Mr. Sedgewick had voluntarily moved his family to London, for no son, however loving, could be expected to live comfortably with a mother like this. Her long-held vision of the Sedgewick's domestic bliss was shattered, and she wondered how Laura could have shared a home with such an ill-tempered woman and yet give no hint of any household strife in her letters.

She was exceedingly grateful to Mr. Blythe for stepping forward to extricate her from this hopeless situation. "We will be putting up at the George for the present," he told the weeping lady. "If you should receive any communication from your son—or his wife—within the next day or so, Miss Newby would like to be informed of their direction."

Mrs. Sedgewick's only response was to hide her face in her handkerchief.

A few minutes later, dazed and despondent, Nerissa found herself standing in the middle of Stockwell Street. "I can't begin to think what I'm supposed to do with myself now," she said.

It was, she realised, the first time she had admitted defeat. Throughout her father's illness and after his death, she had found the strength to go on, knowing he would expect her to be brave. Somehow she had survived the ordeal of being the favourite subject of gossip in Olney, and she'd had the courage to break her engagement to Andrew Hudgins. And throughout the strange events of the past two days she had displayed what she considered to be a remarkable degree of fortitude. But all along she'd been sustained by hope and the certainty that at the end of the road she would find a respite from the troubles that had plagued her of late. Now it turned out that the safe, happy refuge she had sought did not exist, and her one friend was lost to her.

Turning to her only possible source of consolation and comfort, she confessed, "I've never felt so completely alone in all my life."

"You didn't fail me in my hour of need," the gentleman reminded her. "Don't despair, my dear, for you are not without a friend. Did no one ever tell you that good deeds sometimes come home to roost?''

When he held out his arm to her, she placed her trembling hand upon it, and let him lead her down the street.

5

WHEN THEY RETURNED to the George, Nick parted from Nerissa in the vestibule, with the promise that they would meet again at dinner. She nodded absently, gave him a lopsided smile, and made her graceful way towards the staircase. As soon as he heard the faint opening and closing of her chamber door, he left the inn.

The skies were ominously grey and the wind on the rise. He walked aimlessly along the busy streets populated by strangers, occasionally pausing to look into a shop window. The parish church, Leek's most notable landmark, crowned a piece of high ground, and he strolled in that direction. He climbed to the summit, from which vantage point he was able to count the brick smokestacks belonging to the various local manufactories, a grim contrast to the gentle hills beyond the town. For some minutes he gazed upon the miniature world spread out before him, marvelling that its ceaseless rhythm was unaltered and quite unaffected by the small tragedies in the lives of the individuals inhabiting it.

The churchyard was graced by a sandstone monument, a pyramid engraved with curious images. After a brief, disinterested examination, Nick sat down upon its base and leaned his back against the solid surface. The wind was merciless, but he hardly felt it; the constant, dull ache in his heart effectively blotted out the sensation.

His perusal of the *London Gazette* had made it pain-fully clear that he was still an object of notoriety. Col-umn after column had been chock-full of details—all false—of his purported *affaire* with Lady Titus. Public outcry against duelling was great, according to the pa-per, and he guessed that the less reputable printers of Grub Street were producing sensational and incendi-ary pamphlets, which would destroy any chance of a fair trial, should it ever come to that. All along, in the back of his mind, he had believed he could return to London at any time and clear his name of the murder charge. Recalling the disturbing accounts he'd read thus far, he knew that to make an attempt now would be sheer folly. Perhaps someday—but perhaps never, and it was better to accept what there was no chang-ing.

At least, he thought, trying to cheer himself, his possessions were protected. For the remainder of his life, no other person could lay claim to his title and fortune. However long he must remain in exile, his lawyers would continue to act on his behalf, and his steward, a trustworthy man, was well qualified to manage his Wiltshire estate. Moreover, because the property was not entailed, none of his family—and here he thought of his cousin Ramsey, who most needed the money—could profit from having him de-clared legally dead in the future. But in the event of his untimely demise, everything he owned would go to his nearest male relative, as specified in the only will he had ever made. It had been drawn up long ago, when his only assets had been his horses and his books and the legacy his mother had left him, and it had not been updated at the time of his father's death. There was no way to prevent his title from devolving upon Ramsey. But the thought of his cousin selfishly squandering the substantial Blythe rents on hunters and hounds angered him beyond reason. He'd always intended to name Justin the heir to his real property but had never quite got around to doing anything; this oversight tortured him, helpless as he was to remedy it.

Lifting his head, he stared out at the panorama of town and country intently, as if it held some answer to the questions tumbling about in his mind. The longer he looked, the more reluctant he was to leave England for Ireland, that alien land. And why should he? This journey from hamlet to village to marketplace had reminded him of that vast world beyond London, and as he gazed upon the distant hills, he wondered if hiding himself in some remote, rural corner of England would be preferable to seeking refuge across the channel. He had already created a new identity, and as Nick Blythe, Esquire, he ought to be able to build a whole new life for himself.

And who better to share it with him, he thought, smiling, than that lovely, lost creature back at the inn, who by her own admission had no home, no friends, and no relations to speak of?

He could not marry her, of course. Despite her many and manifold charms, he had no desire to be irrevocably bound to her. His family was a respected one; his pride in that ancient name and lineage would not permit him to take just any female to wife. Nerissa Newby was beautiful and well mannered, and she possessed a striking intellect, but he required something more in the way of pedigree. If she was indeed a product of the merchant class, which seemed to be the case, that in itself would be no real impediment to a union. But there was also the fact that she had borne a bastard child, and the future Lady Blythe could not carry so indelible a stain into matrimony. Someday his need for an heir would compel him to take a wife, for a son would be an undisputed claimant to his title and lands. That being so, it was unfortunate that his scruples prevented him from marrying Miss Newby, who was, if nothing else, a proven breeder.

That evening he dressed for dinner with as much care as if he were about to tender a genuine offer of matrimony. Before putting on one of the new shirts Cat had procured for him in St. Albans, he washed himself, energetically splashing soap and water from the basin, his mind still busy fashioning arguments that might induce Miss Newby to throw her lot in with his. If she had thought him mad when he begged her to shelter him in Lutterworth, he could just imagine how she would react to his proposal that they live together without benefit of clergy. She might not regard him as any great bargain, but certainly she was in no position to pick and choose when it came to protectors.

He elected to wear his kerseymere breeches rather than the travel-worn buckskins he had been sporting for so many days. After arranging the folds of his cravat with precision, he fastened it with a gold pin, a gift from his father. Surveying himself in a looking-glass smoky with age, he wondered if Miss Newby would be inclined to look upon him with favour.

When she joined him in his private parlour at the appointed hour, he saw that she, too, had taken some pains with her appearance. She wore a cambric gown the colour of fine burgundy, with a low, square neckline and long sleeves. He led her over to the table, its snowy cloth nearly obscured by an array of dishes and utensils, and told her, "I ordered several courses, and the first of them should arrive at any moment. Although I have much to say to you, I would prefer to wait in order that we may avoid any interruption."

She nodded her assent, and took her seat.

As he filled her glass with wine, he asked pleasantly, "How did you pass the afternoon?"

"Idly, I'm afraid. I kept to my bedchamber—with a young rogue named Tom Jones as my companion," she added with an impish smile.

"And did he entertain you well?"

"Certainly he put me in a rather more cheerful mood than my circumstances would seem to warrant." Nerissa picked up her napkin and placed it in her lap. "It's my misfortune that whoever occupied my room before me left behind only the first volume of Fielding's novel."

"You are fond of reading?" Nick asked.

"Very. I had free run of Papa's library from an early age. He always said that if I was able to reach a book, then I was old enough to be permitted to read it. So my Aunt Portia made sure to keep the most titillating forms of literature on the topmost shelf, and she placed all her housekeeping and cookery books well within my grasp!"

The waiter entered the room at that moment, and their conversation suffered his intrusion. The first course that was laid before them included a roast chicken smothered in wine sauce, a raised pie, and a hasty pudding. Nerissa sampled everything yet ate little, but Nick, as a result of the day's mental and physical exertions, applied himself to the task of polishing off his share of the meal. When the dishes were cleared away and the cloth removed, Nerissa took a few sugared almonds before retiring to the settee.

When Nick asked if she would mind if he smoked, the lady said promptly, "Not in the least. Papa always did so after dinner, and I quite like the smell of tobacco."

He selected a long-stemmed clay pipe from the case on the mantel and reached into his coat pocket for his tobacco pouch. He filled the bowl with the aromatic weed, tamped it down, then lit it with a spill. After summoning up all the persuasive speeches he had been memorising all afternoon, he sat down in an aimless chair across from the sofa. ''I've been trying to determine how I can best help you, Nerissa,'' he began.

''That must have been a singularly unrewarding pastime,'' she commented. ''But you may be easy, Mr. Blythe, for I assure you that I don't depend upon you to help me.''

''Perhaps not, but still I feel some responsibility towards you. I did place you in a position of danger—remember, I am yet a hunted man. The law is seeking me even as we sit here, cosy and safe in the wilds of Staffordshire.''

''Laura Sedgewick's untimely absence from Leek is hardly your fault,'' she persisted. ''I would have found myself at *point-non-plus* whether or not you had accompanied me to that house this morning. But you mustn't concern yourself—I daresay I shall simply go to London.''

Nick drew thoughtfully on his pipe, wondering if she would seek out her former lover, the father of her child. ''Do I perceive a certain reluctance to take that step?''

''I think we may deal in reality rather than perception, Mr. Blythe,'' she said crisply. ''The facts of my situation are very, very clear. For reasons that I shall not go into, I managed to scandalise my village to the extent that I was obliged to leave it. My reputation is shattered, perhaps irreparably. My friend is out of reach. And though I do have a little money of my own, it hardly matters, for in every other respect I am quite destitute.''

He was impressed by this speech, for she had managed to deliver it without investing a single syllable with self-pity. ''People are so fond of saying that money can't purchase happiness,'' he mused, ''but for a moment let's pretend that it could. I wonder what sort of life would most content you, Nerissa. Tell me, what would you ordain for yourself, if you were able?''

Softly she replied, ''I would want to live quietly, as I did in Olney. Although I should like to feel useful— I'd want some sense of purpose—I would require a reasonable measure of independence, for I've always had that. As for material things, well, I would be happy with a pleasant house and plenty of books, and per- haps a garden to work.''

The simplicity of her catalogue delighted Nick, for he instantly saw how he might use it to his advantage. ''But surely you would need a companion to share your Arcadia. I don't believe we humans are capable of be- ing completely happy in solitude. Hermits are very rare, Nerissa.''

A shadow passed over her face. ''But no power in the world can restore my father to me. I am destined always to be alone, for no one can ever take his place in my life. Andrew Hudgins would have been a sorry substitute, and I was far from being the proper woman for him—he wanted perfection in a wife, something Papa never expected from his daughter. His tolerance may well have been responsible for my downfall, but I cannot regret it. My mistake was imputing a similar tolerance to others of my acquaintance.''

Nick supposed this was the most she would ever tell him about her disgrace, even though she hadn't men tioned her child directly. It was apparent to him that the broad-minded Captain Newby had accepted the re- sult of his daughter's indiscretion, but her Mr. Hudg- ins had not. Now, bereft of father, fiance, and child, this brave, unbowed girl had left her home, intent upon making a fresh start, only to be thwarted at the outset.

''What is your age, Nerissa?'' he asked her.

''Twenty-three.''

''You are at once too young and yet too old to find

yourself so alone in the world." He lifted the pipe to his lips and inhaled deeply, expelling the smoke in rings. He watched them dissipate, then said, "You say you seek some peaceful retreat, but I fear you will never find it in London. I have lived there, and I know. Nor can you, as impulsive and strong-minded as you are, ever be happy living a highly restricted life with some paid companion to lend you a false respectability." He abandoned his chair, and after taking a turn about the room he told her abruptly, "I have changed my mind about going to Ireland. There will be a watch on at Holyhead port, and the constabulary on the other side of the channel may have been alerted by now."

Remembering his determination to be frank, he gave her a slight smile and said ruefully, "The fact of the matter is, I simply don't *wish* to leave England, any more than you want to go to London."

Her fathomless blue eyes stared back at him. "But what will you do?"

"I've decided to continue travelling north, as far as the Scottish border. I've funds enough to set up as a gentleman farmer in some remote area where no one can connect me with my crime. And," he concluded, his heart already pounding in anticipation of her reply, "I want you to go with me."

For the space of several seconds, she hardly seemed to breathe. Finally, after a startled intake of air she echoed faintly, "Go with you? In—in what capacity?"

"As my companion in adversity."

He was encouraged by the smile that played at the corners of her generous mouth. "That is certainly a vague reply," she said.

"I'm asking you to live with me," he elaborated. "I cannot hold out false promises merely to soothe your sensibilities, so I tell you quite frankly that ours would be a sham marriage. But in the eyes of the world you would be my wife, and for the sake of convention,

I would expect you to take my name." He read the shock in her face and strove for a soothing note when he said, "I don't demand an immediate answer. You must take the time to consider very carefully, for I am content to wait, if I improve my chances by so doing." Satisfied that he had been as forthright as he vowed to be, he walked over to the fireplace to empty the ash from his pipe and deposited it on the mantelshelf.

While his back was turned he heard her say, "Mr. Blythe, I want to be quite sure that I understand the terms of this—this partnership you are proposing. You offer me your protection and your name, in return for which I am to keep your house and cook your meals?"

Nick shook his head. "No, no, I certainly don't demand that you become a household drudge! You will be the wife of a gentleman, we will have servants—as many as you like. If you want to raise hens or dirty your hands in the rosebeds, it will be your decision, not by my command."

"But we hardly know each other."

"Time will soon remedy that." Despite this assurance, she frowned slightly, so he said, "Do not mistrust my motives; for I don't think I've ever given you cause to do so. I don't require that you become my mistress, Nerissa."

Privately, however, he had his hopes. From the very beginning of their association he had been conscious of her opulent beauty, and tonight her lavish figure was revealed to his eyes as never before. She might be wary of him now, but she was no virginal miss. She had already sampled the pleasures of love, and he could not doubt that she had found them to her liking. He would not force her to his bed, but neither did he believe it would remain empty for very long. But more than anything he wanted her to feel comfortable with him, and in order to settle any lingering concerns he added, "I seek your friendship and your companionship, Nerissa. In whatever fashion they come to me, I will be satisfied."

She did not answer immediately. Finally she said, "I appreciate your candour, for I value it above anything. Except tolerance," she amended.

"I am tolerant, too," he said silkily, "and generous. And patient and kind and anything else you most admire in men." The sudden blaze of reproach in her eyes chastened him, and he said, "Forgive me, I know you won't be won over by tricks and stratagems. Nor will I try to convince you with unceasing argument. If you cannot come with me willingly, then it is best you do not come at all."

The lady's thick, dark lashes swept downward. After a brief study of the carpet, she looked up and said, "I promise I will think on all you've said—I daresay I shall think of nothing else. But for now, if you will be so good as to excuse me, I would like to return to my room."

Just as she reached the door, he stopped her, saying, "Before you go, Nerissa, will you answer me one question?" She signalled her willingness by facing him, but her expression was wary. "If I offered to make you my wife, legally and by church rite, would you accept me more readily?"

"No," she said, "I don't think I would. I'm not sure that a true marriage of convenience is preferable to a pretend one, Mr. Blythe. In some ways, I think it might even be worse."

She left him, and as he watched her go, Nick warned himself that he would be wise to prepare for a disappointment.

For the third night in a row, Nerissa could hardly sleep for thinking about Nick Blythe, tossing and turning in yet another unfamiliar bed in yet another strange inn. Despite her uncertainty, one thing was apparent to her: she could do whatever she pleased, for there was not a soul alive who cared where she went, or with whom.

Her de Tourzel relations were simply too far away to be of any use to her, nor was Jersey a suitable or a safe haven for a solitary young woman—or anyone else, these days. When Uncle Claude had written to her after her father's death, he had described the island as a place where the people lived in constant fear of French invasion. The peace of St. Helier, the principal town, was forever disturbed by the brawling pirates and privateers who had made the port their headquarters. The de Tourzels were well off, they owned farmland and town property, but they were strangers to Nerissa. No doubt they would welcome a visit from Gabrielle's only child, but would any of them be willing to provide her with a permanent home?

On her paternal side, her prospects were only slightly better. Her papa's first cousin, the Duke of Solway, had four grown children of his own, and he was guardian to his fatherless niece and nephew. Besides, he and his duchess moved in the highest circles of society, and Nerissa would be woefully out of place in their exalted world. She had made a few, brief visits to the duke's country seat during her youth, and he had been a frequent visitor to the house in the Adelphi Terrace. But upon leaving Olney she had been reluctant to seek His Grace's protection, and after several days of travelling through England's heartland with a notorious duellist, she was even less eager to do so. There would be no covering up the unhappy fact that she was doubly ruined now.

She did not doubt that if she were deathly ill or in grave danger, her relations would come to her aid. But she was not in such dire straits as that; her problem was simply that she didn't know what to do with herself. Her trustees, a banker and a lawyer, were busy men, far more interested in her assets than her personal welfare. Mr. Halpern and Mr. Rose spoke the language of Funds and Consols and shares and capital, and not once since her papa's death had either of them asked if she was unhappy, or lonely—or bored. In their eyes she was simply a collection of documents in a black tin box with the Newby name painted on the lid.

She could acquit Mr. Blythe of coveting her fortune, because he did not know she was an heiress. And he had not asked her to do anything that she had not already done; she had passed herself off as his bride during their first night together, in Lutterworth, and for the whole of the following day. Being a fugitive, he would want to live very retired—something that appealed to a young woman who was weary of being stared at and gossiped about. He held out the promise of the sort of life she had known at her father's side, and that was a strong inducement indeed.

It was not even an alien notion to her, that a couple should share a home without being married. As a child she had known the poet Mr. Cowper and his devoted friend Mrs. Unwin, the widow who had kept house for him. They had lived together in unwedded bliss for some three decades, and despite the irregularity of their liaison, Nerissa's aunt and everyone else in the neighbourhood had received them.

But Nick Blythe would be bound to make advances, sooner or later, no matter what he'd said to the contrary, for he couldn't be completely impervious to the quality in her that had attracted so many others before him. This troubled her, but she knew her powers of resistance, and besides, he could easily find some other female to supply the kind of companionship she was unwilling to provide him.

Try as she might, she was unable to churn up any strenuous objections to his scheme. The odd thing was, she had no real reason not to accept Nick Blythe's offer, and ironically, that was why she found it so difficult to do so.

In the morning she faced the looking-glass with trepidation. As she had feared, she wore her woes in her face, and soap and water went only a little way towards lessening the ravages of another sleepless night. To her own critical eyes she looked infinitely older, and without the advantage of feeling any wiser. When she went down to breakfast, she still did not know how she would answer Mr. Blythe's inevitable question. She entered the parlour with a skipping pulse, but when she took her place at the table he did nothing more alarming than wish her good morning, adding that it was the day of the village fair. This was unexpected, so far removed from the thundering "Well?" for which she was still so miserably unprepared, that she had trouble thinking of a reply.

"Should you like to go with me?"

"To the fair?" she asked, fearing that he had suddenly and unceremoniously reverted to the subject that had kept her awake for so many hours.

"I thought we might disport ourselves among the locals, for it would be a shame to waste such a day as this." He gestured towards the window with his knife.

Where, she wondered, was the lust-driven ogre that had figured in her worst imaginings during the long night? The man who obligingly passed her the butter was the same polite, handsome gentleman she had known for the past—why, could this really be the fourth day of their acquaintance? Surely an eternity had passed since the afternoon their paths had crossed in the inn yard at Northampton.

Meeting his eyes, clear and grey, she smiled. "Yes, I would." And then, lest he had mistaken her answer as she had his question, she elaborated, "I'd like to go to the fair. Very much."

Later, when they joined the country-folk who had

converged upon Leek, Nerissa could almost believe
her escort had forgotten their conversation of the night
before. But while she followed him from stall to stall
and pretended to admire the cabbages and parsnips on
display, she was still wrestling with the question of
whether or not she ought to accept his offer.

She was so much distracted that she failed to notice
that they had become separated. As soon as she did
realise he had left her side, she was seized by the fear
that he had deliberately abandoned her. The cries of
the hawkers and the roar of the multitude rang in her
ears, intensifying her panic, and she was continually
jostled by the press of bodies all around her. After
fighting her way to a market stall, she rose on tiptoe
to scan the crowd with anxious eyes, but Nick Blythe
was nowhere to be seen. An apple-woman began a
long-winded harangue, praising her wares, and since
Nerissa had no intention of buying, she had to move
on. A Punch and Judy show loomed ahead of her, so
she joined the group of children and adults that clus-
tered around the booth. They shouted with laughter at
the puppet play, but Nerissa could barely muster a
smile, not even when the argumentative Punch took
up his cudgel and flailed everything in sight.

Although she saw the appreciative leer on the face
of the burly man standing next to her, she ignored
him. When he began to sidle up to her, she pretended
not to notice, but this cavalier reception of his attentions emboldened him to fling his arm about her waist.

''Come with me, pretty one,'' he drawled, his hot
breath searing her cheek, ''and I'll buy you a fairing.''

''Let me be, damn you!'' she cried.

''Mind your language, wench, we mustn't shock the
wee ones.'' A ripple of laughter greeted his words;
some of the audience had turned to see what was going
on at the rear. When she tried to escape his impris-

oning hold, her grinning admirer gave her an admonitory pinch.

Nerissa stopped struggling. "Good sir," she said sweetly, *"Here's* a fairing to remember *me* by." He leaned forward expectantly, and she dealt his red, sweaty face a resounding blow with her open palm. There was a burst of applause from the onlookers, and the man walked off, muttering curses and rubbing his cheek.

"Well done," said a familiar, husky voice from behind.

Nerissa whirled around to find Nick Blythe smiling down at her. "There you are," she breathed in relief.

"I'm happy that you chose to decline his invitation—it would be quite lowering to lose you to such a rival as that."

She tossed her head. "Fie, sir, I'm never the sort to run off with just any man who asks."

"No, of course not," he agreed, but his eyes were gently mocking. "Naturally you are very selective, or you would not be in my company now. Come along, minx, before you get into trouble again. There's a sight you cannot miss—the most famous juggler in all Christendom!" He took her by the hand and led her to a nearby platform where a man in a tunic and particoloured hose was tossing apples. Although a placard described him as a favourite at every court in Europe, the sadly bruised fruit bore testimony to his lack of skill—and veracity.

After watching him bend down again and again to retrieve his apples, Nerissa and Nick, their sides aching with laughter, finally abandoned the fair. They found a pleasant, tree-lined footpath that led away from the village, and followed it, neither much caring where it might take them. The afternoon was typical of October, sunny and clear, but a faint chill in the air was a reminder that this month of abundant harvest was also a time of preparation for the grimmer season to come. As they walked along, Nerissa, locked in that continuing battle with her conflicting desires, kept her eyes fixed upon the colorful, haphazard patchwork of fallen leaves.

Something occurred to her, and she came to a sudden stop. "If I agree to go north, to live with you in obscurity, could I not pretend to be your sister?"

"I'm afraid you don't look very much like a sister," Nick said bluntly.

His reply wounded her a little, but she knew exactly what he meant by it. "I suppose not," she sighed.

"I would be honoured to acknowledge you as my kinswoman," he said when they walked on, "but you are intelligent enough to understand why that might arouse suspicion. If we are to live the sort of anonymous life I envision, you will have to put your mother's wedding ring back on your finger."

He was right, of course. Keeping her voice light, as though her question were merely a hypothetical one, she asked what would happen if they discovered that they weren't compatible.

"We can always dissolve our partnership and go our separate ways," he replied. "If someday you decide that you prefer to go to London, I can easily move on to some other remote locale and begin anew."

She was surprised that he made no further attempt to persuade her; surely he must see how close she was to capitulation. But he had, she recalled, told her that her decision must be a voluntary one, and clearly he was a man of his word.

Their stroll ended abruptly at the edge of a river, and so did Nerissa's arguments with herself. "I will go with you," she said, and when she turned to look at him, she caught the flash of triumph in his eyes. It was gone so quickly that she decided she must have imagined it, for surely he couldn't care so very much whether she accepted or refused him.

"You are quite sure?" he asked.

"I hate to think what my fate would be if I went to London. I prefer to take my chances with you, Mr. Blythe. What is the best method for sealing a bargain such as ours?"

"This, I think," Nick said, extending his hand, and his fingers closed over hers, even as his eyes strayed to her mouth. "Unless," he added daringly, "you regard a handshake as too formal and unfeeling."

Nerissa looked up at him curiously, never guessing he might accept it as an invitation to him to do what he did. The kiss lasted for the space of a heartbeat, but it was quite long enough to warn her, too late, that she was condemned to build her new life upon the very brink of temptation.

WHEN IN LONDON, Ramsey Blythe lived in a set of rooms in Carrington Street, a convenient situation for a man of his tastes, being but a short walk from the sacred precincts of Tattersall's Repository. He seldom missed a sale-day, and one Monday morning in the middle of October he could be found standing in the shade of the graceful colonnade, watching the progress of a handsome bay gelding that was being paraded around the enclosure.

He had often stood in that same spot with his father, a gambler and an avid huntsman, who had all but beggared himself pursuing his ruinously expensive hobbies. The family coffers had been too empty to permit an Oxford education; Ramsey had received his schooling on the hunting field and at the gaming tables. Viscount Cavender, after raising his eldest son in his own image, had broken his neck in a fall from his horse, and at eighteen Ramsey found himself responsible for his father's massive debts, his widowed mother, and his young brother Justin. Lady Cavender had long practised stringent household economies in a futile attempt to make up for her husband's excesses, but the extent of his obligations was such that Ramsey wondered why she had bothered. Knowing he could never hope to keep it up, he had offered to sell the freehold of the London house to Baron Blythe, his paternal uncle, nearest neighbour, and sole trustee. The imposing mansion in Grosvenor Square, duly renamed Blythe House, passed to the other branch of the family, and the purchase price permitted Ramsey to settle with the most pressing of his father's creditors.

Shortly after attaining his majority, he made up his mind to seek a tenant for Cavender Chase. The thought of strangers living there was abhorrent to him, but he needed more money than the encumbered estate could produce. His mother stoically agreed to vacate her home, but she had demanded one thing, that her younger son be allowed to continue at Eton. She made it clear that she would spend her own jointure, if necessary, to send Justin to Oxford and she was equally determined that one day he should read jurisprudence. Ramsey, no less eager to see his brother established in a profession that would ensure his self-sufficiency, promised to contribute what he could to Justin's education. Satisfied, Lady Cavender went to live with Lord and Lady Blythe in that same London house she had once been mistress of, and Ramsey leased his ancestral home to a wealthy Cit at a very high rent.

He had just been able to afford a small string of hunters, and was thus able to follow his predecessor's example, spending the greater part of the year in the shires, riding to hounds, and the rest of it at boxing matches and prize fights and race meetings. And that October afternoon at Tattersall's, he found himself in the sort of company he most liked. He was one of a large group of men of all ages and every degree of fashion, which included courtiers and commoners, grooms, stableboys, kennel-masters, coachmen, jockeys, and horse-dealers. And as his brown eyes scanned the crowd, he could count numerous friends and acquaintances. Feeling the need of some refreshment, he went to the spacious taproom, and there fell in with a party of younger men who solicited his opinion on the bay gelding, and a fine chestnut filly that had been on show earlier in the day.

"We missed you at Melton a fortnight ago," said one fellow, the scion of a noble house.

Ramsey shrugged diffidently, but a flush stained his tanned countenance as he recalled the reason for his absence. He had lost a great deal of money at the August Meeting at York, when he had backed Allegro, ridden by the famed Newmarket jockey, Mr. Buckle, against the filly Louisa, ridden by a noted equestrienne, the wife of Colonel Thornton. The lady rider had won the race, and to cover his bets Ramsey had sold off three of his best hunters. And although he admitted this fact to Lord Albert, he hoped his presence would encourage everyone to think he'd come to Tattersall's to replace his horses. He kept to himself the dismal truth, that he lacked the funds—or the credit—to purchase any of the handsome animals being shown, or the meanest of the many phaetons and curricles for sale.

"Bought one of your cast-offs myself," one gentleman declared, "that long-tailed grey you were always so proud of—Samson. Carried me on a capital run our last day at Melton—can't imagine why you didn't keep him. What stamina the poor brute had," he said, shaking his head sorrowfully.

"Had?" Ramsey choked.

"My groom was exercising him t'other day, and the beast broke his knees taking a five-barred gate. I had to shoot him on the spot—the horse, not the groom, though I vow I was sore tempted!"

He fought to conceal his chagrin and disgust. The most beloved of all his mounts was now rotting in some ditch—or had he received that mark of distinction reserved for faithful hunters, and been fed to the hounds? Ramsey would not ask, nor could he, for his

friends had begun to talk of the duel, as nearly everyone seemed to be doing these days.

"I heard that his ladybird finally accepted *carte
blanche* from Tarrant," said the young lordling who
had remarked on Ramsey's absence from the Melton
hunt. "She must've given up hope that Blythe will return. Or else she's clever enough to know he'll have
scant use for her if he lands in Newgate!"

"Have a care, Bertie," someone cautioned him.

"What? Oh, sorry, Cavender. But it's no secret he
might have to stand trial for murder in the House of
Lords. Peers have been tried before, and have even
gone to the gallows. Think of Lord Ferrers," Lord
Albert added darkly.

"That was nearly fifty years ago," protested the man
who had bought and destroyed Samson. "I can't believe Nick Blythe killed a man in cold blood. Some
say the duel was forced upon him—Sir Algernon had
a damnably short temper, and a history of settling
grievances at pistol-point. And that jade he took as a
wife was flirting with half a dozen fellows I can name,
before and after the wedding."

"Well, if she had a lover, it couldn't have been
Blythe," Lord Albert pointed out. "He was perfectly
content with his doxy, the little Ellen. Ain't that so,
Cavender?"

"I—I believe he was," Ramsey faltered. His throat
suddenly felt dry, and he lifted his tankard. Ever since
that infamous duel, he'd fallen prey to the curious,
who, like Lord Albert, were eager to question him.
Day after day he'd read the newspaper accounts of his
cousin's alleged infamy, for the London printers had
sunk their teeth into the juiciest scandal to come their
way in years, and as yet had not grown sated. Reluctant to join in the speculation about where the Baron
had run to, Ramsey mumbled an excuse about an ap-

pointment with his tailor and made his escape from the taproom.

His cousin's duel had quite cut up his peace, for the whole world was buzzing about Lord Blythe and Lady Titus and poor, dead Sir Algernon. Ramsey wasn't much concerned that he could be connected with the recent unhappy events, for he'd been careful to keep his *affaire* with Georgiana a secret, and she wouldn't care to make it known, certainly not now. But perhaps he would be wise to call in Clifford Street, ostensibly to offer his condolences, just to make certain that her husband hadn't uttered some incriminating deathbed confession.

A domed temple housing a life-sized statue of Rey-nard stood in the courtyard, and as Ramsey passed it he heard a gruff voice exclaim, ''By God, the very man I've been looking for this half hour!'' He turned slowly, steeling himself for another encounter with one more person eager to talk of his cousin. But the man who accosted him was none other than his Uncle Isaac, who was accompanied by an impassive, black-eyed In-dian manservant.

It was at Newmarket that Lord Cavender had first met the black sheep of the family. Mr. Isaac Meriden, after amassing a sizeable fortune during his two-score years in India, had returned to his native shores with the intention of purchasing a property in Leicester-shire, where he would be close to his favourite hunts. When Ramsey had learned that his uncle required a female relation to keep house for him, he was quick to suggest his mother, and the long-suffering Lady Cavender left Blythe House and went to live with her brother.

''Good day to you, sir,'' he said, shaking hands. ''I had no notion you were in town. Does my mother accompany you?'' The old gentleman shook his head, to Ramsey's great relief. He was not close to his widowed parent, and supposed it was because he reminded her so much of his father. "Did you see that bay gelding?" he asked.

"Too rich for your blood, m'boy," Mr. Meriden said severely. "And it's a pity, he'd carry you well. Or me, only I'm not in the market for a hunter—came to Tatt's for a neat little mare, one that will be gentle in harness. I found her, too, and now I must buy a dogcart. I thought your mother might enjoy tooling herself around the country." Ramsey dutifully enquired about his mother's health, and received a favourable account. "She's very well, very well indeed," the nabob said cheerfully. "It's lucky I met you here—saves me the trouble of calling in Carrington Street. I wish to discuss a business matter with you, provided you are at leisure this evening."

"I am."

"Then join me at Boodle's eight o'clock. We'll dine together. This afternoon I'm meeting with my solicitor, and afterwards I must go to Lincoln's Inn and see if I can run young Justin to the ground; your mother has messages for him that I must deliver in person." The old gentleman frowned. "Lately his letters have been very full of Damon Lovell—I trust he ain't been getting into trouble now that the wild young marquis has taken him up?"

"Not that I know of," Ramsey answered.

"Glad to hear it. One scandal in the family is quite enough," said Mr. Meriden sternly.

That night Ramsey arrayed himself in his evening togs and presented himself at Boodle's in St James in obedience to his uncle's wishes. He was not himself a club man, his meagre income did not provide the same luxuries that his fellow peers took for granted, but he spied several acquaintances as a footman led him to the coffee room where Mr. Meriden awaited him.

He did not look forward to this interview; he preferred any one of his sporting cronies to the whole pack of his relations—except for Justin, the only person who looked up to him. Ramsey, who believed that he was similarly devoted to his brother, never quite realised that his affection was more selfish than self-less. For a time Dominic Blythe had supplanted him as his brother's hero, and then at Oxford, Justin had met Damon Lovell, so much closer to him in age. Ramsey envied his cousins not only Justin's affection, but also their looks and their popularity with the fair sex—and their large fortunes.

The dinner was excellent, but he had to compete with the chops and puddings for his uncle's attention. After the covers were removed and a bottle of brandy placed on the table by one of the serving men, the conversation improved.

"How long will you be in town, Uncle?" Ramsey asked, after hearing a long, dull report about his mother's recent activities.

"I'm leaving tomorrow," Mr. Meriden announced. "After a week of putting up at Fladong's, I shall be glad to return to Leicestershire. My business is completed—or will be when I've talked it over with you. There's a meet at Swanborough Abbey at the week's end, and I don't want to miss it. D'you mean to attend?"

Ramsey shook his head regretfully, for the Swanborough pack and the country it hunted were renowned. "I've no longer got horses fit for that terrain, just a pair of cover-hacks."

Mr. Meriden narrowed his eyes. "A pity. You should've done as I did and gone to India to repair your fortunes, Ram. The place would suit you down to the ground. No one works terribly hard—too hot for that—and the society is lively. And there's a decent amount of sport to be had." He was silent for a few seconds, then said, "I came back from the East with more money than most men dream of, and as you know, I've no son to leave it to. Oh, I sired two bastards in Calcutta, and made provision for them before I left. Naturally I've never contemplated leaving my money to either of them, not when I've got a bevy of nephews, without even counting my second sister's brood. She refuses to receive me, so I feel no compunction to remember her or her brats in my will."

Ramsey began to listen more attentively.

"Sir Robert Meriden is a worthy fellow, but he's to be wed to one of Lord Rowan's girls next spring, which makes him ineligible."

"I believe my mother mentioned the engagement," Ramsey said diffidently. He couldn't imagine why his cousin's marriage should serve to put him out of the way of inheriting the nabob's fortune, but he couldn't be sorry for it.

"I must confess that at one time I considered making Celesta's son my heir," Mr. Meriden continued. "You won't remember her, but she was a sweet creature and always fond of me. But now I know young Damon rather better, I fear he's growing too much like his father—a cold, harsh man, who made my poor sister most unhappy. And the marquis needs none of my brass, for he's undoubtedly one of the wealthiest men of his generation."

That left only two other possibilities, and Ramsey's heart began to pound. It couldn't be Justin, he told himself, Justin was a younger son, he had a profession—or would have, when he completed his law studies.

"You, Ram, are the eldest of all my nephews, and although you are a Blythe, Meriden blood flows in your veins. You are yet unwed, which is something to the purpose, and you possess a title. So I have made up my mind to make you my heir."

Ramsey hardly knew what to say. His brain was reeling from the sudden and entirely unexpected news that one day he would be an extremely rich man. Striving for a sober note that would conceal his exultation, he replied, ''Your generosity overwhelms me, sir.''

Mr. Meriden shook his head. ''I haven't finished. The inheritance would be conditional upon your acceptance my terms. For I'm not only offering you a fortune, but a bride as well. If you want the one, you must agree to take the other. The young lady's birth is impeccable—she's the daughter of an earl and niece to a duke.'' Mr. Meriden's sallow face softened, and his voice was gentle when he said, ''You needn't worry that she's lacking in beauty, or charm, for she has both. In abundance.''

''I am all eagerness to make her acquaintance,'' Ramsey said. He didn't greatly care what the chit was like; he'd agree to wed a gorgon if he could enrich himself by so doing.

''For all I know, you may have met her already. You've hunted with the Swanborough pack, and she is the earl's only sister.''

But Ramsey, an infrequent visitor to Swanborough Abbey, had no memory of any young lady there. Lord Swanborough was yet a child, and the ward of his uncle, the Duke of Solway. ''I do believe I helped his lordship onto his pony once, but he is so young that I never thought he might have a sister of marriageable age.''

''Lady Miranda Peverel is only seventeen,'' Mr. Meriden replied. ''She and the little boy make their home with the Marchants.'' In a confidential tone he said, ''It is not generally spoken of, but the birth of young Ninian was hard on his mother. The Countess of Swanborough is a complete invalid and lives in Bath in the constant care of a physician. She was the Lady Hermia Marchant, the duke's prettiest sister and my own sweetheart. I'd have married her, too, if I hadn't fallen into a scrape and been shipped off to India by my father.''

Ramsey, amused by his uncle's sentimental reason for promoting the match, stated his willingness to enter into an engagement. ''But, sir, this bud of perfection might prefer to choose her own husband. I believe girls of seventeen can have very definite notions about suitors. And I doubt that her guardian will welcome the addresses of a penniless peer so many years her senior.''

''Oh, Duke William and I are old friends,'' the nabob said airily. ''I will drop a word in his ear about your prospects. As for your age, there's nothing can be done about it, and anyway it's common knowledge that young ladies will often develop a *tendre* for an older gentleman. You're a hunting man, and she grew up among such—your horsemanship will win her, I'll be bound. And you are no longer penniless, far from it.'' Mr. Meriden reached into his coat pocket. ''Here's a draft on my bank. It should enable you to purchase as many hunters as you please. As soon as the banns are published, I'll undertake to provide you with an independence—then you can take up residence at Cavender Chase again. I can't let you house Lady Mira in your Carrington Street lodging, now can I?''

Ramsey, delighted by the vast sum scrawled upon the face of the cheque, thanked his uncle profusely. But he could not help saying, ''An allowance and a bride all in one day—you go much too fast for me, Uncle.''

''Not fast enough,'' his uncle contradicted him. ''It so happens that the lass is very friendly with her Marchant cousins. Both are well-looking young men, and the elder will be duke someday. Besides which, a multitude of other eligibles have descended upon Leicestershire this autumn, and as soon as word goes 'round that Solway's niece is an incomparable, you'll be left in the dust." He rubbed his nose with his forefinger and said morosely, "And there's something else that troubles me—this damned mess Nick Blythe's got himself embroiled in."

Ramsey's hand jerked on his brandy glass, sending a shower of amber liquid across the table. As he mopped it up with a napkin, he said hastily, "I fear my cousin's case is quite hopeless—the newspapers predict that if he is ever caught he will have to stand his trial for murder."

"Pshaw," was the older man's disgusted reply. "This scandal is a nine days' wonder, no more, and in time this ridiculous furor will subside. The press may have whipped the public into a lather, but who among us has not fought a duel in his time, or wanted to? It wasn't the first one and it certainly won't be the last. Everyone knows Blythe's pater was a King's man, and the Crown will never prosecute the son of one of its most prominent servants. I don't know your poor cousin very well, but for your sake—and Lady Mira's, since she will one day be related to him by marriage—I'm determined to help him. I have a deal of money, and you must have some influence—between us we should be able to reinstate him in society's good graces, before it's too late."

"But how? No one knows where he has gone," Ramsey said. But his uncle hadn't heard him; a ruddy-faced gentleman had stepped forward, and the two men were already reminiscing about days long gone.

Left to his own thoughts, Ramsey stared into his glass as he considered what had happened that afternoon. He had finally screwed up his courage and called upon Georgiana, only to find that she was the merest shadow of the woman who had been his eager mistress. But even though she had seemed distant and a trifle cool, she hadn't accused him of anything. And why should she? He'd done nothing wrong. Oh, he'd tried to cloak his own sins by encouraging Sir Algernon to believe that Dominic, not he, was her ladyship's lover, but how could he have guessed that a fatal duel would be the result? Everything that happened on the following morning was shocking, regrettable, tragic, but to step forward now and confess his part would benefit no one, least of all himself.

Yet each time someone mentioned Dominic's name, Ramsey was reminded that his cousin might have to live out his life in exile. And now, just when he was beginning to think himself completely safe, his Uncle Isaac had commanded him to set everything to rights. If he succeeded, like the knights of old he would be rewarded with a fair bride and sufficient monies to reclaim his ancestral home, but no dragonslayer had ever faced a more formidable foe than his own unquiet conscience.

It might be, he thought hopefully, that by finding Dominic and helping to establish his innocence he would wipe the slate clean. But would it be possible to accomplish that without also putting his own reputation at risk? This question further depressed Ramsey's spirits, and even though he reached instinctively for the decanter, he knew that no amount of brandy could completely banish his fears of discovery and dishonour.

The following week, Ramsey visited the sale-rooms of an auction house in Tavistock Street, where a nobleman's vast library was being dispersed. He was not an avid reader, but reportedly a number of books on the turf and the chase would be offered for sale, and those he did collect in a desultory fashion. He was looking for a first edition of Beckford's *Thoughts on Hunting*, now that he could afford to indulge himself.

He had already spent some of his uncle's largesse

on new raiment, which had greatly improved his appearance. His hunting clothes, however well made, had never displayed his stocky, muscular figure to advantage, and it was remarkable what a clever—and expensive—tailor could achieve. On this day he sported a green swallow-tailed coat and nankeen pantaloons. He had also visited a skilled barber, who had shorn his sun-streaked brown curls and coaxed them into a flattering and fashionable crop. These changes had been wrought with an eye to pleasing that seventeen-year-old girl upon whom he had pinned his hopes, but he had not yet paid his visit to Swanborough Abbey, where, according to his uncle, she was spending the autumn. Each day he found a new excuse for putting off his intended journey to Leicestershire. During the afternoon he haunted the subscription room at Tattersall's, by night he courted the favours of a pretty opera dancer, and he spent the early hours of the morning at gaming tables of one of the many halls to be found in the neighbourhood of St. James.

Although he submitted the catalogue of books on sale to a painstaking perusal, he failed to find the one he wanted. He was on the point of leaving when the Marquis of Elston entered the sale-room, a lady in black on his arm. The couple walked past Ramsey as if they were quite oblivious to his presence, and he saw that his cousin's companion was the widowed Lady Titus. They had given him the cut indirect. Striving to maintain his composure, Ramsey was more than ever inclined to agree with his uncle that Damon was as cold-blooded as his late father, who, according to rumour, had banished his wife and only son to his country estate in order that his debauchery in town might continue unchecked. The unhappy Lovells—dubbed the Loveless by the London wits—had been united in death if not in life, for they met their end simultaneously, in a carriage accident.

Feigning an interest in a calf-bound book on cattle breeding, he eyed the handsome young nobleman malevolently. The marquis was drifting towards a table displaying the volumes dealing with foreign travel; Georgiana had wandered off to another part of the room. Taking advantage of her absence, Ramsey approached his relative and enquired whether he was planning a journey.

"Not any time soon," Lord Elston disclaimed in a bored voice. "But then, one never knows."

At least he had not delivered a cut direct; he was simply being his usual enigmatic self. Ramsey felt confident enough to say, "I didn't know you were so well acquainted with Lady Titus."

"My attentions are philanthropic, not amorous, dear coz. You would be surprised to know how many of her ladyship's former friends have cast her off since Sir Algernon's unfortunate demise."

Ramsey flushed, reading in this caustic remark a criticism of himself. If Georgiana had told Damon about their liaison, he would have to be very careful indeed. Thinking it best to change the subject, and quickly, he asked, "Have you seen Justin lately?"

"I regret I've not had the pleasure for several days. This week he seems to spend all his time reading briefs or following some barrister in and out of the courtrooms. But why am I telling you this, when you must surely be aware of your brother's habits?"

Ramsey, who had avoided Justin in the weeks following the party in Clifford Street, didn't care to admit that fact, certainly not to his supercilious and possibly suspicious cousin.

"By the way, Ram, I've been wondering if you've received any communication from Lord Blythe."

"I have not," Ramsey replied, more sharply than he intended.

"I daresay you are quite anxious to learn how he has fared since leaving the Metropolis."

Ramsey resented this kind of quizzing by someone so many years his junior. "I *am* concerned about Nick, and I would very much like to help him out of his present difficulties." He was pleased with this speech, and hoped his cousin would be similarly impressed.

"You astonish me," the marquis murmured, and Ramsey flinched. The deep blue eyes were hard and merciless, more so than was customary. "I did not realise that your devotion to Lord Blythe ran to such lengths. Justin, on the other hand, would give his life for the so noble Dominic. And very nearly did, a fortnight past."

"What do you mean?"

Lord Elston smiled, but not very pleasantly. "Did Justin fail to tell you of his great adventure? I never thought him a secretive fellow—unlike others I could name. Your brother acted as Blythe's second in the duel."

"You can't be serious!"

"Ask him, if you doubt my word. But you shouldn't, for I was also present."

"*You?*" Bemused, Ramsey shook his head. "I had no idea."

"That, dear coz, is perfectly obvious. I offered to serve as Sir Algernon's second not because I supported his accusations against my good friend Blythe, which I know to be quite false, but in order that their dispute might be kept as quiet as possible."

"But if Nick should ever stand trial, Justin might also be implicated in the case!"

"And so would I be. Though naturally I don't expect you to be much concerned with my fate." Lord Elston sighed.

But Ramsey scarcely heard him, for he was still struggling with the dread fact of his brother's involvement in the duel. As his horror receded, it was replaced by rage. He resented the fact that Dominic— and Damon—had permitted Justin to endanger himself, and his career. But wasn't he also at fault, for telling that damned lie about Dominic in the first place?

"I must find my cousin," he said desperately. "Will you help me?"

The marquis raised his malacca walking-stick and tapped the viscount on the chest with its golden knob. "I think, Ram, that you would do better to leave Dominic alone. Haven't you troubled him enough for one lifetime?"

The willowy nobleman turned and walked away, and Ramsey, thoroughly alarmed by the implication left hanging in the air, had no opportunity to refute it.

THE FINE WEATHER seemed a favourable omen to Nerissa on the day Nick took her to see her new home, the farm they now invariably referred to as their Arcadia. A hired horse and gig carried them from Carlisle, whose long history of strife could be traced in the remains of her battle-scarred castle, and into the surrounding countryside. The Cumbrian mountains and moorland were no longer shrouded by the thick, low-hanging mist of the past several days, and Nerissa was charmed by the strange, stark landscape, so unlike that of her part of England. She had already learned that the north could sometimes be chilly and forbidding, and sadly damp.

During their drive on that bright morning, she was glad to see that the strain had left Nick's eyes, and his air of despondency was gone. Their alliance had effectively reduced the degree of desperation each of them had felt at various stages of their journey, he at Lutterworth and she at Leek. During their travels, he had described his ideal farm to her so many times, in such minute detail that she had easily believed it really existed, although his initial lack of success in locating it had seemed to prove otherwise. Each day he'd left their inn in Scotch Street in hopes of finding the place where they hoped to live together in peace and harmony and perfect amity, but not until yesterday had the land agent shown him Mr. Haslam's untenanted property near Wetheral, only a few miles from the city.

This hamlet, Nerissa discovered, was a cluster of houses built around a triangular common, with an ancient church set a little distance away, by the river. The main road followed the broad sweep of the Eden, and beyond the village the gig passed by the ruined gatehouse of the Benedictine priory that had once stood there. Nick reined in so she could admire the distant view of Corby Castle on the opposite bank, but she was more enthusiastic about the river itself, prompting him to say, "This affinity for water must be a legacy from your father."

"And of my mother's as well," she laughed.

"Oh? I don't think you've ever mentioned her before now."

"She died when I was but a week old," Nerissa explained, "so I know very little about her. I've always thought her name quite beautiful—Gabrielle de Tourzel. Papa met her on one of his voyages."

"Was she a Creole?"

"Goodness no," she laughed, "nothing so exotic. She came from Jersey."

"That sounds exotic to me," he said, urging the horse into a walk.

"A storm in the channel once forced my father to dock on the island, at St. Aubin harbour. During his time on shore he visited the marketplace, where he saw a beautiful red-haired girl. He was so enraptured that he followed her home and alarmed her family by requesting permission to pay his addresses. His courtship lasted as long as the storm, and by the time he sailed for Madras, they were engaged. The following year he returned to Jersey and wed her and brought her to England."

Just as her tale ended, they rounded a bend in the road that brought them to the farm. The rocky land, decorated with clumps of heather and gorse and dormant fern, was dotted with sheep and criss-crossed with drystone walls. The house of weathered stone was hardly the cottage she had envisioned, but a rambling structure at the base of a hill, dominated by a square pele tower. It lent a pleasing air of antiquity to the place and, Nick said, had been erected centuries before in defence against the Scots.

The drive was rutted from recent rains, and the stable yard, bounded by several outbuildings, was choked with mud. McNab, the wiry Scotsman who served as caretaker and farm manager, was at work laying in a supply of straw. He issued a laconic greeting and took charge of the horse and gig. Nick escorted Nerissa to the front door of the house, where they found Mrs. McNab on her knees, scrubbing the steps. More solidly built than her spouse, she possessed a sharp nose and a jutting chin, and was slightly more talkative.

"The place is a reet mess," she informed her new mistress, shaking her head. "I've sent for Sally from the village to help me put things in order, but even with two pair of hands it's a hard task."

They left her to her work, and Nick conducted Nerissa over the house himself. The rooms were irregularly sized, although the parlour was spacious enough; much of the furniture was at least two centuries old, solid and well made. Fearing that the wooden chairs with carved backs, great oaken chests, and old-fashioned settles might not be to her taste, Nick told Nerissa she had *carte blanche* to make whatever improvements seemed necessary to her. The bedchambers were more sparsely appointed, the largest with only a four-posted monstrosity hung with moth-eaten brocade.

Manfully preserving his countenance in the face of the lady's blushes, Nick commented, "A bit gloomy," don't you think? I daresay you'll prefer the tower room, which lies down the hall.''

This small, quaint chamber did indeed take Nerissa's fancy. "But won't the servants wonder at my failure to share your quarters?" she asked him.

"I shouldn't think so," he replied gravely, although his eyes were bright with amusement. "Do you not know, Nerissa, that married persons of the Quality commonly sleep in separate bedchambers? We will be following a custom established by the highest in the land." Their sleeping arrangements thus established, they made their cautious way down the uneven stone steps of the spiral staircase.

A short time later, when he showed her the apple orchard behind the house, Nerissa surveyed the crop and observed, "My first task will be to make cider—provided we can find some local lads to pick all of this ripe fruit.''

"Do you know how?" Nick asked doubtfully as he ducked to avoid a heavily laden branch.

"I most certainly do—my Aunt Portia taught me well. I can't boast that I'm as excellent a housekeeper as she was, but I assure you I managed to keep Papa tolerably comfortable after we moved to Olney.''

He reached up to pluck an apple and took an experimental bite. Looking over at Nerissa, he smiled and said, "So tell me, wife, what do you think of your new home?''

"I think, husband, that you have chosen well.''

"In all things," he murmured, his eyes on her lovely face.

But she didn't hear him; she was already composing mental lists in preparation for her assault upon the cabinetmakers, upholsterers, and china warehouses of Carlisle.

* * *

"Do you take cream in your tea, Mrs. Blythe?"

Nerissa was now so used to being addressed by the false name that her heart no longer skipped a beat every time she heard it. "No. Thank you," she answered, and stretched out her hand to receive the cup Mrs. Haslam passed to her.

She and Nick had spent the afternoon in Carlisle, and had dined at their landlord's mansion in Abbey Street. After dinner, the banker had lured Nick into his study and Nerissa, bereft of his bracing presence, had followed the lady of the house and her daughter to the drawing-room. Silently praying the gentlemen would not be long over their port, she fastened a smile upon her face and complimented Mrs. Haslam on the excellence of the tea. "Indian, is it not?" she ventured, knowing herself to be on firm ground. Her father had taught her a great deal about the commodity on which so large a part of his fortune had been founded.

"You like it?" the lady asked. "I had it from one of our local merchants." After a sip from her own cup, she leaned forward to say, "Although Maria and I are not in the habit of receiving Mr. Haslam's tenants, this time we are happy to make an exception. Maria, dear, please be so good as to shift the fire-screen for Mrs. Blythe."

Miss Maria Haslam, a tall, spare woman on the shady side of forty, obediently performed this office.

Said Mrs. Haslam, her full-moon face set in serious lines, "Truly, Mrs. Blythe, it breaks my heart to think of you stuck out on that dismal little farm. Could you not persuade your husband that a townhouse would have been more to your liking?"

"Now, Mama," Miss Haslam said warningly.

"No, Maria, I mean to speak my mind," the plump matron declared. "I know it may seem a very romantical notion, love in a cottage, and of course the poor French Queen set a fashion for that sort of thing. But the inconvenience of living at such a distance from town! You may think me a frivolous creature, Mrs. Blythe, but I would simply perish without the shops to visit and friends to call upon, to say nothing of the assemblies that are held during the Assizes!''

Her daughter gave their guest an apologetic smile, saying cheerfully, ''But the farm is no more than half a dozen miles from Carlisle, Mama. You make it sound like the ends of the earth!''

''It might as well be,'' her parent persisted, shaking her head until her cheeks bobbled. Nerissa assured her that living in the country was no hardship. Mrs. Haslam said, ''I suppose you know best,'' but she didn't seem convinced. ''Have you had any luck hiring servants, my dear?''

''Mrs. McNab cooks for us, and Sally Willis, a girl from the village, lives in.''

''Only one maid?'' the older woman cried, horrified. ''But I could never manage with fewer than three!'' And Nerissa dared not admit that she performed a number of household tasks with her own willing and capable hands.

The conversation would have foundered at this point, had not Maria Haslam expressed her admiration of Mrs. Blythe's gown, a lovely plum-coloured silk with a lace overdress. Talk turned to the current London modes, and not long after, the gentlemen returned.

Mr. Blythe moved to his wife's side with an alacrity that caused the Haslam ladies to exchange a speaking glance. Mrs. Haslam heaved a sentimental sigh at this proof of the young husband's devotion, then said, ''I hope you won't think it an impertinence, but have you and Mrs. Blythe been married long?''

Nick, standing by Nerissa's chair, placed one calming hand on her shoulder. With perfect ease—and a marvellous lack of precision—he replied, ''For less than a year, ma'am.''

He was conscious of a curious sense of pride when the ladies begged Nerissa to visit them often; obviously they were much taken with her. And why should they not be, he thought, for her company manners had proved to be impeccable, and no one could fault her appearance. But when, during their drive back to the farm, he tried to compliment her, he found her to be a great deal concerned with the stirrings of her conscience.

''What *fiends* we are,'' she said mournfully, ''treating those nice people so shabbily! I think I shall never feel easy about deceiving everyone we meet.''

Nick heaved a sigh that shook his large frame, and his voice was especially uneven when he said, ''With all the larger sins in my dish, our pretending to be married doesn't seem to me such a terrible one.'' Hoping to cheer her a little, he added, ''By the by, our affable landlord has swelled the ever-growing ranks of your admirers. Before we broached the first bottle of port, old Haslam said heartily, if rather inelegantly, that I was a lucky young dog. And naturally I agreed with him.''

This comment failed to win him the smile he had counted on. His occasional gallantries inevitably fell flat—as puzzling as it was disappointing. And their initial foray into local society had left her so dispirited that he knew it was not an auspicious moment to begin the seduction that was increasingly on his mind.

He owed her this life, he was fully conscious of it, but shorn as he was of title and estate, he had very little to offer by way of recompense. At least, he reflected, he could provide her with the security of a permanent home, and with that in mind he had mentioned to Mr. Haslam that he was interested in purchasing the freehold of Arcadia Farm. The canny old banker, knowing the amount his tenant, also his client, kept on deposit, had named a figure so large that Nick declined to meet it. But at least the bargaining had begun, and soon he must write Cat Durham and recover the money he had left with her.

When they arrived home, Nick bid Nerissa his usual polite, impersonal good-night in the upstairs hall, and they entered their respective apartments.

Nerissa had made her tower room a cosy place, but it was drafty nonetheless, and she quickly changed into her nightshift and dressing gown, a handsome, gaudy garment of blue silk with bamboo leaves picked out in gold thread. She sat down to brush and braid her hair, and as she dropped the combs and pins into her lap she wished, not for the first time, that she had been blessed with her friend Laura's smooth, blonde tresses. Unbound, her heavy chestnut mane turned her into that wild gypsy girl her father had so often called her.

She had not troubled to lock her door, for Nick had never sought entry to her room, so when she heard a soft knock, she experienced a frisson of panic. After a moment of indecision, she tied the corded sash more tightly about her waist and called, "Come in." To her own ears the invitation sounded tentative at best.

He was still fully dressed, she was relieved to see, and his purpose in coming was to bring her a book she had purchased that afternoon in Carlisle. "McNab found this in the gig," he said, placing it on a table.

This reminded her of something she had forgotten to tell him earlier. "There is a registry office next to the bookseller's," she said, "and persons seeking employment sometimes gather at the area railing and accost the passers-by. Today I was approached by a young man—a boy, really, for he can't be more than seventeen. He had the reddest hair I've ever seen, and wanted to know if I required a footman. It was all I could do to keep from laughing, for he was so young, and *so* shabby, but I told him there might be work for him here.''

''If you are bent on hiring on a manservant, you would do better to hire a trained one than some stray cub,'' Nick said.

''I don't like footmen, they don't seem human to me. Besides, any decent one would hold up his nose at our menage.'' She picked up her brush and plied it with such vigour that her hair cracked.'' This Alec Hewes had an honest face, and he's country bred. He might be useful for odd jobs like carpentry or looking after the cows. And I expect Mrs. McNab would like having someone to order about besides Sally—she has such an autocratic disposition.''

Nick, who had been wandering about the room, paused to pick up her silver hand-mirror from the dressing table. Running his forefinger over the initials engraved upon its back, he asked her what the R signified.

''Rosalind. Nerissa Rosalind.''

''The captain must have been exceedingly fond of the Bard.''

''It happens that he was, but he was obliged to name me for one of Shakespeare's ladies—it's a tradition in his family,'' Nerissa told him. ''His sister was Portia and his mother was Beatrice, and his aunts were Viola and Ophelia—oh, it goes back for generations. I have always been thankful for the names I was given. I might easily have been called something quite horrid, like Hippolyta or Calpurnia.''

''Or Goneril.'' He looked over at her, frowning slightly.'' I believe there is a noble family that follows the same custom.''

Nerissa, knowing all too well which noble family he meant, suddenly averted her eyes. ''How very interesting, to be sure.''

Should she reveal her connection to the Duke of Solway? She considered this, but in the end rejected the notion. She and Nick had met as equals, and she preferred that they continue as such. To tell him that she was related to the Marchant clan—and was an heiress besides—would serve no good purpose, and it might conceivably damage their easy relationship. At present her aristocratic kinsman played no part in her life, and her inheritance was held in trust until her marriage, or her twenty-fifth birthday, a full eighteen months away. Being quite unaffected by both circumstances, she could see no reason why she should admit to either.

Nick broke the quiet by saying, "I must cull *The Merchant of Venice* for suitable quotations to address to you. Did you remember to purchase a set of Shakespeare at the bookseller's?"

"Among other things," she replied in a voice of doom. "I'm afraid I've run up quite a bill in the name of Mrs. Nicholas Blythe of Arcadia Farm, Wethcral. Who doesn't even exist."

"No, she certainly does not," he agreed. "My parents, less literary minded than yours, christened me Dominic."

Her hairbrush paused in midstroke, and she eyed him accusingly. "You might have told me!"

"I'm sorry, I forgot you didn't know. You needn't call me Dominic if you don't like it," he said, amused by her fierce expression.

"It isn't the *name* I dislike, but the not knowing." She began to plait her hair, biting her lower lip in concentration, and forgot her momentary annoyance.

Nick watched this operation in silence, and when it was over he said teasingly, "I never guessed that the night transformed you into a mandarin, pigtail and all."

Without looking up at him she said, "My robe belonged to a mandarin—or so Papa always said. I was never entirely sure he was telling the truth."

"It is vastly becoming, wherever it came from."

When he was gone, Nerissa considered this new habit of making such personal remarks. At times he seemed to be pursuing something more than a platonic friendship, although he had yet to say or do anything that could be construed as an advance. He would, of that she was certain. But she was experienced in fending off amorous gentlemen, she thought with some pride, and was both fully prepared and perfectly able to do so.

"Unseemly, I call it," Mrs. McNab grumbled as she surveyed the wreck of her kitchen, littered with pots and pans and utensils. "Why should decent, godly folk want to build bonfires, I'd like to know?"

Sally Willis, a pretty country girl with dusky curls and pink cheeks, paused on her way to the scullery to say shyly, "Alec said it's to fright the witches." She brushed back a lock of dark hair, her hand white with flour.

Nerissa laughed, but she hastened to correct this false impression. "He was thinking of All Hallow's Eve. Tonight, we'll be honouring—or rather, *dishon-ouring*—Guy Fawkes, the Catholic gentleman who conspired with others of his religion to blow up Parliament." She opened the door of the bread oven to remove the first of two apple pies, using a dishcloth to protect her hands from the hot plate.

"And for that we must go to all this trouble and encourage the farm folk to roister all the night?" Mrs. McNab fumed. She cast a darkling glance at the kitch-enmaid and said bitterly, "And Sally forgetting to dust the downstairs rooms because she spent all morning sewing a big dolly and stuffing it with straw! Heathen-ish doings, mistress, and I like it not!"

"Part of the fun is burning Guy in effigy," Nerissa explained. As she reached for the second pie, her cloth slipped, and when her palm touched the edge of the tin, she jerked it back with a cry of pain.

"Now you've gone and burned yourself over this foolishness," the Scotswoman said, aggrieved. "Sit you down, mistress, I've a certain remedy. Sally, lass, fetch me the alum powder and some water—be quick, now!"

She mixed a paste which she applied to Nerissa's wound. "You needn't bind it," she said gruffly, "and the pain will go off soon, or my name's not Martha McNab. Rest ye easy, there's nothing more needs doing that Sally and I can't manage between us."

Nerissa reminded Sally to fetch two bottles of claret from the cellar and gather together the spices Nick required for the punch he insisted upon making, before hurrying to her room to dress for the simple country fête, her first in her new home. Not knowing which of her gowns was Nick's favourite, she put on her grey silk, and in honour of the occasion unearthed a pair of kid dancing slippers and bound her hair with cherry ribbons.

At dusk the company began to straggle in, and a handsome feast was laid out upon the dining-room table. After everyone was wonderfully stuffed with mutton, parsnips, baked custards, and pie—all washed down with liberal doses of ale—Nick announced it was time to repair to the top of the hill.

Alec Hewes had built a bonfire of such startling proportions that upon seeing it, Nerissa observed that it would likely take all night to burn away. "I shouldn't be surprised," Nick replied with a laugh, before going to take the torch from the young man. He kindled the vast pile of wood, and as soon as the fire was well established, the cloth and straw figure of Sally's making was strung to a long pole and held over the leaping flames. The children watched, open mouthed, as the effigy was consumed, but seeing that their elders laughed and clapped, they followed suit.

As the children capered about, chasing each other and shouting gleefully, Nerissa thought of Samuel, and a seemingly distant time when her days had been filled with the sweet sounds of lullaby and baby's cry.

When the party returned to the house, Alec Hewes said to her, "'Tis a treat the wee bairns won't soon forget, mistress.''

"They wouldn't have had it if you hadn't built such a grand bonfire,'' she replied. The grass on the steep hillside was already coated with frost; it crackled beneath the soles of her slippers, and although she made her way cautiously, she very nearly lost her footing. The young man reached out to take her arm, preventing a fall, and when she turned her head to thank him she was startled by his besotted expression. He mumbled something unintelligible and suddenly bolted, half running and half stumbling down the hill. At that moment Nick stepped out of the shadows, and she greeted him thankfully and a trifle desperately.

"Another admirer, Nerissa?" In the wavering torchlight she could not read his face, but she guessed it was disapproving. "Come along,'' she heard him say, "you should not be standing out in the cold.''

Their company reassembled in the parlour, which Nerissa had rendered more comfortable by removing the straight-backed settle and wooden stools and re-placing them with a cosy sofa and several wing chairs. The men shoved these against the wall to make room for dancing and rolled up the fine Turkey carpet that was her pride and joy. When Mr. McNab took up his instrument, everyone cried out for the master and mistress to begin the dancing. Nerissa let Nick lead her onto the floor before it occurred to her that he had never partnered her before, which might well be obvious to the onlookers.

"As we are unacquainted with the northern reels," he said, "perhaps we had best let the locals show us the way. Alec, Sally," he called over his shoulder, "Mrs. Blythe and I cannot manage this business without you."

The little maidservant blushed rosily and Alec swallowed, his Adam's apple rising and falling. But the younger couple heeded their employer's command, and to the accompaniment of the pipes they executed a simple step. Nerissa linked hands with Nick and they joined in, tentatively at first, laughing at their mistakes, but with every measure they grew more confident. The warm glow of the candles and the firelight softened the harsh planes of his face, easing the lines of tension about his eyes and mouth, and Nerissa forgot that he and she were no more married than Alec and Sally. He swung her around with dizzying speed, and she let out a most undignified shriek. And when the reel ended, she collapsed against his broad chest, breathless from exertion.

"You dance very well, wife," he whispered, before releasing her.

At his invitation, the others joined in the dancing. He busied himself with concocting the punch, while Nerissa sat down at the hearthside with the young people to roast chestnuts. More food was served—and more drink—and the party did not break up until midnight, by which time the children were half asleep and their fathers none so steady on their feet. When everyone had gone, Nerissa dismissed Sally to her garret room and sent a yawning Alec to his bed above the stables, which he shared with the brown-and-white rat terrier which kept the place free of vermin. Then she repaired to the silent kitchen to tidy up. She had just locked the meat safe when Nick entered the room, a pewter tankard in hand.

"Best have a care," she warned him, "else your

head will pay the price tomorrow.'' She reached out
to take the vessel from him and her long sleeve fell
back, exposing the red mark on her hand.

''What've you done to yourself?''

''It's a trifling burn—Mrs. McNab rubbed some
salve on it, and it doesn't even hurt now.''

He shook his head at her. ''What a one you are for
getting into trouble.''

Something in his comment seemed to her to go beyond her injury and she blurted, ''I wasn't flirting with
Alec tonight.''

''I never suggested that you had been.''

''But you must have been thinking it,'' she said unhappily.

''Oh, no,'' he replied, his eyes dark with some emo-
tion she could not quite define, ''I've been too busy
thinking how very much I would like for you to flirt
with *me*.'' He placed his hands on either side of her
face and drew it towards him. His mouth, she discovered, tasted of oranges and spices and wine, and his
kiss was more intoxicating than the punch he had im-
bibed so freely. Gradually, without her being aware of
it, her fingers uncurled from the handle of the tankard,
until it slipped free and fell to the floor with a loud
clatter.

For several seconds they stared at one another with
a new awareness, and the only sound in the room was
the faint hiss of the banked fire.

Nick stared down at his hands, lost in the thickness
of her hair; the dark tendrils curled around his fingers
as if to bind him to her. He said ruefully, ''I've never
done this in a kitchen before.''

''Done what?'' she asked witlessly.

''Seduced a lady. For that, you know,'' he said in
his foggy voice, ''is exactly what I am doing.'' He
took a deep breath, then quoted softly, '' 'The first
interrogatory that my Nerissa shall be sworn on is,

whether till the next night she had rather stay, or go to bed now, being two hours to day.' ''

"You are drunk," she sighed.

"Not at all, or I'd never have managed a speech like that one. I've been waiting for just the right moment to use it, but to speak more plainly, will you lie with me tonight, sweet Nerissa?"

She took a backward step. "I'm not your wife." But how lovely if she could be, for then there would be no shame in his invitation. "It isn't part of the arrangement," she reminded him.

"True," he agreed, "but I hoped you might be interested in renegotiating the terms. If not, then I must be patient a little while longer."

When he turned to go she realised, belatedly, that he had received the impression that someday she would be willing. She wanted to call out to him that she would never, ever change her mind, but the words stuck in her throat and remained unspoken.

It was a good thing, Nerissa told herself as she scrambled into her clothes one cold morning, that she did not mind keeping early hours. At Arcadia, she generally left her bed at the rise of the sun, and returned to it only an hour or two after supper. She was occupied every minute of the day, but as she often told Nick when he took her to task for working so hard, she simply didn't have enough time to feel tired.

After all of these days and weeks living with Nick Blythe, she knew virtually nothing of his history, or what family he had left behind. Although they slept beneath the same roof and ate at the same board like any married couple, they were wholly independent of one another. She kept busy within the house; he accompanied Mr. McNab on his daily rounds. They shared a life, but nothing of themselves. It was as if they were both waiting for some outside force to tear down the barrier they had erected, by tacit consent, on the night of the bonfire, when she had stepped out of his arms.

She put on a practical kerseymere gown and coiled her hair at the nape of her neck, all the while comparing the still mysterious Dominic to her worthy, respectable Andrew, and concluded that she much preferred being a pretend Mrs. Blythe to a lawful Mrs. Hudgins. Her existence had never been sufficiently ordered by the rules of society, by considerations of convention and propriety, for her to miss them now. The safe path had never held any charms for her. If it had, she would not be living in an isolated Cumbrian farmhouse with a man she had known slightly less than a month.

When she hurried down the spiral staircase, ready to begin the tasks of the day, she found Nick standing in the hallway. "Good morning, Mrs. Blythe," he said, his eyes dancing as they always did when he called her by that name. "I didn't expect to see you abroad so early."

"There's cider to be made, and I wouldn't want to miss the fun," she said, so much like an eager child for a promised treat that he laughed. "Will you be away all day?"

"Only for the morning—there's a prize bull on show at Warwick village, and McNab wants to look him over. Why don't you pack up some bread and cheese for a picnic—we can walk over to the caves when I return. At this season, we can't expect too many more fine days." And with a wave, he was off.

Nerissa spent her morning in the cellar, supervising Alec's labours with the ancient apple press. The young man's violent infatuation showed no signs of abating; she suspected his feelings alarmed him far more than they did her. Trusting to time to effect a cure, she was careful to treat him with a combination of kindness and disinterest.

At noon an excited Sally called her upstairs to receive a visitor.

"Pray forgive my intrusion, Mrs. Blythe," Miss Maria Haslam said when Nerissa entered the parlour.

"It is a welcome one," Nerissa said cordially. "Mrs. McNab has put the kettle on, and we shall have tea and cake directly. Today we have begun making the cider, and I fear the place is much disordered as a result."

"I quite understand. Is Mr. Blythe at home today? I think he will be particularly interested to hear what I have come to tell you, for I know how closely gentlemen follow the progress of the war."

"He and Mr. McNab have gone to Warwick to inspect a bull. Do you have news—have our armies lost a battle?"

"I cannot say, but the Navy has lately won an engagement against the French fleet, off Cape Trafalgar." The spinster's voice sank when she said, "Yet this longed-for victory came at a terrible cost. My dear, our gallant Lord Nelson was killed!"

Nerissa felt as though she'd just been told of the death of someone she had known well, and even loved.

"It happened a fortnight ago—I should have brought you Papa's paper, which told the number of ships involved and explained the particulars of the engagement, but in my haste to leave the house I left it behind."

It was just as well, Nerissa thought; a newspaper never had any good effect upon Nick's spirits. "I will tell Mr. Blythe when he returns from Warwick," she said. "You were very kind to remember us, Miss Haslam."

The other lady's dark eyes were lit with their characteristic twinkle when she said, "Oh, I often think

of you, Mrs. Blythe. And, I might add, with considerable envy. You live here in this grand ruin, which I
confess I have always adored, and you are exceedingly
fortunate in your choice of a husband. I can't think
when my father has taken such a fancy to anyone as
he did to Mr. Blythe.''

This speech gratified Nerissa, but it embarrassed
her, too. Fortunately she was saved the trouble of a
reply by Sally, who carried in the tray. As the two
ladies nibbled seed-cake and drank their tea, the conversation become more general and less personal.
Nerissa's guest requested a tour of the house, and expressed her admiration of the kitchen and the still-
room.

Before climbing into her carriage, Miss Haslam said
warmly, ''I do hope you will visit us in Abbey Street
very soon, Mrs. Blythe. Not only am I eager to repay
your hospitality—I should very much like for us to be
friends.''

But Nerissa knew the risk of developing a close relationship with any stranger, even one as well meaning
as Maria Haslam; familiarity might breed careless-
ness. The lie she was forced to live had closed her off
from all others save her fellow conspirator, and she
could never let down her guard, not in front of her
servants and certainly not with the daughter of their
landlord. She accepted the hand the other lady held
out to her but did not commit herself to anything, saying only, ''You are very kind.'' And she made a silent
vow to stay away from Carlisle.

Later that day, when she and Nick set out on their
excursion, she told him what little she knew of the
naval battle, but he had already heard the news. ''They
were talking of nothing else at Warwick,'' he told her.
''The whole nation is mourning the hero.''

''And well they should,'' she sighed, pulling her
wool shawl closer about her shoulders. ''Poor Lady

Hamilton, I wonder what will be her fate now she has lost her Lord Nelson? People speak ill of her, but I think she is very much to be pitied now.''

Their exploration of St. Constantine's Cells, as the locals called the three caves cut into the sandstone bank of the Eden, was brief. Although they found that it was possible to stand and move about each of the manmade chambers, the dark and the cold were unpleasant. "I should have brought a lantern," said Nick when they emerged.

He spread a horse blanket in a pool of sunshine on the ridge overlooking the river, and Nerissa looked up from unwrapping their meal to enquire, "Why were the caves built?"

"No one seems to know who was originally responsible," he replied, "but I believe they were sometimes used to conceal the priory's plate and money whenever the Scots raiders came calling."

After breaking a piece of bread from the loaf she passed it to him. "This is such a quiet part of the world that it's hard to conceive of so much pillaging and plundering going on here. Those must have been exciting times," she said wistfully.

"I wonder how excited you'd have been if Bonaparte had successfully invaded our shores last year?"

She laughed and acknowledged, "Not very—I was as terrified as everyone else. I suppose the distance of time makes the past infinitely more romantic than the present." When he handed her the jug in exchange for the loaf, she held it up to her lips and drank. The ale was bitter, but pleasantly so, and it brought back happy memories. "When we first moved to the country, Papa and I used to play at being gypsies, and often ate our dinner on the ground. We would walk by the river and talk for hours and hours, till the sun went down. My aunt spent the latter part of her life teaching me to be a lady, but he managed to undo all her hard work in a very short time!'' She looked out at the river, its rippling waters gilded by the Midas touch of the sun. ''I still cannot accustom myself to his being gone.''

''I know something of what you must feel,'' Nick told her, ''for I lost my own father last year.'' When she looked over at him in surprise, he said, ''Nerissa, you must learn to look to the future, not the past, if you hope to be happy. I offer myself as your tutor—and let this be your first lesson.'' He took her chin in his hand and gave her a swift, hard kiss on the mouth. He would have ended with that, but gazing into her eyes, so deeply blue that he fancied himself drowning in them, he felt the stirring of desire. ''You smell of apples,'' he murmured, before kissing her again. And when she turned her face away, he said, his voice thick with passion, ''Do not deny me—this is what you were made for, you know.''

Taking her by the shoulders, he pressed her gently down to the ground, and began to peel back her shawl before drawing her back into his embrace. But when he felt the wetness of her cheek and tasted the salt of her tears, he could not go on. Looking down at her, he realised that this was no token show of reluctance. He had known her in many moods, but never before had he seen such despair in her face. ''I'm sorry,'' he said quietly. ''I didn't mean to frighten you.''

Nerissa drew several laboured breaths. ''It isn't your fault,'' she panted. ''I knew, the day I accepted your offer of protection, that this was inevitable. I'm not afraid of you, Nick, and in truth I like you very well, but—''

''But you prefer to be admired from a distance,'' he finished for her.

He rolled over onto his back and stared up at the blue dome of the sky. She was so temptingly made, with her provocative face and generous form, but she was still not ready to accept him as a lover. For the first time he began to wonder whether she would ever be able to do so. This partnership of theirs seemed to be so seriously flawed that it might never flourish in the way he had originally hoped. He wasn't even sure how he could continue living with a woman who was so eminently desirable and at the same time so devilishly elusive.

He supposed he would have to resign himself to her stubborn determination to withhold the secrets of her body, but he could not permit her to close her mind against him. Her quietude was thoughtful rather than sulky, but he was troubled by it nonetheless and for the rest of the afternoon he exerted himself to put her to ease again.

That night after dinner they retired to the cosy parlour, according to their habit. When Nick went to the secretaire to begin his long-overdue letter to Cat Durham, Nerissa curled up on the settee and hid her face between the marbled covers of a book. Nick recognised it as one of a set of four she had bought for herself in Carlisle, a collection of the writings of Mary Wollstonecraft, and he could appreciate why she might find solace in it. Like Nerissa, the authoress had been characterised by independence and intelligence, and she had flouted convention by living with a gentleman who was not her husband. And, he thought as he trimmed his quill, Mary had also borne a child out of wedlock.

When he heard her get up, he looked around to ask, "Going upstairs so soon?"

"It is well past my usual time, as you would know if you'd looked at the clock lately." Her eyes followed him anxiously when he vacated his chair and came towards her.

"Do not worry, I am not going to do anything improper, I promise." She permitted him to kiss her cheek, and just to make her blush, he said, "You *still* smell of apples."

And then, hoping he had proved that he was a man of his word, he went back to the desk to finish his letter.

=== 8 ===

ONE AFTERNOON NERISSA devoted her full attention to refurbishing Nick's chamber, for ever since coming to Arcadia he had complained that the dust-heavy brocade curtains gave him sneezing fits in the night. As she vigourously pulled the rings from the old ones, she reflected that if there had been any danger of his interrupting her work, she would have postponed it indefinitely, for there was no telling what he might do if he chanced upon her in such proximity to his bed.

Before hanging the blue damask curtains she and Sally Willis had sewn, she polished the intricately carved bedposts. When she set her cloth impregnated with beeswax on a walnut chest of drawers, she noted that it cried out for similar treatment. First she had to remove a collection of Nick's personal belongings—an empty tobacco pouch, scraps of paper, a silver button which she recognised as belonging to his dress coat, and a letter. Setting these aside, she rubbed the wood until it threatened to blind her with its shine, then she replaced each item where she had found it. The letter, a single sheet, was not folded, and she could see that the writing was neat and regular—very feminine, in fact—and it bore a St. Albans postmark.

Curious to know the identity of his correspondent, she hunted for the signature. The closing words of the final paragraph leapt up at her: ''Your past kindnesses to me have been so much greater than I deserve, and there is nothing you cannot ask. Be easy, you shall have your thousand pounds as soon as I can contrive to get them to you, and more if you need it. I trust and pray you are well, and that no great hardship prompted the request of your funds, which I am happy to restore to you. I remain, as ever, your devoted Cat."

Nerissa couldn't bring herself to read anymore; she dared not, knowing it was wrong. It was bad enough to know that in St. Albans there lived a woman named Cat who had control of Nick's money. Was she a relation, some sister or a cousin to whom he had applied for assistance? Try though she might—try though she did—she could not shove aside her fear that the relationship was other than a familial one. Perhaps this Cat was a sweetheart or a mistress he had left behind. And then it came to her with heart-stopping clarity, and the letter fell from her fingers, fluttering to the floor.

Dominic Blythe was a married man.

Her fledgling hope that he might someday make her his wife curled up and died, and in that moment she also discovered, to her shame, that she had fallen so deeply and desperately in love with him that the simple, dreadful truth of his marriage could not alter her feelings. To him she had only been a prospective mistress, and she could never expect to be anything more. Casting her mind back to that night in Leek, when he had asked her to come north with him, she recalled his frankness about his inability to offer matrimony. She might have asked him why, but instead she had acted with her usual impulsiveness, flinging herself headlong down the road to ruin.

She hurried from his room, stepping blindly past the pile of discarded brocade curtains, and made her way to her own chamber. When she had wrapped herself in a warm, protective cloak, she left the house stealth-ily, without alerting any of the servants, and walked towards the river. To get there she had to cut across a meadow where sheep grazed; the animals darted nervously out of her way. The day had been particularly fine, but now the sun had begun its westerly descent, leaving behind long streaks of pink and orange on the pale azure palette overhead. Nerissa trudged on, heedless alike of the brambles that caught at her skirts and the wind which swept along the fells and across the moors.

Of all the many trials she had undergone in the months since her father's death, this was surely the worst. She longed for a broad masculine shoulder to rest her head upon, but Nick's was denied her. She needed someone to talk to, but she had no other friend. And however much she might love him, she could not continue living with him—nor could she bring herself to admit that she had seen his wife's letter. She would encourage him to believe that she was weary of the deception, and so bored by their restricted life that she had made up her mind to go to London after all.

The advance of dusk was swift and merciless, and in minutes the world changed from brilliant gold to dismal grey. Nerissa drew her cloak more tightly about her and sat down upon a rock at the edge of the water.

Mary Wollstonecraft had been correct when she wrote that nothing destroyed peace of mind more than platonic attachments. Nerissa was now convinced of her favourite author's assertion that such relationships often ended in sorrow; having succumbed to that "dangerous tenderness" Mary had alluded to, she could no longer be satisfied by mere friendship with Nick Blythe. Her traitorous heart had not remained disengaged, and on the day of their picnic at the caves her treacherous passions had been stirred. His skilled and seductive assault upon her person had been nothing like Andrew's tentative demonstrations of affection, and it had answered many questions about who she was and what she wanted in a lover. For a brief, lovely moment she had given in to that wild, wanton creature dwelling inside her, whose existence she had never intended to reveal to any man, least of all to Nick. When tempted, her salvation had not been her conscience but that stronger fear of becoming what the people of Olney had called her.

In time, she might have given herself to him, in the expectation that she would one day be his bride. He was a man of honour, and she believed he would have wed her had there been no impediment to a legal union. She felt she was more truly his wife than the woman who had expressed her devotion so sweetly yet hadn't had the decency to accompany him into exile. The real Mrs. Blythe was safe in St. Albans, with plenty of money at her disposal, and whatever she might be suffering, it was Nick who had paid the higher price—banishment, no less.

The discovery that night had fallen heavily around her startled Nerissa out of her abstraction, and when she walked slowly homeward, the path before her was barely visible and the noises of the countryside seemed louder because of the darkness. A sheep's cough made her jump, and there was an ominous rustling in the reeds along the river. But it was only the brown-and-white terrier which seldom strayed very far from Alec's side, and Nerissa, glancing over her shoulder, saw the young man following behind and paused to let him catch up. "Shouldn't you have been home a long time ago?" she asked. "I hope Mrs. McNab saved you some supper."

"She gave me leave to go 'cross the river," he assured her. "The ferry was delayed, or I would not be so late in coming home from the castle. I heard they may be hiring on a new groom, and went to enquire."

The youth whistled to the dog; it scurried up the bank.

"Mr. Blythe would be very sorry to lose you," Nerissa said kindly as Alec fell into step beside her.

He ducked his head self-consciously, avoiding her eye. "The master has been good to me, but I've been thinking it might be best to find me a new place."

She hadn't believed she could feel any worse, but knowing that his guilt over his attachment to her compelled him to leave Nick's employ depressed her spirits even further. "Oh, Alec," she said, and the words came out as a mournful sigh.

"Mistress?"

"Don't—don't make up your mind too hastily." She couldn't tell him she was leaving; he would hear about it soon enough. But now there was yet another reason not to delay her departure from Arcadia Farm.

Mrs. McNab gave Nick the news of Nerissa's disappearance when he returned from his day in town. His mood was not the best, for none of his business there had been successful. The chaise he had ordered from the Carlisle carriage-maker was not yet ready, and he had failed to find a suitable pair of horses at an auction. His landlord still demanded a purchase price that he knew to be far in excess of what the farm was worth. Now Nerissa had gone missing—it only needed that, he thought morosely as he stood at the parlour window, watching and waiting and worrying. His vigil ended when two figures approached the house, with a small dog tagging at their heels.

"Where the devil have you been?" he growled at Nerissa when she stepped into the room. No sooner had he spoken the rough question than he wished he could call it back, because it sent the colour flying from her cheeks. Her pallor made her eyes seem even more blue, and the black mole stood out starkly against her white skin.

"I—I went for a walk by the river," she faltered.

''I never meant to be so late returning.'' She went to kneel before the fire, and after a moment looked up and asked him to close the door. ''There is something I must say to you, in private.''

When he had complied with her request, he sat down in his favourite chair, saying lightly, ''I hope you aren't about to tell me that you're planning to run off with the stableboy.''

She closed her eyes, her expression one of anguish, then opened them again. Staring at the dancing flames, she said quietly, ''No, not that. But I *am* going away. I simply cannot go on living here, pretending to be what I am not. Once I thought I could, but I was mistaken.''

Nick abruptly abandoned his chair. ''Nerissa, I would never harm you, surely you know that. Are you so afraid of me?''

''More afraid of myself, I think. But we are neither of us saints.''

''That we are not,'' he agreed, holding her so close that he could feel her breasts rise and fall against his chest as she laboured for breath. ''Don't go,'' he whispered.

''It's no good,'' she said, although she made no attempt to break away. ''You won't change my mind with a few kisses and a caress or two. Remember, before we ever began this charade, you said I would be free to end my part in it at any time.''

But he didn't want to be held to some rash promise he'd made so many weeks ago, before he had grown to depend upon her—to love her. For a long time now he had desired her, but it was possible to want a woman without really knowing her. It was the knowing that made all the difference.

When she stepped out of his embrace, she continued, ''I have a cousin in London, the Duke of Solway.

He is a good-hearted man, so perhaps he will not judge me too harshly when I throw myself upon his mercy.''

"The Duke of Solway," he repeated. "How can you possibly be related—I thought your father was a sea captain?''

The corners of her mouth lifted in a smile. "Even a sea captain can come from a ducal house. My grandmother was Lady Beatrice Marchant, for all she married a plain Mr. Newby. Papa was first cousin to the present duke, and the two were excellent friends as well.'' Nerissa wandered over to the window to draw the curtains, and when she was done she faced Nick again and said, "You mustn't think I am intimate with the Marchants, for nothing could be less true. They go in for hunting and balls and other pursuits for which my father had no time or interest, but sometimes he took me with him to Haberdine Castle in Northamptonshire. The duchess was so toplofty she scared me half to death, and Gervase and Edgar and Ophelia and Imogen were always racing about on their ponies. They deemed me very poor company, and I think in their eyes I was a little tainted by my father's trade. But Cousin William—the duke—was always very kind to me, and I hope he will be again.''

If Nick had doubted her, which he didn't, the way she rattled off these names and titles would have convinced him of her claim. Her very name, taken from Shakespeare, was proof of her tie to the Marchants. Nevertheless, it was disconcerting to discover that this daughter of an obscure merchant seaman was related to one of the noblest families in the realm. "Why didn't you tell me before now?'' he asked her.

"I didn't want you to misunderstand, to think me something I am not. I've never moved in the same exalted sphere as my cousins do, nor will I do so in future.'' Moving towards the door, she said, "I mean to leave for Haberdine in a few days. I'll have to think

up some plausible excuse to explain my sudden departure . . . a sick relative or something." She prevented
further discussion by saying hurriedly, "Pray excuse
me, but I am tired from my walk. Mrs. McNab has
made some soup—could you tell Sally that I'd like
some brought up to me in a bit?"

Privacy Dominic would grant her, but never her
freedom, he told himself as the door closed behind
her. The prospect of living at Arcadia without her, of
doing anything at all without her, was insupportable.
He had lost too much already—his title, his friends,
his property—and he would not lose her too. For none
of those things he had formerly valued so highly had
any worth at all when set against the lady he was determined to keep by his side.

Nerissa, kneeling on the damp stone floor of the
cellar, placed her ear to the wooden cider cask and
listened carefully. When she heard the faint hiss from
within she looked over at Sally, standing on the top
step. "Yes," she said, "fermentation has begun. Tell
Alec it's time for him to rack the juice off into another
cask, and remind him that when he pours, he must be
very careful not to disturb the dregs."

The maidservant vanished, and Nerissa climbed to
her feet, wiping her hands on a skirt that was already
soiled from her labours in the dairy and the poultry-
yard and the kitchen. Keeping busy was the best way
to keep her sorrows at bay, so she had thrown herself
into the role of housewife with even greater fervour
than she had done formerly. Two days had passed since
she had told Nick of her plans, and only two more
remained before she would leave this house forever.
Picking up her taper, she lit her way up the steps, and
mentally ticked the task she had just performed off her
list of things to do. Time to move on to the next one:
the household mending.

She was startled when, upon emerging from the dark depths of the cellar, she came face to face with Nick. He had left for Carlisle immediately after breakfast, and usually he did not return until late. He was, she noted, dressed in his newest and best clothes, a dark coat and oyster-coloured breeches. "I'm taking you on an outing," he announced. "Run upstairs and comb those cobwebs out of your hair, and put on a fresh gown. A blue one, I think, to match your eyes. Hurry now, we haven't got all day!"

"Oh, very well," she said, poised between frustration and curiosity. "Are we going to visit Hadrian's Wall?" She had expressed this desire more than a week ago, but he had apparently forgotten it.

"Ask me no questions, I'll tell you no lies."

Her blue gown was sadly wrinkled, so she put on a white one instead, fulfilling the spirit of Nick's request by covering it with her blue pelisse. When she went back downstairs, she found him in the hall. As he held the front door open for her, he nodded approvingly and murmured, "White—now why didn't *I* think of that?"

She had assumed that they would take the gig, but there was a neat chaise and a pair of horses waiting at the door, along with a postboy in drab livery. "Did you hire it in Carlisle?" she asked.

"Only the horses," he answered, handing her into the vehicle, which smelled of leather. "I've purchased the chaise."

"Oh, Nick, such extravagance will ruin you!" It was really none of her business, so she said nothing more, but as the carriage lurched forward, it occurred to her that the money must have come from his wife.

They followed the road to Carlisle, proving wrong her guess about Hadrian's Wall, and beyond the city they passed a flat, barren stretch of land where the only dwellings were rudely built of sod and wattle.

''Where *are* we going?'' she asked, and when he refused to enlighten her she heaved an exasperated sigh
and turned her head towards the window to gaze at the
golden sands and grey water.

''That is Solway Firth,'' Nick said. ''From which
your kinsman takes his title?''

''No, it came from the Border town of Solway Moss.
There was a battle, in the sixteenth century, I think,
and the Marchant of the day distinguished himself in
the fighting and was ennobled as a result. Papa used
to tell me the story when I was a child.'' She wondered if her ancestor had been as struck by the bleak-
ness of the flat marshland as she was.

''We are very nearly in Scotland, and the next town
on this road is Gretna Green. That being the case,
perhaps you might like to take part in the most popular
local custom?'' When she turned an astonished face
upon him, Nick smiled and said, 'I'm asking you if
you will marry me, and I do hope you'll agree, or else
I've abducted you to no purpose.''

As the import of this speech became clear to her,
Nerissa went rigid with shock. What he suggested was
an abomination—how could he be so callously cruel,
so utterly shameless?'' ''You must be mad!'' she
gasped.

''I've never been more serious in my life.''

Hot fury mobilised her and she drew back her arm
to strike him, a futile attempt, for he caught her hand
just before it connected with his cheek. ''Let me go,
damn you!'' she cried. ''Do you expect me to say I
am *honoured* by your proposal? What you suggest is
hateful, disgusting! It would be bigamy!'' She tried to
pull free of him, but his grip on her tightened.

''You are *married?* For God's sake, answer me, Nerissa!''

Cowed by the dangerous glitter in his eyes, she
shook her head. ''Not I—you.''

During her disjointed explanation about finding the letter, Nick's face gradually regained its colour, and the wild light died out of his eyes. "You didn't read very much of it, did you?" he said when she fell silent. "Because if you had, you'd know that Cat is *not* my wife."

If he lied, he was a master of the art, because his words rang with sincerity. Nerissa eyed him uncertainly. "Who is she, then?"

"For most of the years I've known her, she was my father's mistress. But she has also been my friend. After the duel I stayed the night at her house in St. Albans and entrusted some of my funds to her keeping. Our correspondence has been financial, not amorous." He smiled over at Nerissa as he said warmly, "My dear, I am so much a bachelor that I have never even come close to offering marriage to any lady. Until today."

"Yet not so long ago you said you could never marry me," she reminded him.

"You are wondering why I've changed my mind?" he asked, leaning close to her. "I think you'll agree that this is reason enough."

While he kissed her, she could not think, and when he stopped, his husky words rendered all thought unnecessary.

"Nerissa, why should we continue to live a lie when a simple exchange of words can make us honest? In your heart you must know this is right—and I have decided it is time." As the chaise jolted across a bridge, its pace slowed, and Nick said, "The fame of this place is such that the postboy will think nothing of our stopping here—fully half of Gretna's visitors are tourists. Although," he added, surveying the straggling village of whitewashed, thatch-covered houses, "it appears that none have come today, which is fortunate for us. We have the choice of being married by a fisherman, a smuggler, a joiner, a tobacconist, or the traditional blacksmith, and he will ask whether you have come here willingly."

"I do. I have," she said breathlessly, her lips still throbbing in reaction to his kiss.

"Then take off the ring you are wearing now, because I am going to replace it with another very soon."

A few minutes later, Nerissa stood in a dimly lit room facing a shabby individual who wore a coat liberally flecked with ash from his pipe and appeared to represent several of the professions Nick had named. Although he declared he was a professional "joiner," the local slang for a priest, the walls of his humble cottage were lined with the jars of tobacco and snuff he offered for sale. A liberal stock of whiskey barrels confirmed Nerissa's suspicion that he supplemented his income by smuggling the goods of some local, unlicensed distillery, but she saw nothing to indicate that he was a blacksmith, though he did conduct the ceremony over an anvil, as required by custom.

Six guineas was the price demanded of the groom, who readily paid the sum. "Ye must treat my friends to a glass of whiskey apiece," the Scotsman said, nodding in the direction of the witnesses he had called in. "And if ye've brought a ring, give it to the lady."

When Nick had done this, he barked, "What's yer name?"

"Dominic Sebastian Charles Blythe."

"A reet mouthful, that, Lassie?"

"Nerissa Rosalind Newby," she replied.

"Where d'ye bide?"

"London," Nick answered.

In the periphery of her vision, Nerissa saw a coin change hands; obviously it was the habit of the witnesses to wager on the outcome of that question.

"Are ye both single folk?"

"We are," said Nick.

Turning to Nerissa, the old man asked if she had come of her own free will and accord, and she replied in the affirmative. There was a brief pause in the proceedings while he quaffed the contents of his tankard. Then, "D'ye take this woman to be your lawful wedded wife, forsaking all others, and keep to her as long as ye both shall live?"

"I will," said Nick.

After Nerissa had answered the same question, the Scotsman asked her for the ring, which he then transferred to her bridegroom, who placed it on her finger. Nick repeated the vow, saying, "With this ring I thee wed, with my body I thee worship, with all my goods I thee endow, in the name of the Father, Son, and Holy Ghost, amen."

"Now, lassie, ye must say 'What God joins together, let no man put asunder.' " The words were hardly out of Nerissa's mouth when the old man said hurriedly, "Forasmuch as this man and this woman have come together by giving and receiving a ring, I therefore declare them to be man and wife before God and these witnesses."

When all was done, a dazed Mrs. Blythe asked, "Aren't we supposed to sign a register?"

"Only if ye want to."

She was about to insist upon it, but Nick suggested that they dispense with the formality. She nodded, for to leave behind any proof of their belated nuptials might result in discovery and embarrassment. And Nick, being a fugitive from the law, could not run the risk of signing his true name.

He bought their well-wishers the promised dram and purchased some pipe tobacco for himself from the Scotsman, and when Nerissa followed him out of the cramped dark house, she was surprised to find she felt no different than she had upon entering it.

"Being wed at Gretna is not nearly as romantic a

procedure as one is led to expect," he commented. "I hope you aren't disappointed?" Nerissa, thoroughly disoriented from all that had occurred in so short a time, shook her head and let him lead her back to the waiting chaise. Their postboy, none the wiser, climbed into his saddle and pointed the horses to the south.

As the carriage retraced its earlier path, Nerissa inspected the gold band Nick had placed on her finger; it was chased with a delicate pattern of hearts and flowers. There was an inscription, too. "Love me and leave me not," she read aloud. "Why, it's the same motto from Nerissa's ring in *The Merchant of Venice!*"

"A jeweller in Carlisle engraved it," Nick told her. "I had intended to give it to you at Christmas, but I decided to put it to a better use." His voice was pitched very low as he said, "I do not demand your love, Nerissa, it may yet be too soon for that. But at least I need no longer fear you will leave me."

The tide of Nerissa's joy ebbed. Had he married her only for the sake of convenience, because he could not get her into his bed any other way? She banished this thought at once, and tried to look on the bright side— she was wed to a man she loved beyond reason, and furthermore, she could now claim her inheritance, although by law it belonged to her husband. Who, she suddenly recalled, was entirely oblivious to her prospects.

Nick, whose watchful eyes were fixed upon her troubled face, said quietly, "I hope you aren't regretting this step."

"Oh, no, it's only that I—" She broke off, uncertain about how to proceed. At last she plucked up her courage and said boldly, "Now that I am your wife, there is something I ought to tell you, Nick. It wasn't important before, but you do deserve to know the truth about me."

She had no way of knowing that this tentative pre-
amble was exactly what he had been dreading, and
although it was not unexpected, it was most definitely
unwelcome. Nick did not want to begin his married
life by listening to his bride confess her liaison with
another man. It would be kinder, perhaps, to tell her
that he already knew about the child, but he couldn't
bring himself to do it.

Peering up at him, she said, "I've never discussed
this—everyone knew it, you see, which makes this a
trifle difficult. I suppose I should just say it straight
out and be done." She took a breath, then blurted,
"I'm an heiress. My father's estate was considerable,
and he left the whole to me—it has been administered
by my trustees, but their power expires upon my marriage, and would have done so on my twenty-fifth
birthday had I remained unwed. The principal is in-
vested in Consols—the three percent consolidated an-
nuities. And I have India stock, and Bank stock as
well. But the larger part of the income derives from
the ships—when Papa sold them, he retained part interest. He was very successful in his business ven-
tures," she said with more than a trace of pride, "and
I believe I may have as much as half a million pounds,
though I've never known for sure. But he told me once
that I would be dowered with one-tenth of his fortune,
and my portion alone is fifty thousand."

Yes, Nick thought bitterly, it would take that much
money to buy a husband for a wayward daughter, heiress though she might be, and obviously Captain Newby
had known it.

Nerissa bit her lower lip in consternation. "You
don't appear to be much pleased."

"I am not a mercenary man," he told her, more
harshly than he had intended.

"I never meant to suggest that you were," she replied calmly, but he could read the pain in her eyes.

His expression softened. Gently he drew her head down to rest upon his shoulder and said, ''Today I have gained something of greater value to me than mere money, Nerissa, and I am content.''

Within the hour the carriage swung into the drive leading to the farmhouse, and he smiled down at his silent companion. ''Home at last.''

''Just in time for tea,'' she murmured prosaically.

''A pity we won't be able to enjoy it in privacy,'' Nick commented. ''It appears we have company.''

Nerissa lifted her head and saw that a mud-splattered chaise stood in the yard. ''Not the Bow Street Runner?''

''Travelling post? I doubt that very much,'' her husband replied. ''I hope it's not the Runner—surely he wouldn't intrude upon our *second* wedding night!'' He pinched her rosy cheek and laughed as if he hadn't a care in the world.

Upon entering the hall they found a trunk and a bandbox, and the parlour was occupied by a short, dark-haired lady. Nerissa paused on the threshold, watching as Nick swept the stranger into an embrace that nearly lifted her from her tiny feet. ''Why didn't you warn me that you meant to come north?'' he asked when he released the lady, who smoothed her chignon with one dimpled hand and glanced uncertainly at Nerissa. ''Come and meet Mrs. Durham,'' he invited her, before turning back to the lady. ''What brings you here, Cat?''

''I had to see for myself how you were faring,'' she told him.

Nick draped a careless arm around his bride's shoulders and said merrily, ''Very well indeed. Since you and I last met, this lady has honoured me with her hand in marriage. And she will be glad of your company, for I am kept busy all the day long—I am no longer the idle fellow you once knew.''

He silently blessed his wife when she supported him, saying easily, "Mrs. Durham, I am most happy to make your acquaintance, and I hope you are able to make a long stay. I'm sure the two of you have much to discuss, so if you'll excuse me, I'll tell Alec to carry our guest's trunk to the spare bedchamber and order some tea brought in."

After closing the door behind her, Nick turned to Cat, his expression one of comical dismay. "I hardly know where to begin."

"You said nothing in your letter about being wed!"

He placed a warning finger over his lips, and said softly, "I wasn't, not until two hours ago. We've just returned from Gretna, the only place where the deed could be accomplished with ease, and in complete secrecy." He crossed to the fireplace to take his clay pipe from its rack on the hearth. "Do you mind?" Cat shook her head, so he drew his newly filled tobacco pouch from his coat pocket.

"Lady Blythe is very beautiful," she commented as he tipped some of the mixture into the clay bowl.

"Isn't she? But you must take care not to expose me, Cat, for despite our having lived together as man and wife—or very nearly—all this while, Nerissa is quite unaware that I'm anything other than plain Mr. Blythe. I dispensed with my title many weeks ago, and it was better that she believe in my alias implicitly."

"Surely you mean to tell her the truth," Cat interjected. "I accept that it might have been more prudent to conceal your identity when there was some danger of discovery, but now—"

"No," he said firmly. "She'll need time enough to grow accustomed to our marriage. I can't burden her with the fact of my being a nobleman just yet."

With a sigh of resignation, she replied, "Oh, very well, I suppose you know best. But trust me, for I speak as a woman, you had better tell her soon, or you'll rue it." Reaching for her fringed reticule, she said, "I've brought your thousand pounds in the form of a draft drawn upon my bank in St. Albans."

"Your arrival is most timely, for my resources are sadly diminished. Living isn't cheap, not even in this remote part of the world, and I had no very clear notion what it would cost to set up housekeeping. My word, the things I've had to purchase—furniture and a carriage, and milk cows and a horse, and a host of other things."

"Which you've always taken for granted, spoiled fellow that you are—or were," Cat said, dimpling up at him.

"Was I? Well, those days are long gone." Nick sat down in his usual chair and stretched his legs out comfortably. "Nerissa, I've lately learned, is an extremely wealthy woman in her own right. I could probably purchase half of this shire with her dowry, but I don't know when I'll have access to her funds. Her trustees won't be pleased to learn that she's Lady Blythe, although they cannot withhold her inheritance. My marriage will have to be made public, for I may have to remain here for a very long time, and I can't have the legitimacy of any issue open to question. Tomorrow I will go to Carlisle to have a new will drawn up. I'll have to reveal my legal name, but it's a risk I'm obliged to take—I must make provision for my wife. Fortunately there's no entail on Blythe; I can leave it to her outright. Ram is heir to the title until I have a son to follow me, but—"

"Oh, how *could* I be so forgetful!" Cat interrupted. "I meant to tell you the moment you walked in the door, and here we sit talking of money and wills and such! Nick, he visited me!"

"Who?"

"Your cousin, the viscount—and I was never so amazed in my life, or so frightened!"

Nick lifted his brows. "Did he offer you *carte blanche?*"

"Don't be absurd, of course he didn't. But I'd almost rather he had, for then I should have known what to say!" she said fiercely. In a calmer voice she explained, "He came to St. Albans last week, and wanted to know if I could tell him where you're hiding. Finding you appeared to be a matter of some urgency to him."

Nick puffed thoughtfully on his pipe. "What did you say?"

"Very little. He did most of the talking, and I didn't understand the half of it. He kept saying he hoped you hadn't fled the country, because it would hurt your case."

"*What* case?" he asked wryly. "I have none, as he must surely know."

"I confess, he made me feel very ill at ease. I cannot but wonder if he intends some sort of mischief."

But Nick cared very little about his cousin's reasons for visiting Cat, and he listened to the rest of her tale with only half an ear. As glad as he was to see a familiar face, her arrival on the scene would prevent him from pursuing that greater intimacy he hoped to achieve with Nerissa. He had wanted her, he had wed her, and yet, he reflected, he had not really won her trust if she was still unwilling and unable to reveal the fact of her son's existence. Luring her to his bed had long been his goal, but as soon as he got her there he would face the inevitable explanation of why she was no virgin.

At least, he told himself as he idly blew a perfect ring of smoke, the drawing up of his new will and the negotiations for the purchase of Arcadia Farm would serve as much-needed distractions. Although nothing could prevent him from regretting his present inability to claim the lady who was now his wife.

ALTHOUGH NERISSA, WHO spent her wedding night alone, was perplexed by her bridegroom's failure to come to her, it encouraged her to hope that he'd had other reasons for marrying her apart from the obvious one. At breakfast the next morning, it almost seemed as if she had dreamed the event of the previous day, for Nick did not allude to the change in their circumstances. When he explained that last night he and Mrs. Durham had sat up talking till the candles guttered, she wasn't sure whether he intended it as an explanation of why he had not sought her bed, or an excuse. And by the time he rose from the table, saying he must hasten to Carlisle, it was even more clear to her that the hurried ceremony at Gretna had effected no material alteration in the structure of their life at Arcadia.

Her first official task as a married lady was taking care of the household mending she had neglected the day before. She was working in the parlour when Sally Willis came to announce that Mrs. Durham was awake but still abed. "I've just taken a tray up," said the maid, "and she bade me give you good morning and say she'd be downstairs soon. Oh, and Mrs. McNab is wanting to know if she should dress some of the fowls master killed t'other day."

Frowning at a tiny, jagged rent in the sleeve of her husband's shirt, Nerissa said, "We'll have them for our dinner. I'll make a syllabub—you must remember to reserve some of the new milk for it.''

"Aye,'' Sally said absently, her attention caught by something in the window. Wringing her apron, she reported, "There's a gentleman riding up the drive, wearing shiny boots and a tall hat, like the town-folk.''

Nerissa laid Nick's shirt across the arm of the sofa and went to see. The man, a stranger to her, was exactly as Sally had described him, and his fashionable garb stilled her instant fear that he might be a Bow Street Runner. When he dismounted, he carelessly tossed a coin to Alec, who had darted out of the stable yard to take charge of the horse. "Answer the door,'' Nerissa told Sally over the insistent hammering of the knocker, "and if he wishes to speak to Mr. Blythe or me, you must remember to ask for his card.''

"What will I do with it, mistress?'' the country-bred girl asked dubiously.

"Bring it to me,'' Nerissa instructed her. "Don't worry, it's what he will expect.''

But the maid returned empty-handed, saying breathlessly, "He's got no cards with him, but he told me he's a *lord!* Am I to let him in?''

Nerissa nodded, thinking that he must be one of the Howards from Castle Corby, for there was no other noble family in the neighbourhood.

When he stepped into her parlour, she realised that he was not as impressive a figure as he had seemed on horseback; though his riding clothes fit well and his boots were highly polished, he was no taller than she, and squarely built. He removed his hat, revealing close-cropped brown hair with tawny streaks in it. "Is this Arcadia Farm?'' he asked, and she affirmed it with a nod. "I'm Cavender—Lord Cavender. Dominic must have mentioned me.''

"I'm afraid he didn't,'' she said apologetically.

This appeared to amuse him. "I daresay old Nick

didn't want to bore so charming a creature by reciting the dull particulars of his family relationships.'' His brown eyes raked her from head to toe, pausing at her bosom in a way that caused her cheeks to flame.

She was quick to clarify the precise nature of her connexion to Nick by saying, with quiet dignity, ''Mr. Blythe and I were but lately married, my lord, so I still have much to learn about him.'' She expected him to leave off staring at her in that rude fashion, but his leer grew even more pronounced.

''*Mr.* Blythe, is it now?'' Lord Cavender drawled. ''Well, if you do not mind, I shall await his return, but I won't trouble you for anything more than a glass of wine. Though I confess I'm sore tempted.'' Nerissa glared at him, and he gave a sharp, derisive laugh. ''Ah, but the game is up, my beauty—I cannot be bamboozled. If Nick chooses to pass his doxy off as his wife, it's all the same to me. Although if he wanted you to be completely convincing, he ought to have given you leave to make use of his title. Mayn't I call you '*Lady Blythe*'?''

He was drunk, Nerissa thought frantically, or demented. She couldn't decide which would be worse. It was no wonder Nick had failed to tell her about this relation, for nobleman or not he must be a great embarrassment to the Blythe family. Stiffly she said, ''I fail to comprehend your jest, my lord.''

''Did he not even bother telling you he's a baron? How very remiss of him, to be sure.'' Lord Cavender moved closer to her, and tipped his head to one side. ''D'you come from these parts? What luck for old Nick, finding so fine an armful to warm his bed in the cold north.''

There was a startled gasp from the doorway. Nerissa and her visitor turned to see Cat Durham, who cried, ''For shame, Lord Cavender! You must not say such things to this lady!''

"Lady, my eye!"

"Mrs. Durham," said Nerissa faintly, as she eyed the unrepentant viscount, "do you know this gentleman?"

"Enlighten the wench, Cat. Tell her who I am. Clearly she thinks me something less than sane, and I gather you two ladybirds speak the same language."

"I will not bandy insults with your lordship," was Cat's quelling reply. "When Lord Blythe returns—" She hesitated, realising what she had just said.

"Never mind," Lord Cavender laughed. "I've already revealed the terrible truth about her so-called husband, the fictitious Mr. Blythe."

Through lips that were stiff and dry with shock, Nerissa whispered, "Is it true, then, what he said about Nick being a baron—it was *not* a jest?" And when Cat bowed her head in confirmation, the room spun sickeningly around her. She tried to focus on the faces of the lady and gentleman, one so anxious and concerned, the other blatantly mocking, and struggled to gather her scattered wits together. The effort proved to be beyond her.

"You are amazed," Cat said sympathetically, "and well you should be. I told Nick, I warned him how it would be, but he is so stubborn."

"It is not your fault. I think," Nerissa heard herself say, "that I must excuse myself. I suddenly feel the need to—to lie down."

She was halfway up the stairs when Lord Cavender said, in a carrying voice, "D'you suppose she meant that for an invitation, Cat? Ought I to follow her?"

But his malice could not wound her; she was too numb.

Ramsey Blythe, tense and out of temper, twirled the long stem of a wine glass between his fingers. He had the parlour to himself now—first Nick's bold-faced beauty had disappeared, and then Cat Durham, after waving her little paws and mewling at him, had stalked off. Eventually he had induced the shy little maidservant to bring him some wine, quizzing her about where her master had gone. To Carlisle, she had replied, and his glowering reception of this news sent her scurrying from the room. The irony of it was most irritating: Ramsey had just come from that city, riding over one of the worst roads he had encountered during the whole of the past week.

He could have come here sooner, but he had preferred to remain in London, enjoying his new riches and the pleasures they provided. Then his benefactor had demanded his instant attendance at the Swanborough hunt. Fearful of having offended Mr. Meriden, Ramsey had sent his horses ahead to Leicestershire and travelled there himself a few days later, but without expecting Lady Miranda Peverel to live up to the accolades the old nabob had heaped upon her unsuspecting head. To his amazement and delight, he discovered her to be everything his matchmaking relative had promised, and more. Only seventeen years old, with black hair and deep blue eyes that proclaimed her Marchant blood, she was as lovely as she could be, the embodiment of grace and charm—all in all, a piece of perfection. After a single day of basking in her sweet smiles, he made up his mind to wed her, only to have his uncle remind him that he had not yet made a push to find Lord Blythe, as he had promised.

Cat Durham's extreme nervousness at the time of his visit to her house had alerted him that she knew a great deal about his cousin's whereabouts. One of her servants had let it slip that she was planning a journey, and when she left St. Albans early the next day, he had travelled in her wake, risking discovery by putting up at the same middling inns along the way in order that his postboy, a born spy, could glean information from hers. Upon reaching Carlisle he lost track of her, but sheer luck led him to the Blue Bell in Scotch Street. When he asked the proprietor if a gentleman by the name of Blythe lived within the radius of the great border city, the man replied that Mr. Blythe and his lady had stayed at the inn before taking up residence at Arcadia near Wetheral.

There would be a lady, of course, Ramsey thought as he shifted a sewing basket aside so he might sit down on the sofa. Sipping his wine, he marvelled that even in this remote place his cousin had managed to fill his cellar with decent vintage and his bed with a lovely female. Count on Nick to land on his feet, for rustic though his hideaway turned out to be, it was a surprisingly snug one. The land surrounding the vast stone pile was scrubby and sparse, useless for hunting and fit for nothing but sheep, but those it seemed to support by the hundreds.

He glanced impatiently at the clock. What the devil was keeping Dominic in Carlisle all this time? And a full hour went by before he had the opportunity to put that question to his cousin, who, Ramsey noted with resentment, didn't seem at all surprised to see him.

"It was imperative that I visit an attorney," the baron said as he pulled off his driving gloves. "But my landlord, with whom I also had business, has been called away to Dumfries, so I'm back much sooner than I meant to be."

Ramsey had expected—even hoped—to find Dominic had changed, but saw no sign that he was bowed by his misfortune. His handshake was firm, his carriage as self-assured as ever, and the grey eyes remained bright with good humour even when Ramsey said cuttingly, "Are there no barbers in the north of England? What a shaggy fellow you have become!"

Dominic reached up to shove his ragged hair out of his eyes and retorted, "And you are looking more spruce than I remember. Cat said you'd be nosing 'round and asking questions, so I knew you were on my scent, but I never guessed you would run me to ground. Well, now that you're here, you must let me show you the farm.'' He forestalled Ramsey's intended objection by saying in a subdued voice, ''I think we had better postpone any discussion until there is no danger of our being overheard, don't you?''

During a very thorough tour of the pigsties and the dairy, Ramsey feigned a polite interest, bobbing his head sagely as Dominic enthused over the hardiness of the herdwick sheep swarming on the fells and dales. He cared nothing for farming, only for horses, and it almost broke his heart when he saw the sole occupant of the stables, a placid grey mare that pulled the humble gig and carried his cousin to the village or the town. He dutifully admired the new chaise, but when he heard that Nick intended to buy carriage horses, he couldn't help saying disparagingly, ''I doubt you'll find anything to suit you in *this* neighbourhood. Now where are we bound?''

''There's an excellent view of the country from the top of the hill,'' Dominic said as he vaulted over a low stone wall, and Ramsey could do nothing but follow him. ''Justin is well, I trust?''

''I seldom see him now he has become Lord Elston's boon companion.''

''You've never liked Damon very much, have you? Or me,'' Dominic added grimly, but without rancour. ''Which is why I have to wonder at your taking the trouble to visit me—a taxing and expensive journey.''

Now the time had come for Ramsey to state his business. ''I've come here in the hope of persuading you to return to London.''

''And risk having my neck stretched with a silken rope? Your concern for my welfare is most endearing, coz.''

"It's concern that brings me here," Ramsey puffed, trying to keep pace with his taller cousin's stride. "Dominic, the longer you remain in hiding, the harder it will be to convince the world of your innocence."

"I doubt it can ever be convinced. Haven't you looked into a newspaper lately?"

Ramsey gave a dismissive shrug. "I've spent most of the past two months in town, and I assure you that very few people—important people—have been swayed by the lies that have been printed."

"You relieve my mind considerably," Dominic said dryly. "As for the other million or so souls in London, do you suppose I care nothing for what they must think?"

"Popular opinion will change as soon as you've been cleared of the murder charge," Ramsey was quick to point out. "But for that to happen, you must first come forward to defend yourself, or at the very least, seek to have the coroner's verdict overturned. We'll find a pliant magistrate to do it for us, and a year from now hardly anyone will remember that you killed a man."

They halted at the crest of the hill, beneath a spreading oak with gold-brown leaves valiantly clinging to its branches. Dominic turned to Ramsey and said, "I have no intention of leaving this place. I won't say I never will," he went on thoughtfully, "for I'd like to be able to return to Blythe—someday." Leaning against the trunk of the tree, he crossed his arms over his chest. "We've never had much in common, Ram, yet I think I know how you must have felt upon giving up Cavender Chase. But at least you have the freedom, if not the funds, to live there."

"It happens that I do have expectations of reclaiming my estate, for my Uncle Isaac Meriden has designated me his heir."

Dominic, who had been stirring the ground with the toe of his boot, looked up. "The nabob?"

"He has given me a generous allowance, and even put me in the way of a suitable marriage," Ramsey answered. His new sense of superiority was too sweet, too heady to keep him from puffing off his own good fortune to the very man whose life he had ruined. But deep down, he despised himself for it.

"Are you seriously thinking of matrimony? You are hardly the stuff good husbands are made of, Ram."

This criticism prompted him to retaliate by saying, "And what of you? That ramshackle house down there is filled to the rafters with females—and one of them your own father's fancy-piece!"

"You're sadly off the mark if you think there's anything shameful about my relationship with Mrs. Durham," his cousin replied with a maddening smile.

"And what about the other one?" Ramsey taunted him. "Oh, yes, I've seen her. A showy bit of goods, not in your usual style at all—she casts your little Ellen into the shade. Have you finally outgrown your deplorable fancy for plain, simple fare?"

His voice dangerously quiet, Dominic said, "Mark me well, Ram, I will not permit you to attach such slanders to Lady Blythe."

"You don't mean to say you've actually *married* that doxy?" Perceiving that his cousin's face was rigid with anger, Ramsey took a nervous, backward step. "I do earnestly beg your pardon, if she is indeed your wife."

"Surely Nerissa told you we are wed?"

"She tried," Ramsey admitted, avoiding his eye.

"And you didn't believe her?" There was a brief silence. "Well, I'll smooth things over somehow—fortunately my bride has a sense of humour. But you are very much mistaken in thinking Nerissa was my mistress, for she has only ever been my wife."

Feeling his way cautiously, Ramsey said, "You can't have known her very long."

"We met soon after I left London. And even if that

damned duel hadn't placed me in her path, I'd have found her—I like to think so, anyway. We were made for each other."

Ramsey had never heard that warm note in the rough, uneven voice; his lip curled derisively. At the same time, he was conscious of the stirrings of the same envy he'd always felt for his cousin. In an attempt to bolster his own ego, he conjured up the image of Lady Mira—sister to an earl, niece to a duke, and superior to Lady Blythe in every way. "What is her ladyship's family?" he asked loftily.

"Her name was Newby. Her father, although something of an original, was a gentleman, although you may not believe that when I add that his fortune derived from trade."

Suddenly it occurred to Ramsey that he might use Dominic's strong feelings to his own advantage. He tried for a concerned, reasonable tone as he asked, "Is it quite fair to your lovely lady, keeping her hidden away in this northern fastness? She is a baroness, she deserves to take her rightful place in society."

"You are sadly off the mark if you think Nerissa pines for London and high life. She was brought up to value other things besides the shallow pursuits our tonnish friends delight in." Dominic added quietly, "Her life has not been easy of late, and I will not make her uncomfortable by stirring up my own sad scandal."

"You are a fool, Nick," Ramsey spat, "and your refusal to face the charges against you makes me wonder if you are not also a coward."

Head high, his eyes as hard as agates, Dominic said, "Call me a murderer as well, then, and begone. Your insults mean nothing to me, Ram. This may be difficult to understand, but I've never been happier in my life, and this northern fastness, as you call it, is very much my home now. Here I will remain, with or without your approval."

Ramsey protested, but to no avail; his cousin was adamant in his refusal to leave Cumberland.

By the time he rode away from Arcadia Farm, he was blazingly angry. Dominic was stupid, stubborn, selfish, and lost to all consideration of how his continued exile went against the interests of the Blythe family. And it was particularly galling that he should regard himself as a happy man, when to his own relations and to the majority of his acquaintance he was an object of pity. But Ramsey's defeat went far beyond his failure to convince Lord Blythe to return to London, for he had not yet relieved himself of that torturous, gnawing sense of culpability for his act of spite on that long-ago October night. He was responsible for the death of one man and the ruin of another, and whatever happened, he knew he would carry that burden to his grave.

After waving Ramsey off, Dominic returned to the house, trying to think of some way to make Nerissa laugh at his cousin's foolish misapprehension about her status in his household. The door to her bedchamber was closed, so he knocked, calling her name. There was a muffled, indistinguishable reply, and he turned the handle.

Nerissa reclined on the low wooden chest covered with a goosedown bolster which she'd fashioned into a windowseat and to which she often repaired with one of her books. But she was not reading. In a dead and distant voice she said, "My lord?"

If she had thrown something at him, or wept, or raged, he might have known how to respond, but her complete inaction left him at a loss. "I can explain," he began, wondering if she would give him the chance. "You mustn't think I didn't trust you enough to tell you, for I never doubted your loyalty, I swear. But you were better off not knowing the truth about me—if I'd been captured, taken up by the Runner, you would have been questioned, too. So long as you remained ignorant of my identity, no real harm could come to you. I was planning to tell you, and Cat warned me I shouldn't put it off, but I wanted you to have time to adjust to the marriage. And part of my reluctance was because of the way you reacted when you learned my name is Dominic and not Nicholas.''

"It hardly matters now," she said dully. "I accept that you had your reasons. But I confess, it is unsettling to learn that the man I thought I married yesterday does not even exist. I am wholly unacquainted with Baron Blythe." She tilted her head away from the window and said, "What were all the names you gave when we were wed? There were so *many.*"

"Dominic Sebastian Charles Blythe," he repeated.

She tilted her head away from him. "And where is Lord Cavender?"

"He has returned to Carlisle."

"You should have invited him to stay to dinner. Or didn't your lordship think he would sit down at the table with your doxy bride? Of course," she continued on a harsher note, "he must be eager to return to London and tell all of your grand friends about this misalliance.''

"You refine too much upon the title, Nerissa," he said with ill-concealed impatience. "I am only the second person to hold it, and my father was ennobled a mere decade ago. What difference if I am a nobleman? It doesn't stop the people in the streets of London from calling me a murderer.''

"When you believed me to be naught but a lowly merchant's daughter, you refused to wed me," she said venomously. "And it doesn't require much in the way of the imagination to guess just why you suddenly chose to regularise our liaison. You felt sorry for me, poor, ruined creature that I am—but in case you have forgotten, I lost my reputation before you ever met me. Your sense of obligation must have been especially keen after I revealed that I'm related to a rich and powerful duke, for only then did you bother to rush me to the altar—or rather, to the anvil," she amended.

"I had many reasons for marrying you," he said, but she stilled him with a glance.

"Oh, you wanted me in your bed, too—you have always been honest about that. And you must require a legitimate heir to your title and whatever estate you may possess." Nerissa bounded up from her seat and faced him, her body quivering with rage. "Well, I may be your wife, but if you lay a finger on me, you will rue it."

"You did not refuse the terms," he shot back. "It takes two to make a marriage."

"Or to unmake one."

Her cold words sent a shiver down his spine. "And are you perchance implying that you would seek to have this union annulled?"

Without quite meeting his eyes, she asked, "Could I?"

It was not exactly the answer he had dreaded, but it was bad enough. "I won't deny that you could make a very convincing case, for I misrepresented myself to you, and the marriage hasn't been consummated. Yet no court, temporal or ecclesiastical, will set you free." On a note of cruel triumph he concluded, "Because, my dear wife—and so you will remain, like it or not—you cannot dissolve a marriage if you are unable to prove that it ever took place."

And with that, he turned and walked out of the room, leaving her to think of him what she would.

10

THE DAIRY, A squat stone building behind the farmhouse, was Nerissa's refuge, the one place where she could be alone with her thoughts and yet make herself useful. One chill December morning she was there, and troubled though her mind was, her hand was steady and sure as she propelled the tin skimmer, scraping the thick, yellow cream from the top of the milk pans. With a deft flick of her wrist, she tipped the cream into an earthenware container at her elbow and moved on to the next pan.

She and Dominic had not made up their quarrel, and the opportunities to do so diminished each day as they grew farther and farther apart—and without ever really being together, she thought unhappily. Now that the scales had been lifted from her besotted eyes, she saw quite clearly that their union was nothing more than an act of condescension on his part. However well connected, the reckless daughter of the eccentric Captain Newby was no proper bride for Baron Blythe. Constrained by his sense of duty—and of honour—he had elevated her to a position for which she was unworthy, and to which she was most ill-suited. For the present he might be willing to overlook her lack of birth and proper upbringing, for he was an outcast, detached and displaced from his privileged, titled circle of friends. But one day he might resume his former mode of life, and although for his sake she would be glad when that time came, for her own, she dreaded it.

When she had taken all of the cream from the pans, she emptied the skimmed milk into a pail, where vegetable parings and table scraps would also find their way before the whole was fed to the pigs at the end of the day. She rinsed the pans with spring water and strained the morning's milk into them, covering each one with a cheesecloth. She was washing her utensils—the skimmer, strainer, and ladle—when the outraged cackle of the geese in the yard warned her that someone had trespassed upon their territory, and hers.

A moment later, Cat Durham stuck her head into the dairy to say with satisfaction, "*Here* you are—I've been looking everywhere! Mrs. McNab is growing impatient and wants to know when she can begin making her butter. Can I be of assistance?"

"I'm almost finished, but you may dry these wet things." Nerissa tossed the cloth to Cat.

"You ought to have Sally do that," the other lady commented as Nerissa swabbed the stone floor with a mop.

"Mrs. McNab keeps the poor child busy enough in the kitchen. Besides, a lady ought not to set her servants to any work that she is not prepared to undertake herself."

"Whoever said so?"

"My Aunt Portia. She was the most compleat housekeeper."

During the past fortnight, the two ladies had grown close, and although Nerissa had never expressed it, she was grateful to Cat for extending her visit. She kept Dominic well entertained, playing piquet with him of an evening, or relating the bits of town gossip which had come her way, and at table she maintained an even flow of conversation. Nowadays, the only time he smiled was when Cat made a jest, or told him an amusing story about some society person he knew. In the rare times when the Blythes found themselves alone together, they spoke scarcely a word, but in Cat's presence they were forced to behave as a couple, however ill-matched they might be.

"Do we go to church tomorrow?" Cat asked, shaking the water from the milk strainer before applying her cloth. "A collection will be taken up for the Trafalgar wounded, and for the widows and orphans of the men who died. And there's to be a great thanksgiving for the victory, by the King's decree."

Never in her life had Nerissa felt less thankful, although naturally she was glad that the French navy was no longer the threat it had been before the great battle. "Yes, I suppose we ought to attend," she replied.

"Nerissa," said Cat, for the two women were now on terms of familiarity. "I am glad of this opportunity to talk to you in private, about something that has been on my mind for many days. I'm afraid I've outworn my welcome at Arcadia—I have imposed upon you and Nick entirely too long."

Nerissa's face was a mirror of dismay. "Cat Durham, if you go away now, I think I shall never forgive you!"

"I must not stay," Cat replied, shaking her head. "Really, I cannot bear to see you and Nick hurting each other this way— your silence, your anger, are breaking my heart as well as both of yours. Can't you forgive him for deceiving you, Nerissa? Not once in all the years I've known him have I seen him so—so miserable."

"It is not only the deception," Nerissa said uncomfortably. "He should never have wed me, Cat. Our marriage was made too hastily, and for all the wrong reasons. I ought not have accepted him, but on the way to Gretna he was so persuasive, he said all the things

I most wanted to hear. He even kissed me." She placed her fingers on her lips, then removed them to say, "But he hasn't done it since."

"Well, how *can* he, when you have not given him the chance?" Cat pointed out reasonably.

"If he really wanted to, he would not wait for that."

"Be kind to him," Cat pleaded. "He lost his reputation, which is everything to a gentleman, and he had to leave his friends and family and every one of his possessions behind. You could be his comfort now—his helpmeet."

"I will try to be," Nerissa promised. "But it is harder than it was before, because I know he only wanted me as a mistress, not a wife. And now," she said softly, to herself, "I am neither."

For most of the afternoon the skies had been spitting snow, and now that it was December the days were short and darkness fell early. With scant consideration for his own or the mare's safety, Dominic spurred her on to greater speed, impatient to reach the warmth and shelter of the farmhouse. What sort of welcome would he get upon his arrival, he wondered as the horse lunged ahead. Cat, bless her soul, would probably greet him at the door, her face wreathed in smiles to make up for Nerissa's failure to summon up even one. Where had she gone, that bold, laughing girl who had stolen his heart? He'd entered this marriage with the best of intentions, only to see it fail before it ever had a chance to succeed. Within twenty-four hours of speaking her vows his bride had spoken of an annulment, and he had heard himself state the impossibility with a brutality he never ceased to regret. Not that he expected her to congratulate herself on the match—he might be a nobleman, but he was an exiled one, and known to the world as a murderer.

Seeing her as she had been these past two weeks, so

grave and troubled, he had resolved to remove the stain
of scandal from his name. What he would not do for
Ramsey, or even himself, he had to do for Nerissa.

Today he had revoked his offer for the farm and had
given notice to quit when the term of his lease expired,
whereupon Mr. Haslam had proposed a figure that was
more in line with what Nick would have willingly paid
only a few weeks ago. He had wearied of life on an
upland sheep farm, he had said mendaciously, but in
the end he had told his landlord a partial truth, that
family business required that he return to London.

The more Dominic considered his position, the
stronger it seemed to him. He had not murdered Sir
Algernon Titus, and at least three others beside himself knew it: Justin, Damon, and Georgiana. If any
one of them came forward to verify his claim of innocence, he might well be able to salvage something
from the wreck of his reputation. The blot upon the
Blythe escutcheon would never be completely erased,
but to be able to pick up the threads of his old life, to
pass his days at Blythe or in town as he pleased—that
would be freedom indeed. Society might not welcome
him back with open arms, no doubt people would always whisper about him as soon as his back was
turned, but he could, he decided, live with that.

Crouching over the mare's neck to avoid the snowflakes slanting into his face, he wondered what Nerissa
would say when she learned he was leaving her behind. It would not be easy for him, but he really had
no choice; he could not thrust her into the nightmare
of his own making, not after everything she had en-
dured. As soon as he cleared his name he would send
for her—and what a stir she would cause in London,
where her dramatic looks would attract notice and
comment. And when they wearied of town life, they
would retire to the country, to his beloved Blythe, with
its green and rolling parkland and fertile hills.

Through the thick veil of snowflakes he could make out the farmhouse, so different from the graceful brick mansion which figured in his thoughts. There was a light shining in the parlour window, and a figure silhouetted there. He guessed it was Cat who was watching for him, but was pleased to discover it was his unclaimed bride, her lovely face so white and strained that he knew she'd been wearing herself out with some household task. Her determination to keep busy was further proof, not that he needed it, of her discontent. He was glad to see the teapot waiting; he was chilled to the marrow of his bones. While Nerissa poured out his cup, he told her he had called in Abbey Street, although he did not tell her why. "Miss Haslam sends you her warmest greetings, and she hopes you will visit her soon. Did you and Cat have a pleasant day? Where is she?"

"In her room—packing." When he frowned, Nerissa said hastily, "I did beg her to stay, Nick, but she's adamant about returning to St. Albans."

This was worrying; Dominic had counted on his dear friend and only ally to keep Nerissa company during his absence. Thinking aloud, he said, "Well, neither of us will be able to travel south until the weather improves."

Nerissa could not have looked more stricken if he'd slapped her face. "You are going away?"

"To London."

"Oh. Of course." Her hand shook so badly that she had to set down her cup.

"It is time I answered the charges against me—I must try to establish my innocence. You understand that, don't you?" She nodded, and he said gravely, "I don't know what the future holds—I can't be entirely sure that I won't be clapped into prison within the week. And I know I'm leaving with many things unresolved between us. Perhaps I have no right to ask, but will you stay here, and wait until I send for you to join me in town?"

"No," she said firmly, "I will not."

His heart thudded to a standstill. If she had closed her heart and mind against him, he was a lost man.

With her distinctive, sensuous grace, she came to stand before him, and then she gave him back his life by adding, "I will not wait, my lord, because I intend to go to London with you."

During the week it took to make all the necessary arrangements, Nerissa and Cat Durham bustled about the house, making inventories and putting it in order for the next tenant, Miss Maria Haslam, who would take possession as soon as the Blythes vacated.

"My mother is horrified, of course," the spinster said merrily, when she drove out to the farm to bid Nerissa farewell. "But at the age of forty-five, I hope I am not dependent upon her permission when it comes to pleasing myself. I have always loved this old place, and my father, knowing that, has generously let me have it for my very own."

The day of departure dawned. Two chaises had been hired for the journey, and at first light the two ladies climbed into the first one; Lord Blythe and most of the baggage would follow in the other. Cat tried to comfort her despondent companion with the reminder that she left Arcadia in very good hands. As the carriage bumped along the rutted drive beneath the ancient oaks, their branches heavily laden with mistletoe, Nerissa turned her head for a final look at the house that had been her haven and her home.

The southward journey was swift and unattended by any of the discomforts and alarms of her earlier travels with Dominic, and nothing occurred to hinder the progress of the two chaises, which passed town after town in rapid succession. Each night they stopped at a comfortable inn, and over dinner Nerissa and Cat joined in the effort to lift the spirits of their escort, playing cards with him and taking turns reading aloud. But theirs was a forced gaiety, and it dissipated as soon as each lady retired to her private chamber. As she drew nearer to the metropolis, Nerissa's anxiety increased, and not only on Dominic's account. Her life was about to undergo a drastic change, a prospect that was nearly as daunting as his impending ordeal.

No longer would she fill her days with butter-making or furniture polishing. She had no friends in London, except for Laura and Henry Sedgewick and their brood, and in a city so large it would be difficult to discover where they might be living. She would visit Lucy and Samuel, of course—it was pleasant to think that she was now in a position to do something for them. She hoped there might be a vacant cottage on Dominic's Wiltshire estate, similar to the one in Ol-ney. But with her husband's future still so unsettled, it was hardly the time to reveal her tie to the baby, nor the nature of her obligations to him.

Late on the fourth day, the cavalcade drew into Northampton. It was already dark, but Nerissa could make out streets and houses familiar to her. They stopped at the George, which Dominic preferred to the Angel; he was instantly recognised by the landlord, who exhibited no real surprise upon seeing him. That night, as she prepared for bed, Nerissa thought about her old acquaintance Mr. Gudgeon, and Ned the ostler. When she counted the weeks since she and Dominic had met in that very same town, she was surprised that they numbered only ten; it seemed to her that whole years had passed since that October afternoon.

The next morning, while waiting with Cat for the carriages to be readied for the final leg of their jour-ney, she voiced some of her concerns about what the future might hold. ''I was not brought up to be the consort of a nobleman,'' she said, pleating her napkin nervously. ''Despite my kinship with the Marchants, I know nothing of how lords and ladies conduct themselves. Oh, I've lived in London, but on the fringes of fashion, and although I was nominally my father's hostess, his dinner parties were exclusively male, and I was more likely to meet artists and philosophers and men of commerce than aristocrats. Lord Blythe's friends will think me some kind of adventuress—or worse.''

''You make too much of the differences between you,'' Cat said soothingly. ''I doubt that they have occurred to his lordship.''

''I daresay Lord Cavender pointed them out to him,'' Nerissa murmured. Whenever she recalled that gentleman's disdain, she wished she'd had the wit—and the nerve—to strike his mocking face.

A little while later, when the proprietor of the George saw his distinguished customers off the premises, he said vaguely, ''Didn't someone tell me that you had gone abroad, Lord Blythe?''

Dominic laughed mirthlessly, and denied it. ''No, no, I've been in the north country.''

Shaking his head dolefully, the other man said, ''The whole world will be London-bound soon enough, to pay respects to Lord Nelson. He's to be given a grand state funeral come New Year, and there may be another ere long, for they say poor Mr. Pitt has fallen ill at Bath. 'Tis sad times for old England, milord, sad times indeed.''

At St. Albans they paused just long enough to deposit Cat Durham on the doorstep of her brick-fronted house on Holywell Hill. ''I will be thinking of you both,'' Cat assured Nerissa, and the two ladies clasped hands through the open window of the chaise. Glancing up at Dominic, who had climbed out to bid her good-bye, she said, ''If there is anything I can do to help you, my lord, you must be sure to let me know.''

''I will—and thank you, Cat.''

After signalling to his postilion, he startled Nerissa by climbing into her chaise, taking the place Cat had vacated. They had not been alone together since the day he announced his decision to return to London, and she was painfully conscious of their estrangement. He appeared to be occupied with troubling thoughts of his own, so she gazed out the window, watching for familiar landmarks as they neared London. At the bottom of Barnet Hill they stopped at the Red Lion to have fresh horses put to for the final stage.

Dominic said hoarsely, when the lights of the city began to be visible in the distance, ''There have been times when I wondered if I'd ever see London again.''

''I, too,'' she sighed, and he looked over at her.

''Tired? We've not much farther to go, only a few miles now. My servants will have prepared the suite of rooms that belonged to my mother, and I hope you will find them tolerably comfortable.''

''I'm sure I shall.'' Nerissa felt her stomach curl at this reminder that she was now the mistress of a great establishment.

''I doubt the state of Blythe House is desperate enough to warrant that grave face,'' he said lightly.

Dredging up a smile, she replied, ''It's only that my Aunt Portia trained me to manage three or four servants at most, not to organise an entire staff.''

When the two carriages halted before Blythe House, one of the many magnificent residences which bounded Grosvenor Square, a trio of liveried footmen came rushing down the steps. One held a branch of candles high, another opened the door of the chaise, while the third took charge of the baggage. ''Welcome home, my lord,'' said the man with the candelabra.

"Thank you, James, we are glad to be here safely, and in good time. Ah, there you are, Drummond."

"My lord, my lady," intoned a black-clad individual as the couple stepped into a high-ceilinged hall flagged with black and white marble. He tendered a folded sheet of paper. "This just arrived for your lordship."

Dominic broke the seal and scanned the few short lines. "Send 'round to the mews and tell Coachman I want the town carriage," he told one of the passing footmen, before turning to Nerissa. "I'm afraid I ought to go—my cousin and Lord Elston are dining together tonight and invite me to join them."

Even as her spirits sank, she said stoically, "I'm sure you are anxious to hear whatever news they may have."

"Drummond will show you to your rooms, and if you desire refreshment, you have only to ask. Do not wait up for me, for I don't know how long I must be gone."

She followed the butler up the graceful, curving staircase, taking note of the allegorical paintings which lined the wall. When he asked if she had brought her personal maid with her, she admitted the truth and hoped it would not diminish her in his eyes. "I have no abigail, but now I am come to town, I mean to engage one."

"Tomorrow I will undertake to visit the registry office, if my lady wishes it, to seek suitable prospects for the position," said Drummond, as he preceded her down a long hallway hung with more paintings.

Her suite was composed of three rooms, a parlour which contained delicate giltwood furnishings and a handsome Aubusson carpet, a bedchamber which was appointed in a similar fashion, and a small dressing room. Nerissa's mood was much improved by the sight of her new domain, with its hangings of pale blue

damask and white marble chimneypieces, and her appetite, which had fled the moment the chaise had
pulled into Grosvenor Square, suddenly returned.

"Drummond," she said with decision, "will you be
so good as to have a bowl of soup sent up to me, and
perhaps a piece of fowl, if it is to be had. And I think—
no, I am sure that I would like a glass of wine as
well."

The butler inclined his silvered head and murmured
respectfully, "Yes, my lady."

The moment he was gone, Nerissa collapsed onto
the pretty blue sofa in her sitting room. One of her
worries could be discarded, because judging by her
first attempt, being a great lady wasn't going to be
difficult after all.

= 11 =

As HE WAS borne eastward along the fog-enshrouded
streets, Dominic remembered his last visit to Lincoln's Inn when, as a fugitive, he had taken sanctuary
in a district where most persons sought to uphold the
law. The carriage stopped in Chancery Lane, and he
walked to Southampton Buildings, where he found
the narrow house where his cousin lodged. The rickety
staircase creaked warningly, and before he reached the
landing, Justin flung open the door and called a greeting down to him.

"Come in, come in," the young man invited him.
"We had nearly given you up—I've lost my wager with
Damon, because I said you'd be too tired from your
journey to join us, and here you are. But I'm glad of
it—we have so much to tell you!"

"But first," said a cool, familiar voice, "we must
congratulate the fellow upon his marriage. You've been
a busy man, Blythe."

"I have indeed," Dominic agreed, gripping the
hand Lord Elston held out to him.

Justin Blythe shared his apartments with two fellow
students at Lincoln's Inn, and in the cramped common
room the signs of their habitation were conspicuous: a
black woollen gown had been discarded on a chair,
casebooks were piled upon the floor, and dustballs had
gathered around the skirting boards. "Is she pretty,

your bride?" he asked eagerly, pressing a wine glass upon the new arrival.

"You'll have the opportunity to judge for yourself soon enough." Eyeing the table dubiously, Dominic said, "When you bid me to dine with you, I never expected a feast fit for a king!"

"A prodigal, rather," said Lord Elston. "It comes from Serle's Coffee House—I ordered the supper and the wine myself, knowing all too well that our ascetic Justin keeps nothing but bread and cheese and ale."

"That's because they feed us so well at the Lower Table, though not as well as the Benchers!"

The three gentlemen sat down to their meal, which was enlivened by Dominic's description of his flight to Cumberland. The Marquis shook his blonde head in disbelief and said it must have been a great adventure.

"Too much of one, at times," Dominic said feelingly. "In fact, I met my wife when she shielded me from a Bow Street Runner."

"A Runner? Are you sure of it? Well," he certainly wasn't chasing you, Nick, for to my certain knowledge Bow Street was never set on the case."

Dominic frowned across the table at his friend. "Yet the papers made it plain that the authorities were seeking me high and low."

Lord Elston shrugged his shoulders. "Oh, that report was naught but a sop to the common people, who were crying for your blood. No one made the least push to find you—not until Cousin Ram took it into his head to do so. I don't mean to imply that your flight was unnecessary," he hastened to say, "for had you remained in town the authorities would have been compelled to act. But your departure saved them the trouble—and the embarrassment—of taking a peer into custody."

"And now that I've returned, where do I stand with regard to the law?"

Justin replied, "Two magistrates, Blodgett and Crane, of the Marlborough Street court, have already agreed to conduct an enquiry into Sir Algernon's death."

"What are the chances of having the inquest verdict quashed?" Dominic asked.

"That's difficult to say at this stage," was his cousin's evasive reply. "Mr. Peale, for whom I clerk, is willing to discuss the matter with you. I think he will take your case, and you need not worry about having to give evidence, for we'll find some way around that. You did fight a duel, and your opponent did die—these facts cannot be concealed or altered."

"*And* there was a witness," Dominic said, "that damned medical man who told the coroner's jury that I murdered Algy in cold blood. I hardly think he will recant his earlier testimony."

"My effort to locate him has failed," Lord Elston interjected. "And making some enquiries, I ascertained that he has left London, but for reasons that are quite unconnected with your duel. He was in the pay of a band of body-snatchers and worked as a middle man, delivering bodily remains to surgeons and anatomists for dissection. His activities in support of the Resurrection Men had been so *very* sordid that the magistrates are not likely to credit his account of what occurred at Chalk Farm."

Dominic, having eaten his fill of the chops and savoury puddings, leaned back in his chair and said gloomily, "I had hoped this business would be easier, but I see it promises to be very messy."

"I'm afraid so," Lord Elston agreed, "but I don't doubt you possess the resolution to see it through."

"If only Nerissa might be spared . . . I would send her down to Blythe if I weren't reasonably certain that she would refuse to go." Dominic smiled as he recalled his wife's stubborn determination to accompany him to London. ''I daresay my leaving town is out of the question?''

''You can ask Mr. Peale,'' Justin replied, ''but you may be sure he will advise against it. I have also consulted with Hill, Serjeant-at-Law of Lincoln's Inn—Serjeant Labyrinth, as we call him. He can cite cases and precedents by the dozen, and although his arguments are complex and generally impossible to follow, he was quite clear about one thing—we must convince the magistrates of the strength of your friendship with Sir Algernon.''

''And how,'' Dominic sighed, ''am I to do that, if your Mr. Peale fails to call me as a witness?''

It was Lord Elston who answered his question. ''The fair widow possesses a great deal of information that would benefit you, although whether she is willing to reveal it all is yet to be determined.''

''Georgiana has already suffered too much—can we not leave her in peace?''

''It's to save your neck, man,'' the Marquis said testily.

Justin hastened to throw himself into the breach. ''The case is not so desperate as all that, Damon.''

Dominic turned on his cousin. ''Tell me, exactly how desperate is it? You've managed to skirt that issue quite neatly, in your lawyer fashion.''

''We cannot expect miracles,'' Justin told him frankly. ''If the magistrates bring in a verdict of manslaughter this time, we will have to be satisfied, for in all likelihood you would not be committed to trial. Even though it is a capital offence, the officers of the court are notably lax when it comes to prosecuting duellists, knowing all too well that juries often acquit in such cases.''

''Manslaughter,'' Dominic repeated, and his optimism, faint though it had been, faded away, leaving him prey to a pervading sense of doom.

* * *

At midmorning Nerissa, clad in her Chinese dressing gown, her hair lying loose about her shoulders, ate her customary breakfast of tea and toast in the privacy of her sitting-room. Her husband's entrance took her by surprise and brought the colour rushing into her cheeks; not since their marriage had he seen her *déshabillé*, and she felt unaccountably shy. When he enquired politely if she had slept well, she answered him with a nod, and her eyes followed him as he wandered about the room.

Pausing at the window, he said critically, "These hangings are faded."

Now that she had seen her new surroundings in the light of day, she was inclined to agree, although she said, "By comparison to our former abode, Blythe House is a palace."

"You must have Drummond show you all 'round it—I honestly believe he is prouder of the place than I am, though it was my ancestor who built it. It was known as Cavender House, until Ramsey, ever pressed for funds, sold it to my father, who acquired his fortune in the established way of younger sons. But he married an heiress by design, not by accident, as I did," Dominic said, inspecting one of the china ornaments on the mantel. "Lord Cavender, you will no doubt be glad to know, is safely out of the way, paying court to some young lady in Leicestershire. As he's a hunting man, I'm not surprised he should seek a bride from the shires."

But Nerissa cared nothing for the viscount; she was more interested in what had transpired last night. When she asked him, he shrugged, as if unwilling to discuss it with her.

"Oh, we talked for many hours, Damon, Justin, and I, and managed to come up with a reasonable motive for my damning flight to Cumberland." When he replaced the figurine, he looked over at Nerissa and smiled. ''You may save my neck yet again.''

She tipped her head to one side. ''How so?''

''I've already written the announcement of our marriage and sent it to the papers, and by the end of the week the whole of fashionable London will have heard that we spent a protracted honeymoon viewing the lakes—among other things. That is what we will let them believe, and I beg you to keep silent about the truth of my admittedly unconventional courtship.''

Nerissa bit back the retort that there had been no real courtship, for she didn't want to quarrel. She was his wife; it was her duty to support and defend him, and although silence was the only thing he had asked of her, if he required her to perjure herself, she would do it, and gladly.

''I must not linger,'' he said suddenly. ''Mr. Peale, Justin's mentor, is expecting me in his chambers, and after I confer with him I'll be off to the city to present myself to your trustees.'' After telling her that he would leave the town-carriage at her disposal, he hurried from the room.

Where, Nerissa wondered, did he expect her to go? She had no one to visit except Lucy, and to go rushing to Chelsea hard upon her arrival in London, or to have Samuel brought to Blythe House might well stir up the kind of speculation that had driven her from Olney, and Dominic would inevitably demand an explanation that she was not yet ready to make. From now on she must act prudently. But despite this resolve, she dashed off a letter to Lucy, explaining her new circumstances, and folded it around a ten-pound note. Then she rang for James the footman, and lest he puzzle over her correspondence with someone living in so unfashionable a street as Jews Row she said, with perfect truth, that Lucy Roberts was a former servant.

For someone who was, ostensibly, a lady of leisure,

she spent a busy morning. The butler took her over
the house, from garret to cellar, and presented the staff
to her with grave formality. The housekeeper, hastily
summoned back from a holiday, was taken aback when
the new mistress expressed a preference for a tea other
than the sort presently served at Blythe House.

"But I've laid in pounds of the stuff, my lady,"
Mrs. Rogers protested.

"You can serve it at the servants' table," Nerissa
said firmly. "I am not particular about most things,
but in this I insist upon a change." She was a little
afraid she had alienated the woman, but when she supplied the name of a merchant who could be depended
upon to carry her favourite blend, the housekeeper
regarded her with respect and said she would send
someone to make the purchase right away.

Unlike Mrs. Rogers, the gentleman-cook had remained in residence during Lord Blythe's long absence
from town. Nerissa's brief encounter with him made
her think longingly of Mrs. McNab, for she knew she
would not be called upon to help Mr. Anson knead
the bread or stir a stew or make a white sauce. And
his kitchen, with its row of crockery and collection of
gleaming pots and pans, was quite as intimidating as
the chef himself.

To her surprise, Drummond's visit to the registry
office turned up two excellent candidates for the position of lady's maid. The first of these was a woman
of mature years with excellent credentials, but Nerissa
feared she might be inclined to despise her mistress's
ignorance. And therefore, quite unknowingly, she endeared herself to the footmen in her husband's employ
by engaging a young, pretty, buxom lass named Rose.

She didn't need an abigail to point out the sad fact
that her wardrobe required attention. Few of the gowns
that had been made up for her marriage to Andrew
Hudgins were suited to her new estate, so she dis-

patched the ubiquitous James to the nearest booksell-er's shop to procure a selection of the latest fashion journals. After poring over them and making a list of things she required, she went to the library. Its many glass-fronted bookcases were filled with tempting vol-umes, and she was turning the musty pages of a sixteenth-century florilegium when Dominic found her.

"I should have known you would find your way into this room," he commented. "Have you spent the en-tire day studying my shelves?"

"Oh, no. I managed to restrain myself till now," she laughed. "Is this your private retreat?"

"It is, but I am perfectly willing to share it. What have you found there?" She carried her book over to him, and after a brief examination he handed it back to her. "A fine specimen—I'm forever finding trea-sures I never knew about. Sometimes I make the mis-take of removing them to Blythe, which has another fine collection, so the existing inventory is rather less than completely accurate. I'll try to find a copy of it for you, if you like."

"I would." Curious to know how much of her dowry would be reserved as a jointure, or whether he would make some settlement upon her, she asked, "How did you prosper at your meeting with my trust-ees? Did you persuade Mr. Halpern and Mr. Rose to release my fortune into your hands?"

He had crossed to the knee-hole desk at the far end of the room, and was gathering together some of the many papers strewn across it. "Everything is all ar-ranged—it was a simple, straightforward business. And the gentlemen, though no longer your trustees, will continue to administer your father's estate as they have always done, for their management has been ex-cellent. I keep my own solicitor busy enough with my affairs. As for the disposition of your house in Olney,

I recommend that you sell it, unless you object for sentimental reasons, in which case a tenant must be found.''

The thought of being tied to Olney in any way made her say hurriedly, ''No, I do not object to selling. What happens to my dowry?''

''It will be tied up in a trust. For the benefit of our children, if our union should be so blessed.''

This was the first time he had ever mentioned the possibility of issue. Nerissa's cheeks burned, and she was relieved when he glanced down at the sheaf of papers in his hand. ''You will have a great deal of correspondence to catch up on,'' she said, and made her escape.

The next morning, in common with the rest of the town, she read the notice of her marriage in a column in the *London Gazette*, which stated that Baron Blythe had wed Nerissa, only daughter of the late Captain Richard Newby, in a private ceremony. Recalling the particulars of that ceremony, its tipsy witnesses and disreputable Gretna priest, she had to smile at the way the conventional phrasing hid the truth. The repercussions were immediate, and for the remainder of the day, footmen clad in the livery of various noble houses delivered congratulatory notes. Nerissa even received one from Laura Sedgewick, now residing in Bloomsbury. But the most notable of all the many well-wishers called in person.

The Duke of Solway's greying hair was thinner than Nerissa remembered and his flesh appeared to be somewhat reduced, but otherwise he was the same Cousin William she had always known. He kissed just as kindly as when she had last seen him, on the occasion of her father's funeral, and she said ruefully, ''How mortifying to think you learned of my marriage in such a way—my only excuse for not calling at Solway House is that I had no idea you were in town. Are you terribly, terribly shocked?''

''Not that, although I admit to some considerable surprise,'' the duke replied, taking a chair. ''Everyone believed Lord Blythe had fled the country, and natu-rally I had no idea that you and he were at all ac-quainted. I seem to recall you were planning to marry some neighbour fellow in Buckinghamshire.''

''At one time I was, although it came to naught.''

''Change of heart, eh?''

''I fear that at the time I accepted that proposal I was too distraught to know my own mind,'' she said candidly.

The duke wagged his grey head. ''I quite miss the pleasant little talks Dick and I used to enjoy when I visited him in the Adelphi Terrace.''

''The grand arguments, you mean,'' she said with a roguish smile. ''How is the Duchess?''

''As magnificent as ever—she's coming up to town later this week. My word, but she's having a busy time of it! Our little niece Mira will be making her come-out this spring, and already Her Grace is planning balls and I don't know what. You remember Mira, don't you?''

''Swanborough's daughter is old enough to be pre-sented? I recall that she was a very pretty child.''

''And has grown into a lovely young lady. I suspect that the period of my guardianship will quickly run its course, for I've already had an offer for her hand. Co-incidentally, it came from a member of your husband's family. Have you met Lord Cavender?'' She nodded, and he asked, ''And has he told you he's dangling after Mira?''

''Is he? No, the subject never came up. At the time, his lordship was quite ignorant of my connexion to the Marchants and the Peverels, and may still be, for all I know.''

"I confess to you, Nerissa, I like it not. Mira is too young for a man of his years and habits, although to say so to either of them would do more harm than good at this stage."

Seeing how distressed her relative was, she changed the subject. "Tell me about the rest of your family—I am counting on some happy news about the Ladies Ophelia and Imogen—I believe both were in an interesting situation last winter."

"I've two grandsons now," His Grace reported. "But can you credit it, my Gervase still hasn't been caught by any of the lures cast out to him! Edgar has just matriculated at Oxford, for all he's no scholar— his mother has hopes it may steady him." It wasn't long before the duke touched upon Lord Blythe's difficulties, but his words were ones of comfort, not censure. "Your husband is fortunate in having the support of many friends," he said, "and a man who is capable of inspiring such loyalty will surely prevail."

"I pray you may be right, sir, but I know nothing about the particulars of the case. Lord Blythe has not discussed it with me."

"Well, that's because he doesn't want you to worry. Nor should you," he said, pinching her cheek. "Take my advice, and don't encourage him to hide his face, my dear—be sure he goes to his clubs and is seen about town. If you like, you may have use of Her Grace's box at Drury Lane. That little lad who causes so much stir, Master Betty, is playing in *MacBeth* tonight."

The popularity of the youth who had been London's favourite player for the past year was on the wane, but that evening the theatre was crowded with his admirers. Dominic pointed out several famous personalities to Nerissa, among them the Duke and Duchess of Bedford, Lady Holland and Mr. Luttrell, and the Devonshires. The gouty duke and his once-lovely duchess were there in the company of their intimate friend Lady Elizabeth Foster, dressed from head to toe in funereal black out of respect for the departed Nelson. Nerissa derived much amusement from the parade of persons in the box-lobby, and found the audience even more diverting than the actors. During the interval the Marquis of Elston joined the Blythes, and begged to be presented to Nerissa. The extraordinarily handsome young man then embarked upon a light, one-sided flirtation with her, and spun some choice tales about her husband. In the morning, she penned a letter to her noble kinsman, thanking him for the loan of his box.

The following week His Grace's carriage returned to Blythe House, and this time it brought his wife and niece. The Duchess of Solway was, as her fond spouse had said, a magnificent woman; she had passed her fiftieth year, but her hair still retained its rich brown colour and her complexion nearly rivalled that of her companion, a girl of seventeen.

She embraced Nerissa, saying, ''My dear, so now you are Lady Blythe! I was astonished when the duke wrote to tell me the news. Mira, my love, make your curtsey to her ladyship.''

''Oh *please* do not,'' Nerissa begged her young cousin. ''It makes me feel ancient, and anyway, I've been studying tables of precedence as if my life depended upon it, so I know I should be the one to curtsey to you. The daughter of an earl outranks the wife of a baron!''

Lady Miranda Peverel gave a soft laugh and said in her pretty voice, ''Tables of precedence, indeed! And I remember you as being so lively and care-for-nothing.''

''Dear me, what a character to live down,'' Nerissa cast a chagrined glance at the duchess, who, to her surprise, smiled benevolently upon her.

"You were ever like your father in spirit as well as looks," the great lady said. "I do confess that Miss Portia Newby had all my sympathy! I don't doubt that she would be gratified by this match you've made—to think that Dick Newby's daughter snagged Dominic Blythe! Let me tell you, my dear, if your husband had ever shown the least interest in either of my girls, I would have been in transports. Although I must say that Ophelia and Imogen did quite well for themselves. And so, no doubt, will Mira."

Nerissa hardly recognised the poised young beauty as the pale, quiet child she had met years before. Lady Miranda wore a simple white muslin gown that flattered her fragile figure, but Nerissa suspected her appearance of delicacy was deceptive, for she'd been raised among hardy, horse-loving Marchants. The blue eyes were bright with intelligence, and Mira's black hair fell to her slim waist in a cascade of long curls.

The duchess continued, "We have come to invite you and Blythe to attend our Twelfth Night dinner, although I'm afraid it will be less gay this year—we cannot give our usual grand ball afterwards, not with Nelson being interred in the same week. But what say you, will you join us on the sixth of January?"

However honoured Nerissa was to be asked, she could not accept before discussing the matter with Dominic; the magistrates' enquiry would take place the following day.

"Yes, yes," the duchess said briskly when she mentioned this circumstance, "the duke heard the news at his club. He feels—and I agree—that you and Blythe might be glad of something to take your minds off all that unpleasantness. We'll expect to see you, then," she concluded, her tone indicating that as far as she was concerned, the issue was settled. "The progress of the war, that's all anyone cares about these days. The one name on all lips is poor Nelson's—for which you and Blythe must surely be glad. Trafalgar quite eclipsed the scandal of the duel, and now the state funeral will overshadow the inquest.''

Nerissa was prevented from making a reply by her butler, who came to announce the arrival of another caller. ''Lord Cavender is here, my lady, and is wishful of speaking with his lordship.''

''Oh, dear.'' The words slipped out before Nerissa realised it, and she strove to cover this lapse by adding swiftly, ''I mean, how unfortunate that Lord Blythe has already gone out. Drummond, please inform Lord Cavender that I will be happy to receive him.''

When the viscount entered the saloon she went to meet him, her head held high—not even the duchess could have outdone Nerissa's show of pride as she welcomed this most unwelcome of visitors. ''Good afternoon, my lord,'' she said graciously, extending her hand.

He bowed over it. ''I hope I haven't come at an inconvenient time, Lady Blythe.''

''Not at all,'' Nerissa said, thinking that this civil encounter was the antithesis of their previous one. ''I'm afraid Lord Blythe has gone to one of his clubs with Lord Elston. In the absence of your cousin, I invite you to make do with some of mine—I believe you are acquainted with Her Grace, and Lady Miranda.'' His startled reception of this speech gave her a perverse satisfaction; he was clearly taken aback.

The duchess gave him a long, assessing look. ''Lord Cavender, surely you know that her ladyship's father was first cousin to the duke?''

''No, I did not,'' Ramsey faltered, for he had never guessed that the bold-faced creature he'd met in Cumberland might be a lady born. He hoped she did not hold his past rudeness against him, although if she did, she gave no sign of it. When she invited him to be seated, he took the place nearest Lady Miranda.

"I presume your lordship has come to London in connexion with the inquest," said the duchess, "for certainly you will be much affected by the outcome."

. Although Ramsey had suffered a shock upon learning of Lady Blythe's connexion to the Marchants, it was nothing to what he felt now. For one panicked moment, he thought the duchess was hinting—more than hinting—that he was responsible for the baronet's death. He managed to recover his voice, and with a tolerable show of calm he said, "I join with all of my cousin's friends in hoping he may be able to clear his name." Demonstrating a concern for Dominic would surely redound to his credit in Lady Mira's eyes.

It was not long before the duchess and her lovely charge departed, and he took this as his cue to leave as well; Lady Blythe made no attempt to detain him. As he walked away from Grosvenor Square, he wondered if he had been wise to follow his inamorata to town. Perhaps he should have waited until after the New Year—after the magistrates' enquiry into the circumstances surrounding the death of Sir Algernon Titus. But he had been pressured into leaving Leicestershire—not only by his uncle Isaac Meriden, impatient to see him wed to Lady Mira, but also by Justin, who had urged him to support Dominic. His brother so seldom asked anything of him that Ramsey hadn't been able to refuse the request, however disturbed he was by the prospect of attending the hearing. He took some comfort from the fact that nearly three whole months had passed since the party in Clifford Street, so it was quite unlikely that anyone would even remember he'd been present. And as he strolled along Brook Street, his frown of concern was replaced by a smile of triumph.

CHRISTMAS CAME AND went, but few hearts were made happier by it. Entertainments and celebrations were rare; a pall seemed to lie over the vast metropolis. The British people, already mourning the loss of Lord Nelson, were pitched into deeper gloom upon receiving grim news from the Continent, where the French armies had soundly defeated the Austrian and Russian allies. London's weather was as dismal as the mood of her inhabitants, and in the final week of 1805 an epidemic of influenza attacked the upper reaches of society, keeping many tied to their homes.

On Christmas Day, as Nerissa watched her husband carve the goose, she had to remind herself that this was supposed to be a festive, joyous season. She saw him so rarely that she could have fancied herself single again, their activities kept them apart during the day, and at night he generally dined out. When their paths did cross, he made some comment about her attire, or quizzed her about what book she was presently wearing out her eyes with, and he avoided the subject of the inquest altogether. He made no real effort to break through the seemingly impenetrable barrier of silence that had grown up between them, but what pained her most of all was that this man who had once been so eager to be her lover was a most disinterested husband.

The next day, still feeling low, she supplied her ser-

vants with the traditional gift of money, and wrote a
falsely cheerful note to her friend into which she
placed three shillings as a Boxing Day remembrance
for the Sedgewick children. And she was thinking of
another child this Christmas, for she had received a
smudged missive from Lucy Roberts, containing numerous spelling errors, along with a lock of black hair
and a vivid description of the lively young gentleman
in her care.

As the old year waned, Nerissa had to put off her
visit to Chelsea, for a multitude of callers, mostly female, descended upon Blythe House. All were long-
time acquaintances of Dominic's who were eager to
pass judgment on his wife—or to see how she was
bearing up as the date of the inquest drew near. What
these fashionable ladies thought of her Nerissa knew
not, nor did she greatly care.

On New Year's Eve, she received a more welcome
visitor in Justin Blythe, whose devotion to his cousin
had endeared him to her. The young student of law
resembled his brother neither in looks nor disposition;
his smile was warmer than the viscount's, and his sensitive, fine-boned face more attractive. And although
she had initially supposed him to be quiet and grave,
she was now able to detect the faint, mischievous light
in his brown eyes.

She cast aside her book when he was admitted to
the saloon and said in surprise, "Mr. Blythe, I thought
you'd gone into the country!"

"I returned this morning, and bring happy news for
Nick. But first I had to wish you a happy Christmas,
Lady Blythe."

"You really must call me Nerissa," she urged him.
"We are cousins by marriage, and I refuse to let you
stand upon formality. I have long wanted to thank you
for working so tirelessly on my husband's behalf. Mr.
Peale is a very capable barrister, I'm sure, but I know

you have done much to assist him in constructing the defense.''

Justin said soberly, ''Well, I don't think you'd approve of some of the stratagems by which we hope to convince the magistrates of Nick's innocence. Until now, I never guessed my chosen profession was as much one of stretching the law as upholding it!''

Not until the day of the Duchess of Solway's Twelfth Night dinner did Nerissa pay her long-overdue visit to Chelsea. She left the house in the afternoon, unaccompanied and on foot, walking all the way from Grosvenor Square to a hackney-coach stand in Picadilly. When the humble conveyance deposited her in Jews Row, she lifted the veil that she had worn over her bonnet to avoid being recognised, and approached Lucy's dwelling.

''Oh, I *do* wish you'd warned me you meant to come!'' said the former laundry-maid as she admitted Nerissa. ''Sam could do with a washing-up—he's that untidy I hate for you to see him!''

''Do you think I care for that?'' Nerissa laughed. ''Where is he?''

''In the kitchen, and a rare mess he is. Come along, miss—my lady, I should say, though 'tis so odd to be calling you so!''

Nerissa followed the young woman down a dim, narrow corridor. ''How is your mother?'' she asked.

''Her joints are something stiff in this weather, but she's in spirits. I'll take you upstairs to see her in a bit—she'll be so pleased.''

The kitchen smelled pleasantly of fresh-baked bread. In the corner a child sat upon the floor, playing with a collection of wooden spoons. He had curly dark hair, and his face was liberally smeared with soot. Turning wide blue eyes upon Nerissa, he clapped his chubby, dirty hands and cried, ''Lady, lady!''

"I don't think he knows me," she said forlornly, as she held out her arms to him. "Come to me, little rogue—you owe me a kiss." The boy regarded her doubtfully, then crawled across the floor to her. "Isn't he walking yet?" she asked Lucy.

"Aye, but he's a lazy lad today. He'll show you his steps when he's more used to you, I'm sure."

Nerissa knelt down and managed to coax the child into her lap. She hugged him close with one arm and used her handkerchief to clean his face. When he tugged at it she let go, and as he examined the lace-edged square of linen curiously, she sighed, "I ought to have brought him a toy."

"Your ladyship mustn't spoil him. Why, I couldn't even bring myself to spend the money you've sent, and put it safe away." Lucy's expressive face wore a troubled frown as she watched Nerissa enjoin Samuel in a game of pat-a-cake. "There's something I left out of my note, being as I don't write so smooth. You won't believe it, my lady, but Will Darcy has returned."

"Has he indeed?" Nerissa exclaimed, looking up. "After all this time? Why, it's been more than two years!"

Lucy's eyes filled, and she wiped them with the corner of her apron. "When he was took from me, I never thought to see him again. And I very nearly didn't. He was serving on the *Ajax,* one of the ships that fought at Trafalgar—in the vanguard, he says, though I'm sure I don't know what that means. During the battle nine men were wounded—Will was one of them—and two of his mates got killed. They put him on a transport, and when it docked at Portsmouth he was given leave to come up to London. Oh, my lady, when I saw him standing there at the door, his arm in a sling, I fainted clean away." The young woman smiled through her tears. "But I think *he* was near to swooning when he met my Sam and learned he was a papa! And he's

going to be a husband, now, for the banns have already
been cried twice, and on Monday morning we'll be
wed. As soon as my mum is well enough for the journey, we'll be going to live at Portsmouth. Will's getting his discharge, and means to work in the shipyards
there.''

Nerissa tightened her hold on the child in her lap.
She couldn't let Lucy see how painful the joyous tidings were to her, so she strove for a cheerful note
when she said, ''How lucky it is that I came here today.''

''Oh, I wouldn't have left Lunnon without bidding
your ladyship farewell, not after all you've done for
us—and the captain, too, God rest his soul. But you'll
not be alone now you've got a husband of your own—
and him a lord, no less! And just think, one day you'll
have wee ones of your own.''

But would she, Nerissa wondered, as Samuel
squirmed out of her embrace and toddled over to his
mother.

She tried to imagine a son of hers and Dominic's.
He would have dark hair, most likely, and perhaps her
husband's fine grey eyes, which dimmed and lightened
with his changing moods. Oh, yes, a child would bring
great happiness into her life, and especially if it bound
her to the man she loved in a way that their belea-
guered, strife-ridden marriage had not done. But at
whatever the cost to her pride, she would have to take
the initiative. For too long she had cowered in the
background of Dominic's life, waiting for him to make
some conciliatory move. By doing so she had not, she
realised, been true to her nature.

It would not be easy. But Nerissa—who had been
bold enough to invite a strange gentleman to travel
with her, reckless enough to share a room with him,
brave enough to marry him—decided then and there

that she could find in herself the requisite strength to
confess her abiding love for him.

Restless and uneasy, Dominic paced up and down
the elegant saloon, clad in full dress for the duchess's
party—dark blue tailcoat with silver buttons, silk
waistcoat embroidered with silver thread, and satin
breeches. With each glance at his timepiece and every
chime of the long-case clock, the lines in his face grew
deeper and harsher. He had planned to present Nerissa
with a selection of his mother's jewelry to wear this
night; that pleasure had been soured by her delay.
When she had left the house that afternoon she had
not taken the town carriage, and that hinted at con-
cealment—of what, he didn't like to think. So he had
left the jewel-case on her dressing table with a brief
note which contained none of the warm regard that
had prompted him to make the gesture.

At half-past seven a hackney-coach pulled up at the
door. A moment later Dominic heard Nerissa's voice
asking James to pay off the driver, and he hurried into
the marble-flagged hall to intercept her.

When she saw him, her smile illuminated her face
and she said breathlessly, "I'm late, I know—I rather
lost track of time. How *elegant* you look! Poor Rose
will have to work miracles upon me." She glanced
down at her rumpled pelisse.

It was on the tip of Dominic's tongue to ask where
she had been, and why she had returned in a hired
carriage instead of her own, but he forced back those
questions, fearing the answers. Not once in all the time
he'd known her had she looked so gloriously alive, so
wondrously happy, confirming his worst suspicions. It
broke his heart to see that her clandestine reunion with
her son had wrought the kind of transformation that he
had hoped to achieve himself.

Within the hour she reappeared, wearing a gown of

dark blue satin cut low at the breast to display a glittering necklace and an abundance of white flesh. The
diamonds in the crescent she wore in her dark hair
shimmered in the light of the chandelier. "Is it too
much?" she asked him. "I wasn't sure what would be
appropriate, for I've never dined at Solway House."

"You do me great credit," he said, going to assist
her with her velvet opera-cloak. As he draped the heavy
garment across her shoulders, his fingers grazed her
warm, bare flesh and she smiled up at him. He ached
to take her in his arms, but the carriage was waiting,
they were expected—and anyway, he wasn't at all sure
that she would welcome his advances. She'd given him
no cause to suspect she was anything other than satisfied with their present arrangement.

Solway House sat at the corner of Mount Street and
Park Lane, across from Hyde Park, and its classical
white stucco facade was particularly impressive when
lit by flambeaux. The great ballroom at the back of
the house was far from being full, for this was but a
family party, but Dominic saw many familiar, friendly
faces.

"I hardly expected to find you in this company, Damon," he said when he came abreast of his friend and
fellow peer. "Most of the guests are related to the
Marchants by blood or marriage."

"Yes, that is precisely why my attendance here is
so very compromising," Lord Elston said. In a mock-
conspiratorial whisper he said, "I am a front-runner
in the stakes for Lady Miranda Peverel—or don't you
read the betting-book at the club?"

"Since when are you hanging out for a wife?"
Dominic accepted a glass of wine from the tray held
out to him by a passing footman.

"I'm not, of course," the younger man confessed.
"But it does one's reputation so much good to be seen
at Solway House—I fancy that's why you were asked

here on the very eve of the inquest. That other aspirant to Lady's Mira's hand, your cousin and mine, was not honoured with an invitation. So if Ramsey accuses me of stealing a march upon him, I beg you to deny it."

"I will," Dominic promised.

"You know, Nick," said the marquis, as he looked towards the sofa where Nerissa sat with Lady Miranda Peverel, "if they should clap you in prison, I fear I will not repine with my whole heart. I would dearly love to be the one to console Lady Blythe."

"That is a singularly uncomforting prospect," Dominic said drily.

"I might have guessed that of all of us, you would be the one to settle into a love match. Ram is too selfish, he cares for no one but himself. I'm too much aware of my parents' failures to look upon the institution of marriage as anything but a form of entrapment. And poor young Justin is just that, too poor and too young to think of taking a wife."

"You know, Damon, whoever advised you to cultivate your innate cynicism did you a great disservice," Dominic said, and his friend let his mantle of sophistication slip just long enough to let out a genuine and boyish laugh.

When dinner was announced, the guests made their way into the dining-room in a formal procession which followed the strict rules of precedence. Dominic's partners for the meal were Gervase, the duke's heir, and Lady Miranda Peverel; Nerissa sat on the opposite side of the long table, at His Grace's right hand, with Lord Elston on her other side. She appeared to be well entertained, and so was Dominic. The little Lady Mira, who had not yet been officially presented to society, was proficient in the art of conversation. She deserved a better husband than Ramsey; it was a pity that Damon wasn't going to come up to scratch, but soon there would be plenty of likely fellows hanging about her.

There was much laughter and merriment when the Twelfth Night cake was borne in by a quartet of footmen. The duchess cut it with her own fair hand, and the plates were passed down the table until everyone had one. Lady Miranda's slice contained the pea and the Marquis of Elston found the bean; it was obvious to Dominic that this outcome had been planned ahead of time. The couple were given pinchbeck crowns to wear, and despite his lordship's dismissive remarks about marriage, his blonde head was never very far from Lady Mira's black one, and when she sat down at the pianoforte he gallantly offered to turn the pages of her music. Out of consideration for Lord Nelson's memory, there was no dancing, but card tables were provided for the guests, and Dominic was solicited to partner his host at whist. The duke turned out to be a skilled and indefatigable player, and the game went on until supper was served.

It was several hours past midnight when the Blythes finally returned to Grosvenor Square, and Nerissa, looking delectably sleepy, could not quite hide her yawns. As she and Dominic walked up the staircase she said apologetically, ''I know we ought to have come home long ago. Several times I looked into the cardroom to say we might leave, but you and Cousin William were so engrossed in your game that I didn't like to disturb you.''

They came to the door of her bedchamber. Dominic wished he might go in with her—he needed so much to be with her, to talk, but her abigail was there, waiting to undress her. So he bade her good-night and continued down the hallway to his own room.

He shrugged out of his evening coat and tugged at his neck-cloth. Before disrobing further he paused to pour a glass of brandy and tossed it off in the hopes that the fiery liquid would ease him into sleep. His state of mind and present wakefulness reminded him of that agonising, endless night before his duel with Sir Algernon. With the prospect of another one before him, he reached for the decanter once again, putting it down with a guilty start when he heard a faint rap upon his door. He supposed it was his officious valet, come to pester him, but when he opened it he found his wife standing in the corridor.

She was still clad in her satin ball gown, but the jewels were gone. So, too, were her shoes and stockings, and he smiled at the sight of her pink, high-arched feet. "May I come in?" she asked, and he stepped back to permit her to enter. As she did, she glanced about curiously, and he recalled that she had never seen his room before. "I know it is late, I will not stay long, but I wanted to talk to you about something. Something very important."

Dominic's mouth suddenly went dry. She had seen the child; now she was going to ask if she might bring it into his house. Before he could stop himself he said, "I know already, Nerissa. I've known ever since the day we met. Shall I prove to you how far my knowledge goes? He is rising two—or was. He may well have attained that age by now. Someone named Lucy looks after him for you, and she, I believe, lives in Chelsea." As she stared at him, perplexed, he explained, "That afternoon at the Angel when I first saw you, I overheard everything you said to the young man who drove you there in the gig. Don't you remember? When you told him good-bye you gave him a ten-pound note—for your son."

She drew a long, sobbing breath, and when he reached out to her, she backed away. "Don't touch me, don't even speak to me—I must think. Northampton, John—yes, I did give him some money, I remember, and asked him to send it to Lucy. And so you

thought—" As realisation dawned, she began to trem-
ble all over. "You offered me your protection, you
even *married* me, believing me to be unchaste?" Her
hands curled into fists and she pressed them against
her mouth.

"I wanted you," he rasped.

"Nick, I have no child."

"You can't deny his existence, Nerissa."

"Oh, I don't. But Samuel isn't *my* son, I swear it."
Dominic's giddiness had nothing to do with the advanced hour, or the brandy. But before fierce exultation completely overwhelmed him, he had to make sure
he'd understood her. "You're telling me that you've
borne no child—had no lover?"

She smiled wanly. "And all this time I thought I'd
left that old scandal behind in Olney. But none of it is
true—Sam's mother is Lucy Roberts, who was one of
our maids in the Adelphi Terrace. Because she and I
were very near in age, we became friends, and it was
her habit to confide in me. She had a sweetheart, a
coal-heaver, and they planned to be wed in the summer." Nerissa paused to take a breath, then asked him,
"Do you remember how very active the pressmen were
in the spring of 1803?"

"Vaguely—I seem to recall that there were reports
of it in the papers." He listened closely as she described the events of a Sunday afternoon in May of
that year, when a press gang had descended upon Hun-
gerford Stairs by the river to take recruits by force.

"Will Darcy and his mates were on the wharf
nearby, and threw coal and bottles at the pressmen to
chase them off. In retaliation the gang took Will and
one of his friends. Papa had connexions at the Admiralty, and learned that Will was transported to Dept-
ford, where he was taken aboard the *Enterprise*. Later
on he was sent to the Nore, where he was assigned to

some other ship, but Papa could never discover which one.''

"And your maid was already with child by her young man," Dominic said quietly.

"About six weeks later, she came to me. I knew she'd been ill, and I also knew that she and Will had—" Nerissa broke off and flushed. "Well, it was no surprise that she was breeding. I went to my father, and he agreed that we couldn't turn her off—he was, as I have told you, exceedingly liberal in his notions and agreed that Lucy should continue in our employ until her lying-in, and after. When the baby was born, I stood as godmother, and even chose his name." Nerissa quoted softly, " 'And the child Samuel grew before the Lord.' That winter, when Papa and I removed from London to Buckinghamshire, Lucy went with us to be our laundress. She lived in a cottage of her own down the lane from our house."

She sat down upon the edge of the great bed. "Everyone in the neighbourhood guessed Samuel was baseborn, and that I doted upon him was no secret. The world being what it is, this gave rise to the rumour that he was not Lucy's son at all, but mine. I don't know exactly when the gossip began, but I first learned of it soon after Papa died. I was inclined to scoff, thinking the talk would die down in time, but it didn't. When it touched Andrew's family—he had unmarried sisters—he sent Lucy and the baby away. And that's when I knew that I, too, had to leave.''

"What sort of man was your gentleman, that he would let you go, and in disgrace?" Dominic asked savagely.

"It was my decision. Lucy's sudden departure, to say nothing of the broken engagement, would have confirmed the gossip rather than refuted it. So I wrote a letter to Laura and closed up my house and let Andrew's brother John drive me to Northampton. The rest of it you know."

"Why," he said, shaking his head, "did you never tell me all this?"

"At first I only wanted to forget. As you know better than anyone, it is a hard thing to be driven from your home by scandal and gossip and nasty specula-tion. And later, when we were at Arcadia, I *did* for-get—for a time. I might have told you everything after we were married, but then your cousin came and I learned you were a lord and we quarrelled. If I had known then that you were harbouring such dreadful suspicions about me—but I didn't." Gazing steadily at him, she said, "I can understand why you found it easy to believe in my lack of virtue. I am not stupid, and I *do* have a mirror."

Sitting down beside her, Dominic reached for her hand and said huskily, "There is one thing I have to know, Nerissa. If you had it to do again, would you still marry me?"

She lifted her head and gave him a radiant smile, the one he had yearned to see for all the weeks of their marriage. "I regret only that I haven't been the wife you deserved."

When he folded his arms around her, she expelled her breath on a long, blissful sigh, and as the first light of dawn crept into the room, they both tried to forget, for the moment, that their present happiness might be snatched away during the course of this new day.

13

MANY HOURS LATER, Nerissa opened her eyes and discovered that she was lying in her husband's bed. She sat up, shoving her hair out of her face, and looked down at her blue satin gown, now crushed and creased, possibly beyond repair.

"What's the time?" Dominic enquired sleepily.

The bracket clock on the mantel showed the advanced hour. "Oh my," she gasped, "it's nearly eleven!" But when she felt his fingers idly tracing a path up her bare arm, she decided that it didn't matter.

"Good," he said, pulling her back down to him, "then I have a little while yet to wish my wife a good morning. I think I shall begin just here." He placed his lips on the beauty mark so close to her mouth.

"Nick," Nerissa said when she was able, "we cannot lie abed all day. When are we expected at the magistrates' court?"

"Oh, no," he said, when she wriggled out of his embrace. "You aren't going with me."

"Indeed I will," she informed him.

"I never guessed you would be such a shrew in the morning," he sighed. She made no reply, but went to stand before a looking-glass. He watched as she struggled vainly to repair the wreck of her coiffure. "It might be very awkward for you—Justin says the best we can hope for is a verdict of manslaughter."

She shook her head at him. "I'm not some weak,

helpless creature you must shield from all unpleasantness, surely you know that by now.''

Dominic ran his fingers through his own disordered
locks. ''Very well, then. Order some breakfast brought
up to your room, enough for two. And coffee. I'll join
you as soon as I can. And tell Rose to begin packing
for you, because later today, if fortune favours me, we
are leaving for Blythe.''

She didn't ask what they would do if he should be
committed to trial for murder; it was something she
couldn't even consider. And as much as she wanted to
believe that all would be well, she was exceedingly
nervous about the ordeal that lay ahead. After first
making sure that no servants were loitering in the hallway, she returned to her own suite, where she removed
her crushed clothes. She performed the ordinary, ev-
eryday business of washing and dressing with a sense
of urgency, and although it was Rose's habit to linger
over the arrangement of her hair, she hurried this delicate operation along as best she could.

When she went to her sitting-room, where James
had just laid the breakfast tray on a table drawn up to
the giltwood sofa, she found her husband waiting for
her. Dominic handed the footman a sealed letter.
''This goes to Elston House,'' he said, ''and you
needn't wait for a reply.'' The servant bowed, then
hurried off to do his bidding.

Nerissa joined him on the sofa and poured his coffee, presenting it to him with a whimsical smile. ''It
is curious, but this morning, for the very first time, I
feel as though I am *truly* your wife.''

''Not quite in every way, but I shall remedy that,
you may be sure—as soon as we reach Blythe.''

She experienced a surge of delight, which she covered by saying spiritedly, ''You needn't make it sound
like a threat.''

''I meant it as a promise,'' he told her, smiling.

Could this be happening, she asked herself. Last night they had reached a promising state of intimacy before she had fallen asleep in his arms, and now he was making love to her over breakfast, on this of all days. It was like being in the middle of a dream and a nightmare all at once. Her senses thoroughly disordered, she looked down at the array of foods before her and said, "I don't think I can eat a thing."

"You will," Dominic replied, in a tone that brooked no argument. "And you'd better, unless you want to swoon in front of the court. While it might well soften the magistrates' hearts towards me, I had rather win my appeal on the evidence."

When it was time to go, she put on a mulberry velvet pelisse and wound a black fur tippet about her throat; to hide her shaking hands, she carried a large muff. If they had been bound for the scaffold, she could not have been more afraid, but she was determined not to show it.

The town carriage, which bore the Blythe crest upon its panel, conveyed them to the police office in Great Marlborough Street, and its arrival was greeted with shouts and exclamations from the waiting public. Nerissa glanced worriedly at Dominic, who said calmly, "You cannot blame them, it isn't every day that a lord comes into this court." And, they soon discovered, not one lord, but many had come. At the front of the crowded chamber they found a host of peers: the Duke of Solway, Viscount Cavender, and the Marquis of Elston. Dominic shook hands with each one and thanked them for coming.

"I have saved two places," Lord Elston announced. "I wasn't sure if her ladyship would come, but I thought it likely." He cast an approving smile upon Nerissa, and she gave him a weak one in return. "Lady Blythe, you shall sit here, between your husband and Lord Cavender."

She took the chair he indicated, and while the gentlemen continued to talk among themselves, she glanced around the room. Seated where she was, she commanded an excellent view. An iron railing separated the spectators from the court, and on the opposite wall was a fireplace, flanked by two doors. The officials of the court were seated behind a wooden desk covered in green baize, and she took careful note of these men who would decide her husband's fate. One was fat and wore a powdered wig that was much too small and a tight, ill-fitting coat, which gave him a comical appearance; the other was old and frail, and his white head trembled with palsy. Neither looked especially fearsome, and both appeared to be considerably bored by the case they were hearing. Dominic's grim-faced barrister, Mr. Peale, was conversing with Justin Blythe, who was there in his capacity as clerk; their black robes lent a decidedly sombre note to the scene.

When the case was called, Mr. Peale rose and approached the bench. There was a continual buzz of voices which prevented Nerissa from hearing what was being said, but at last the noise all around her abated, just as the two magistrates began to review the finding of the initial inquest into the shooting death of Sir Algernon Titus, baronet.

The portly one, whose name was Mr. Blodgett, said, "Mr. Peale, we understand that you have come before us today to argue that Dominic Sebastian Charles Blythe, Baron Blythe, is innocent of the charge of willful murder. Is that correct?"

"It is, sir. Moreover, I can prove that his lordship's purpose in leaving London on fifth October was not to evade the law officers."

Mr. Blodgett glanced at the papers in his hand. "A surgeon who attended at the duel gave the evidence which placed Lord Blythe at the scene. But as that individual had been connected with other vile crimes, Mr. Crane and I chose to disregard his testimony." He nodded at the constable standing on the other side of the room. "You may bring in the first witness."

One of the doors was opened to admit a neatly dressed gentleman of middle years, and Nerissa listened closely as he swore that his testimony was true. She felt certain she had seen him before, but could not recall when or where.

Mr. Blodgett asked the man to state his name and business, to which question he replied, "I am John Frank, proprietor of the Denbigh Arms, an inn at Lutterworth."

"Mr. Frank, do you recognise that gentleman seated just behind the railing, the one in a black coat?"

"I do, your worship," the man answered. "He stopped at my inn one night in October—I believe it was the first week of that month. He came with a lady, and they'd just been wed."

The older magistrate asked in a quavering voice, "How do you know that, Mr. Frank?"

"The gentleman told me so, before he asked to be shown to the best bedchamber." There was a murmur from the crowd, but it subsided when Mr. Frank added, "*And* his lady was wearing a veil over her hat. I'm afraid the young gentleman was rather the worse for drink, and I clearly recall that he said he'd made too many toasts to his bride."

Laughter greeted this statement, and Mr. Blodgett said curtly, "Thank you, that will be all. Mr. Peale, the court has heard that Lord and Lady Blythe spent their wedding night at the Denbigh Arms at Lutterworth. I suppose the gentleman's story can be corroborated?" The barrister inclined his bewigged head and the magistrate said, on a long-suffering note, "Constable, bring in the next witness."

The person who was subsequently led into the court

was a plain-faced young woman clutching a shawl tightly about her hunched shoulders. ''State your name and occupation,'' Mr. Crane told her none too gently.

''Nan Holden, sir.''

''And your occupation?'' he repeated.

''I'm chambermaid at the Denbigh Arms, sir.''

When the elderly magistrate asked if she could iden-tify anyone in the court, she glanced fearfully at the immense crowd. After a moment she said, ''The lady and the gentleman there.''

''Can you tell me where you last saw them?''

''At the inn.''

''Did you wait upon either of them?''

The girl considered this. ''I took the lady water for washin', and then I helped her to dress, and I arranged her hair. I remember breakin' her scent bottle, too, but she didn't scold me for it.''

''Did she address any remarks to you at that time?''

The girl stared stupidly at her inquisitor, and her ugly face wore a puzzled frown. ''Did she speak to you?''

''Oh aye,'' she said, bobbing her head. ''She asked me where was her husband, and I said he was bein' shaved.''

Nerissa heard the rumble of amusement behind her, but she didn't care. The first two witnesses established a reasonable motive for Dominic's flight from London. She remembered that he had told her she might well save his life a second time, and now she understood: because they had passed themselves off as newlyweds in Lutterworth, he had an alibi. The date of their marriage had never been publicised, and there was no proof anywhere, not even in Gretna, that it had occurred in November, not October.

''Is that the sum of the evidence you mean to pre-sent, Mr. Peale?'' the portly magistrate asked.

''If it please your worship, there is one more witness, whose evidence will establish beyond doubt that Lord Blythe had no intention of murdering Sir Algernon Titus. I request permission from the bench to undertake the examination myself.''

"Permission is granted, Mr. Peale." Mr Blodgett heaved a sigh and gestured to the constable.

Nerissa was conscious of Dominic's sudden intake of breath, and he reached inside her muff to take hold of her hand. She did not know if he intended to provide reassurance, or whether he sought it for himself.

Although the next witness was also a female, she was nothing like poor Nan Holden, being blonde and quite attractive, and fashionably but soberly attired in dove grey silk. When she was sworn to tell the whole truth, Nerissa heard Viscount Cavender, seated on the other side, make an odd, strangled sound low in his throat.

"Madam, will you please state your name," the barrister said politely.

"I am Lady Titus."

Both magistrates eyed her with considerable interest, as did everyone else in the court. Mr. Crane asked if she was the widow of Sir Algernon Titus, baronet, and she nodded, whereupon he instructed Mr. Peale to proceed with the examination.

"Lady Titus, are you acquainted with Baron Blythe?"

The widow glanced at Dominic and it seemed to Nerissa that her tense expression softened. ''Indeed I am, sir, for he was a frequent visitor to our house.''

"How long was Sir Algernon acquainted with his lordship?" Mr. Peale asked.

Lady Titus shrugged her shoulders. ''For all of Lord Blythe's life, I should think—and that would be upwards of thirty years. His lordship's name was at the top of the list of those persons we invited to our soirée on the fourth of October.''

"And did Lord Blythe attend?" the barrister enquired.

"He did."

Mr. Peale took a turn around the room before continuing with his questioning. "Lady Titus, do you know of any reason why Lord Blythe might have wished to kill your husband?"

"No, none," she said firmly, clearly.

"Can you tell the bench whether Lord Blythe did, in fact, kill your husband when they met at Chalk Farm on the morning of October fifth?"

"He did not."

"And how do you know that?"

"Because my husband was very much alive when Lord Blythe and two other gentlemen brought him home."

Mr. Peale paused to let the magistrates—and the rest of the court—digest this. "And was Sir Algernon conscious? Lucid?"

"Both, I sat with him until the doctor arrived, and he was talking to me all that time."

"Do you remember what he said?"

For the first time during her recital, the witness exhibited signs of distress. Her generous bosom rose and fell, then she said, "He begged me not to be angry with him, and explained that he'd met Dominic Blythe at Chalk Farm, although he did not appear to attach any blame to his lordship for what had happened."

"You are sure of that?"

"Quite sure," she said, "otherwise I would not be standing here now."

Mr. Peale seemed to be unaware that he had just received a setdown, but a ripple of amusement gave evidence of the spectators' appreciation of her ladyship's remark. "Lady Titus," the barrister continued, "when the physician ministered to your husband, did he give an opinion on Sir Algernon's chances of recovery?''

"His opinion meant nothing to me," the lady said harshly. "For it was the doctor killed my husband, and not Lord Blythe."

This outburst resulted in an intermission, during which the two magistrates conferred with the barrister, and then with one another. At first Nerissa thought the examination was over, but Lady Titus had not yet been dismissed—she still stood before the bench, her chin held high. Her testimony was so precise that it gave the impression of being entirely accurate, and Nerissa was sure it would go a long way towards exonerating Dominic. He must have known that Lady Titus would be present; unlike Lord Cavender, he'd exhibited no surprise when she had stepped into the court. Deep within the warm recesses of her muff, she could feel her husband's hand gripping her own, and she forgot about Ramsey Blythe. "Do you think everything will be all right now?" she whispered.

Dominic smiled down at her. "I am hopeful. Georgiana sounded very convincing, don't you think?"

"Oh yes," she agreed.

When the court officials concluded their brief colloquy, Mr. Blodgett signalled to Mr. Peale to resume the interrogation.

"Lady Titus," he began, "just now you stated that the physician was responsible for Sir Algernon's demise. Would you explain exactly what you meant by that?"

"The doctor insisted that my husband be bled," the lady said wearily. "I protested, but to no avail— medical men dislike having their advice contradicted, especially by a female. If Sir Algernon had been in a high fever, it would have been a different matter entirely, but he was already weak from loss of blood. After being cupped, he grew even weaker. At first I thought he was falling asleep, for the doctor had also given him some laudanum for the pain. And then I was told that he was dead," she concluded in a lifeless voice.

"Do you recall where Lord Blythe was during the time you were with your husband?"

"Lord Blythe?" Georgiana repeated, as though she'd never heard the name before. "I believe he was downstairs."

"He did not rush away, or attempt to hide himself from the law?"

"Oh no, he was there. I remember that I went to find him after Sir Algernon—I went to him after it was over. I don't know exactly what I said, but I didn't tell him about—" Suddenly Georgiana was quiet, and very still.

"About what, Lady Titus?" Mr. Peale prompted her.

"Forgive me, sir, I'm afraid my mind was wandering," she said apologetically. "Could you repeat your question?"

"What did you say to Lord Blythe?"

"I really can't tell you with any degree of certainty, sir. Very likely I expressed my amazement that Sir Algernon had challenged him. You see, at our party the night before, someone told my husband that Lord Blythe had—had betrayed him. And his lordship was certainly entitled to defend himself against such a base lie."

Nerissa had the impression that Mr. Peale lost control of the witness, for he seemed to be forming his question as it occurred to him. "Are you saying that the duel did not result from a quarrel, but was provoked by malicious gossip? Wouldn't Lord Blythe have denied any charge laid against him?"

"I suppose he must have done, only my husband didn't believe him. Sir Algernon was very stubborn—

and of a jealous disposition. I assure you the man who slandered Lord Blythe knew that,'' she said acidly.

"Did your husband have some enemy, was there any person who would have profited from his death?''

Georgiana lifted her golden head. "An enemy?'' she repeated, a strange smile playing about her lips. "I can't be sure of that. But my husband and Lord Blythe were equally his victims.''

"Can your ladyship be more specific? Do you know the name of the individual who lied to your husband, thereby inciting his anger?''

"I do. He is in the court.'' On a note of high triumph, she declared, "The blackguard who was responsible for that duel is Viscount Cavender, Lord Blythe's cousin.''

14

Mr. Blodgett possessed a booming voice, but not even he had the power to control the din created by the outraged spectators. Lady Titus, clearly shaken by the uproar her accusation had created, looked as though she might fall to the floor. Mr. Peale waited patiently for order to be restored, and everyone else was staring at the viscount.

Finally the witness was led away by the constable, and Nerissa heard Lord Cavender mutter, "*Bitch!*" through his teeth.

Said Lord Elston curtly, "Be still, Ram, for God's sake."

"I won't," Ramsey flashed back. "You cool devil, did you put her up to this? I'll not sit by and let some whore insult me in public!" He leaned across Nerissa to speak to Dominic. "Surely *you* don't believe her, Nick!"

"Which of us did you want out of the way, me or Sir Algernon?" Dominic asked, his grey eyes hard and implacable.

"Neither!" Ramsey protested in a fierce whisper. "Let us say it was both, and damn you for a lying cur!" Dominic felt his wife grasp his arm as if to restrain him, but he paid no heed. "Call me out if you dare—or does the knowledge of your own sins prevent that? You robbed me of my honour," he said savagely, "and by so doing you have dishonoured yourself past all reclaim."

His face ashen, Ramsey rose stiffly and hurried out of the court.

After his lordship's abrupt departure, an expectant hush fell over the room as everyone waited to learn what the magistrates would make of this development.

Mr. Blodgett leaned back in his chair. "Mr. Peale, under the present circumstances, I believe we should give our opinion at once."

"I concur," Mr. Crane said faintly. "We need not withdraw, I think, for the matter does not require further deliberation on my part."

His brother magistrate nodded, then said, "In this case, as in all capital cases, the rules of evidence must be strictly observed. At the initial inquest, no one testified that Sir Algernon did not expire upon the duelling ground, and the coroner therefore concluded that the gentleman's opponent not only intended murder, but committed it. After hearing Lady Titus's description of the events of October the fourth and fifth, the bench decrees that the verdict must be overturned." There was an approving hum from the crowd, but Mr. Blodgett quelled it with a glance. "Furthermore, this examination has revealed that after the obligatory exchange of fire, Baron Blythe demonstrated his concern for the baronet's welfare. He conveyed his wounded friend to London, at some risk to himself—hardly the act of a ruthless murderer. As to the lady's charge that a physician is responsible for her husband's demise, this court has no authority to have the accused bound over for prosecution. It's not the first time a man has been doctored into a premature grave, nor will it be the last. Our finding is accidental death. This case is dismissed."

Dominic turned to Nerissa and murmured, " 'O wise and upright judge.' "

"It's over," she breathed, although she couldn't quite accept the truth of it. He assisted her to her feet, and they found their exit impeded by the many well-wishers who crowded in upon them.

The Duke of Solway said, "I'm vastly relieved—this is the outcome your friends hoped for. Still, Blythe, you would do well to remove from town as soon as possible."

"That is my intention, Your Grace."

"Good, good. There's nothing you can—or should—do for Cavender. If he is cut by the whole of his acquaintance tomorrow, it is no more than he deserves. Well, I must be on my way—the duchess will be anxious to learn what has transpired. My dear," he said, smiling at Nerissa, "we hope to have the pleasure of seeing you and your husband at the Haberdine Castle very soon."

As the duke departed, Justin Blythe stepped forward to claim Dominic's attention. His bony face was a mask of strain, but his voice was steady as he said, "My hasty trip to Lutterworth was quite unnecessary, it seems—for Lady Titus won the case for us. But at such a cost—" Turning on Lord Elston, standing behind him, he said, "Damon, you are the one who persuaded her ladyship to give her evidence. Did you know she would implicate my brother?"

"I warned her that no good would come of introducing Ram's name, but evidently Georgiana is ruled by a very strict sense of justice."

Justin's brown eyes were sombre. "I must find Ram—he will need me."

As the young clerk made his solitary way out of the court, Lord Elston observed, "I suspect Justin's ambition to become a barrister has received a grave setback this day. What can we do for him, I wonder? Have someone pull a string or two at the Foreign Office?"

"The diplomatic service? Yes, a posting abroad might be just the thing for him, especially now," Dominic said thoughtfully, his eyes still following the black-gowned figure.

Nerissa, who had kept silent all this time, spoke up. "I can't believe Mr. Blythe would agree to leave the country—he won't want to desert his brother at such a time."

Lord Elston said grimly, "That is why it will fall to Ramsey to persuade him to take whatever position we find for him. Well, Nick, shall we be off? I had your note this morning, and I must say I went to some considerable trouble to arrange everything as you requested."

"What is he talking about?" Nerissa asked, glancing from her husband to the marquis, and back.

"Come with us, and you shall see," Dominic invited her.

Their short walk took them to the stately, columned edifice of the church which dominated George Street. There was a post-chaise standing at the curb, an array of luggage strapped behind. Nerissa demanded to know why it was waiting for them there, but neither of her escorts would give her a direct answer.

They halted beneath the portico of St. George's, and her husband said to his friend, "Will you kindly stop ogling my wife and inform the vicar that we will be with him presently?" When the marquis had withdrawn, Dominic took Nerissa's hand. "Today my life and my honour have been restored to me—I am a free man, Nerissa. We began so badly, you and I, and although that ridiculous ceremony at Gretna may be legal and binding, it was frightfully ill-managed. I had Damon procure a special licence for us—it occurred to me that you might wish to have our union blessed by church rite."

"But I don't."

Perplexed by her unequivocal reply, he asked, "Whyever not?"

Her blue eyes bright with mischief, Nerissa said, "Because a marriage which cannot be proved can *never* be dissolved."

"You can't seriously think I would ever take such a step!"

"Oh, I do hope not," she said fervently. "But I rather like the security of knowing that it would be quite out of your power." She lifted her smiling face to his and reminded him, "I already gave you my vow to abide with you, for better or for worse, at Gretna. And, Nick, the worst must surely be behind us now."

When Lord Elston returned, he enquired, with exaggerated politeness, if they were coming inside, and Dominic, beaming at his wife, replied, "We have made up our minds to dispense with the services of the vicar after all."

"Afraid I would demand the privilege of kissing the bride?" was his friend's mocking rejoinder.

"Something of the kind," Dominic laughed. "Will you give the reverend gentleman my compliments, and my apologies, and—"

"A handsome fee," the marquis sighed.

After discharging his duties, he followed Lord Blythe and his lady to the chaise. "I'm sure you're impatient to be gone, but I really *must* have that kiss," he said slyly, and before Dominic could say him nay, he embraced Lady Blythe and bussed her soundly on the cheek. "Have a safe journey, my dear, and if your husband should turn out to be a brute, you have only to let me know and I'll come to rescue you!"

"I have no such fear, my lord," she assured him.

"As for you, Nick," Lord Elston continued, "you mustn't worry about Justin, for I will see to it that he doesn't suffer his brother's disgrace."

As the chaise moved forward, Dominic leaned back

against the seat and said, "I think you will like Blythe, Nerissa. For a very long time now I've wanted to take you there, but my case seemed so desperate I thought this day would never come." He paused to put his thoughts in order, for her joyous smile threatened to wipe from his mind the many important and necessary things he wanted to tell her. "You saved my life, not once but many times—and my sanity, because you gave me hope when I'd lost everything else. And when I nearly lost *you*, I realised that nothing else mattered very much, not even the possibility that you had a child. Last night I discovered, to my horror, that I have wronged you, and for that I am more sorry than I have ever been in my life. I married you, believing you were something you are not, and loved you despite that." He caught the past tense and amended hastily, "And will always love you, although I don't really know you as I thought I did."

"But you *do* know me," Nerissa hastened to say, "for I haven't changed. I'm still as impulsive and stubborn and wild and willful as I ever was. But there is something you have yet to learn about me," she realised suddenly. "In all my twenty-three years I've been fond of very few people. Papa and my aunt are gone now. Andrew was a good friend, but could never be anything more to me. For a time I had Samuel, but he isn't really mine to love. My heart would be quite empty, Nick, if I hadn't met you. I first knew my own feelings at Arcadia, when I found Cat's letter. And then, when I saw my godson yesterday, I thought that perhaps by giving you a child I might be able to win your love."

"You stand in no need of help, Nerissa," he assured her. "Any child of ours would be proof of my love." He took her face in his hands and said huskily, "From this time and forever, you must be happy. If you aren't, it won't be through any fault of mine, for I intend to do everything in my power to make you so."

And he began by kissing her long and longingly as they left the great city behind and followed the road to a new and brighter future together.

About the Authors

The author of more than thirty romance novels, **Barbara Metzger** is the proud recipient of two *Romantic Times* Career Achievement Awards for Regencies and a RITA award from the Romance Writers of America. When not writing romances or reading them, she paints, gardens, volunteers at the local library, and goes beachcombing on the beautiful Long Island shore with her little dog, Hero. She loves to hear from her readers, care of Signet or through her Web site, www.BarbaraMetzger.com.

Margaret Evans Porter is the award-winning author of Regency and historical novels, nonfiction, and poetry. She studied British history in England, trained as an actress, and later worked as a producer for film and television. A dedicated traveler, she spends part of the year in Britain, Ireland, or France, and most of it in New England, where she lives beside a woodland pond with her husband, two dogs, and a variety of wildlife. For information, visit http://members.aol.com/MargEvaPor/.